THE
AUTUMN
REPUBLIC

THE
AUTUMN
REPUBLIC

THE POWDER MAGE TRILOGY:
BOOK 3

BRIAN McCLELLAN

www.orbitbooks.net

Copyright © 2015 by Brian McClellan
Map by Isaac Stewart

Orbit
Hachette Book Group
1290 Avenue of the Americas, New York, NY 10104
www.HachetteBookGroup.com

Printed in the United States of America

RRD-C

First Edition: February 2015

10 9 8 7 6 5 4 3 2 1

Orbit is an imprint of Hachette Book Group, Inc. The Orbit name and logo are trademarks of Little, Brown Book Group Limited.

The Hachette Speakers Bureau provides a wide range of authors for speaking events. To find out more, go to www.hachettespeakersbureau.com or call (866) 376-6591.

The publisher is not responsible for websites (or their content) that are not owned by the publisher.

Library of Congress Cataloging-in-Publication Data

McClellan, Brian, 1986-
    The autumn republic / Brian McClellan.—First edition.
      pages; cm.—(The powder mage trilogy; 3)
    ISBN 978-0-316-21912-9 (hardback)—ISBN 978-0-316-21911-2 (paperback)—ISBN 978-1-4789-2933-8 (audio download)
    I. Title.
    PS3613.C35785A95 2015
    813'.6—dc23

2014023159

For Mom,
For pushing me in the right direction and
making all of this possible

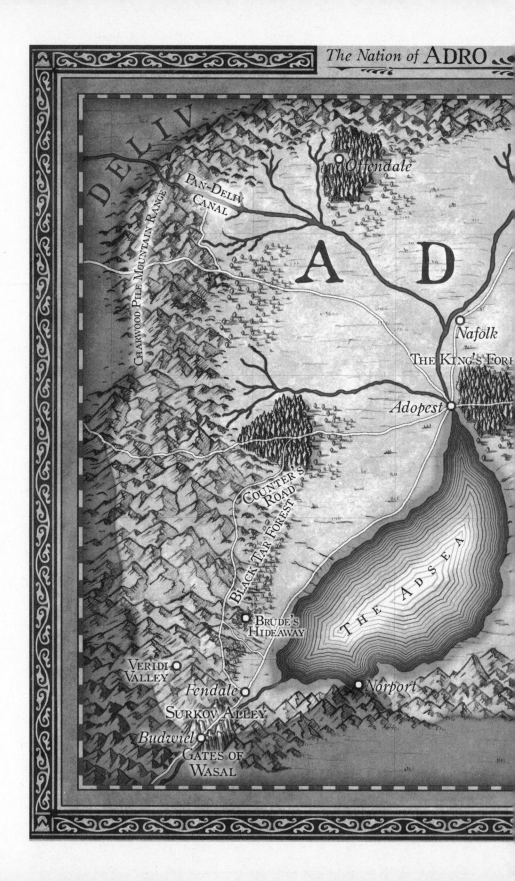

DELIV

Offendale

A D

PAN-DELIV CANAL

CHARWOOD PILE MOUNTAIN RANGE

Nafolk

THE KING'S FOR

Adopest

COUNTER'S ROAD

BLACK TAR FOREST

THE ADSEA

BRUDE'S HIDEAWAY

VERIDI VALLEY

Norport

Fendale

SURKOV ALLEY

Budwiel

GATES OF WASAL

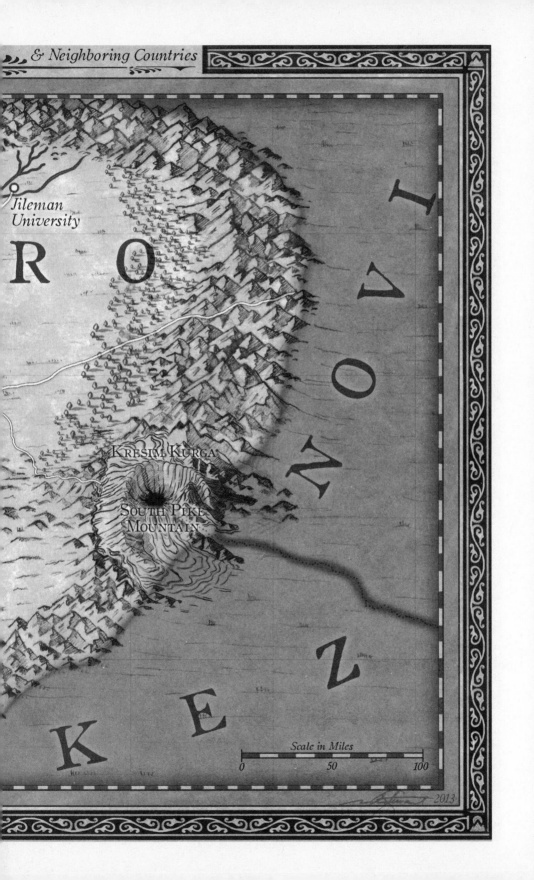

CITY OF
ADOPEST
AND SURROUNDINGS

1. Kirkamshire
   Adopest University
2. Adom's Wall
3. The Samalian Market
4. Samalian District
5. Laughlin Square
6. Kinnen Hotel
7. Kresim Cathedral

8. Baker's Town
9. The Routs
10. Elections Square
11. Public Archives
12. Centestershire
13. Black Street
14. Hrusch Ave.
15. Skyline Palace

16. Union Headquarters

HIGH
TALIEN

NEW
CITY

FACTORY
DISTRICT

WEST
LADEN

OLD CITY

Scale in Miles

0   1   2

THE ADSEA

2013

THE
AUTUMN
REPUBLIC

CHAPTER

1

Field Marshal Tamas stood in the ruins of the Kresim Cathedral in Adopest.

What had once been a magnificent building with golden spires that rose majestically above the surrounding buildings was now a pile of rubble being picked over by a small army of stonemasons in search of usable marble and limestone, and birds that had built their nests in those spires now wheeled aimlessly overhead as Tamas inspected the ruin by the light of the rising sun.

The destruction had been wrought by Privileged elemental sorcery. Granite keystones had been cut apart with an almost casual indifference, and entire sections of the cathedral were melted away with fire hotter than the center of any forge. The sight turned Tamas's stomach.

"Looks worse from far off," Olem said. He stood beside Tamas, hand resting on the butt of his pistol beneath his greatcoat, eyes scanning the streets for signs of Brudanian patrols. He spoke around the cigarette clenched between his lips. "This must have been the column of smoke our scouts saw. The rest of the city seems intact."

Tamas scowled at his bodyguard. "This cathedral was three hundred years old. It took sixty years to build. I refuse to be relieved that the damned Brudanians invaded Adopest *just* to destroy the cathedral."

"They had the chance to level the whole city. They didn't. I call that lucky, sir."

Olem was right, of course. They had ridden hard for two weeks, dangerously far ahead of the Seventh and Ninth brigades and their new Deliv allies, in order to determine the fate of the city. Tamas *had* been relieved to see Adopest still standing.

But now it lay in the hands of a Brudanian army and Tamas was forced to sneak about in his own city. There were no words to describe the anger he felt.

He pushed down that rage, trying to get control of himself. They'd arrived on the outskirts of the city only a few hours ago, sneaking in under cover of darkness. He had to get organized, to find his allies, scout his enemies, and find out how an entire city could fall into Brudanian hands with no sign of a fight. Pit, Brudania was eight hundred miles away!

Had another one of his council betrayed him?

"Sir," Vlora said, drawing Tamas's attention to the south. She stood above them on the remains of a buttress, watching the Ad River and the old quarter of the city beyond it. Like Tamas and Olem, she wore a greatcoat to conceal her Adran uniform, and her dark hair was tucked beneath a tricorne hat. "A Brudanian patrol. There's a Privileged with them."

Tamas eyed the rubble and considered the lay of the street to their south, formulating a plan to ambush the Brudanian patrol. He forced himself to stop that line of thought. He couldn't risk any open conflict. Not without more men. He'd only brought Vlora and Olem ahead of the army and while they might be able to cut through a single Brudanian patrol, any kind of firefight would bring more running.

"We need soldiers," Tamas said.

Olem ashed his cigarette on the ruins of the cathedral altar. "I can try to find Sergeant Oldrich. He's got fifteen of my Riflejacks with him."

"That would be a start," Tamas said.

"I think we should make contact with Ricard," Vlora said. "Find out what happened to the city. He'll have men that we can use."

Tamas acknowledged the advice with a nod. "In good time. Pit. I should have brought the whole powder cabal with me. I want more men before we go see Ricard." *I don't know if he's turned on us.* Tamas had left Taniel's unconscious body in Ricard's care. If someone had harmed his boy, Tamas would…

He swallowed bile and tried to gain control of his pounding heart.

"Sabon's trainees?" Olem asked.

Before Sabon's death he had been tasked with setting up a school for powder mages just north of the city. Early reports were that he had over twenty men and women with some talent and that he was already teaching them how to shoot and fight and control their powers.

They'd had only a few months of training. It would have to be good enough.

"The trainees," Tamas agreed. "At the very least we can get Telavere before we go to Ricard."

They headed across the Ad River in the cool dawn as the streets began to fill with people. Tamas noted that Brudanian patrols, while they were frequent and the street guards plentiful, seemed to leave the citizens unmolested. No one questioned him or his companions as they passed through the old city's western gates or as they left the city once again to reach the suburban northland.

Tamas saw Brudanian ships in the harbor along the river and

their tall masts out in the bay to the south. The mountain-crossing canal that Ricard's union had been building must have been a success, he noted wryly. It was the only way oceangoing vessels of that size could reach the Adsea.

Tamas lost track of the number of destroyed churches and monasteries. It seemed as if every other city block had a pile of rubble where a church had once been. He couldn't help but wonder what had happened to the priests and priestesses that staffed them and why they in particular had been targeted by the Brudanian Privileged.

It was something he'd have to ask Ricard.

Their journey took them an hour north of the city by foot, where the school stood on the bank of the Ad River. It was an old brick building, a decommissioned clothing factory with a field off to one side that had been turned into a firing range. As they came off the road, Vlora grasped Tamas's arm. He sensed panic in her touch.

Tamas felt his chest tighten.

The windows of the dormitory above the school were shuttered, and the main door hung off its hinges. A wooden placard, emblazoned with the silver powder keg of a powder mage, had been knocked from its place above the door and lay broken in the mud. The grounds around the school and the firing range beside it were quiet and abandoned, the grass overgrown.

"Vlora," Tamas said, "take the south side by the river. Olem, swing around to the north."

The two moved off with a "yessir" and no further questions. Vlora removed her hat and crept through the tall grass, while Olem continued up the street past the school, sauntering casually, before cutting across the firing range to approach the school from uphill.

Tamas waited for them to be in position before he continued cautiously down the path to the school. He opened his third eye to look into the Else, searching for signs of sorcery, but it revealed nothing about the contents of the building. If anyone lay waiting inside, they weren't Privileged or Knacked.

Nor could he sense any powder mages, for that matter. Why was the school empty? Telavere had been left in charge. She was a powder mage of little raw power but excellent technical skill, a perfect choice to teach the recruits. Could she have taken them into hiding when the Brudanians arrived? Had they been attacked?

Tamas drew his pistols as he neared the school, pausing only to sprinkle black powder on his tongue. A powder trance gripped his body, his eyesight, hearing, and smell sharpening and the pain of the ride ebbing away behind a curtain of strength.

A low sound filled his ears, almost drowned out by the sound of the gentle flow of the Ad River. He couldn't quite place the sound, but he knew the smell that filled his nostrils. It smelled of iron and decay. Blood.

Tamas checked the front window of the school. The glare of the morning sun prevented him from piercing the darkness within. The low sound seemed a roar now in his trance-enhanced hearing, and the scent of death filled him with dread.

He kicked the front door off its hinges and dove in with both pistols ready. He froze in the entryway, eyes adjusting to the dim light.

His caution was unwarranted. The foyer was empty, and the silence stretched throughout the building—but for the low drone of what he now saw were thousands of flies. They buzzed and churned in the air, dancing against the windowpanes.

Tamas shoved both pistols into his belt so he could tie a handkerchief about his mouth and nose. Despite the flies and the smell, there were no bodies in the entryway, and the only sign of violence was the smear of rust on the floors and splatters on the wall. Men had been killed here, and the bodies dragged away.

He followed the trail of smeared blood from the entryway and proceeded deeper into the old factory building, one pistol held at the ready.

The factory floor, an immense room that had no doubt once been home to dozens of long tables where seamstresses worked at their sewing by the hundred, was empty now but for a dozen desks along one side. There were fewer flies here except for the ones hanging out around a half-dozen stains and rusty puddles where men had died.

The smears continued along the factory floor and out through a door in the back corner.

Tamas whirled at a sound, leveling his pistol, but it was only Vlora coming down the stairway from the dormitory above. He noted plenty of blood on the stairs as well.

"What did you find?" Tamas asked. His voice echoed eerily in the large room.

"Flies." Vlora spit on the floor. "Flies, and half the back wall of the school is missing. Plenty of scorch marks. Someone detonated at least two horns of powder up there." She swore under her breath, the only crack in her professional demeanor.

"What happened here?" Tamas asked.

"I don't know, sir."

"No bodies?"

"None."

Tamas gritted his teeth in frustration. Plenty of blood—that's what the flies were attracted to—and more than a little gore. Dozens of men had died in this building and not all that long ago.

"They dragged the bodies out the back," Olem said, his voice echoing in the large room as he stepped through a small doorway at the far corner of the room.

When Tamas and Vlora had joined him, Olem pointed at the floor where the lines of rust overlapped each other all the way out the back, disappearing into the tall grass between the school and the Ad River. "Whoever did this," Olem said, "cleaned up after themselves. They didn't want any bodies to tell a story."

"The story tells itself," Tamas snapped, striding back inside. He went to the front of the school, scattering flies in his wake. "They came in through the front." He pointed to blood spatter and bullet holes in the wall. "Overran whoever was standing guard, then took the factory floor. Our mages made a last stand upstairs, using whatever powder was at their disposal..."

He heard his voice crack. These men and women were his responsibility. They were his newest mages. Some were farmers, two of them bakers. One had been a librarian. They weren't trained for combat. They'd been slaughtered like sheep.

He could only pray that they had been able to take a few of the enemy with them.

"Death is a bloody painter and this is his canvas," Olem said quietly. He lit a cigarette and drew in a deep breath, then blew smoke against the wall, watching the flies scatter.

"Sir," Vlora said, stepping past Tamas and snatching something off the ground. She handed Tamas a round bit of leather with a hole in the middle. "Looks like it was behind the door. Whoever cleaned this place up must have missed it. Do you know what it is?"

Tamas spit to get rid of the sudden bitter taste in his mouth. "It's a leather gasket. You have to keep spares if you carry an air rifle. It must have fallen out of someone's kit."

An air rifle. A weapon used specifically to kill powder mages. Whoever had done this had come prepared.

Tamas threw the gasket away and stuffed his pistol into his belt. "Olem, who all knew the location of this school?"

"Aside from the powder cabal?" Olem rolled his cigarette between his fingers, considering. "It wasn't a closely guarded secret. They put up a sign, after all."

"Who all knew *directly*?" Tamas said.

"A couple members of the General Staff and Ricard Tumblar."

The General Staff were men and women who had been with him for decades. Tamas trusted them. He *had* to trust them.

"I want answers, even if someone has to bleed to give them. Find me Ricard Tumblar."

CHAPTER

2

The Holy Warriors of Labor, the biggest workers' union in all the Nine, kept their headquarters inside an old warehouse in the Factory District of Adopest not far from where the Ad River spilled out into the Adsea.

Tamas watched the building with some trepidation. There were hundreds of people coming and going. It would be almost impossible to get in to speak with Ricard without being seen—and probably recognized—by someone. The coming conversation could very well become bloody, and Tamas didn't want to have it where Ricard's guards were within screaming distance.

If not for the urgent pressure of his heart pounding in his chest, Tamas would have waited until nightfall and followed Ricard home.

"We could make an appointment, sir," Olem suggested, leaning casually against the stoop. Across the street, one of the union guards was watching them with a frown. Olem waved to the man and held up a spare cigarette. The union guard cocked an eyebrow and then turned away, his interest gone.

"I'm not making an appointment," Tamas said flatly. "I don't want him to know we're coming."

"I think he's going to know one way or another. He's got more than twenty armed men on this street alone."

"I only counted eighteen."

Olem watched the foot traffic pass them with a feigned air of indifference. "Marksmen in the window above the shop thirty paces to your left, sir."

"Ah." Tamas saw them now out of the corner of his eye. "Something has Ricard spooked. The old headquarters had no more than four guards at any time."

"Could be he's worried about the Brudanians?"

"Or that I'll return. There's Vlora. Let's go."

They worked their way down the street, doing their best to avoid the attention of the union guards, and joined Vlora in the doorway of a small bakery. Tamas looked over the loaves stacked on the counter and wondered where Mihali had ended up. Was he still down south, with the main army?

Of course he was. If Mihali wasn't holding Kresimir at bay, then Adopest would have been leveled by now. Tamas felt himself wishing for a bowl of the chef's squash soup just about now.

Vlora led them through the bakery and out the back into a narrow alley filled with refuse and mud. "Down here," she said over her shoulder as they picked their way down the alley. Tamas's boots squelched as he walked and he tried to ignore the smell. The Factory District was by far the dirtiest part of the city—and the alleys were always the worst.

They navigated three more alleys, then climbed an iron ladder over a two-story building before they found the back entrance to the union headquarters.

A pair of union guards sat with their backs to the wall beside the door, their heads bowed beneath their hats as if they were asleep. A brief glance at the mud told Tamas that a quick scuffle had taken place, but Vlora had taken the two men without trouble.

"Are they dead?" Olem asked, flicking his cigarette into the mud before drawing his pistol.

"Unconscious."

"Good," Tamas said. "Try not to kill anyone on the way in. We don't know for sure whether Ricard has betrayed us." *And if he has, I'll do the killing.* Tamas set his hand to the door only to have Olem stop him.

"Pardon sir, but we'll go first."

"I can..."

"It's my job, sir. You haven't been letting me do it lately."

Tamas bit his tongue. This was a terrible time for insubordination from his own bodyguard, but Olem had a point. "Go on."

He didn't have to wait for more than about three minutes before Olem returned for him. "Sir. We have him."

They passed through the back hallways and two servants' rooms before slipping in the side entrance to Ricard's office. Ricard himself sat behind his desk, his jacket stained and his beard wild, his eyes narrowed in anger. Behind him, Vlora stood with the barrel of a pistol against the back of his head.

When he saw Olem, Ricard slammed both hands on his desk. "What is the meaning of this? What do you think..." His jaw dropped and he made to stand. Vlora put a hand on his shoulder to keep him in his seat. "Tamas? You're alive?"

"You don't sound too surprised," Tamas said. He holstered his own pistol and nodded to Vlora to let go of Ricard's shoulder. Olem took up a position beside the main office door.

Ricard swallowed hard, looking between Tamas and Olem. Tamas tried to decide if it was the nervousness of a man caught in betrayal or just the shock of his sudden presence. "I had heard you were still alive, but none of my sources were reliable. I—"

"What happened to my powder mage school? And where's my boy?"

"Taniel?"

"Do I have another?"

"Do you?"

"No."

"I . . . well, I don't know where Taniel is."

"You better explain quickly." Tamas drummed his fingers on the ivory handle of one of his dueling pistols.

"Of course, of course! Can I offer you some wine?"

Tamas tilted his head slightly. Ricard seemed unaware that he was two wrong words away from a bullet cleaning out his skull. "Talk."

"It's a very long story."

"Sum up."

"Taniel woke up. Not long after you went south, the savage girl brought him back. The two of them went to the front line and Taniel helped to hold against the Kez but then was court-martialed on charges of insubordination. He was kicked out of the army and was hired by the Wings of Adom, but then killed five of General Ket's soldiers in self-defense. He then disappeared."

Tamas rocked back on his heels, head spinning. "That's all happened in the last three months?"

Ricard nodded, glancing over his shoulder at Vlora.

"And you don't know where he is now?"

"No."

"And what happened to the school?"

Ricard frowned. "I haven't heard from them for a few weeks. I assumed everything was fine."

Tamas tried to read Ricard's face. This was a man who had made his fortune by being likable—smoothing things over and getting people to work together. Despite this, he was a terrible liar. The fact that he didn't seem to be lying now only deepened Tamas's concern.

Olem's startled shout was Tamas's only warning. He whirled to see a woman kick Olem in the side of the knee, sending him to the ground with a curse. The woman leapt upon Tamas, a stiletto in one hand, moving with impossible speed. Tamas caught her by the wrist and swung her past him—or at least he tried. She stepped back suddenly, flicked the stiletto into the air, and caught it with her other hand, stabbing it at Tamas's throat.

The knife missed by mere inches as Vlora slammed into the woman from one side, and they both hit Ricard's bookshelf with enough force to bring the whole thing down on them. Olem, back on his feet, waded into the mess to grab the woman by her collar, only to receive a punch to his groin. He doubled over and fell back against the wall.

Tamas stepped up behind the woman, ready to shoot her to keep her down.

"Fell, stop!" Ricard bellowed.

The woman immediately stopped struggling.

Still with a pistol trained on the woman, Tamas pulled Vlora and then Olem to their feet. The woman lifted herself to a sitting position in the middle of the collapsed bookshelf and stared sullenly at the pistol in Tamas's hand.

"Damn it, Fell," Ricard said. "What the pit was that?"

"You were in danger, sir," Fell said.

"Were you trying to kill the field marshal?"

Fell's cheeks grew slightly red. "I'm sorry, sir. I didn't recognize him from behind. And no, I was only trying to incapacitate them."

"You swung a knife at my face!" Tamas said.

"It wouldn't have gone deep. I am very precise."

Tamas glanced between Vlora and Olem. Vlora had a darkening bruise on one cheek from the bookshelf and Olem cursed softly as he clutched at his groin. This woman had faced three armed strangers without fear, and she had only meant to incapacitate them? She had dropped Olem in a split second and nearly gotten the better of Tamas himself, even though he was burning a low powder trance.

"You've been hiring better people, I see," Tamas said to Ricard.

Ricard returned to his desk chair and put his head in his hands. "You could have made an appointment, you know."

"No, sir. He couldn't," Fell said from her spot on the floor. "He's been out of contact for months. The city is in foreign hands. He wouldn't know what to think."

Ricard scowled at her for a moment, only for the scowl to slide away, a look of realization replacing it. "Oh. You think I sold the city out to the Brudanians, don't you?"

"I know," Tamas said, "that a foreign army holds my city and that I left you, the Proprietor, and Ondraus with the keys to the city gates."

"It's bloody Lord Claremonte."

It was Tamas's turn to scowl. "Lord Vetas's master? Adamat didn't root out that mongrel?"

"Adamat did an admirable job," Ricard said. "Lord Vetas is dead and his men dead or scattered. We broke him only for his master to arrive with two brigades of Brudanian soldiers and half the Brudanian Royal Cabal."

"No one defended the city?"

Ricard's nostrils flared. "We tried. But... Claremonte didn't come to conquer. Or so he says. He claims his army is only here to help defend us from the Kez. He's running for the office of First Minister of Adro."

"Like pit he is." Tamas began to pace. This army in control of Adopest posed too many questions. If Tamas was going to find out answers, he'd have to do it backed by an army of his own. The Seventh and the Ninth, along with his Deliv allies, were still weeks away.

"Get me a meeting with Claremonte," Tamas said.

"That might not be the best idea."

"Why not?"

"He has half the Brudanian Royal Cabal behind him!" Ricard said. "Can you think of any group that hates you more than the royal cabals of the Nine? They'll kill you outright and dump your body in the Ad."

Tamas continued to pace. He didn't have the time for this. So many enemies. So many facets to consider. He needed allies badly. "What news from the front?"

"They're still holding, but..."

"But what?"

"I haven't had any good information from the front for almost a month."

"You haven't heard from the General Staff for that long? Pit, the Kez could be at the city gates by tomorrow! Damn it, I..."

"Sir," Fell said to Ricard. "Have you told him about Taniel?"

Tamas whirled on Ricard, snatching him by the front of the jacket. "What? What about him?"

"There have been...I mean, I've heard rumors, but—"

"What kind of rumors?"

"Nothing substantial."

"Tell me."

Ricard studied his hands before saying quietly, "That Taniel was captured by Kresimir and hung in the Kez camp. But," he said more loudly, "they're just rumors."

Tamas could hear his heart thundering in his ears. The Kez had taken his boy? They had hung him like a piece of meat, some macabre trophy? Fear coursed through him, followed by the fire of white-hot fury. He found himself sprinting from Ricard's office, shoving his way through the crowd out into the building's main hall.

Olem and Vlora caught up with him in the street.

"Where are we going, sir?" Vlora asked.

Tamas gripped the butt of his pistol. "I'm going to find my boy, and if he's not alive and well, I'm going to pull Kresimir's guts out through his ass."

CHAPTER
3

Adamat was on his way to arrest a general.

He sat in the back of a carriage, the ground bumping away beneath him, and stared out the window at the fields of southern Adro. The fields were golden with fall wheat, the stalks bent by the weight of their fruit and swaying gently in the wind. The peacefulness of it all made him think of his family; both his wife and children at home and the one sold into slavery by the enemy.

This might not go well.

No, Adamat corrected himself. This *could not* go well.

What kind of a madman goes to arrest a general during wartime? The government was in disarray—practically nonexistent—and it was a miracle that the courts were still operating on a local level. All federal cases had been suspended since Manhouch's execution, and it had taken bribery and cajoling to get Ricard Tumblar, one of the interim-council elders, to sign a warrant for General Ket's arrest. They'd strong-armed two local judges into signing the same warrant. Adamat hoped it would be enough.

The driver of the carriage gave a terse command and the carriage suddenly slowed to a stop, lurching Adamat forward in his seat. A glance out one window showed him the wheat fields and rolling hills that gradually gave way to the mountains of the Charwood Pile, their peaks far in the distance, while the other window gave him an unobstructed view of the Adsea stretching off to the southeast.

"Why have we stopped?"

One of Adamat's traveling companions stirred from her slumber. Nila was a woman of about nineteen with curly auburn hair and a face that could charm its way into a king's court. Adamat was under the impression that she was a laundress. He still wasn't quite sure why she had come along on this journey, but Privileged Borbador had insisted.

Adamat opened the door and called up to the driver. "What's going on?"

"The sergeant ordered a stop."

He ducked his head back inside. Why would Oldrich call for a stop? They were too far north to have run into the Adran army already. They still had over a day to travel before they reached the front.

The carriage lurched ahead again suddenly, only to pull off to one side of the road in order to let traffic continue past them. A stagecoach rumbled on, and then a trio of wagons filled with supplies for the front.

"Something is wrong," Adamat said.

Nila rubbed the sleep from her eyes. "Bo," she said, poking the man sleeping on her shoulder.

Privileged Borbador, only surviving member of King Manhouch's royal cabal, gave a start and then went back to snoring loudly.

"Bo!" Nila slapped Bo's cheek.

"I'm here!" Bo sat upright, bare hands dancing in the air in front of him. He blinked the sleep out of his eyes and slowly lowered his hands. "Bloody pit, girl," he said. "If I had been wearing my gloves, I could have killed both of you."

"Well, you weren't," Nila said. "We've stopped."

Bo ran a hand through his ruddy hair and pulled on a pair of white gloves covered in archaic runes. "Why?"

"Not sure," Adamat said. "I'll go check." He hauled himself out of the carriage, glad to be out of close confines with the Privileged. Bo's elemental sorcery could kill Adamat, Oldrich, and the entire platoon of Adran soldiers that made up their escort in mere seconds. Adamat had watched Bo snap the neck of Manhouch's executioner with a flick of his wrist. For all of his charm, Bo was a cold-blooded killer. Adamat glanced back into the carriage once and then trudged up a slight incline toward where Sergeant Oldrich and several of his men conferred beside the road.

"Inspector," Oldrich said with a nod. "Where is the Privileged?"

"Better start calling him 'counselor,'" Adamat said.

Oldrich snorted. "All right. Where's the *lawyer*? We've run into something unexpected."

"Oh?"

"There's an army just over that rise," Oldrich said.

Adamat felt his heart leap into his throat. An army? Had the Kez finally broken through? Were they marching on Adopest?

"An Adran army," Oldrich added.

Adamat's relief was short-lived. "What are they doing here?" he asked. "They're supposed to be in Surkov's Alley still. Have they been pushed back this far?"

"What's going on?" Bo arrived, stretching his arms behind his back. Adamat was reminded again just how young Bo was—not far into his twenties, at a guess. Certainly not yet thirty. Despite his youth, the Privileged had worry lines on his brow and an old man's eyes.

Adamat looked pointedly at Bo's gloves. "You're supposed to be a lawyer," Adamat said.

"I don't like going without my gloves," Bo said, cracking his knuckles. "Besides, no one will see. The army is still a ways off."

"That's not quite true," Oldrich said, jerking his head toward the rise in the road.

Nila had caught up to them. "With me," Bo said to her. They headed up to look at the army over the rise.

Oldrich watched them go. "I don't trust them," he said when they were out of earshot.

"We have to," Adamat said.

"Why? Field Marshal Tamas has always got on without Privileged to hold his hand."

"Tamas is a powder mage," Adamat said. "Neither you nor I have that benefit. And Bo is our backup. If this doesn't work—if General Ket won't come along quietly to face the law in Adopest—then we'll need Bo to get us out of whatever mess we make."

Oldrich rubbed his temples with both hands. "Pit. I can't believe I let you talk me into this."

"You want justice, don't you? You want us to win this war?"

"Yes."

"Then we need to arrest General Ket."

Bo and Nila returned. Nila frowned to herself, while Bo seemed thoughtful.

"What do you think is going on over there?" Bo asked Oldrich. "That camp should be dozens of miles to our south."

"Could be anything," Oldrich said. "Could be the wounded from the front. Could be reinforcements. Could be that our boys were routed and they're retreating."

Bo scratched his chin. He had removed his Privileged gloves. "It's afternoon. If our boys were routed, then they'd be marching toward Adopest right now. I don't know what it is, but something is wrong. There's no more than six brigades in that camp. Too many for reinforcements, too few to be the whole army."

"We should find out what's going on," Adamat said.

"How?" Bo demanded. "We will only know what's happening by riding into that camp. Which we have to do, by the way. If I want to save Taniel—pit, if he's even still alive—and if you want my help saving your son, then we're heading down there."

Bo strode off toward the waiting carriage.

Nila remained, looking between Oldrich and Adamat.

"If this thing goes bad," Oldrich said to Nila, "will he back us up?"

Nila turned to watch Bo. "I think so."

"You 'think'?"

Nila shrugged. "He might also burn his way through a few companies of soldiers and leave us in the wreckage."

Oldrich asked, "What did you say you do?"

"I'm Bo's—the *counselor's*—secretary," Nila said.

"And before that?"

"I was a laundress."

"Ah."

They returned to the carriage and were soon moving again, heading over the hill, where the sight took Adamat's breath away. The Adran camp spread out across the plain in a sea of white tents. It seemed to move and wriggle, like an anthill viewed from above, thousands of soldiers and camp followers going about their day.

The carriage came to a stop once more a mile later as they reached the camp's pickets. Adamat heard one of the guards call out to Oldrich.

"Reinforcements?" a woman's voice asked.

"Eh? No, escorting a lawyer down here on the orders of the interim council."

"A lawyer? What for?"

"No idea. I'm supposed to bring the lawyer down here and convene a meeting of the General Staff."

Bo had his head near the window, listening intently to the conversation. He had pulled his Privileged gloves back on, though he held them below the window, and his fingers twitched ever so slightly.

"Well," the guard said, her voice bored, "that's going to be harder than you think."

Oldrich groaned. "What's happened this time?"

"Uh, well…" The guard cleared her throat, and what she said next was too low for Adamat to hear. Across from him, Nila had a look of concentration on her face.

Oldrich whistled in return. "Thanks for the warning." A moment later and the carriage rumbled on. Adamat cursed under his breath.

"What's happening?" he asked Bo. "Did you hear that?"

Instead of answering, Bo looked at Nila. "Did you listen like I showed you?"

"Yes," Nila said. She ran her hands over her skirt and stared hard out the window. "It seems," she said to Adamat, "that General Ket has been accused of being a traitor. She has taken three brigades with her and split off from the main army. The army is now in a state of civil war."

The General Staff command post was a commandeered farmhouse about a mile from the main highway. It sat at the center of the army, some six brigades strong, white soldiers' tents spiraling outward in an organized but ultimately loose formation of a camp.

Adamat and Bo were left waiting, confined to their carriage, for almost three hours before they were finally led inside. Their guards made it clear that the General Staff were all very busy and that their appointment would take up no more than five minutes of the general's time.

The farmhouse consisted of just one large room with stone walls, a squat fireplace at one end and two neatly made sleeping pallets in the corner. The table in the center of the room had one leg too short, and there were no chairs to be seen. Several maps lay on the table, their corners weighted by pistols. Adamat glanced over the maps briefly, committing them to his perfect memory, where he could study them later at his leisure.

"Inspector Adamat."

Adamat recognized General Hilanska from a portrait he'd seen once in the royal gallery. He was not a tall man, and significantly overweight due to complications resulting from the loss of his arm when he was a young soldier. Well into his forties, Hilanska was a celebrated hero who had made his name as an artillery commander in the Gurlish Wars. Rumor had it he was one of Tamas's most trusted generals.

Adamat nodded to the general and stepped forward to clasp his remaining hand. "This is Counselor Mattias," he said, introducing Bo. "We've come on urgent business from Adopest."

Bo swept off his hat and gave the general a deep bow, but Hilanska barely graced him with a glance.

"That's what I've been told," Hilanska said. "You should know that we are still at war. I've turned away dozens of messengers from Adro because I simply don't have time to deal with domestic issues. You're only here now because I know you were on special assignment from Field Marshal Tamas before he died. I certainly hope you have something important to tell me. Sergeant Oldrich was rather sparse on the details, I'm afraid, so if you could—"

Bo moved forward quickly, cutting Adamat off. "Of course, General," he said, drawing a sheaf of documents from the case hanging from his shoulder. He flipped through several papers before producing one signed and stamped by Ricard Tumblar and the judges in Adopest. "I'm sorry we couldn't provide your men with more details, but this is a delicate matter. You'll see here that we have a warrant for the arrest of General Ket and her sister, Major Doravir."

Hilanska took the paper from Bo and looked it over for several moments. He handed it back. "Adopest has not been apprised of the situation here?" he asked.

"What situation?" Adamat said.

"I have sent several messengers over the course of the last two weeks. Surely you've been informed..."

"We have not, sir," Adamat said.

"The army has gone to war with itself. General Ket has taken three brigades under her command and split with the main army."

Though Nila had told Adamat exactly that, he still didn't have to fake the shock on his face. "How? Why?"

"Ket has accused me of treason," Hilanska said. "She called me a traitor. Said that I was in league with the enemy, and when the rest of the General Staff stood behind me, she took her men and broke with us."

Bo stiffened at Hilanska's words and his hands twitched toward his pockets—to his gloves, no doubt. "And there is no basis for this accusation? No evidence?"

"Of course not!" Hilanska snatched his cane and climbed to his feet. "She based her claim on the report of an infantryman who said he saw me conspiring with enemy messengers."

"And were you?" Bo asked. Adamat shot him a look, but the damage had been done.

Hilanska snapped back, "Of course not. It was one of her Dredgers, a convict from the Mountainwatch. The worst kind of scum. To think she believed him over me..." He shook his head sadly. "Ket and I have known one another for decades. We've never been friends, but we certainly haven't been enemies. I never thought she would make such a baseless accusation. Unless..." He held his hand out for the arrest warrant and Bo obliged him. His eyes skimmed the page. "Unless she's trying to cover her tracks."

Adamat exchanged a glance with Bo. "We came to a similar conclusion ourselves, but in regard to the court-martial of Taniel Two-shot. Taniel sent Ricard Tumblar a message asking him to look into Ket's accounts, and it was what put us onto her track."

"Tamas's boy did that? He's twice as clever as Ket thought him. Incredibly sad, that."

Bo slipped to one side of Hilanska, moving casually, a hand dipping into his pocket. "What's sad about it?"

"Taniel was captured by the Kez," Hilanska said. "Raised above their army like a trophy."

"No." Bo swallowed hard, his hand coming out of his pocket without his gloves.

"The whole army saw it. Rumor has it he tried to go after Kresimir himself." Hilanska shook his head. "I watched that boy grow from a lad. I'm just glad Tamas wasn't alive to see it."

Adamat tried to focus on Hilanska's tics—the way his left hand fiddled with the empty right sleeve of his jacket, the way his eyes moved around the room. The general was working his way around the truth. He'd told him some of it, but not all.

Unfortunately Adamat had no way of discovering what Hilanska was leaving out.

"And he's dead?" Bo asked.

"They took his body down quickly after his capture. He was only displayed one day, but he was certainly dead."

Adamat shot Bo a glance. The Privileged's face had gone deathly pale. He blinked as if there were something in his eyes, and his breath grew short. Adamat stepped toward him and offered him his arm, but Bo waved him off before suddenly rushing from the room.

Hilanska watched him go. "Strange man. Did he know Two-shot?"

"Not that I'm aware of," Adamat said smoothly. "I was told he's very sensitive to talk of death."

"I see." Hilanska chewed on this a moment, a frown crossing his weathered face.

"Sir," Adamat went on so as not to give Hilanska time to consider Bo's behavior, "do you have a plan to close this schism and face the Kez?" If Two-shot was truly dead, Adamat would have to salvage the situation. Would Bo still help Adamat recover his son? Or was Adamat now on his own? Regardless, Adamat felt some duty to country that he should do what he could to reunite the army.

Hilanska headed to the table, where he swept his hand to clear the brigade markers and began to awkwardly roll up one of the maps with his one hand. "I don't think I should talk of tactics with you, Inspector."

"Tactics? Will there be a battle?" Adran fighting Adran? The Kez greatly outnumbered the Adran army, and infighting would be sure to doom them all. It was a miracle that the Kez had not yet taken advantage of the infighting to attack. Adamat's thoughts whirled as he tried to reorganize his priorities.

"Of course not. We are doing everything within our power to settle this amicably. In fact, with this new evidence I may be able to sway Ket's allies away from her. If that lawyer can get his stomach back, have him bring me every bit of paperwork he has. We can show the officers that Ket is just trying to cover up her own crimes. At the very least it will reassure the men that we are on the side of the right."

"Certainly," Adamat said. "But the Kez—"

"We have this in hand," Hilanska cut him off. "Don't worry yourself any further. I trust that you will return to Adopest and assure the council we will heal this fracture and turn back the Kez threat, and then we will return to deal with the Brudanians."

It was the first time Hilanska had mentioned the foreign army that held Adopest. Adamat opened his mouth to ask him what he meant, but the general waved his hand to signal an end to their meeting and turned his back.

Adamat found Bo sitting outside the farmhouse, his back to the stone wall and the tails of his jacket in the mud. Adamat grabbed him under the elbow. "Come on."

"Leave me be."

"*Come on*," Adamat insisted, pulling him up. He spoke in a fierce whisper to get Bo's attention, leading him away from Hilanska's guards. "We still have work to do."

"Bugger it all. You heard him. Taniel's dead." Bo jerked away from Adamat.

"Quiet down! He may not be dead."

Bo looked as if he'd been slapped. "What do you mean?"

Adamat felt instant guilt at giving Bo any false sense of hope. "Well, let's at least confirm Hilanska's story before you go into mourning. Taniel may be a Kez captive, or he may have escaped, or..." He trailed off. Bo regarded him with suspicious skepticism.

"Why the optimism?" Bo asked. "Shouldn't you be hoping that Taniel's dead so we can go about finding your boy? Or are you just afraid that I'll go back on my word?"

Adamat *was* afraid that Bo would go back on his word. "Something is bothering me about Hilanska. The maps on his table." Adamat pictured them in his mind, turned them around, and considered them before speaking. "The only experience I have with battle planning is from my time at the academy, but I'd bet my pension that Hilanska is planning on sandwiching Ket's force between his own and the Kez."

"It would be sound reasoning on his part," Bo said.

"Not if he's trying to reunite the brigades, as he claims."

Bo shrugged and looked off into the distance, his face sullen.

"Bo," Adamat said. "Bo!" He reached around and grabbed Bo by the front of his jacket, turning them face-to-face. Bo jerked his jacket out of Adamat's hands and stepped back. Adamat followed him forward and slapped Bo across the face.

A thrill of fear went up his spine. He'd just slapped a Privileged. Holy pit. What had he done? "Pull yourself together," he said, trying not to let his voice quake.

Bo's mouth hung open, one Privileged glove in his hand ready to be pulled over his fingers. "I've killed men for less."

"You have?"

"Well. I've thought about it. I'm sure other Privileged have. You have seconds to tell me why you thought that necessary."

"Because we have a duty here. This is bigger than one man. This is the fate of our family and our friends and our country."

"You don't understand why I'm here, do you, Inspector?" Bo said. "I'm here because Taniel Two-shot is my *only* friend. He's my *only* family. Privileged normally do not have the luxury of either, and I'll be damned if you think this country means more to me than that."

Adamat took a deep breath, relieved that Bo didn't try to kill him then and there. He whispered, "If Hilanska butchers these proceedings, my children will wind up as slaves to the Kez. I have to try and make sure that doesn't happen. If the best way to do that is to help you find your friend, then so be it. You need to get a hold of yourself and *discreetly* ask around about Taniel. I'm going to look into Hilanska."

Bo blinked several times, taking shaky breaths, and seemed to regain some of his composure. "We're forgetting the mercenaries."

The turn of conversation was so quick it took Adamat a moment to catch up. Of course. The Wings of Adom, the mercenary company in the employ of Adro. They should have had several brigades on the front. Adamat pictured Hilanska's map once more, looking for the flags: a saint's halo with gold wings. There they were, up in the corner. "They're camped about ten miles from here. Probably trying to keep out of this internal spat."

"Smart of them."

Bo flexed his jaw and stuffed his Privileged glove back into his pocket. "Start asking around. Find something out, and do it quickly. Or I'm going to go back in there and question Hilanska *my* way."

"Are you all right?"

"My cheek is a little sore."

"I meant about Taniel."

Bo looked as if he'd swallowed something sour. "A moment of weakness, that's all. I'll be fine. And Adamat...?"

"Yes?"

"If you lay your hands on me again, I'll turn you inside out."

CHAPTER

4

Nila waited beside the carriage for Bo and Adamat to return from their meeting with General Hilanska.

Downhill from her a small stream wound its way through the camp, its banks muddied from the tramp of a thousand boots. Nila watched as a laundress filled a bucket with the dirty water and hauled it back to her fire, where the uniforms of half a dozen soldiers sat piled on her bench. The woman filled her washing pot with the water and sat back to wait for it to boil, drawing a soiled hand across her brow.

A different choice sometime in the last few months and Nila knew that might have been her. She glanced down at her hands. For years they had been cracked and worn by the soap, water, and lye she'd used to do laundry. Now they seemed remarkably smooth to the touch and, Bo told her, they would be put to better use.

A Privileged. She still couldn't believe it, not even after seeing the fire spring from her own fingertips the first time and during all their practice since.

Privileged were creatures of great cunning and strength. They commanded the elements and made armies quake. It seemed so crass that a laundress without family or connections could suddenly hold such power.

She couldn't help but feel cheated as well. Had she known it lay dormant within her, she might have used that power to escape from Vetas or to protect the royalists. Nila clenched her fist and felt a slight warmth on the back of her hand—fire, blue and white, dancing across her knuckles as if they were at the center of a hearth. Glancing around to see if anyone had noticed, she shook her hand to put out the fire and then hid it behind her back.

She thought about her time with the royalists and remembered Rozalia, the Privileged who had fought for them. Had Rozalia sensed the latent power within Nila and simply chosen not to mention it? Or had she been kind to her for some other reason? Would Nila become like her someday—old, wise, and powerful? Would people be nervous around her as she had been nervous around Rozalia?

"Risara!"

Nila emerged from deep within her own thoughts, and it took her a moment to remember that was the name she was using as she pretended to be a secretary to Bo—who himself was masquerading as a lawyer. She turned her head to see him hurrying toward her from across the camp. There was an urgency to his step that concerned her.

"Did you find Taniel?"

"No." Bo took her by the arm and stepped around to the far side of the carriage, where they were less likely to be overheard. "General Hilanska says that Taniel's dead."

The dispassionate way Bo spoke the words made her step back. Taniel had been his obsession ever since he had taken her and Jakob under his wing. His only friend, he claimed. He had been searching for Taniel for months now with a passion that Nila had found inspiring. And now this? Bo could be distant at times, even cold, but this...

"There's something else?" she asked.

"We're going to find out for sure. Adamat thinks there's a chance he's still alive, and Hilanska is only one man."

Nila realized he wasn't dispassionate—he was dazed.

"Where do we stand?"

"Hilanska has dismissed us, but I'm not leaving until I can confirm that Taniel is dead. I want a body or a grave or something more than just Hilanska's word. I'll even go to the Kez camp if I have to. Adamat is corroborating Hilanska's story with the soldiers. I'm going to do the same." He paused and looked her up and down. "This will be dangerous. If Hilanska finds out who I am, I may be killed outright—along with you, Adamat, Oldrich, and his men."

"Just for impersonating a lawyer?"

A smile tugged at the corner of Bo's face, but he stifled it quickly. "I'm serious. Hilanska doesn't like or trust Privileged. He's a man with something to hide, and the mere fact that we're snooping around is going to gain his suspicion. He's like Tamas—he'll do what's expedient. Even if it means killing a whole lot of people."

"That seems like something you would respect."

"And I can respect it by not letting him know what I really am. Or what you are, for that matter." He glanced down at her hands and fell into a long silence. He had told her that no Privileged but the gods could touch the Else without runed gloves to keep them from being burned from the inside out by pure sorcery.

Except for her, apparently. And she was far from a god.

She had no doubt that if she said the word, Bo would send her back to Adopest today. This was her opportunity to run. She could fetch Jakob and go into hiding, using the funds that Bo had left for her. She would be able to get out of danger.

If she left now, she would never learn how to control her new powers. She would never find a Privileged as patient or thoughtful or just downright human as Bo. And she would never get the chance to repay him for the kindness he'd shown her and Jakob.

"What can I do?" Nila asked.

Nila waited inside the small wood-and-stone building that had, according to one of the soldiers, at one point been a stable.

The building barely had a roof, and the door was nothing more than a scrap of cowhide, but it seemed that the quartermaster of the Twelfth Brigade was making do. The floors were covered in straw and every available space was stacked with wooden crates and powder kegs.

Bo had told her to ask around about Taniel Two-shot, stifling her protests that his instructions were rather vague, and left her to her own devices. He wasn't exactly the image of rousing leadership.

She didn't know how to go about asking soldiers about the death of their own. It seemed crass. So she thought she'd put what she *did* know to good use.

Despite the horror of being Lord Vetas's prisoner, she had learned many valuable lessons. One of those was the worth of good record keeping, and how it could be used against the very people who kept those records.

The cowhide was swept aside and a woman of about fifty ambled into the room wearing an Adran-blue army jacket with the quartermaster's pin on her collar. She was a slim woman, carrying most of her weight around her hips, and her graying hair was tucked into a bun behind her head.

"How can I help you, my dear?" she asked, dropping carelessly onto a powder keg.

"My name is Risara," Nila said, smoothing the front of her skirt. "I'm the secretary to Counselor Mattias of Adopest and I need access to the brigade records."

"Well then." The quartermaster sniffed. "I'll have to clear that with General Hilanska."

Nila produced an attaché case from beneath her arm and opened it on her lap, taking great pains to leaf through the official-looking documents within. She withdrew one in particular and handed it to the quartermaster. "This is a warrant granting me access to whatever records I wish to see. Do you think this is something the general wants to deal with during the current turmoil?"

The quartermaster read the warrant over twice. Nila tried not to let her nervousness show. The warrant was perfectly valid, but Bo had warned her that the army operated outside civilian judicial purview—whether legal or not.

"All right," the quartermaster said, handing the document back to Nila. "What do you want to see?"

Nila tried not to show her surprise at being granted access so easily or to let on that she didn't actually know what she was looking for. What would help her track down Taniel? His movements before his reported death? "Give me a copy of all requisition reports of the last two months."

"All of them?" The quartermaster rocked back on her powder keg. "That's several hundred pages."

"Get a scribe in here. I'll wait."

The quartermaster grumbled under her breath and began sorting through the crates piled in one corner. Nila waited, trying to put on as patient an air as possible. Lord Vetas had forced her to run many of his errands—not all of them strictly legal—and she had quickly learned that if she only acted like she belonged someplace most people would assume she did.

"Is there anything else you need?" the quartermaster said, wrist-deep in sheaves of paper. "I don't want to have to go through all this again."

"What records do you have on individual officers?"

The quartermaster lifted a pile of worn yellow paper almost as thick as Nila's hand was wide. "You'd have to see the general's adjutant for that."

"Of course." Nila took the records from the quartermaster and leafed through them. "Do you need to make copies?"

"They're all in triplicate. That's why the column for order signatures is blank. I'll have another copy made up when someone has time. Anything you're looking for in particular?"

Nila hesitated a moment. If she mentioned her goal, it might raise suspicion. But the idea of combing through all those reports was incredibly daunting. "Do you know if Captain Taniel Two-shot made any requisition orders?"

"He did." The quartermaster scratched her head for a minute as if to run through her memory. "There are a few dozen, I think. I can't tell you the exact days, but any requests made by a powder mage are marked with a 'pm' in the order column."

"You've been most helpful. Thank you. Do you mind if I look through the copies here?"

The quartermaster shrugged her bony shoulders. "Fine by me. You'll have to excuse me for a moment, though. I'll just be takin' a piss."

Nila was left alone with the records. It took her a few minutes to get a feel for how the pages were organized. They were covered in small script and several columns. Names, dates, orders, and whether they were fulfilled. There were notes in half a dozen different handwritings—various quartermasters, she assumed. Once she found the first 'pm'—a request by Taniel for more powder, which was denied—it wasn't hard to spot more.

She had just found the fifth powder request when she heard the old quartermaster behind her.

"Right there," the woman said. Nila glanced up out of politeness, only to see herself trapped in the small building by two big soldiers. The men wore dark-blue Adran uniforms with red trim and tall bearskin hats. Not regular soldiers. Grenadiers.

"Ma'am," one of them said, "would you come with us, please."

Nila's heart was in her throat. "Is something the matter?"

"Please," he said again. "Come with us." He glanced behind him, as if nervous. "Try not to make a ruckus, ma'am."

Nila didn't see that she had much choice. She could yell and scream, with only a small chance of attracting Bo. But even then, what could Bo do? For the purpose of this mission they were not in a friendly camp. "Of course, just let me gather my things." Nila scooped up the requisition orders, securing the whole thing with a string, and forced them into her attaché case before following the men out of the building.

"Stay with us, please," one of the men said in a low voice before moving on ahead. The other, Nila noted, fell back some ten paces. It was almost as if they didn't want to be seen with her.

She was led past General Hilanska's headquarters and over a slight rise and into another part of the camp. She examined the various standards, trying to remember the brigades and regiments of the Adran army and failing completely. If not General Hilanska, who were they taking her to see? Or were they taking her straight to the stockade?

The man in front of her suddenly stopped beside a white-walled tent and turned as if taking up the guard. He gestured to the flap. "Go on in."

The other soldier had disappeared. Nila stared at the tent for a moment, both curious and fearful about what she'd find inside. She clenched her jaw. She was a Privileged now. She was going to have to get used to danger—and taking risks. She ducked inside.

A man sat in the middle of the tent, scribbling furiously in a notebook on his lap. He didn't look up when Nila entered, only pointed to the chair opposite him and continued to write. Nila looked around carefully. No sign of danger here, though that could all change in a moment in a camp full of soldiers. She took the offered seat.

By the size of the tent, Nila guessed that this man was an officer. He was a big man, well over six feet tall standing, with wide shoulders and thick arms. He had a face that looked like it had been punched one too many times, with a crooked nose and high cheekbones. His chair was wheeled, of the kind used by invalids.

She spotted the man's army jacket hanging in one corner, with two hawks over the Adran Mountains emblazoned on the shoulder. It also held four bars over a chevron—Nila knew enough to recognize he was a colonel. Had she read something in the newspaper recently about a colonel being paralyzed in a heroic action?

He finally stopped writing and pushed himself up straight in his chair. "You're the girl that came in with the lawyer this afternoon?" he asked.

"I am Counselor Mattias's secretary."

"How long have you been with the counselor?" The colonel watched her face intently.

"I'm not sure what you're asking."

"It's a direct question," the colonel said. "How long have you been with him? Are you in his confidence?"

Nila knew she had to make a decision. Throw everything in behind Bo—be there if he was exposed and killed—or pretend that she was nothing more than a hired secretary.

"Some time. I am in his confidence, sir."

The colonel's eyes narrowed. "Indeed? Then what's the Privileged up to?"

Nila forced herself not to bolt for the tent flap. "I don't know what—"

"Stop," the man said. "I've known Taniel Two-shot since he was a boy. You think I wouldn't recognize his best friend?"

"I'm sorry, sir," Nila said. "I don't know your name."

"Colonel Etan."

"Colonel Etan. If you think you know someone, shouldn't you invite them to your tent directly?"

The shadow of a smile touched Etan's face. "Is Borbador here looking for Taniel?"

Nila couldn't avoid a direct question like that. This man claimed to know Taniel. This may be the best way to get information out of him. Or it could all be a trap. "Yes," she said.

Etan gave a soft sigh, closing his eyes. "Thank Adom."

"I'm sorry?"

Etan opened his eyes again. "I've spent the last several weeks trying to find out what happened to Taniel. Nobody has seen him since he was raised up like a trophy above the Kez camp. Hilanska has refused to ask any questions. He won't even request Taniel's body back from the Kez."

Nila's throat felt dry. "So Taniel *is* dead?"

"I don't know," Etan said. "He was alive when he was raised up on that beam. He was alive the last time anyone saw him up there, and then when Kresimir killed Adom, he—"

"Wait, what?" Nila couldn't help herself. She leaned forward in her chair. "Kresimir killed Adom? What are you talking about?" Was this man mad?

Etan waved his hand. "It's a very long story. One that hasn't gotten back to Adopest, it seems. Pit, Hilanska is keeping a tight lid around here. To answer your earlier question, I deemed it unwise to bring Borbador here. I'm hoping that you are being watched less closely than the supposed 'lawyer' is."

"You want me to pass him a message?"

"Yes. Don't trust Hilanska."

"I don't think Bo trusts anyone."

Etan scowled at his legs. He didn't seem to hear her. "Hilanska is a superior officer and I do him a disservice, but he's been acting very strangely lately. As I said before, he won't look into Taniel's whereabouts. He adamantly refuses to believe that Tamas might still be alive. What's more, he's been putting all of Tamas's most loyal men into their own companies and promoting his own longest-serving soldiers. And he's been raving about a Kez pincer movement that could come over the southern mountains—he sent two whole companies into the valleys in the southwest, where they won't be able to do a damned thing when the Kez do attack."

Nila couldn't pretend to understand the inner politics of the army, but she imagined it not unlike anywhere else that people were constantly jockeying for rank or status—even like the noble household where she had been employed before the coup. She *did* know that Bo wouldn't care one whit for the army politics. But Etan was clearly distraught, and she didn't think it would help to tell him that.

"Are you able to help us find Taniel?" she asked gently.

Etan glanced at the attaché case in her hands. "I've gone through all of Taniel's requisition forms. I was there when he made some of them. I don't think they'll help you, but I suppose another set of eyes wouldn't hurt. I've done everything within my power to discover his fate—I've been watching for anyone who might come asking, as well. Bo might have to go to the Kez to get any more information."

"That would be suicide," Nila said. Not that it would stop Bo.

"It might. I'm sorry that I could not be more help. I'm leaving for Adopest in the morning. If there's anything I can do to aid your search, contact me through one of the grenadiers of the Twelfth."

"Thank you," Nila said.

She left the colonel and headed back across the camp toward where they had left their carriage. What else could she do now but wait for Bo and tell him about Etan? Etan's advice had been unhelpful, but she hoped it would make Bo more optimistic to know they had a friend in the camp and that Taniel had last been seen alive.

Their carriage had been moved off the road and down into a gully and the horses unharnessed. She sat in the carriage to read through the reports, going through every page one by one, carefully examining each line to be sure she didn't miss any of Taniel's requisitions. The column that interested her the most was the one where the quartermasters entered their own notes about the requisition. Up to a certain point in time, each of Taniel's requests for black powder had been denied "by order of the General Staff."

Until about a month previous. He was given powder, and the note column said, "Special permission, General Hilanska." Nila set that page aside to show to Bo.

It grew dark, and Nila finally had to set aside her work. It seemed strange to her that neither Bo nor Adamat had returned yet. In fact, she hadn't seen Sergeant Oldrich or his men either. She leaned her head against the wall of the carriage, wondering if she should go look for them or just rest here until they returned.

Nila thought she heard a soft click from the opposite door of the carriage. She turned, but the carriage door was still closed.

"Hello?" she asked. When there was no response, she put her hand to her door latch and it occurred to her that in a camp of many tens of thousands, there didn't seem to be anyone close to her carriage.

The opposite door suddenly swung open. Nila glimpsed a dark coat, a covered face, and the dull glint of steel in the moonlight. The carriage rocked as someone dove inside. A hand darted toward her.

Nila threw herself across the carriage, felt a knife catch in her skirts. She twisted away and heard a low curse in a man's voice as her attacker tried to drag his blade from the cloth. She rolled onto the flat of the blade and kicked out at the man's shoulder.

He pulled back with a grunt, the knife no longer in his hand, only to leap bodily upon her.

She caught him under the shoulders. He batted at her arms, pushing them down, one hand snaking around her neck. She felt his fingers close about her throat and remembered Lord Vetas's hot breath upon her shoulder when he had done the same.

The man hissed suddenly, jumping away from her, his jacket on fire. Nila felt the pressure leave her throat, saw the flame dancing on her fingertips, and she leapt on top of the man, fueled by the coals of her rage. He tried to grapple with her, his attention taken by his burning coat, but Nila forced herself inside his guard.

Her hand still aflame, she grasped the man's face and pushed.

Skin and bone seemed to give way beneath her fingers. The man's scream died in his throat and his body stopped moving. The cushion and the man's clothes were still on fire and she beat at the flames with her skirt until they were gone.

The body, most of its head melted into a sickening black goop on the carriage bench, lay still beneath her. Nila slowly backed away. Her head hit the roof of the carriage and she ducked down, unable to pull her eyes away from the corpse lying in the smoldering remains of its own clothing.

She looked down at her hand. It was covered in cooked bits of bone and flesh.

"Nila, are you—"

Bo jerked open the door she had been resting against just a few moments before and stared down at the body. His face was unreadable in the darkness.

"Come here," he said gently, taking her by the wrist and pulling her outside. She only noticed the acrid smell of smoke and burned flesh, hair, and wool as Bo led her away. He pulled a handkerchief from his pocket and gently cleaned her hand, emptying some of his canteen onto her fingers. He went back to the carriage and fetched her attaché case.

"I..." She seemed barely able to take a breath. Her heart thundered and her hands shook.

She'd just killed a man by burning through his entire head. *With her hand.*

"We'll leave the luggage. I'd set fire to the carriage, but it would just attract attention all the sooner. They've arrested Oldrich and his men. We have to go find Adamat."

Nila looked at her hand, clean now of the charred gore. The phantom stickiness of the blood clung between her fingers. She forced herself to look up into Bo's eyes. She had to be strong. "And if he's captured as well?"

"We'll save him if we can. If not, he's on his own."

"And all of Oldrich's soldiers?"

Bo looked about them furtively. "Not even I can get fifteen men out of an army encampment. They'll have to face the firing squad for us. Now, let's go." He pulled at her arm.

"No," Nila said.

"What do you mean, 'no'?"

"You—we—brought them into this. We'll get them out."

"Damn it, Nila," Bo hissed. "We'd have to have help, and we simply don't have it."

Nila tilted her head to one side. "Yes we do," she said.

CHAPTER
5

Adamat was only able to spend about three hours asking questions before the provosts came for him.

He was in the middle of speaking with a young sergeant about her cousin in the Third Brigade under General Ket's command when he felt a hand at his elbow. He turned, expecting to find Nila or Bo there with some kind of news, but instead looked over and up—and up some more—at the military police officer standing beside him. The man had a barrel chest, and when he spoke, his voice sounded like an echo.

"Inspector Adamat?"

"Yes."

"You're to come with me."

Adamat grasped the head of his cane tightly and raised his eyebrows. "I'm sorry, I'm just in the middle of an interview. You'll have to wait." He turned back to the sergeant, hoping that was enough to put off the provost.

"*Now*," the man's voice rang out.

The sergeant leaned over to Adamat. "Inspector, you better go with him."

Adamat let out a small sigh, gathered his hat in his hands, and faced the provost. "What's this about?"

"You're to come with me."

"Yes, I gathered that much. I'm an Adran citizen and I have the right to ask why I'm being gathered by an officer of the peace."

The provost tilted his head to one side. "This is a military jurisdiction and you have no such rights as would be afforded to you by an Adran provost. Now, will you come along or shall I drag you?"

Not as daft as he looked, unfortunately. Adamat gave him a firm nod. "I'll come along, but under protest."

"Protest all you like. This way."

Adamat made sure to grumble loudly in an inconvenienced sort of way as they headed through the camp. Inside, though, his heart was hammering. He had expected the provosts to come after him sooner or later. After all, if Hilanska was indeed keeping secrets, he wouldn't want someone snooping around. Adamat hadn't expected them to be so quick about it.

Had Hilanska questioned Oldrich? Or perhaps one of his soldiers had recognized Bo? There were too many things that could go wrong, it was impossible to plan for them all. Perhaps the girl had lost her nerve and run to Hilanska herself.

Adamat dismissed the last option. That laundress, whoever she was, had steel in her eyes.

The camp stockade was nothing more than a trio of prison wagons near where the brigade's cavalry hitched their horses for the night. Adamat was led over to the closest and one of the guards unlocked the door.

The big provost took Adamat by the shoulder and pushed him toward the wagon. Adamat gritted his teeth, wanting to reprimand the man, but knew this was no time to be making enemies. All three wagons were already full—of Oldrich and his men.

Adamat's cane was taken away and he stepped inside.

Oldrich regarded him sourly. "I see the Privileged's plan is off to a wonderful start," he said when the guards had gone on to do their rounds.

"When did they come for you?" Adamat asked.

"Not more than half an hour ago."

"Did they say why?"

Oldrich shook his head. "They got us while we were split up. Some of the boys were at the mess, two others at the latrine. It was all done very quiet, and they were sure to outnumber us by three to one." He leaned over to the bars of the prison wagon and spit. "It's bad when they come quietly. The provosts love to flaunt their power."

"They're acting like we're enemies of the state," one of the other soldiers said. There was a round of nods, and he added, "We wouldn't get treated like this by the field marshal."

Oldrich looked over his shoulder. "The field marshal isn't here," he said. "You boys just remember—you were following orders. If anyone's going to take the fall it'll be me." He examined Adamat, as if wondering if it was worth getting court-martialed or worse on his behalf.

By the sullen silence among the men, Adamat guessed that they'd had this conversation already.

"When are they going to question us?" Adamat asked. He had little experience with provosts, but he could only imagine the worst: Hilanska wanted to cover something up. He'd torture them all to find out what they knew, and then have them executed quietly.

"Depends on how big of a hurry they're in. And how big of a hornet's nest you kicked by asking questions. Could be they'll just hold us a couple of days and then let us go." Oldrich didn't sound optimistic about that outcome.

The night drew on and Adamat watched the tents, waiting to see Hilanska's provosts return to collect them for questioning. The hours passed. The more he thought about it, the more he realized Oldrich was probably right: Hilanska just wanted to keep them from complicating things. He needed them out of the way and that was it. They were still in a tight place, but the belief helped Adamat to relax.

He was just beginning to doze, his shoulders up against the cold steel of the prison wagon walls, when he heard a hiss behind his ear.

He turned to find Bo right behind him. "How long have you been here?" Bo asked through the bars.

Adamat shook away the sleep. "A few hours, I think."

"The sentries are unconscious. We have a few minutes until the guard makes their rounds. We have to go. Now."

Adamat hesitated. If Hilanska only wanted to hold them for a time, an escape attempt would only make things worse. Bo moved around to the front of the prison wagon and licked the end of his gloved finger. He twitched his fingers twice and then set it against the steel of the lock.

"Are you sure this is a good idea?" Adamat asked.

"They tried to kill Nila," Bo said. "They don't want us quiet— they want us dead. Nila! Get the other wagon."

Adamat turned to see Nila rush over to one of the other prison wagons. She glanced around, as if self-conscious, then held one hand out in front of her, palm up as if holding a fruit. Adamat frowned at the gesture. What was she doing?

A cold blue flame danced over the palm of her hand. She reached out and grabbed the lock. Steel melted in her hand, dripping to the ground with a sizzle. One of the soldiers swore under his breath.

This girl was a Privileged? No wonder Bo had insisted on bring-

ing her along! But where were her gloves? Adamat didn't have time
to think about it as he was pushed out the front of the prison wagon
by whispering soldiers.

"How the pit are we all getting out of the camp?" Adamat hissed
to Bo.

"With help," Bo said. He gave a low whistle, and two men suddenly emerged from the blackness near the hitching posts. They
both stood well over six feet tall and each carried a bundle of blue-
and-crimson uniforms in their arms. "Oldrich," Bo said. "Get your
men dressed. They've just joined the grenadiers of the Twelfth Brigade. You too, Adamat. Over your clothes, boys. We can't leave
them any sign of how we escaped."

Adamat snatched one of the uniforms and pulled it on over his
suit. It was an awkward fit, the uniform was made for someone far
larger. The jacket followed, and he was handed a bearskin hat.

Nila went down the line, straightening uniforms and tugging
them to fit here and there. She joined Adamat and Bo and gestured over the two grenadiers. "You're part of Colonel Etan's honor
guard," she said to Adamat, "escorting him up to Adopest. He was
going to leave in the morning, but word of a sickness in his family
has him riding out tonight."

"And we can trust this Colonel Etan?"

Bo hesitated for a moment, and then nodded. "One of Taniel's
friends."

Adamat looked between Bo and Nila. Neither was wearing a
uniform. "And what about you?"

"We're making our own way out," Bo said. He didn't elaborate
further.

"And this civil war?" Adamat asked.

"Not my problem."

Nila gave Adamat an apologetic look.

"Get a move on," Bo said. "The guard changes in an hour. We'll wait here to make sure your disappearance isn't noticed before the colonel can get you out, then I'll make a false trail running for the Adsea. They'll assume you've escaped by boat."

Adamat suppressed the urge to thank him. After all, he wouldn't be here if it weren't for Bo's urging. "And my boy?" He needed to get his son back, and Bo was the only one who could help him do it.

"I'm going to find Taniel, and then I'll come get you in Adopest. You have my word."

Adamat gave the Privileged a tight nod and followed Oldrich and his men after the two grenadiers. They were led through the camp at a double march and Adamat struggled to keep up. Oldrich's men were Adran soldiers. They might not have been as big as grenadiers, but they could play the part without too much of a stretch. Adamat was older than most of these men by ten years, softened by his own age and family life. He was used to riding in carriages, not marching.

He remembered a time in the academy when Tamas, then a colonel, had first begun to pave the way for the rise of commoners among the ranks. Adamat had considered joining as a career.

Three minutes into the march and Adamat said a grateful prayer that he had not done so.

They soon arrived in the section of the camp occupied by the grenadiers of the Twelfth Brigade. Adamat recognized their standard, two hawks over the Adran Mountains, and tried to recollect what he knew about Colonel Etan.

Etan was a career military man. Just over thirty, he had risen through the ranks by distinguishing himself in battle during one of the many small wars in Gurla after the Gurlish campaigns had supposedly ended. His rise might have seemed swift, but was less strange when Adamat considered how short an average grenadier's career normally was. Shock troops didn't often last long, and few enough of the big men were known for their intelligence.

Adamat also remembered reading in the papers just a couple of weeks back that Etan had been wounded in battle. Paralyzed, the article had said.

His breath sounding ragged in his ears, he caught sight of a waiting carriage near the edge of the camp, surrounded by an honor guard of some fifty grenadiers. Several grenadiers stood by with rifles and kits. Adamat, Oldrich, and the rest were hastily outfitted.

"Fall in, men!" a captain called. "Damned dogs, arriving late! You're not worthy to carry the colonel on your backs! Not worthy to bathe his feet. It'll be latrine duty for all of you when you get back!" He ran up and down the line, slapping at their knees with his riding crop. Adamat felt the sting across his calf and bit back a curse. He was playing a character now. He dared not drop it.

"Yes sir!" he said with the others.

The captain stopped beside him and leaned forward, speaking low. "If you cause trouble for my colonel, I'll kill you myself." He moved on before Adamat could reply.

A hand reached out of the carriage and thumped the side. Adamat had barely begun to catch his breath before they were marching double-time again.

Sweat was already pouring down his face when the carriage trundled off the hard-packed dirt of the camp thoroughfare and onto the cobbles of the main highway to Adopest. They came to a slow stop beside the northernmost checkpoint. Two sentries approached the carriage.

Adamat wasn't close enough to hear the ensuing conversation. He stood with rifle shouldered, the pack on his back pressing against his spine, and hoped that they wouldn't notice how short he was for a grenadier—or that his uniform was already soaked with sweat and they hadn't even begun their march.

One of the sentries shrugged and they both stepped back, waving Etan's carriage on. Adamat wasn't even given a second glance as he trotted past them.

His legs burned as they continued on into the night, and his lungs felt on fire. Every wound from the last six months seemed to flare up—his nose ached, cuts on his stomach and shoulder itched, and bruises he'd not even known existed began to throb. He felt himself lagging behind the other grenadiers—both Oldrich's men and Etan's real soldiers—and struggled to push himself harder.

What a miserable existence. Who could stomach putting their body through this kind of abuse? Adamat used his indignation to propel himself forward. This whole trip had been a waste. Taniel was likely dead, and it could be weeks or months until Bo returned to help Adamat look for Josep. If he returned at all. Why had he ever agreed to this in the first place?

And this whole affair between Hilanska and Ket. It would prove Adro's undoing, he had no doubt. The more he thought over the map he'd seen in Hilanska's command post, the more he was convinced that the general wasn't just preparing for a fight—he was looking for one.

Would Ket really accuse Hilanska of being a traitor just to cover her own tracks? Perhaps she'd thought more of the General Staff would side with her? Or perhaps she'd thought to sway the Wings of Adom. Regardless, she would be crushed between Hilanska and the Kez.

Did she know that three brigades of Adran infantry would die because of her? Was she that selfish?

Adamat didn't realize he'd stopped marching until he noticed the carriage and its escort some forty paces ahead of him. He ran to catch up, forcing himself to ignore the pain in his knees, and arrived at the back of the line just as the captain called for a stop.

Adamat shouldered his way through the soldiers, heading toward Etan's carriage, and felt a hand on his chest.

"I didn't say to fall out," the captain said to him. "Back into line before I give you a beating."

"I have to speak with the colonel," Adamat said.

"You'll do no such thing. Back in line!"

Adamat didn't have time for this. His heart beat with a sudden urgency that had nothing to do with this quick march. "I'm not one of your damned soldiers and you know it," Adamat said. "I appreciate your help, but get out of my damned face. I'm on assignment from Field Marshal Tamas himself."

"Field Marshal Tamas is—" the captain started, drawing himself up.

"Captain," a voice called from the carriage. "Settle down. Let the inspector ride with me."

Adamat suppressed a triumphant grin. No need to antagonize the man further. He pushed past the captain and opened the door to the carriage, stepping inside.

In the darkness it was difficult to see any of Etan's features. Adamat was certain he was a large man. He was propped in his seat—probably strapped in place, due to his condition—and leaned on a cane.

"You can get rid of the uniform now," Etan said. "If someone comes after us now, it won't be much of a disguise."

Adamat removed the bearskin hat and the crimson jacket and breathed a sigh of relief. He immediately regretted it as the cold night air reached his soaked suit underneath, chilling him to the bone. "Thank you for this help, Colonel," Adamat said.

"It's the least I could do." Etan thumped on the side of the carriage and they began to move again. "Taniel saved my life. He was a good friend. I know that you are trying to help him. I just wish we could all have done more."

"There may be more we can do yet," Adamat said, and quickly added, "for the army, that is."

Etan made a noncommittal grunt.

"This affair between Ket and Hilanska could be the end of Adro," Adamat said.

"I've washed my hands of the whole thing. I'm returning to the north, quietly going into retirement. No one has use for a crippled grenadier, whether or not we win the war."

"But..."

"No 'buts,' Inspector. I'm glad to help you escape Hilanska's machinations, but this is the end of it for me."

"I understand." Adamat smacked his fist into his palm in frustration.

Etan's next words were hesitant. "If there's anything I can do to speed you on your way, I'll do it."

"There is," Adamat said, feeling a surge of renewed hope. "I could use a letter of introduction."

"To whom?"

"Brigadier Abrax of the Wings of Adom. I think I know how to save General Ket's troops."

CHAPTER

6

Taniel watched the squad of Adran soldiers as they searched the canyon floor far beneath him.

He had been trailing them since they left the Veridi Valley, breaking off from the main company two days before. There were twelve of them in all, dressed in Adran blues and carrying a full kit on their backs and rifles under their arms. They proceeded warily up the valley, covering less than a mile a day and searching every deer trail and crevice along the way.

At this rate it would take them two more days to find Ka-poel's hiding place.

Taniel fought the urge to stand up and shout. He wanted to rush down the side of the mountain, sliding on the scree, waving his arms to be seen. It had been weeks since he'd had a good meal and a soft bed. His skin was cracked and dirty, his body still aching from the beating at the hands of Kresimir's soldiers.

He'd long since stopped noticing his own smell—a sure sign that he was too used to the foulness.

The only thing that kept him silent was the nagging doubt of suspicion. It was more than likely these men were looking for him; the mountains of southwest Adro were nigh impassable and their immense network of valleys led to nowhere important. Why else would Adran soldiers be up here? The real question was: *Why* were they looking for him?

No one in command had reason to send two companies to find him. General Hilanska had betrayed Taniel, betrayed Tamas, and betrayed Adro. These could be his picked men. Or perhaps Tamas had returned and they were friendly.

Surely they would be shouting for him if they were friendly. He was wracked by indecision. At a mile away, it was impossible to recognize any of them. Taniel cursed quietly under his breath. If he'd had any black powder left, he could have seen them clearly from five miles away.

It took him several hours to move down the mountain with enough stealth to avoid notice. His boots were full of grit and his calves burned from the descent, and it was nearly dusk when Taniel finally crouched in the shadow of a boulder some hundred and fifty feet above the squad, his body hidden. Sweat poured from his brow. He swore again.

Each of the soldiers carried a rifle with the bayonet fixed. From a distance the rifles' basic shape could be mistaken for any flintlock, but from here Taniel could very clearly make out the sleek, streamlined barrel and the rounded stock. These weren't flintlocks. They were air rifles—they fired bullets not with the combustion of black powder but with compressed air.

They were delicate, unreliable weapons. Soldiers only carried air rifles when they needed to kill a powder mage.

Taniel waited in his hiding spot until after dark, watching the soldiers set up camp, and then headed back up the steep side of the mountain.

Taking goat paths, he crossed over the ridge and then followed it to the east for almost a mile, back into a narrow crevice wedged under two great, flat boulders.

Ka-poel sat cross-legged with her back against the wall of their cave. Her ashen freckles were obscured by mud, her long black duster ripped and worn. There were large, dark circles under her eyes. She looked up at Taniel and her head bobbed slightly from exhaustion.

"A squad of Adran soldiers," Taniel said. "Armed to the teeth with air rifles." He lowered himself down beside her, unwilling to look at the wax figure lying on the dirt before her. "No doubt Hilanska's men." He felt the fatigue deep in his bones. Every muscle ached and his hands shook from the lack of gunpowder. It was progress. A few days ago he had barely been able to stand from the withdrawal symptoms. "They're working their way up the valley. They'll reach the curve soon, then come up this direction. It won't take them longer than two days. I can't sense an ounce of powder on them."

He forced a smile onto his face. Ka-poel leaned her head on his shoulder, and Taniel tried to sit up straight. He couldn't show his own weariness. It wouldn't be fair to her.

Not after she had rescued him. Her very sorcery gave him strength.

She who kept a god in check by the power of her will alone.

Taniel finally looked down at the wax figure lying in the dust. He recognized that face, from the delicate chin and the golden hair to the ugly black pit where one eye used to be. A rock the size of Taniel's fist sat in the center of the wax figure's chest and one long needle stuck out from its head.

Gently, Taniel pushed Ka-poel's head off his shoulder. "It's time," he said.

She looked up at him, a question in her eyes. He wondered briefly how her voice would sound if she were able to speak. He kissed her on the forehead and climbed to his feet.

"I have to go kill my countrymen."

*   *   *

Taniel crept down the mountainside just after midnight. The night was deep, thin clouds obscuring a quarter moon. His whole body shook from the effort of the descent, holding himself back so that he wouldn't disturb the scree or startle small animals out of hiding, and his eyes ached from squinting hard into the darkness.

He had the musket that he'd taken in their mad dash from the Kez camp as his only weapon. Bayonet fixed, it would be little use to him except as a spear, as he lacked both powder and ammunition. He'd left his jacket behind with Ka-poel, as the silver buttons might have caught errant moonlight and betrayed him to the enemy—his belt buckle he had wrapped in leather to hide it.

He felt the lack of powder keenly. A single hit of black powder would have sharpened his senses and allowed him to see clearly in the darkness. It would have dulled the ache in his bones, the soreness of his back and feet, and would have given him strength and speed, so that dealing with a dozen men would have been...

Well, certainly not easy. But not outside the realm of possibility, either.

Crouched on the mountainside, he examined his quarry.

The squad of Adran soldiers camped in the shadow of a ten-foot cascade with their backs to a shallow recess in the cliff wall. One stood guard at the top of the cascade. After several minutes of careful examination Taniel was able to spot the second sentry below the camp, about thirty paces down the valley. It was a good defensive position, impossible to flank.

But Taniel wouldn't be flanking anyone. Not on his own. The waterfall would be the only thing serving to cover his approach.

His lack of vision in the darkness was a blow, but he had been planning for the possibility of this ambush for over a week. He knew the lay of the terrain by heart. This was one of a half-dozen locations along the valley where scouts might have camped, and he'd been right in his assumptions all the way down to where they positioned their sentries.

Their Adran blues were difficult to see in the dark, but the silver buttons gave them away. Taniel felt a sudden misgiving. He'd been raised among these men and women—perhaps not those hunting him, but certainly their comrades. These were his brothers and sisters.

Then why were they hunting him with air rifles? Only Hilanska would have been able to get ahold of so many air rifles in Adro. Only he would be able to gather this many Adran soldiers loyal enough to him that they'd be willing to go after a powder mage. *I've killed Adran soldiers before*, he reminded himself. General Ket's vile soldiers, sent after him and Ka-poel. *I can do it again.*

The gravel shifted beneath his feet as he worked his way down to the top of the cascade. The sentry's head turned slightly and the barrel of her air rifle came up. Taniel paused, his breathing shallow. An eternity seemed to pass until she lowered the barrel of her rifle back toward the ground and she turned to the east, looking down the length of the valley.

Taniel stepped into the stream and felt the cold water leak in through a hole in his boot. Stepping lightly, he worked his way toward the sentry. He put one hand to the end of his musket to unfasten the bayonet.

A cold sweat broke out on the nape of his neck. The bayonet wouldn't budge. He twisted harder, but with no success.

He fought down a rising panic. He could still do this with his bare hands, but the lack of a weapon made it both less certain and more personal.

He set his musket carefully down on the bank of the stream and took three long steps forward, snaking one arm around the soldier's neck and putting the other against the base of her spine. He squeezed instantly, flexing his arm to cut off the flow of air and blood to the brain.

She made a quiet choking noise and dropped her rifle with a clatter into the stream. Taniel's heart leapt at the sound, and he watched over her shoulder for signs of alarm in the camp below them while he counted quietly in his head.

Twenty seconds for unconsciousness. Four minutes to be sure of a kill.

Her desperate clawing slacked off after just eight seconds. Taniel continued to count, and when it was apparent that no alarm would be raised, he squeezed his eyes shut.

Why should he spare any of these soldiers who were hunting him? If a single one lived through the night, they'd raise the alarm with the company back down the valley and Taniel would have two hundred men or more coming straight for him. For Ka-poel.

The soldier stopped struggling entirely at eighteen seconds. Taniel kept his grip tight, pulling her close. The killer's embrace, Tamas had called it.

He felt moisture on his cheeks.

He remembered a time not so long ago, in the mountains far to the east of here, looking down the barrel of his rifle at his best friend, marked for death because he was a Privileged sorcerer.

At thirty seconds he let go of the woman, his rage not enough to fuel his strength. He let her sag in his arms and lowered her gently down to the bank of the stream.

A hand over her mouth felt her shallow breathing. Taniel cursed his weakness and made his way quickly down and around the camp. He paused once when one of the sleeping soldiers stirred, but the soldier merely mumbled something unintelligible and rolled over, going back to sleep.

Taniel could hear his heart thumping in his ears. His original plan, tenuous at best, relied on removing the sentries and then killing them all in their sleep. Brutal, but efficient.

Now what could he do? They'd wake in the morning and find they'd been attacked. They would know they had found him, and what would his attack have accomplished? Nothing.

His steps became hurried and careless as he approached the second sentry from behind. A rock turned, the scree moved, and Taniel cursed out loud.

The man turned toward him, a question on his lips.

Taniel sprinted forward and slammed a fist against the base of the soldier's jaw. Taniel snatched at the front of his uniform and caught his air rifle as it dropped. The man slumped to the ground.

Taniel examined the man at his feet as the moon flashed briefly from behind a cloud. The sentry's features were soft, young, unworn by years on campaign. He looked about eighteen. A recruit?

He picked up the soldier's air rifle, running his hands over the length. It had a long, smoothbore barrel not unlike a musket, with a firing mechanism where the flintlock would be and a rounded air canister instead of a stock. Terrible weapons to a powder mage, their expense and unreliability had kept them from becoming more common in the Kez army. Tamas had banned them completely from Adro.

To break the mechanism on the weapon was no terrible difficulty. But Taniel needed to send a message.

He held his hand up to the night sky, looking at the moonlight through the gaps in his fingers. He remembered killing those Adran soldiers—the Dredgers. Remembered putting his hand into the man's mouth after he spoke of raping Ka-poel and curling his fingers around his teeth, grasping and pulling. He remembered feeling the tendons of the man's jaw snap as he'd ripped his jawbone from his body.

And all of that without the powder. Only his rage and Ka-poel's strange sorcery to spur him on.

Taniel grasped the barrel of the air rifle in both hands and flexed. Slowly, the barrel gave way. He bent it all the way to a right angle, his muscles screaming in protest at the force required.

He then snuck back up to the camp. He found a burlap sack and gathered all of the air canisters, then stripped the men of their rations and kits—he gathered a knife, a sword, and enough food to feed himself and Ka-poel for over a month.

He left them all sleeping soundly in their bedrolls. They'd wake in the morning—or when their sentries regained consciousness—to find themselves robbed.

And in the center of their camp, just beside the fire, a neat pile of eleven air rifles, each of them bent into an L-shape.

CHAPTER

Nila waited northwest of the Adran camp, her dress damp from the grass beneath her. The stars above were hidden by a veil of clouds, and despite the thousands of cook fires in the camp to the southeast and Bo's warm body by her side, she felt utterly alone in the wilderness.

During the day she knew she would have seen the plains of southern Adopest stretching all the way to the mighty Black Tar Forest that skirted the Charwood Pile Mountain Range to their west. To the east was the Adsea, and the Adran Mountains to the south that separated Adro and Kez.

She had once been told that they were called the Adran Mountains by Adro and the Kresim Mountains by Kez. She rubbed her hands together to get them warm and wondered how these mountains were labeled in the maps of those outside of Adro or Kez. The autumn chill was here and the leaves would fall from their trees any week now. All her clothes were in the luggage on top of their carriage where they'd left it in the Adran camp.

And inside that was the corpse of an assassin with a melted face.

"Are you still going to help Adamat find his son?" she asked. It occurred to her, just after she'd spoken, that if Bo was willing to lie to Adamat, he wouldn't hesitate to hide the truth from her.

Bo shifted beside her. They had slipped out of the camp with little trouble, some trick of Bo's sorcery, stepping around soldiers and sentries as if they were invisible. He hadn't said much since then.

"I keep my word," Bo said. The slight hesitation. The regret in his voice. *He didn't want to.*

"You're thinking you shouldn't have brought Adamat and Oldrich along in the first place," Nila said quietly.

Bo snorted but said nothing.

"Well?"

"Of course I am. It proved nothing but a complication. Certainly it got us a meeting with Hilanska, but I only endangered their lives and made it harder for us to get anything done. On my own I could have slipped into the camp, tortured a few key people for information, and gotten out again."

It was odd the way Bo expressed regret over endangering the lives of those men in one breath and spoke of torturing innocent soldiers in the next. In Nila's mind those two items were mutually exclusive, and yet she still thought of Bo as a good man. Was she wrong, or was it more complicated than that?

Bo waved a hand dismissively, as if in response to something she didn't say. "He's out of harm's way by now."

"Can you be sure?"

"The missing prisoners have certainly been discovered," Bo said. "If Hilanska wanted to make much ado about it, there would be search parties combing these fields already. Perhaps riders going after Colonel Etan. No. Hilanska will sweep it under the rug. Perhaps he doesn't have the time or manpower to organize a search."

Bo's head tilted toward Nila and she thought she could make out the shadow of a smile on his face. "Perhaps the assassin with a melted head has discouraged pursuit."

Nila cleared her throat. She didn't want to talk about that. Pit, she didn't want to remember that. The feel of the man's skull giving way beneath her burning hand would give her nightmares for months. She shuddered. "What are we watching for out here?"

"Spies," he said.

She couldn't help but scoff. "Spies? Out here? It's pitch-black!"

"Don't look toward the fires of the camp. Even at this distance they can damage your night vision."

She had been doing just that, wishing she had someplace warm to sleep tonight. Her teeth began to chatter and she scooted a little closer to Bo. "We're out in the middle of nowhere. Why would a spy come up here?"

"To circle around the sentries," Bo said. She could see the shadow of his arm as he pointed. "Hilanska's camp is down there. And over there," he said, pointing due south, "about seven miles away is Ket's camp. Beyond them are the Kez. And up there"—he pointed to the northwest—"are the Wings of Adom, a mercenary company in the employ of Adro."

"They're keeping their distance while their employers are fighting each other?"

"Exactly," Bo said, sounding pleased. "Now, because of this schism in the army Hilanska probably doesn't trust his own men, so his spy won't go through the pickets to the south but rather head north, pretending to be a courier on his way to Adopest. He'll leave the road a couple of miles north of the camp and cut across this direction, where he can go to either the Kez, the Adran, or the mercenary camps to meet with his liaison."

"How can you possibly know that?"

Bo chuckled. "I grew up on the streets, and then in Field Marshal Tamas's household. I have an education in strategic deduction and guessing that most Privileged never get. Now, stop asking questions. Open your third eye."

Most everyone with magical ability could use their third eye to look into the Else. It allowed them to see the mark that sorcery had made upon the world and to see anyone else with magical ability. It had been the first thing Bo taught her: looking beyond that which was real to see the sorcery beneath it.

She took a few shallow breaths and let her eyes fall halfway shut, focusing on the muscles around her eyeballs. The process itself wasn't all that different from crossing one's eyes. A wave of nausea flowed over her, nearly making her double over, but she forced herself to hold on, opening her eyes all the way to look into the Else.

The world she now saw was faint, as if she were viewing it through a thick veil. She could make out the landscape even in the darkness, but it was as if it had been drawn carelessly in a series of pastel colors, like an artist's sketch.

She turned toward the Adran camp, and for a moment it seemed as if the number of campfires had doubled. The glow of Knacked in the Else. The whole camp seemed almost a smudge.

"I'm going to throw up," she said.

Bo whispered in her ear, startling her. "Don't give in to it. The nausea lessens with practice."

"Is this how we're going to spot the spy in the dark?"

"Yes."

"You think the spy will be a Privileged or a Knacked?"

"Not a Privileged," Bo said. "Likely a Knacked. Many spies are. It gives them an edge. And even if they weren't, it wouldn't matter."

"How so?"

"Powder mages can't see regular people in the Else. Neither can Knacked."

"But Privileged can?"

"Yes. It's very faint. If a Privileged is a bonfire and a Knacked is a lantern, then a regular person is a lightning bug. Their color in the Else will be so faint that you might think you're imagining it."

Holding her eyes on the Else was beginning to hurt. Her eyes felt dry and a headache had begun to form just behind her temples. "How can that possibly be of any use?"

"It takes a sharp eye," Bo said. "And practice."

"If this is practice, I don't want to do it anymore."

"I've always hated practicing," Bo said, his voice warm in her ear. "But that's how you get to be better. That's how you become smarter and tougher than the people who will want to harm you. And when you're a Privileged . . . that becomes everyone."

Nila felt her insides shift uncomfortably. How could anyone keep this up for any length of time? The mere thought of it made her want to vomit.

"You remember how much you hated Lord Vetas?"

Nila nearly lost her grasp of the Else. She didn't trust herself to answer.

"You remember how he made you feel so helpless?" Bo whispered. "Take all that hate and anger and ball it up and put it away. Don't chew on it—that just makes you bitter. Put it aside and use it as a reminder of why you never want to be helpless again. Take your weakness and make it your strength. You'll be a powerful Privileged, Nila. Stronger than anyone I've known. Stronger than me. But you have to work for it."

Nila almost lost her focus again as she bit off a laugh. Powerful? Stronger than Bo? That seemed ridiculous. "How strong are you?"

"Reasonably so. I have my weaknesses, but I make up for them with cunning."

"That doesn't seem honest."

"Lying and cheating are all fair game when your life is on the line. And it always is, in a royal cabal. I might have been cabal head someday. Especially after I learned a number of . . . secrets."

"What kind of secrets?"

"Ancient sorcery. Like folding the Else upon itself so that other Privileged or Knacked can't see me."

"Who taught you that?"

There was amusement in his voice. "A very old woman. She taught me a lot of things that she probably shouldn't have. It came back to bite her in the end." Bo paused. "There's something else you should know about being a Privileged."

"Just one thing?"

"This is rather . . . personal."

Nila's heart skipped a beat. She had wondered when this would come up. "Oh?" She kept her third eye on the dark area north of the Adran camp, watching for anything that could be movement, and said a prayer of thanks that Bo couldn't see her cheeks turning red.

"You'll have urges."

"What kinds of urges?" It was a stupid question. She knew exactly what he meant.

Bo went on in a purely businesslike tone. "You're going to want to take everyone to bed. Constant contact with the Else makes a Privileged like a stag in rut. It affects both men and women, although women have a tendency to control it better."

"And if I don't?"

"You will."

"Do you have any water?"

"Here." Bo put a canteen in her hands. "Drop your third eye. You don't want to pass out."

Nila realized that her whole body was shaking from the effort of looking into the Else. She closed her third eye and took the canteen gratefully. When she finished drinking, she turned to Bo. "Have you had many women?"

"A few."

"I've heard stories about Privileged . . ."

"Most of them are probably true." A pause. She could feel him watching her. "Nila, if I catch a spy tonight or the night after, I'll have to torture him."

She felt relief at the change of subject, but only for a moment. "Do you have to?"

"I need information."

"You can't just magic the truth from him?"

"I wish that were the case."

"There is no other choice?"

"I'm not a good person. No Privileged is."

Nila didn't like the implication. "I'm supposed to become a Privileged."

"You *are* a Privileged. Even if you've only just begun your training."

"And I have to do horrid things to survive in this world?"

"You already have. And you will again."

She remembered the sticky feeling of the blood between her fingers, and the way that assassin's skull had melted beneath her hand as easily as warm wax. "That's the second time in as many minutes you've told me what I'll end up doing. Do you know me so well, Privileged Borbador?"

She felt the feather touch of Bo's gloved fingers on her cheek and then he pulled away.

They sat in silence for some time, listening to the wind rush across the open field. Somewhere nearby an owl hooted in the darkness. Bo stood up suddenly and removed his jacket, putting it over Nila's shoulders.

"I'm fine," she said.

"I can hear your teeth chattering."

She could see the white of his Privileged gloves standing out against the black of the night as he walked down the hill. Struggling against the nausea, she opened her third eye. Was he touching the Else?

The color of his body in the Else nearly overwhelmed her with its brightness. He spread his arms and she waited to see something more, but he just stood there, his face in the wind.

"Bo!" she hissed.

He came back up the hill toward her. "Hmm?"

"I saw it! A movement."

"Where?"

"To the southeast. Moving along the dip between hills. At least, I thought I saw it. Maybe—"

"No." Bo's voice was grim, and she heard him crack his knuckles. "I saw it too. Stay here."

He headed off in the direction where she'd seen the ever-so-soft glow in the Else, striding with the confidence of a man in daylight despite the darkness. She took a few nervous breaths, feeling even more alone in the windy darkness. She looked toward the Adran camp, watching the distant embers of their fires, and wished once more she were in the safety and warmth of her own bedroll.

Bo would say that there was no place safe for a Privileged.

Had he told her to stay behind to spare her the horrors of watching him torture some poor soul? Or because he thought she was weak?

Perhaps both.

She *was* a Privileged, he'd told her. She couldn't afford to be weak to survive in this world. With the power of sorcery came the expectations of others. People would expect her to use her powers—for king or country or wealth. People would try to use her. She wondered if her own power would give her hungers. Not just the sexual urgings Bo had spoken of but the hunger for riches, servants, and authority.

The fear of it niggled at her. What could she do? Flee to some distant land and hope that no one ever noticed her? Or learn to control her sorcery, embrace the power it brought her? She didn't want to be an evil person, yet Bo spoke of Privileged as if they had no choice. She felt as if there were a war inside of her already and that it would determine the kind of person she would be.

Bo, she realized, was in the throes of that very same war.

Nila climbed to her feet. Bo was cresting the next hill, moving farther away. She opened her third eye but could no longer spot the moving shadow of light in the Else. Bo was hidden as well, veiled in whatever trick he'd spoken of earlier.

She closed her third eye and stumbled after him, feeling her way in the dark.

She caught up to him a quarter of a mile and a twisted ankle later, limping up to where he crouched in the long grass. She could feel the intensity as he stared into the darkness like a cave lion stalking its prey. Without turning his head, he whispered, "What is it?"

"I should stay with you."

A hesitation. "Are you sure?"

"Yes."

"Good. Whoever he is, he's coming right at us. Don't touch the Else—I'm going to trip him with earth and bind him with air, but my sorcery will be obscured from any Knacked that might be watching. You don't know how to do any of that, so stay here until I have him."

Nila hunkered down next to Bo, her knees wet from the grass. From the way Bo was facing, she guessed that the spy was traveling in the gully between two hills. She couldn't see a thing, however, and waited for Bo to make his move.

She didn't have to wait long. His arms suddenly came up, two shadows in the night, and she thought she saw a spark when his fingers danced. There was a cry in the gully beneath them that was cut dramatically short, and Bo leapt to his feet. "Come on!" They stumbled down the hill and Bo threw himself forward. "Hold still, damn it. You're not going anywhere." Several muffled grunts followed and then the area was suddenly lit by the beam of a dull light not unlike a bull's-eye lantern. It originated from Bo's shoulder and revealed Bo struggling with a small figure.

"It's only a boy!" Nila said before she could stop herself. Could they have caught the wrong person? Just some innocent messenger, or maybe even a drummer boy who'd decided to run away from the camp?

Bo gave her a dirty look and flipped the boy onto his back. Hands and legs bound by invisible sorcery, the boy thrashed on the ground like an earthbound fish. He couldn't have been more than twelve, with a narrow nose and long brown hair tied back behind his head. He wore a plain black uniform with matching kneesocks, boots, and jacket.

Bo stood up, one finger pointed at the boy as if he were pinning a fly to the ground beneath him, and seemed content to let the boy tire himself out for several minutes.

Nila stepped up beside Bo. "He's just a boy," she whispered in his ear.

"I know that."

"Are you going to torture him?"

"If I must."

"You were a boy once too."

"And I had to learn when to grow up."

The coldness in his words shocked her. "Let me at him first."

He blinked at her several times before gesturing to the boy magnanimously. "Be my guest."

"Give me an extra pair of gloves."

Pulling on the gloves, she knelt next to the boy and held them up to Bo's light. "Do you know what these are?"

The boy nodded fearfully.

"You've the unfortunate luck to fall into the hands of two Privileged. Answer our questions truthfully and we'll let you go. Lie to us, and we'll take turns scouring the flesh from your bones so that there is nothing left of you but a charred shell come morning. I can make certain that no one will hear your screams." She leaned in close to his face. "And no one will help you. Do you understand?"

The boy's mouth worked, but no sound came forth.

Nila glanced over her shoulder at Bo. "Sorry," Bo muttered. One finger twitched.

"Let's try that again," Nila said. "Do you understand?"

"Yes!" the boy gasped. "I do!"

"Good. What is your name?"

"Folkrot."

"Unfortunate name," Bo muttered just loud enough for Nila to hear.

She compressed her lips in a hard line to stifle a laugh. "What are you doing out here?"

"I've run off from my unit." The words had barely left his mouth when Bo's fingers twitched and Folkrot gave a terrified squeal. "I'm sorry! I mean, I'm delivering a message."

Nila tried to keep her composure. Could Bo really sense if he was lying? Or was he testing the boy? "For whom?" she asked.

"General Hilanska."

"Where were you taking it?"

"To the Kez lines. I'm meant to be there by morning."

"And what kind of message are you delivering?"

"I don't know! It's a sealed letter. I'm not allowed to open it." Another squeal, and Folkrot writhed from some unseen twisting of sorcery. "I swear to you it's true!"

Nila slapped Bo's leg and the boy instantly stopped moving. "Where is the letter?"

"Under my shirt."

Nila bent forward and undid the front of the boy's jacket, then lifted his shirt. Strapped to his white belly just below his ribs was a leather satchel. She removed it and handed it to Bo.

Bo stepped away from her and the boy and opened the letter. He stared at it for several minutes before beckoning Nila over.

"It's coded," Bo said. "Damn it. It doesn't help us." He walked around in a circle for a moment before stopping. "The Wings of Adom employ several code breakers. They've fought in just about every country in the world. Their camp isn't far. We can get there by late morning if we walk all night."

Nila didn't like the idea at all. She was already wet, tired, dirty, and she'd twisted her ankle. A seven-mile walk in the dark sounded horrible. "And the boy?"

"I have to kill him," Bo said.

"No!"

"We have no choice. We can't let him go. He'll run back to Hilanska and tell him the letter was taken. I'll make it quick."

"You bloody animal! I will not let you do that."

"And how will you stop me?" There was a challenge in Bo's voice.

Nila felt her hands stiffen and thought of the blue flame that had danced over her fingers. Who was she kidding? She couldn't use sorcery against Bo. He would toss her aside like garbage. "He's an innocent. I'll make you kill me first."

A sour look crossed Bo's face and he looked from her to the boy as if considering how best to move her out of the way.

"We can take him with us to the Wings' camp and hand him over to them," Nila said. "We won't have to kill him and he won't be reporting to anyone."

"I don't like having a tagalong."

"You let me bring Jakob."

"Not here, I didn't. We left him with Adamat's family so he wouldn't be a burden."

"And we'll only have this boy until we reach the Wings' camp. Do you want more blood on your hands?"

Bo stared at his gloves for a moment before giving a curt nod. "Bring him. But we lose him at the Wings' camp."

CHAPTER

8

It was around seven o'clock in the morning, the tall grass still bathed in dew, when Adamat, Oldrich, and their fifteen soldiers trekked into the Wings of Adom mercenary camp.

The mercenaries were camped around a town called Billishire, not more than thirty miles from the edge of the Black Tar Forest. Their standard of a saint's halo with gold wings on a red backdrop waved from the steeple of the town's only church, and the entire camp had been fortified by a hastily built palisade wall and a ditch six feet deep.

Adamat forced himself to put one foot in front of the other, exhaustion weighing him down as the night retreated. He went straight for the first sentry he saw and came up short, letting the man eye him suspiciously for several moments before speaking.

"Inspector Adamat here to see Brigadier Abrax," he said.

The sentry was a middle-aged man with a fixed bayonet. His

red-and-white uniform was clean and pressed, and the gold trim glittered in the early light.

"I've no orders regarding you," the sentry said. He eyed the small troop of soldiers and their trail through the grass that led off into the distance as if not quite sure what to make of them.

"I'm here on behalf of Field Marshal Tamas."

The sentry's skepticism deepened. "The field marshal is dead."

"Is he now?" Adamat asked, giving the man his very best deadpan expression of annoyance. He imagined that it looked like a tired squint. "We've walked all night and I have urgent news for the brigadier. I have a letter of introduction from Colonel Etan of the Twelfth Grenadiers of the Adran army."

The sentry regarded Adamat another moment before looking over Oldrich and his men. The soldiers had shed their grenadier disguises but kept the rifles, and despite not having slept for twenty-four hours, they looked sharp enough to play the part.

"I better escort you in, then," the sentry said.

For the second time in as many days, Adamat was led into the heart of a military camp. They were handed off to another sentry, and then to a major's adjutant—a young woman with blond hair and an easy smile—who took them to the church that Adamat had spotted earlier in the center of the town.

The camp was just beginning to stir, cookpots going over the fires and camp laundresses finishing their night's work. The stillness gradually gave way to the bustle of camp life as the men crawled from their beds.

Adamat caught the sleeve of the adjutant just before they reached the church. "I'm the only one who needs to see the brigadier," he said. "Is there any chance you could show some hospitality to my escort?"

The adjutant gave a quick nod and beckoned to Oldrich. "Take your men over to the Willow Inn, just past that house there. It serves as the officers' mess in the evenings, but they'll be happy to give you breakfast. Tell them that Brigadier Abrax will cover the tab."

"My thanks," Adamat said once the soldiers had gone off in search of the inn.

"Of course," the adjutant said. "We show the same hospitality our brothers-in-arms have shown us. And Field Marshal Tamas has been good to us."

Adamat wondered how, exactly, Tamas had been paying the Wings of Adom. The newspapers had whispered of bankruptcy in the capital for months.

Inside the church, Adamat was shown to one of the pews, and the adjutant disappeared. He sat quietly with his hands in his lap, examining the stained-glass windows behind the pulpit. The largest window depicted Kresimir floating high above South Pike Mountain, his arms spread over the whole of the Nine. His brothers and sisters gathered at his feet, helping him in the formation of the Nine Nations. Adamat wondered how being at war with Kresimir himself would change the Kresim religion in Adro.

"Inspector?"

The voice brought Adamat out of an uneasy sleep, and he realized he'd been leaning his head on the pew in front of him. He rubbed vigorously at his forehead to remove the red line it likely caused and got to his feet. "Yes?"

"The brigadier has just begun her breakfast. She's asked you to join her."

The idea of breakfast nearly made Adamat faint. He'd been so incredibly sore and sleep-deprived all night that he hadn't thought of food, but the very mention of it made his stomach growl as loud as a cave lion.

He was taken across the street to what would have probably been the priest's house, a two-story building with a brick façade and green shutters, and he was shown into the dining room.

Adamat was surprised to see a familiar face sitting at the head of the table: Lady Winceslav, the owner of the Wings of Adom. She wore the white uniform with gold sash of a Wings brigadier—a formality, if Adamat were to guess. She didn't have experience of command.

Brigadier Abrax sat at the foot of the table, also wearing white and gold. She stood when Adamat entered. "Inspector." She regarded him blandly, her stern face unreadable.

"Brigadier," Adamat said, shaking her hand. "And my lady, I didn't realize you were here." This could complicate things. Abrax had a reputation for severity, but Adamat still hoped to cajole her into helping him. Lady Winceslav would stand for no such cajoling.

"Inspector, I'm told that you have word of Tamas." Winceslav raised a cup of tea to her lips.

Adamat swallowed, noting that he had not been asked to sit. "I'm sorry, my lady, but I do not."

Winceslav's face fell. "The adjutant said that you had implied as much."

"I didn't mean to mislead," Adamat said. "I simply said I was here on behalf of Field Marshal Tamas."

"I see." Another sip of tea. Still no invitation to sit. "And what orders has the late field marshal given that you still feel pressed to follow through?"

Adamat filed through his memory, looking for an order, whether spoken or written, that Tamas had given before his disappearance into Kez. "Well, none, my lady."

Winceslav gave a slight sigh. Abrax narrowed her eyes at him. Both remained silent.

"My lady, I..."

"The last time we met," Winceslav said, "you were investigating me for treachery. I understand you were following orders, but it doesn't leave us on the best of terms. I hope you have something good to say."

Lady Winceslav wouldn't be fooled by any stories that Adamat

could spin, and he likely wasn't going to appeal to her patriotism—
she was already doing what she could for her country. What else
would work?

Adamat decided on an appeal to her pragmatism. "I arrived in
the Adran camp yesterday morning with Privileged Borbador and
a squad of Tamas's Riflejacks with the intent of arresting General
Ket on charges of war profiteering and releasing Taniel Two-shot
from imprisonment."

"Two-shot disappeared weeks ago," Abrax said. "Surely you'd
been informed." She said nothing about the charges against Ket.
She didn't even raise her eyebrow.

"We knew he was accused of murdering several of Ket's men in
self-defense. Nothing after that. Until yesterday, of course. General
Hilanska filled us in on the schism in the army, and Taniel's capture and death at the hands of the Kez." Adamat had, not for the
first time, the uneasy feeling that the lack of news in the capital was
not accidental. It was something he'd have to consider more in the
future.

Winceslav's teacup clinked onto her plate. "Did you say Privileged Borbador?"

"Yes, my lady."

"Where is he now?"

"We were separated just before leaving the Adran army." No
need to tell her the specifics about *that*. It would only complicate
matters.

"Two-shot isn't dead," Abrax said.

"Oh?"

"At least," Abrax continued, "no one's seen the body. Before
the...event...between Kresimir and Mihali, Taniel was seen
carving his way through the Kez army with that savage sorceress
of his. My Privileged told me that there was some very interesting
sorcery going on."

Bo would certainly be delighted by that news. But how to get it to him? As far as he knew, the Privileged was in the Kez camp right now—or had been captured and killed by Hilanska. Adamat tried to bring his thoughts back on track. This wasn't about Two-shot anymore.

"That's all very interesting," Winceslav said. She took a bite of a biscuit and chewed and swallowed before going on. "But that doesn't tell us what you're here for."

Adamat's mouth watered. "My lady, I saw Hilanska's battle plans when I met with him. I have reason to believe he will attack Ket within the next couple of days. And I don't think he has any intention of trying to resolve the conflict diplomatically. If the two of them fight, the Kez will only have to sit back and wait until they've destroyed each other and this whole campaign will be in ruins."

"And you have a solution to that?" Abrax asked.

"Yes."

"Well?"

"I want you to draft all three of Ket's brigades into the Wings of Adom mercenary company."

Abrax barked out a laugh. "Absurd."

Adamat put his hands on the table. "It would end this schism and save the lives of tens of thousands of men."

"It's ridiculous. The logistics would be impossible," Abrax said.

"Not impossible. Just inconvenient."

"And," Abrax added, "Ket will have to agree."

"She will. I know exactly what she wants."

Abrax opened her mouth, but Winceslav's raised hand kept her silent.

"Inspector," Winceslav said. There was a note of interest in her voice. "Please sit down and have breakfast with us. I'm interested in hearing more."

CHAPTER

9

Taniel climbed the mountainside, finding a spot several hundred feet above the camp, and settled in to watch the sleeping soldiers until morning.

It was still dark, not long after he'd left the camp, when one of the soldiers climbed from his bedroll and stumbled into the bushes. He returned a minute later and his sudden shouting told Taniel that he had discovered the artwork Taniel had made out of the squad's air rifles. The rest of the infantry were up in seconds.

They were in a panic. Even from this distance Taniel could hear their hoarse arguments, the curses, and then a call of dismay when they found the first unconscious sentry.

It took them another fifteen minutes before a figure—probably their sergeant—made his way to the top of the waterfall and found the second sentry. They carried her down to the group and then huddled in conference, their backs to the cliffside in a defensive perimeter despite their lack of weapons.

The eastern sky was just getting light when they broke camp. Tired, their fright apparent from their body language, they made their way cautiously back down the valley. Taniel waited until he could continue his climb without the risk of being spotted, and then started the long journey back to Ka-poel.

He ducked inside the cave two hours later. His legs ached from the climb and his body sagged with exhaustion. Three times he had lost his footing, nearly falling down the steep side of the valley. His fingers were bleeding from the climb and his trousers and shirt resembled a beggar's filthy rags.

His heart leapt into his throat at the sight of Ka-poel. She was curled up in one corner of the cave, his jacket draped over her, using her hands as a pillow. Taniel skirted the facsimile of Kresimir and knelt beside her.

"Pole," he said, gently touching her shoulder.

Something pressed against his throat. He inhaled sharply and looked down his nose at the long needle clutched in Ka-poel's hand.

"It's me, Pole."

One green eye regarded him for a moment and then the needle was withdrawn. She sat up, shaking the sleep from her head.

"Kresimir," Taniel said urgently. "What has happened with Kresimir?"

She cocked an eyebrow at him for a moment and then her face lit up. She pointed at the doll of Kresimir, which was bound in the center of the cave. She walked her fingers through the air and then chopped the other hand viciously.

Taniel snorted. "He's not going anywhere?"

Ka-poel nodded, a victorious smile on her lips.

"How?"

She tapped the side of her head, then pointed at the doll again.

For the first time, Taniel noticed the symbols written in the dust around the doll: a series of vague lines pointing away from Kresi-mir. They made little sense to him. "What do those mean?"

She made a fist and pointed.

"I don't—" He stopped and frowned. Then he saw it. They weren't symbols, but fingers. Kresimir lay in the palm of a hand— her hand, if Taniel wasn't mistaken. "He's in the palm of your hand. You don't have to be awake to keep him under control?"

A nod.

"How the pit did you figure that out?"

Ka-poel rolled her eyes as if looking into one corner of the cave and made a vague gesture.

"What's that supposed to mean?"

Both of her eyebrows rose and she gave him the flat look she always used when she was pretending not to understand him. He snatched her by the arm. "Pole, what the pit is that supposed to mean?" He couldn't help the urgency in his voice. How did she know that Kresimir was still under control? How did she know what symbols held power?

She shrugged, then drew in the dust with one finger and spread the other hand out toward Kresimir's doll.

"You were *experimenting*?"

A nod.

"*With a god*?"

She gave him a sheepish grin. Whatever sleep she'd managed while he was away had done her a world of good. The lines under her eyes had diminished. Her spirits seemed up. She hadn't smiled in a week.

Taniel released his grip on her arm and ran a hand through his knotted, dirty hair. Several pine needles came away and he tossed them in the corner of the cave.

"How can you possibly know what might or might not work? Pit, I wish I understood something—anything—about your sorcery."

She pointed to herself. *Me too.*

"You don't know anything about your own sorcery?"

She gave him a half shrug, then held up five fingers. She drew in the dust for a moment, then pulled a finger across her throat.

"I didn't catch *any* of that, Pole."

She snorted angrily.

"Be careful experimenting with sorcery, Pole," Taniel said. "I've heard of a few Privileged and powder mages teaching themselves the rudiments. But untrained adepts who try to go further just get themselves killed. They burn themselves to a crisp with the Else or blow themselves up or get powder blindness or... pit, I don't know how your sorcery could kick back at you, but it will happen." He rubbed his eyes. "You're bloody well controlling a god. I'm not sure how you haven't been strangled with your own powers yet."

She made a gesture and a consoling smile. *Me neither.*

Just great.

Taniel fetched the rations he'd stolen from the Adran soldiers. He and Ka-poel set upon them hungrily. The biscuits were hard and salty, the dried beef as stringy as catgut, but he'd never tasted anything quite this good. He went through two meals' worth before he forced himself to stop eating. He'd get cramps something fierce, and...

The taste of hard cheese brought back a memory that he'd wished to forget: Kresimir standing victoriously over where Adom—Mihali—had once stood. These soldiers were only eating marching rations because Mihali was dead. Taniel kicked the pack of rations away from him, feeling suddenly ill. To his great surprise, he felt a tear roll down his cheek.

He quickly brushed it away.

Ka-poel took him by the arm and forced him to lie on the cold of the cave floor, his head in her lap, then began gently rubbing his temples. He stretched out, careful not to touch Kresimir's doll, and felt the pain begin to bleed out of his legs and arms and his mind begin to drift.

He started awake, opening his eyes to find his head still in Ka-poel's lap, her soft hand pressed to his cheek. The cave was well lit by the sun, telling him it was just past noon.

Taniel stifled a yawn and told himself to get up. He needed to be back out there, watching for more Adran squads, but Ka-poel was warm, and despite the cold of the cave floor he felt as if he had been sitting in a hot bath for hours.

"I have to . . . Pole, is that blood on your finger?"

The tip of Pole's finger was smeared with crimson. She pressed it to her lips and looked down at him for a moment, her thoughts elsewhere. She then pressed the finger to his right cheek. He reached up to stop her, but her other hand took his in a surprisingly strong grip and she ministered to first one cheek, then the other. He could feel the blood drying on his face.

She licked the blood off her finger and more welled up in its place. It was her blood, then. What was she doing? Was this sorcery? Some kind of savage ritual?

He pushed her away and got to his feet, feeling strange. "Pole, what are you doing?" He wiped one sleeve across his cheek and looked at it. Nothing. Very strange.

Further questions were met with a yawn.

Taniel left Ka-poel passively regarding the doll of Kresimir. He headed out of the cave and climbed to the apex of the mountain, where he followed the ridgeline.

The canyon down to his right was where he had ambushed the squad of Adran infantry. It would take them half the day to make their way back to where their company camped. If they marched double-time, they would only now arrive.

Taniel didn't need to be that close.

He continued along the ridge, keeping to the eastward side,

where he was least likely to be spotted by any sharp-eyed scouts. The ridge began to narrow dangerously, giving him fewer places to hide, but he continued on until he reached a sharp, flat slab of rock beyond which the sky stretched out like the serene surface of a mountain lake. He crawled to the edge of the rock on his hands and knees and peered over the edge.

Veridi Valley was a jagged rend between two tall, gray-capped mountains. The floor of the valley had to be at least a thousand feet beneath him. A river less than twenty feet across trickled down the middle, and tough mountain brush bristled along the valley floor. The canyon where he'd ambushed the Adran soldiers let out into the Veridi Valley to Taniel's west. The valley, in turn, let out into another, and that led twenty miles or more to the plains of Adro.

On the valley floor were the dots of at least a hundred tents: a company of Adran soldiers. Taniel had little doubt now that they had been sent by Hilanska—and he guessed that every one of them had an air rifle. Where had they gotten the air rifles? From Kez?

Did these men know that they were betraying their country?

Movement caught Taniel's eye. A small group emerged from the canyon and made their way toward the Adran camp. Taniel shifted to get comfortable and cursed his poor eyesight. In a powder trance he'd be able to see the very expressions on their faces. With his normal sight, he could barely count their number.

This was the moment of truth. Would his act of clemency convince them to turn around? Would they realize they'd been duped by their commander into tracking down an ally? Would they be frightened by Taniel's show of strength?

He waited for hours, squinting to see the movement in the camp, not even able to venture a guess as to their plans. No doubt the squad would give their report and the officers would convene. The company major would listen to advice from his captains and make a decision.

Solitary figures began to leave the camp. Taniel tracked their movement as they headed toward the various crags and valleys up and down the canyon floor.

They were recalling the other search parties.

Inside the camp, men fell into ranks. Taniel's heart fell as he watched them. Dozens and dozens fell in with their kits at their hips and their air rifles on their shoulders. Bayonets flashed in the sunlight.

They weren't breaking camp.

A group of between eighty and a hundred—it was hard to tell at this distance—left the camp at a slow march. They were heading deliberately toward Taniel's canyon.

No mistaking their intentions now.

Taniel had begun to prepare for this eventuality from the time he'd first laid eyes on the company trudging their way up the Veridi Valley.

They would proceed slowly, no doubt, but the strength of numbers would give them confidence and they would move faster than the previous searchers. A regular march, with scouts and sentries at all times, would take the group no more than thirty or forty hours to reach the apex of the canyon and from there they would find Ka-poel's cave within hours.

Taniel considered the lay of the canyon, picturing it in his mind. There were three choke points where a single man could hold against an entire army. There were five spots steep and rubble-strewn enough that he could start a rockslide. There were over a dozen prime sniping locations.

But they'd just shoot him in a choke point, the rockslide would give away his position, and he didn't have a rifle.

"Ka-poel," he said, swinging himself into their cave. "We have to go."

She crouched above the doll of Kresimir, her eyes unfathomable as a cat's and a frown on her face. She shook her head slightly.

"They're coming for us," he said. "About eighty infantry, all armed with air rifles. We have two days before they find us here—if we're lucky. There's no way I could possibly fight that many."

Ka-poel shook her head again emphatically.

"What do you mean, 'no'?"

She pointed at the doll, then walked her fingers through the air. *He can't be moved.*

"We have to move him. If we stay here, we die."

Ka-poel stared at the doll for several moments and then rocked back on her haunches, brow furrowed. She scratched in the dirt with the tip of one of her long needles. She cupped her hand and tapped her palm with one finger, as if indicating a pocket watch. *I need time.*

"All right, Pole," Taniel said. "But if they get close enough to turn this into a real chase, neither of us will survive it."

CHAPTER 10

Nila guessed it to be around ten o'clock when they came within view of the mercenary camp. Their prisoner, Folkrot, walked along ahead of them, looking tired and dejected.

He'd tried to escape three times in the middle of the night, making a run to the south. Each time, Nila had chased after him and tackled him to the ground. On the third time Bo caught him with sorcery and all fight went out of the boy.

Nila's feet hurt, her dress was filthy, and she wanted nothing more than a warm bed. Bo showed a dark shadow on his cheeks from not shaving but seemed otherwise unaffected by the lack of sleep.

The sentry was a young woman in the red-and-white uniform of a Wings soldier. She held a rifle on her shoulder and stood in the middle of the road to block traffic—of which there was none—and seemed rather bored. She watched them go past without comment.

"Shouldn't she question us?" Nila asked.

"She's there to watch for the enemy," Bo said. "Soldiers, cavalry. That kind of thing. The next one will ask us our business."

"Oh."

"Do you want to know why?"

"I suppose?"

"Always ask why. It's not enough to know the what of something. A Privileged always needs to know the why. It helps you learn how things work, which aids in your manipulation of the Else."

"All right," Nila said. "Then why?"

"Because the next sentry is a Privileged."

Four mercenary soldiers stood on one side of the road and as Nila and Bo approached, three of them lowered their rifles, bayonets bristling.

"That's far enough," the fourth one said. An older woman, she stood off to one side of the others and held her hands out in front of her so they could clearly see the gloves on her hands. "I know what you are, boy. Explain your presence here immediately."

Bo leaned over to Nila. "The Wings employ several dozen low-strength Privileged. They're good for intimidation, and some of them have skill, but few if any have the strength of a cabal sorcerer. There's a kind of pecking order among Privileged. If I had more time, I might strut and scoff, but now..." He held up both hands ungloved. "I'm here to see Brigadier Abrax," he told the woman.

At the sight of the Privileged, Folkrot had backed away until he bumped into Nila. He turned, panic in his eyes, and would have fled had Nila not snatched him by the collar.

"On what business?"

"My own," Bo said.

The four sentries conversed among themselves.

"Don't open your third eye," Bo whispered. "She'll sense it."

"Can't she see me in the Else?"

"No. You haven't interacted enough with it yet to have an aura. A few months, maybe as much as a year, and you will."

Nila *had* been about to open her third eye. She wanted to see what another Privileged—other than Bo—would look like. Even without doing so, she thought she could feel...something different about the woman. Perhaps she was imagining it.

"Surrender your gloves," the Wings Privileged finally said. "And submit to a search. Then we'll take you into the camp. Brigadier Abrax isn't here, but you can ask for a meeting with Lady Winceslav."

Bo's face immediately lit up. "The Lady is here? Wonderful!"

He submitted to the search with far less annoyance than Nila would have expected, and even handed over all three pairs of his gloves without comment. One of the sentries turned to Nila.

"I'm unarmed," Nila said when he raised his hands.

"I should anyway, ma'am."

Nila squared her jaw and bit her tongue as the man patted his hands down her sides and in the small of her back. When he reached between her legs, she let fly without hesitation, slapping him full across the face.

The soldier stumbled backward. "Bloody pit!"

Bo's eyes glinted dangerously, and Nila saw him tense.

The mercenary Privileged let out a laugh. "Oh, that's grand. Leave off it, she's unarmed. Let's take them in."

They were escorted to the church in the center of the town by two rifle-armed soldiers. Just outside the building, a secretary was called over.

"Where is Lady Winceslav?" Bo asked.

The secretary's eyes flicked to the house just down the lane. "The Lady is unavailable right now. I can ask if she has an appointment..."

Bo pushed past the secretary. "No need!" He was off down the lane without another word.

"Hey!" One of their escorts took off after Bo. Nila put out a foot, hooking his boot, and the man sprawled into the mud. She immediately grabbed him by the arm.

"I am so sorry! That was awfully clumsy of me."

The other escort cursed under his breath and rushed off, but Bo was already disappearing inside the front door of the house the secretary had glanced at. Nila left the first soldier in the mud and followed Bo inside, dragging Folkrot along with her.

Bo was just coming out of the dining room when Nila arrived, their angry escort brandishing his rifle in Bo's face.

"Put that away," Bo said peevishly, shoving the rifle out of his face. "My lady! My lady!"

The soldier shoved the stock of his rifle against Bo's chest. "Outside! Now! Don't make me—"

"Make you do what?" Bo flipped the cuffs of his jacket inside out and slid his hands smoothly into the pair of gloves hidden within. He touched a finger to the soldier's throat and all color drained from the man's face.

"What is all this damned racket?" An old woman wearing a white soldier's uniform with a golden sash came out of the sitting room. She stopped at the sight before her. "Privileged Borbador?"

Bo spun away from the soldier and slipped his gloves off and into his pockets. "My lady!"

"Bo!"

Nila could feel her mouth hanging open as the two embraced like old friends and kissed each other on the cheek.

The old woman—Lady Winceslav, Nila could only imagine—stepped away and looked Bo up and down. "Privileged Borbador, you've certainly grown."

"And you're looking more beautiful than ever." Bo turned the full force of his boyish grin on Winceslav.

Lady Winceslav shooed off their escort and the flustered secretary who had caught up with them. "Come and sit with me! I'll get us some tea. I'm so glad to see you alive. Tamas had assured me that you had not been included in his purges, but I was worried nonetheless."

"I very nearly was anyway," Bo said. "But I made it through. Lady, this is my new protégée, Nila. Nila, Lady Winceslav; owner of the Wings of Adom mercenary company and one of the finest people you will ever meet."

The Lady offered Nila her hand, which Nila kissed. "My pleasure," she said.

"Oh, she is a pretty one," Winceslav said. Nila could have sworn the old woman winked at Bo. She felt her cheeks grow red. "And who is the boy?" Winceslav asked.

"Nobody," Bo said. He snagged the secretary by the sleeve just as she was leaving. "Put the boy in your stocks for two days, then let him go. Feed him well and give him a fiver when he leaves."

Bewildered, the secretary led Folkrot away.

"I'm sorry to cut the pleasantries short," Bo said as they took their seats in the sitting room, "but you should call one of your code breakers right away." He produced the letter he had taken from Folkrot and tossed it on the table.

"And what is that?"

"A missive," Bo said. "From General Hilanska to the field marshal of the Kez army."

The Lady sent for one of her code breakers before returning to her seat. "And how did you come about such a missive? Surely you shouldn't be interrupting lines of communication between Hilanska and the Kez. They might be negotiating a peace treaty."

Nila spoke up. "We took it from that boy at about two o'clock this morning. I somehow doubt, my lady, that he was negotiating a peace treaty at that hour."

"Is this true?" Winceslav asked Bo.

"Yes."

Winceslav shook her head and leaned back in her chair. She

suddenly looked older. "Everything has gone to pit since Tamas disappeared. He was the one thing holding this all together, and..."

"If it makes you feel any better," Bo said, "I don't think Tamas is dead."

"That's awfully optimistic. He was caught with just two brigades behind enemy lines, in enemy territory. I'm no strategist, but the chances of him returning are close to nothing."

Bo's eyebrows danced mischievously, but he said nothing more on the matter, instead asking after Winceslav's health and children. They went on like old friends, and Nila felt infinitely out of her depth.

How did Bo know this woman? Through Tamas, no doubt, but they weren't acting like mere acquaintances. Bo clearly trusted her implicitly—not something the Privileged was wont to do. Nila knew by now that Bo flirted with everybody, so his grinning and compliments were no surprise, but Winceslav was acting a bit like a schoolgirl around him. Had he...had he slept with her?

"Something wrong?"

It took Nila a moment to realize Bo was talking to her. "Hmm?"

"Your cheeks are red."

She fanned herself with a hand. "Just thinking about all the excitement."

Bo gave a chuckle and a knowing smile. Pit! It was like he knew exactly what she was thinking.

It wasn't long before the code breaker arrived with a satchel of papers under one arm. Bo directed him to the letter and continued his conversation with Lady Winceslav. Nila only listened partially to their conversation, as she was watching the code breaker closely.

He opened the letter and smoothed it flat on one of the tables, then turned to his satchel. He leafed through several dozen papers, stopping periodically to lay one flat next to the missive, only to return it a moment later. He finally seemed satisfied with one of them, leaving it next to the letter and then producing a clean sheet of paper and smoothing it out with one hand. "I have a match, ma'am," he said, interrupting Bo. "A lesser-used code, but we have it in our records."

"Go ahead," Lady Winceslav said. "Go on, Bo."

"I was saying it's the curse of war, isn't it? Weeks or even months of waiting for something—anything—to happen. Almost makes you beg for a battle."

"It's terribly boring," Winceslav agreed, "although I wouldn't beg for a battle. I came down here as soon as I heard about the schism in the army. I was just told this morning that no one in Adopest even knows what's going on!" She shook her head. "I can't possibly believe that."

"It's true," Bo said. "May I ask who told you that?"

"A man by the name of Inspector Adamat."

Nila turned away from watching the code breaker. "Adamat was here?"

"He was. He mentioned something about you, Bo, but I'm still surprised to see you here."

"We..." Nila started.

"My lady!" The codebreaker had stood up, his copy of the letter in his trembling hands. "I've finished, my lady. This is urgent."

"Well, go on!"

The code breaker licked his lips. "Hilanska is plotting with the Kez, my lady. He intends to destroy Ket's brigades and then turn on us, working jointly with the enemy."

"Give me that." Bo snatched the translated missive from the code breaker and ran his eyes over it. His face grew grim and he handed the letter over to Lady Winceslav.

The Lady was already on her feet. "I've just sent Abrax and two companies of my men to treat with General Ket. I've sent them to their own end." She paled slightly and then straightened, standing tall. "Send for my colonels. Mobilize the men. We march within the hour!"

The code breaker seemed startled by this. "Whom do you want to march, my lady?"

Winceslav made two fists and gritted her teeth. "Everyone."

Nila put her hand up on the side of Lady Winceslav's coach to keep her head from hitting the walls as they careened along the road together with well over twenty thousand marching soldiers of the Wings of Adom.

Lady Winceslav gazed intently out the window as they traveled, while Bo had become withdrawn almost as soon as the Lady had given the order to muster her troops. There had been no conversation in the coach for two hours already, and Nila wondered how long until they would reach General Ket's camp.

"Do we expect fighting?" Nila asked, if only to break the silence.

Bo glanced toward her for a moment but didn't speak. Lady Winceslav gave her a smile that was only slightly patronizing. "It certainly seems that way," she said.

"Your soldiers mustered quickly," Nila said. "I don't have a lot of experience with armies, but I'd thought it took them longer to get on the march." She *had* been impressed by their speed. Lady Winceslav had given the order and the first companies were leaving camp less than fifteen minutes later.

"The company has spent a lot of time in Gurla," Lady Winceslav said. "Gurlish nomads have a penchant for appearing out of the desert at a moment's notice to harass the camp. The men learn to fall in quickly, or die with their boots off." She fell silent and went back to staring out the window.

"Bo," Nila asked, desperate for a distraction from waiting to arrive, "when are you going to teach me about the elements?"

"When you're ready," Bo said. "Have you been practicing looking into the Else?"

"Yes."

"Good."

"You can't just give me a basic lesson?"

Bo turned toward her, mumbling something under his breath, then lay his hand out flat in his lap and said, "Pay attention. A Privileged manipulates five different elements within the Else; air, water, fire, earth, and aether. Your main hand"—he wiggled his fingers—"can be used to summon those elements from the Else into our world. Your off-hand is used to direct them."

"If I lose a hand," Nila asked, "do I lose all access to sorcery?"

"The Else can be manipulated fully with just one hand, or your off-hand, it's just much harder. Now, each of your fingers corresponds to one of the elements and determines how strong you are in each element, starting with your forefinger for the strongest, and ending with your thumb as the weakest. Do you follow?"

Nila nodded. This was simple enough so far. "How do I know what I'm strongest in?"

"Trial and error. There's no clear way of testing it without having you rub your fingers together all day and pointing your hands at things. Considering the power I sense in you, that's not a terribly good idea in any population centers. We're going to have to figure it out slowly."

"Oh." Nila felt a little disappointed. She wanted to know what she could do now.

"I *can* tell you," Bo continued, "that you're strongest in fire and weakest in aether."

"And how do you know that?"

"When you make a fist, and the fire spreads up your arm, it happens because you've touched the Else and brushed your thumb and forefinger together. You haven't used air to carry the flame anywhere or water to make it behave like liquid fire or your off-hand to direct the elements and so it clings to you like a scared kitten." He smiled at his own analogy.

Fire. She was strongest in flame. She felt a little thrill go up her spine at the thought. "I understand the fire, but what about the aether? And how do you know it's my weakest?"

"Almost everyone is weakest in aether, and that's the thumb. Aether is used to create and destroy bonds between objects and elements, so think of it as an ignition source. It's the spark that starts your sorcery. Thumb to forefinger to begin fire and then moving on down the spectrum."

Nila moved her fingers experimentally, being sure not to let them touch. She examined her middle finger, wondering what power it held. "You said *almost* everyone is weakest in aether?"

"Yes. With some exceptions. The ones who are stronger tend to be healers, as they can knit the bonds between flesh, bone—even blood vessels and brain matter."

"I could never be a healer?" It had been a hope Nila had held on to, despite knowing how rare healers were. After all, being a healer meant she could help people instead of killing them.

Bo gave a shrug. "You can develop some basic skill in healing, but it takes decades of study and practice. I try to brush up on it myself every once in a while for an emergency. I can cauterize a wound competently or remove a bullet without damaging the tissue. Simple stuff. Much more and I'd probably do more damage than good."

"What are you strongest in?"

Bo gave a little chuckle. "Careful whom you ask that. It can be a grave insult."

"What? I just...oh. I didn't know." How was that an insult? It was just a question.

"You couldn't have known," Bo said. "Privileged love secrets. We hoard them like a squirrel does nuts and share them only sparingly. One of those secrets is our strengths and weaknesses. Now, over time, a healer will become known as a healer, or a fire Privileged known to do fire. But at the beginning, when you're most vulnerable as a person, you'll want to keep that information close to you. It could save your life in a duel with another Privileged."

"I see," Nila said. Except she didn't, really. Were all Privileged so mistrustful?

Bo held up his forefinger. "My strongest is air. Then water, fire, earth, aether."

"Well, wait," Nila said crossly. "Why would you tell me that after—"

"Because I trust you," Bo interrupted her. "And because I'm confident in myself and I have enough of a reputation that most Privileged already know my strengths and weaknesses. Once people have heard of you and had a chance to ask around, it's hard to keep that kind of thing a secret."

"Then why is it considered rude to ask them directly?" Nila demanded.

"Because," Lady Winceslav spoke up suddenly, "you're implying that they're fool enough to tell you something that could leave them open to attack. Try to think with that pretty head of yours, girl." Lady Winceslav crossed her legs and turned back toward the window.

Nila stuck her tongue out at her. When she looked back at Bo, he'd already settled back into his corner of the carriage, his mind far away.

Nila thought of trying to start a conversation once more, but neither of her companions seemed to be in the mood to speak. Her window showed nothing but hillside for almost a quarter of a mile, so she turned to the attaché case of papers she still clutched in her hands.

She had read most of the requisition reports from before Taniel was captured by the Kez. With only a few pages to go, she leafed through them slowly, scanning each line.

She had always thought that quartermasters must have the

dullest task in an army, but the way the numbers read on the lines was almost mesmerizing. She imagined that with more experience, she could read these numbers and know exactly how many infantry or cavalry an army had, or the tactical tastes of a particular general.

One line caught her eye about halfway down the page. She read it over a second time, then a third, checking the date.

"Bo..." she said.

"Hmm?"

"Has anyone mentioned Taniel's movements the day before he was hoisted above the Kez camp?"

Bo scratched one of his muttonchops. "I talked to one of the camp cooks—the ones that used to be Mihali's assistants. Taniel visited Mihali in the late afternoon."

"Did they say why?"

"No. But I can take a guess. He's bloody stupid enough to go after Kresimir alone. That's the only way he would have been captured, after all. And he probably went to Mihali for advice."

"And he would have left immediately for the Kez camp?"

"Search me." Bo shrugged. "Why?"

"It must be nothing." Nila flipped the page, reading through the requisitions and dates, but there were no more requisitions reported by Taniel. She felt her breath quickening suddenly. "Bo..."

"What is it?" he asked, shaking his head peevishly as if his thoughts had been interrupted.

"Do you remember me telling you what Colonel Etan had told me? About the two companies of soldiers Hilanska had sent to the mountains?"

"Yes, yes. Get on with it."

She handed Bo the report. "Look at this requisition made by Taniel, about halfway down the page."

"I see it." He ran his eyes over it several times before saying, "This doesn't make any sense. Why the bloody pit would Taniel requisition three hundred air rifles?"

Nila leaned forward. "Back when I was Tamas's laundress, I overheard him say that all the air rifles in Adro had been locked up in an armory in Adopest with strict orders that only a powder mage could order them. Look at the time!" She thrust her finger onto the page. "This was four o'clock in the morning. It had to have been *after* Taniel was captured. The requisition was falsified in his name!"

"Oh, bloody pit," Bo said. He pounded on the roof. "Stop the carriage! Stop it now!"

"What are you doing?" Lady Winceslav asked as the coach came to a halt.

"I need two horses," Bo said.

"Done. What's going on?"

Bo leapt out of the carriage. "A traitor would know Taniel had been captured and that they could falsify the report."

"To what end?"

"If he thought that Tamas might return, perhaps. It doesn't matter. Hilanska has sent his men, armed with air rifles, to hunt down Taniel."

"How do you know?" Nila asked.

"Three hundred air rifles are enough to outfit two companies of Adran soldiers. Two companies sent into the mountains on Hilanska's orders. If that's a coincidence, I'll eat my hat. I have to go."

"I'm coming with you," Nila said.

"No. Stay with the Lady. No one must slow me down. I'm going to rain fire and earth down on those two companies, and anyone near me will be torn apart."

"Then why two horses?"

Bo tugged on his Privileged gloves. "So that when one drops dead beneath me, I can keep riding."

CHAPTER

11

Adamat waited with Brigadier Abrax as General Ket went over the documents he had brought.

They were in Ket's personal tent. The guards outside had been dismissed. Ket slowly leafed through the documents, first reading the arrest warrant issued by Ricard Tumblar and the two judges in Adopest and then looking through the list of charges and evidence presented to the court in the case against her and her sister.

It must have been thirty minutes before she finally shuffled the papers together cleanly and set them on the table in front of her, leaning back. She looked from Adamat to Abrax and then back again.

"Do you deny these charges?" Adamat asked, glad to finally break the silence.

"I do not."

That was a surprise. "I was sent here to arrest you," Adamat said.

"You understand the current situation?" Ket asked.

Beside Adamat, Abrax nodded. "Yes."

"You expect me to recuse myself," Ket said, "hand over command of my men to Hilanska, and go with you to Adopest?" Before Adamat could answer, she continued, "I won't do that. Hilanska is a traitor. He intends on selling us all out to the Kez. Whatever it is that I'm guilty of, treachery is not one of those things."

She had told them as much about Hilanska when they arrived, but had been unable to present evidence. She claimed that her own witness had been poisoned by one of Hilanska's men.

"Actually," Adamat said, "that's not what we had in mind."

Ket cocked an eyebrow, her first change of expression since they arrived. "Oh?"

"I've spoken to Lady Winceslav on your behalf," Adamat said. "She agreed that whatever petty crimes you and your sister are guilty of are secondary to the safety of Adro. As a member of Tamas's council, she has given me the authority to offer you an out."

"And what could that possibly be?"

"You will immediately step down from command. Your sister will step down from command as well. You will be escorted to your estate in northern Adro, where you will have one week to put your affairs in order before you and your households will be exiled. You will be allowed a onetime stipend of one million krana, and your property will be confiscated by the state."

Ket's nostrils flared. "That is not an out. That's a sentence."

"One million is a lot of money," Abrax said sternly. "Do you think Tamas will be so kind when he returns?"

"Tamas is dead."

"He is not." Abrax removed a letter from her pocket and handed it to Ket. "We received this communication just this morning. Tamas has crossed the Charwood Pile with the Seventh and the Ninth and sixty thousand Deliv infantry. He will be here in two weeks."

Adamat felt his jaw drop. Tamas was alive? For certain? Why had Lady Winceslav not mentioned this? It changed everything!

Ket paled visibly. She took up the arrest warrant once more, her fingers shaking, and read it over thoroughly.

"I suggest," Adamat said, "that you be sure to be out of the country by the time he arrives."

"What of my men? Who will take command?"

"I will," Abrax said.

"That is not legal!"

"And you are concerned about what is and isn't legal?" Adamat asked lightly.

Ket rounded on Adamat. "I have covered for my sister's crimes, yes. But I am still a general of the Adran army and I am a patriot. I will only take this 'clemency'"—she spit the word as if it were poison—"on the condition that my men will be safe."

"Your men will be placed under special command of the Wings of Adom," Abrax said. "We will immediately send Hilanska a missive stating that you have been relieved and that your three brigades are under our employ—and protection—until Field Marshal Tamas returns to the field."

Ket's fingers drummed on the table and she stared hard at the air above Adamat's head.

"General," Adamat said, "this is the only way they will survive. Surely your scouts have told you that the Kez are already positioning themselves to attack tomorrow morning, and General Hilanska is positioning for a flanking maneuver."

"More proof that he's working with the Kez," Ket said.

Adamat shared a nervous glance with Abrax. "Even if that's true, he dare not attack once your brigades are under the Wings of Adom flag."

Ket leapt to her feet suddenly. "All right! I agree. I relinquish command. I'll take my sister and go. Just let me address the men one last time." There was a note of appeal in her voice that hadn't been there before, and Adamat could see she was in earnest.

Abrax met her gaze with steel in her eyes. "You will not have the chance to mend your reputation, Ket. Your men will know you as a thief and a liar."

Anger and grief danced across Ket's face—raw emotions of which Adamat wouldn't have guessed her capable.

Slowly, Abrax stood, and with a sigh she added, "I will make certain they know that you stepped down with their best interests at heart."

Ket's only answer was a defeated nod.

Abrax clasped her hands behind her back and squared her shoulders. "General Ket," she said, "you are relieved of command."

Morning came with an unwelcome chill in the Wings of Adom camp.

Adamat stared, bleary-eyed, as Kez infantry began to form just within view, a couple of miles to the south. Their tan-and-green uniforms made them look like acres upon acres of fall wheat ready for the harvest. How many infantry did the Kez have left? Two hundred thousand? Three? Abrax's scouts said that they'd brought up fresh levies from Budwiel during the night.

He jumped at the sudden blast of a cannon. Several more followed, and Adamat knew he should get used to the noise. For now it was just Abrax warning the Kez to keep their distance. It would get worse as the morning wore on and hundreds of cannons opened fire on every front.

Abrax stood beside him, looking out from their vantage on top of a hill where Ket's command tent had been. Instead of the Kez, she was watching to the northeast.

"Any word?" Adamat asked.

The bulk of the Adran army, under Hilanska's command, was hidden by the hills.

"We sent over thirty messengers throughout the night," Abrax said, her voice raw. "At least ten of whom were shot on sight. I don't know what Hilanska has told his men, but he has turned them against us completely. Lady Winceslav would have gone herself if I hadn't prevented it."

"Where is the Lady now?" Adamat asked. The Lady, along with twenty-six thousand Wings infantry, had joined them yesterday evening. They'd brought along news of the intercepted missive—Hilanska's treachery. Adamat had hoped that at least Bo would be with them, but only Nila arrived. What good could a barely trained Privileged do?

"I sent her back to Adopest with a hundred of my best cavalry," Abrax said. "I won't let her die on the field." There was a long silence as Abrax continued to watch the northeast, and then she said, "You've killed us all, Adamat." There was no accusation or anger in the words. Just a dull acceptance.

The realization that they would all be slaughtered by nightfall descended on Adamat's shoulders. He felt his chest tighten and forced himself to take slow, deep breaths. Hilanska was a traitor. He would attack the Wings of Adom, destroying both them and their three adopted brigades of Adran infantry, and then... what? Order his men to surrender to the Kez? Would they follow such an order? Or would the Kez simply swarm and slaughter them as well?

The Adran army would destroy itself, and then the Kez would be fresh to fight Field Marshal Tamas and the Deliv when they arrived.

It was absolutely hopeless. They were hemmed in with no possibility of escape. Abrax had ordered ditches dug and fortifications built. She was determined to make a last stand of it, but Adamat could see the stress lines on her face and the purple circles under her eyes from a sleepless night.

Abrax's head twitched, and Adamat turned to follow her gaze. On the distant hills to the northeast, a horseman had appeared. It paused, watching them, and then Adamat saw the glitter of the sun off bayonets on the crest of the hill.

"They're coming," Abrax said.

CHAPTER

12

Where the pit is everyone?" Tamas demanded.

The corporal before him, standing over his breakfast with a spoon forgotten in his hand, stared openmouthed at Tamas.

The Adran camp was nearly empty. Only a small guard had been left with the thousands of hangers-on, and the sea of tents had been abandoned. That meant only one thing: Battle would be joined today. Tamas could smell it on the wind, and despite his exhaustion and the ache deep in his bones, he felt a thrill course through him.

Olem sawed at the reins of his mount to bring it closer to the corporal. "You heard the field marshal, soldier. Speak up!" Steam rose from their horses from the long, hard ride through the night.

"I'm, I'm . . ." the corporal stuttered. "I'm so sorry, sir. They're . . ." He lifted one arm to point southwest. "They've gone to battle."

"Bloody pit," Tamas swore. Why would Hilanska choose to join battle now? The Kez would still outnumber the Adran army, and on the open plains like this the Kez would be able to bring their superior numbers to bear with devastating effect. "Do you hear that, Olem? Cannon fire."

"I hear it, sir."

"Sir!" Vlora raced toward them through the camp, having gone ahead to try to find the General Staff. She arrived panting and took the reins of her horse from Olem, swinging into the saddle. "Sir, they're not attacking the Kez!"

"Then who the pit would they be attacking?" Tamas asked.

"They're attacking our own men. General Ket had separated her brigades from the army, and Hilanska is attacking her!"

"Ride!" Tamas bellowed, digging his heels in, feeling his stallion leap forward.

The three of them galloped through the Adran camp and then southwest, following the trail of his brigades. The sweat poured down Tamas's face despite the cool wind racing past. What had happened? How could a disaster of this magnitude occur? He was going to find Ket and string her up by her own bootlaces.

They rode several miles along the main highway, and with each crested hill Tamas got a slightly better glimpse of the forces arrayed to their south. His heart thundered in his chest and he clung to the neck of his horse, urging more speed.

They reached the rear of the Adran lines. Soldiers leapt out of their way as they thundered through. Tamas spotted the command tent placed at the height of a hillock overlooking the artillery and veered toward it. Soldiers were beginning to look curiously in his direction, but he ignored them, pushing on.

He leapt from his mount, tossing the reins to a startled infantryman, and advanced on the command tent. He threw back the flaps. "Damn it, Hilanska, what is going on here?"

Several dozen eyes stared at him in dumb confusion.

"Well?" Tamas asked.

Chaos broke out among the assembled officers. There were pro-
testations and exclamations and hands reaching for him. More
than one chair was knocked over as men sprang to their feet. A
cacophony of voices all tried to speak to him at once.

"Quiet down!" Olem roared.

"Thank you, Olem. Now, tell me, what's going on here?" Tamas
searched for familiar faces and was saddened to see so few. Had
they lost that many men since he'd been gone?

"We're about to commence battle with the traitor General Ket,"
a colonel said from the back.

"Like pit we are," Tamas said. "Olem . . . no, Vlora. Take a white
flag across the valley. I want Ket here in person within the hour to
give me an explanation as to what's happening."

"She won't come," the same colonel spoke up. "She refuses to see
our messengers."

"She'll see *me*. Was that the Wings of Adom's colors I saw above
Ket's camp?"

A female general whom Tamas only vaguely recognized gave
him an uncertain nod.

"Then bring me Brigadier Abrax as well, or whoever is in charge.
Dismissed, Captain."

Vlora snapped a sharp salute and left the tent at a sprint.

"Wheel our artillery to face south," Tamas ordered. "I want all
of our cavalry on our eastern flank—and I do mean all of them.
Split them into three groups and wait for my order. The Kez are
preparing to advance. They'll come on at about ten o'clock, or I'm a
horse's ass. Keep our men facing Ket's troops, but make it damned
clear that they are not to engage their fellow Adrans. If the Kez
think we're about to attack our own men, they are going to get a
damned big surprise. Get to it!"

The tent burst into a flurry of motion.

"General Hilanska," Tamas said, "what are you doing? Sneaking
out the back? Get over here."

Hilanska approached along the side of the tent, a wary eye on Tamas. "Sir?" he asked quietly.

"Come with me." Tamas threw back the tent flap. "Move the command tent up the hillside about forty paces," he said to the guards outside. "I want to be able to see everything going on in that valley." He strode up the hill toward the spot he'd indicated, beckoning Hilanska along with him. His body ached from the ride, exhaustion tugged at his muscles, but the excitement of the battle made his fingers twitch.

When they reached the top, he turned to Hilanska, but his words caught in his mouth. "Are you all right?" he asked.

A sheen of sweat had appeared on Hilanska's brow. His collar was already soaked, and he was picking nervously at the buttons of his jacket. Four provosts had trailed them up the hill and stood back at a respectful distance.

"Fine, sir," Hilanska said, dabbing at his cheeks. "What was it you wanted?"

Tamas turned toward the Kez forces. There were at least two hundred and sixty thousand infantry out there, along with twenty thousand or so cavalry. It was a sight to behold, but he couldn't let the grandeur of it impress him. He had work to do.

"Hilanska, I want you to put your best gun crews there and there," he said, pointing. "I want them to rain down everything they have on...Hilanska, are you listening, I..." Tamas felt a sharp pain in his side. He scowled and rubbed at the spot. "Like I was saying, I want them to..."

Tamas felt himself shoved forward suddenly and heard a shout. He whirled, a curse on his lips.

Olem was shouting, his sword drawn, and was suddenly set upon by all four of the provosts who had followed them up the hill. Hilanska was behind the provosts, a dagger in his one hand.

"What the bloody pit is going on?" Tamas demanded. He reached for the butt of his pistol instinctively, but his fingers slipped on it. He held them up, blinking back a sudden dizziness. Their tips were red.

He'd been stabbed.

Hilanska had bloody well stabbed him.

The one-armed general turned and fled down the hill.

Tamas sat in the grass, his jacket stripped from him and his shirt soaked with blood, trying to make sense of what had happened.

A surgeon sat behind him with his hands under Tamas's arms while another cut away his shirt and began to examine the stab wound between his ribs. Not ten paces away, the bodies of two Adran provosts were being carted away, while a third surgeon tended to a gash across Olem's forehead.

Hilanska had betrayed him. That much was clear. But how deep did it go? How long had the betrayal been in the works? Had Hilanska let Budwiel's walls fall, trapping Tamas behind enemy lines months ago? Hilanska had to be behind this schism with General Ket, working to ensure the annihilation of the entire Adran army.

"Olem!" Tamas had to know more. The most important question was, Did Hilanska have accomplices?

Olem appeared a moment later, pressing a fresh bandage against his forehead. "Sir?"

"Fine swordsmanship there," Tamas said. Olem had held off all four provosts until help could arrive. "Did any of them survive?"

"Thank you, sir. Two of them survived. One will die by morning. The boys were rough on them when they saw that you were wounded."

"Rough won't even begin to cover it," Tamas said. "Go find out what they know."

"Shouldn't I go after Hilanska, sir?"

Tamas hesitated. "I don't know whom to trust," he said quietly. "Get two squads together—see if you can find any of your

Riflejacks—and send them after Hilanska. I want you to stay close."

"Yes sir."

Tamas swore under his breath as one of the surgeons poked a finger at his wound. "Bandage it up and get me some black powder. It didn't hit a lung. I'll live." He beat the surgeons back with one hand and got unsteadily to his feet. The pain in his side was sharp now, and he was reminded of a similar wound he'd taken in Gurla twenty years before. He had been bedridden for weeks and nearly succumbed to infection.

He didn't have time for that now.

In the valley below them he saw that the Wings of Adom had taken up a defensive ring around Ket's camp and had dug in with fortifications not unlike the kind Tamas had used against Beon je Ippile's cavalry—though not nearly as deep. He spotted Vlora racing along on her charger, white flag snapping in the wind. She reached the Wings' lines and after a few tense moments was allowed past.

The Kez continued to fall into line. Their army looked immense—and it was—but its size made it ponderous. Tamas adjusted his initial guess that they'd attack by ten. They wouldn't be ready until at least noon. Maybe one. They would attack straight out, using their superior numbers to surround and overwhelm General Ket's camp.

Tamas cracked a powder charge and sprinkled a bit on his tongue. Once the initial shock of the powder trance passed, he felt younger and stronger and the pain from the knife wound was nothing but a tickle in the back of his mind.

Out of the corner of his eye, Tamas saw Olem approaching.

"Anything?" Tamas asked.

"No sir. Both provosts claim that Hilanska warned them you might return but that it would be a Kez trick—a Privileged disguised as you. They also claim he didn't expect your doppelgänger for weeks."

Tamas snorted. "So he panicked and ran when I arrived early? Let's just be glad he wasn't ready for us. Pit, what other rumors has he spread?"

"I can try to find out, sir."

"Do it."

"Permission to search his quarters?"

"Granted."

Olem was off again and Tamas looked around him for someone he could trust. Most of the generals were with their brigades, and it seemed that at least some of Hilanska's support staff had fled with him.

"You there!" Tamas called. "Colonel, come here." From the side, the young man looked fairly familiar, and when he turned to Tamas, he recognized the colonel immediately. "Colonel Sabastenien, it's good to see you alive."

The former Wings of Adom brigadier was a short man in his midtwenties with muttonchops filled with premature gray and a somber face. Tamas noted that the gray hadn't been there the last time they met, and wondered whether it was dyed. He gave Tamas a respectful nod. "Likewise, sir. And it's not Sabastenien. It's Florone now. I've taken my mother's family name. I prefer not to be immediately recognizable to my former comrades."

Tamas understood that. While he'd done nothing illegal or untoward in murdering a traitor in Tamas's defense, Sabastenien had been cast out of the Wings of Adom because the traitor had been a fellow brigadier—and Lady Winceslav's lover.

"All right, Saba...Florone. I need a battle plan. Where are you assigned?"

"I'm with the Twenty-First Artillery."

"And you have artillery experience?"

"Seven years of it with the Wings."

"Good. Congratulations, Florone. You're now a general."

The colonel blinked in surprise. "Sir?"

"Take command of the Second. Bring their artillery around to the south and have the gun crews standing by. Have your infantry dig in to the east and west."

"Yes sir. Thank you, sir."

"Don't thank me yet. I don't know who I can trust in Hilanska's brigades. You might get stabbed in the back by the end of the day. If you have any trusted support staff, take them with you."

"Yes sir."

"And General, have Mihali sent up here, would you?"

Florone hesitated for a moment. "No one's told you yet?"

"Told me what?"

"Mihali is dead. He was killed by Kresimir two weeks ago."

Tamas whirled to look back at the Kez formations and a cold sweat broke out over his body, the back of his neck pricked by an eerie sensation of shock and grief, breaking the calm of his powder trance. If Mihali was dead, why hadn't Adro been swept aside already? There shouldn't be anything left of Adopest or the Adran army but dust without Mihali to balance his brother's power, and yet the country and its capital still stood.

What could possibly be holding Kresimir back?

His attention was caught by movement in the Wings of Adom camp, and soon Vlora was racing back up the hillside. She blew past the Adran sentries and didn't stop until she reached Tamas, leaping from her horse and tossing the reins to a startled messenger.

"Where's Ket?" Tamas asked.

"Gone," Vlora gasped. "She was ousted by Abrax and Adamat just yesterday on accusations of profiteering. Abrax thought it might mend the schism between the camps, but...sir, are you wounded?"

"It didn't mend the schism," Tamas said, "because Hilanska planned a betrayal all along. And what the pit is Adamat doing down here? Damn it all, this is when I needed Ket the most. Aside from Hilanska, she was the most capable commander here. Where's Abrax?"

"On her way here."

"We don't have more than a couple of hours before the Kez attack. Gather the General Staff—I want as many senior officers as you can get within twenty minutes. We'll send orders to the rest via messengers. Olem, what did you find?"

Olem arrived at a sprint and paused briefly to catch his breath. "He left everything. Hilanska's been in bed with the Kez since the beginning. I found dozens of letters."

"Anything to tell us who his accomplices are?"

"I haven't had time to sort through it all."

"Time. Bloody pit, we need time more than anything else. I can't plan a defensive on such short notice, not against that monstrosity."

"Olem," Vlora said, "did you find Hilanska's personal seal?"

"It was there with everything else."

"Get me a fresh horse!" Vlora yelled.

Tamas asked, "Where are you going?"

"I need one of the Wings' code breakers," Vlora said. "Someone who can replicate Hilanska's cipher. If we move quickly, I think I can buy us an extra day."

Tamas dictated a message for the Kez commanders based on the language Hilanska used in his own letters and notes, then had a Wings code breaker translate it into Hilanska's cipher. The message stated that Hilanska would be able to get someone close enough to Abrax to assassinate her if she let down her guard, but that that would require the Kez to appear to withdraw and get ready for an attack the next day.

The whole process took nearly two hours and looked, to Tamas's eye, like a rush job. It would be a miracle if the Kez believed it.

But if they did, it would buy them twenty-four precious hours to prepare for the Kez attack. Time they desperately needed in order to have any chance at winning this battle.

Tamas lifted his eyes to Olem, who was waiting in the entry to the command tent, hand casually on his pistol, as the Wings' code breaker applied Hilanska's own hot wax and seal to the forged message. Tamas took it from him and blew on the wax to cool it, then handed it over to Olem.

Olem snapped a salute. "I've found a few of my most loyal Rifle-jacks, sir. I'll send one of them over to the Kez with it."

"They know it's a terrible risk? If the Kez sniff out the deception, they'll be killed. Or worse."

"Already have a man for the job. He knows."

"Good. That's the only message I want going to the Kez. Tell the sentries they are to shoot on sight anyone who makes a break for the Kez lines. They can't know I'm back."

Tamas nodded a dismissal. When Olem was gone, he turned uncomfortably toward the code breaker, feeling the wound from Hilanska's knife open at the movement and send a stab of pain through his belly that he tried to suppress. Slowly, hoping that the code breaker didn't see his fingers shaking, Tamas broke open a powder charge and sprinkled a bit of black powder on his tongue. The resulting powder trance settled in, stilling the pain.

"Good work, soldier," Tamas said.

"Thank you, sir," the code breaker said. "If I may say so, it's a pleasure to have you back. I know Brigadier Abrax is relieved."

Tamas forced a smile. "I'm glad to hear that. It's good to be back. You know, we didn't have professional code breakers back in the Gurlish Wars. I had to make do with giving some of my clever-est men special duty. It didn't even occur to anyone to make it a regular duty until Lord Winceslav. I've been telling myself for fifteen years that we need our own code breakers in the Adran army, but somehow it always got pushed down the list."

"I had the good fortune to work with Lord Winceslav," the code breaker said. "He was a very intelligent man."

"I agree. It was a shame to lose him. But your Lady is far more clever than her husband was. I always wondered if she came up with the idea for the code breakers and let her late husband take the credit."

The code breaker remained silent, looking down at his feet.

"I'm sorry if I ramble. You don't have to respond to that."

"Thank you, sir."

Olem returned a moment later, giving Tamas a sharp nod to tell him that the messenger had left. "Soldier," Tamas said to the code breaker, "you can head to the mess and get some breakfast. Or lunch. I don't even know what bloody time it is."

"Sir, permission to return to the Wings?"

Tamas glanced at Olem, who stepped up next to the code breaker. "Sorry, soldier, but you're going to have to stay here for a while. We're keeping it quiet that Field Marshal Tamas has returned. It'll make it easier to pull one over on the Kez."

"I won't tell anyone, I swear."

"We'd prefer not to risk it," Olem said.

The code breaker glanced between Tamas and Olem. "Sir?"

"I'm sorry," Tamas said. "We're keeping it quiet even among our own men for as long as we can. We have to weigh the morale boost against the need for secrecy."

The code breaker frowned, then took a deep breath and straightened, snapping out a salute. "I understand, sir."

"Good. I'll let Abrax know how well you did here today."

Olem led the man outside and then returned a moment later with Vlora. She looked dusty and tired, but her step was crisp. He could tell by the smell of her that she had been burning a powder trance all morning.

"How goes it over in the Wings' camp?" Tamas asked.

Vlora saluted, then dropped into a chair across from Tamas. "If the Kez still attack today, it's going to be a rough thing. The Wings have three brigades pointed toward us. Abrax says if this ruse works, she'll have time to wheel them around and be able to throw everything she has at the Kez by the middle of tomorrow morning."

"And so we wait," Tamas said.

Vlora nodded. "We wait." She and Olem exchanged an unreadable glance. Tamas had been too focused on walking the line between going powder blind and managing the pain of his aching body with a powder trance during the mad ride from the Deliv border to Adopest. But whatever they had seemed to have cooled. "Has any word of my presence reached the Wings infantry?"

"Abrax is keeping it to herself and just two of her brigadiers. She agrees that we need to keep it a secret for as long as possible. A couple of the officers may have recognized me, but she's keeping a tight lid on it."

"Good."

"Word's already starting to spread here," Olem said.

"Can't be helped. They saw us ride in."

"I've sealed the camp," Olem added. "No one in or out without orders until morning."

"Excellent work."

Tamas noticed that Olem was fingering the colonel lapel pins that Tamas had given to him outside Alvation. He was going to bring it up again.

"Sir," Olem said.

Tamas snorted. "I'm not going to demote you, Olem."

"I would prefer if you did, sir."

"It's not like I've given you your own command—at least, not beyond the Riflejacks. You're a colonel on special assignment. It's not unheard of."

"But still..."

Tamas raised his hand in a gesture that he hoped would put an end to the argument, though he knew that hope was vain. Olem was utterly convinced he was not colonel material. "I like having you in a position where you can give orders," Tamas said. "Try not to be so glum about it. I won't give you a large command until you're ready for it. Mark my words, you'll be a general—a proper one—within ten years."

Olem looked as if he were about to laugh in Tamas's face. He seemed to quell the urge. "I won't shave, sir. Not even to make general."

"I like the beard," Vlora said. "More soldiers should have them."

"Now, don't you start." Tamas pointed at her. "I'll take that shit from him because he's my last line of defense against assassination. I won't take it from you."

"Fine job he did with Hilanska."

Olem bristled at that, his back stiffening and his face going slack. Tamas glanced at Vlora. That had been coldhearted—she knew Olem had been away, following orders. And Olem took his duties very seriously. Tamas opened his mouth for a rebuke, but closed it when he saw the look on Vlora's face. She had paled slightly and was looking at the floor. She already regretted saying it.

"Sir, is there anything else I can do?" Olem asked woodenly.

"Stay close," Tamas said. "But, speaking of Hilanska..."

"I've got a whole company after him already. They'll catch him and his cohorts and bring them back in chains."

"You did well, Olem. And this minor thing"—he gestured to where the knife wound was hidden beneath his coat—"will heal in time." He felt a twinge of pain when he moved, despite his powder trance.

"Yes sir." The words were stiff.

Tamas rubbed his eyes. He usually used this time before a battle to meet with his commanding officers and plan backup strategies, but he'd already given the orders he'd needed to give, and every-thing was banked on the Kez answer to his fake communiqué. If it worked, they'd have an extra day in which to plan. If it didn't, battle would commence within the hour.

He knew he should be doing *something*. But he just couldn't bring himself to get moving. He tried to tell himself it was just exhaustion from the road—a few moments of quiet and he would be ready to take on the road. But he wasn't just exhausted. His bones ached; every wound new and old hurt; and his mind longed for sleep. Age had caught up with him over these last few months.

And the fact that he couldn't focus on the task at hand meant that he was ignoring something more important.

"Sir," Vlora said quietly, "what of Taniel? We know where Hilan-ska sent his men. Perhaps..." She trailed off.

That couldn't be more important than the task at hand. Taniel might be his son, but he was merely one man. This day determined the fate of an entire country. "I know my duties, Captain," Tamas said.

Vlora looked as if she wanted to say more. Instead, she crossed the room to where Olem stood by the entrance. Olem eyed her, but did not stop her, when she reached inside his jacket for tobacco and rolling paper. She rolled a cigarette slowly, her eyes never leaving Olem's face, then struck one of his matches and lit the end, inhal-ing deeply. The smoke rolled out of her nostrils and she offered the cigarette to Olem.

Tamas thought of telling them both not to smoke in the tent, but he wanted to see how this played out. It was a peace offering, something to take the sting off of what she'd said a minute ago.

Olem took the cigarette and clenched it between his lips. Tamas felt himself letting out a breath he didn't know he was holding.

The tent flap swung open and someone whispered to Olem. "A moment, sir," Olem said, stepping outside.

Tamas found himself alone with Vlora. He knew she wanted

to say something about Taniel. He stared at her, hoping that his expression brooked no argument, but as the silence went on, he almost wished she *would* say something. He could deal with her accusations and disappointment. He could fight that.

He couldn't fight his own.

Olem stepped into the tent once more, letting in a breeze tinged with the smell of cigarette smoke. "Sir," he said, "our man is back. The Kez didn't send back an answer, but their brigades are already leaving the field. We have until tomorrow."

Tamas got to his feet, coughing into his hand to hide the grimace of pain. "Then let's hope the Kez haven't gotten more cunning since we left. How many of your Riflejacks have you found so far?"

"Hilanska sent them all back to their own companies. I've tracked down about two hundred of the picked men."

"Gather them up, would you? We have work to do."

CHAPTER

13

Kresimir—or rather the doll used to control him—couldn't be moved yet.

Taniel had been fighting a growing panic all night. He hadn't slept. He'd barely eaten. The arrival of morning had only deepened his anxiety.

"We have to go," Taniel said.

Ka-poel shook her head adamantly. She crouched over a casket made of sticks and dried grass. It was a box, no bigger than a soldier's kit, meant to contain a god.

"They'll be here by midday," Taniel said.

Ka-poel didn't respond. She'd finished the casket only a few hours ago. Every moment since had been spent painting thin, perfectly straight lines on the outside using a horsehair brush she'd produced from within her rucksack. She used her blood for ink and it dried as a surprisingly bright crimson, not at all the dark rust of dried blood.

The whole thing made Taniel uneasy—more so than usual.

"Half a company of Adran infantry armed with air rifles are camped less than two miles away," he said. "They're climbing from their tents now and breaking camp, ready to continue their search. They'll find us by midday, if we're lucky. We can't possibly fight that many. They'll kill us both and then free Kresimir. We *have* to go."

Ka-poel didn't seem to agree with him. She kept painting, her hand steady and slow, as if she'd not heard a word.

Taniel touched her shoulder. "Pole..."

She whirled suddenly, throwing the brush across the cave and leaping to her feet. He found himself retreating from her advance. Her face was twisted into a scowl and her fists were clenched at her sides. She backed him up against the very edge of the cave and leaned toward him, managing to loom even though she was so much smaller than he. She tapped her hand against her chest, then the side of her head, and made a negative motion. She repeated the series of gestures two more times and then pointed to the casket.

I don't know what I'm doing.

Taniel noticed for the first time that her hair and shirt were soaked with sweat. Her shoulders shook. Unshed tears shone in the corners of her eyes, and Taniel finally realized how much this was taking out of her. He knew that Bone-eyes could create enchantments. They had made enchanted bullets called redstripes for the colonists in Fatrasta, and Ka-poel had even done it once for him—though he'd never witnessed the process. This must be like that.

He glanced at the casket and remembered the thin line of red that encircled the bullets and gave redstripes their names.

Of course. This was *exactly* like redstripes. She had to use her own blood in the enchantments.

Was that what she had done the other day when she wiped her

blood on his cheeks? Enchanted him? How much energy did this take? He saw her again with new eyes, saw the depth of her exhaustion and how her eyes seemed sunken and her cheeks hollow. Her clothes hung off her as if on a tailor's mannequin.

She was killing herself to keep Kresimir from breaking free, and yet she still used some of her power on him.

Ka-poel returned to her project, silent as always.

Taniel collected two knives and a bayonet that he'd taken from the Adran soldiers the other day. He regretted not stealing an air rifle. He could have at least used it as a pike with a bayonet on the end, but in his arrogance he'd broken them all in the Adran camp.

He kissed Ka-poel on the cheek, trying not to be put off by the way she turned away from him, and then left the cave behind, heading up and over the ridge and then following it to the east toward the Adran camp.

It didn't take him longer than an hour to spot the advance elements of the company of Adran infantry. Six of them worked their way up the canyon slowly, cautiously, their rifles clutched in both hands and their eyes on the ridgelines high above them on either side.

He took up a position about three hundred yards above the floor of the canyon and hunkered down to wait.

The vanguard turned out to be fifty paces ahead of the rest of the company. The company was forced to advance in single file and, unlike the vanguard, they weren't apprising themselves of their surroundings. They were fresh and overconfident. Some of the men joked, their chipper voices bouncing off the canyon walls. Taniel had hoped that his display to the squad the other day would make them more cautious, but that didn't seem to be the case.

After all, they were only hunting one man and this was broad daylight.

Taniel knew he couldn't fight all eighty of them. He didn't stand a chance.

He waited until the entire company was within sight, strung out as they were along the canyon floor, and the center of the company was directly below his position. Then he lashed out with one foot at the log beside him and dashed out of the way as twenty tons of rubble immediately began to thunder down the canyon walls.

He couldn't win, but he would damn well take as many of them to the Pit with him as possible.

The canyon echoed with the screams of the dying and the yells of the survivors as the thunder finally subsided in the wake of Taniel's avalanche.

The sound made Taniel sick. He hadn't wanted to kill his own countrymen. These men had friends and family. Children and wives and husbands. He might have fought beside some of them. He might have trained beside them.

It was no different from killing any enemy, he reminded himself. This was war. He had to kill or be killed.

Taniel stealthily stuck his head out from his hiding place to examine his handiwork.

The avalanche had cut the Adran company in half. At least ten of them had been buried by the falling rocks and another dozen or so wounded. A captain was pinned to the floor of the canyon by a boulder on his leg, and Taniel could hear his howls of pain. A lieutenant stood above him, directing a simultaneous defense-and-rescue mission. The infantry had scattered to whatever cover they could find, and now everyone had their eyes on the canyon's walls.

They began to dig out their wounded, and when it became apparent that an attack was not imminent, two squads continued their journey up the canyon.

This was good news and bad news. The good news was that he'd split their forces. The bad news was that those two squads were heading toward Ka-poel's cave.

He set off at a run just beneath the ridgeline, where he could be plainly seen by the soldiers below. A shout of alarm followed him a moment later and he heard the soft pop of air rifles. The distance was far too great for them to actually hit him, but he ducked behind a boulder anyway and took a moment to look back.

The lieutenant pointed toward him, shouting after the two squads. The two squad sergeants conferred, and then one squad headed straight up the steep incline toward Taniel while the other set about looking for a goat path or some other way to flank him.

Taniel had their attention now, and that's what mattered.

He led the two squads on a chase along the ridgeline for over a mile. Of the twenty-four men, only three kept up with his pace, outstripping their comrades in their attempt to catch up. After all, they only had to get close enough for a shot with an air rifle to bring Taniel down. Hilanska must have offered a reward for his head. Soldiers normally weren't this zealous.

The thought hardened Taniel's heart against his reluctance to kill more of his countrymen. These men would gun him down without hesitation. They were hunting him like a dog.

He risked a dash across open ground, flinching at the pop of air rifles and the sound of bullets skipping off of the stone behind him. They were still just out of range, but a lucky shot aimed high might wound him. He leapt a fissure and continued on for some thirty paces before the ground gave way to rockier terrain and he leapt back into cover.

Out of sight of the squad, he doubled back, running in a crouch beneath the lip of a boulder until he was inside the fissure that he'd jumped only moments ago.

Taniel wondered what his father would say if he saw any of his own men being led into such an obvious trap.

Probably that the damned fools deserved to die.

The first pursuer leapt the fissure only a few moments after

Taniel was in position. As the second set of legs flew overhead, he reached up and grabbed a boot, yanking down. The man dropped his air rifle with a clatter and landed face-first on the lip of the fissure, leaving a smear of blood behind.

The third of the group skidded to a stop and knelt beside his comrade. Taniel made a running leap and grabbed this one by the front of his jacket, dragging him back into the fissure. The soldier let out a strangled scream before Taniel silenced him by slamming his face repeatedly against the rocks. He snatched the air rifle from the dead man's hands and checked it for damage.

Air rifles were notoriously more unreliable than conventional muskets and rifles. The mechanisms broke easily and the air reserves leaked. This one seemed sound, and Taniel checked the chamber and shouldered the butt.

"Glouster?" The first pursuer had noticed his companion's absence and turned. "Glouster, are you all right? Allier looks like he's hurt bad. Pit, Glouster, say something!"

Taniel felt a pang at the panic in the young man's voice. The fear must be setting in, overrunning his adrenaline. He'd be wondering if his eyes had tricked him. Hadn't Taniel disappeared into the rocks ahead? How could he possibly be in that dark fissure?

The infantryman came into view, his rifle shouldered, squinting into the fissure.

Taniel shot him in the chest.

He took spare ammunition and air reserves from the dead infantrymen and followed his hidden path back to the rocks. The rest of the squad would catch up any moment, and they wouldn't be as stupid as their comrades.

He ambushed two more infantrymen in the rocks, and then three more after them, using their bulky kits and unwieldy bayoneted rifles against them in the close confines of the rock formations.

He shot another with his captured air rifle just a few moments later, but the damned mechanism broke before he could fire another round, and he was forced to flee, with the remainder of the two squads hot on his heels.

They stayed in a tight formation now, not letting themselves be led on by his tricks.

Taniel knew he was running out of ground. This ridge went on for a couple of miles before it meandered into one of the thousands of valleys that crisscrossed this mountain range. He needed to be rid of the rest of his pursuers before he doubled back and figured out a way to deal with the remaining infantrymen down in the canyon. There was another fissure along here somewhere that would let him get behind his enemy and . . .

Taniel swung around a boulder to find himself staring out into the sky. The drop below him must have been more than two hundred feet down a sheer rock face into a barren streambed. He searched about him for another escape route, but there was nothing but bare, vertical rock to be found. A ledge to his right gave way to more such rock and a narrow outcropping that would doubtlessly give them a firing platform.

Somewhere, he'd taken a wrong turn. He was at a dead end.

He looked back around the boulder the way he came. Maybe he had time to get back and find another route before they caught up.

The flash of Adran blues sent him back behind his boulder. He could hear the shouts of his pursuers.

"He went down this path here."

"Careful on that, no line of sight. He could be hiding anywhere."

"Cover me from above."

"All right, you three with me. Try to go around that way, lads."

Taniel risked a glance to see four soldiers working their way down the goat path he'd followed. They were less than twenty paces away, and would reach him within moments. The other soldiers would find that outcropping sooner or later and he was a dead man.

If this damned air rifle hadn't broken, he might be able to defend himself at range.

When the first bayonet came within sight around the edge of the boulder, Taniel reached past it to grab the barrel and leveraged his weight against the man holding it. Caught by surprise, the infantryman slid and tumbled several feet and then plummeted the rest of the way down into the gorge, the end of his fall punctuated by the silencing of his scream.

"Bloody pit, he's right there!"

"Hold it together."

"He just threw Havin right off the edge! Did you see that? He's going to..."

Taniel didn't wait to find out what the infantryman thought he was going to do. He rounded the corner, gripping his broken air rifle like a pike, and shoved the bayonet into the talking man's chest. The man gave a garbled yell and fell, grabbing the kit of the man behind him as he went and sending them both tumbling over the edge.

Taniel and the last soldier stared at each other for a moment before the man brought his air rifle to his shoulder in one quick move and pulled the trigger.

Click.

"They're so damned unreliable, aren't they?" Taniel asked.

The man swore and jabbed at Taniel with his bayonet. Taniel danced back to dodge the thrust and found himself slipping. He dropped his own rifle instinctively to grab for purchase and listened with a lump in his throat as his best weapon clattered down into the gorge.

Gravel shifted beneath him as he scrambled backward on his hands and feet as the soldier advanced with his bayonet. Taniel backed around the edge of the boulder and snatched for his knife. It wouldn't be worth shit against a bayonet, but he had to try. He drew it just as the soldier was rounding the corner. He wouldn't be able to get to his feet in time. This would be impossible to—

Blood spouted from the soldier's mouth and beneath it something sprouted from his throat like a plant growing in a field. He teetered on his feet, then was helped in his tumble off the edge by a firm shove by Ka-poel.

She held a bayonet in one hand, clutched by the ring, and her ratty clothes were stained by the blood of far more than that one poor infantryman.

Taniel let out a sigh of relief and his whole body sagged beneath him. She'd saved his life. Again. He climbed to his feet and nodded his thanks, not trusting himself to speak. All this adrenaline, this skirting of death, was far harder to deal with when he was not in a powder trance.

A bullet ricocheted off the boulder just above Ka-poel's head. Taniel grabbed her by the front of her jacket and pulled her into an embrace, knowing instinctively that the bullet had come from behind him. He caught a glimpse of two soldiers standing on the outcropping that he'd spotted earlier. The second one was lining up his shot. Taniel could do nothing but put his body in between Ka-poel and the bullet and hope the man missed.

FOOM.

The sound left Taniel's ears ringing. When he managed to pull himself away from Ka-poel, the soldiers weren't on the outcropping anymore. One of their hats lay on its side where they had just been, and a quick glance showed him two more bodies down in the gorge.

What the pit was that?

The crunch of boots on stone made him cringe. More infantry?

A familiar figure strolled out to the end of the narrow outcropping. He wore ruddy muttonchops and a suit of clothes that, if they hadn't been so travel-worn and dusty, would probably cost as much as a horse.

Privileged Borbador kicked the infantryman's hat after its owner and watched it soar down into the gully. He turned to Taniel and waved.

"Hey, Tan. Sorry I'm late," he called.

CHAPTER

14

Nila was going to die.

She wondered if that certainty had ever crossed her mind before, during any of the events of the last six months. It must have. During her time with the royalists, or as Lord Vetas's prisoner, or even her first encounter with Bo. There were a dozen or more times that she had stared death in the face.

Yet none of them seemed more certain than now.

Something had been done to buy the Adran army an extra day. She'd seen a messenger rush from General Hilanska's camp yesterday afternoon, crossing over to the Kez lines, and the anticipated attack had never come. It had given Brigadier Abrax more time to plan and dig in her forces.

And now, with the sun rising over the Adsea, the Kez and Adrans prepared for battle once again. A hundred thousand Kez infantry fell into ranks to the south, their bayonets glittering in the morning sun. To the northeast, General Hilanska's men were already arrayed and ready for battle. Nila stood near the Wings of Adom command tent, where she could see messengers running to and fro and hear the bark of Abrax's stern alto.

The Wings of Adom and the three brigades of Adran soldiers that Ket had handed over would be crushed between the two enemy armies.

There wasn't even any place to run.

Rumors swirled among the Wings of Adom. A captain claimed that they'd seen one of Field Marshal Tamas's powder mages. An infantryman claimed that Deliv had entered the war and were sending reinforcements, but that they were still weeks away. Another said that this was all a ruse by Hilanska and that once the Kez forces advanced, Hilanska's army would swing around and hit them in the flank.

Soldiers would say anything to keep up morale, it seemed.

Even if all of those things were the case, they would still be crushed by the Kez. There were just too many of them. Their army could swallow the entirety of the Wings of Adom mercenary company five times over and still have room for more. The Wings' infantry—impressively—kept up a professional front, but she could see the panic in the eyes of the rank-and-file soldiers and their officers.

They would all be dead by morning.

"Ma'am," a voice said at Nila's elbow, startling her.

She regained her composure and turned to the young lieutenant. He couldn't have been much older than Nila and he wore his black hair slicked back under his bicorne and tied in a bow behind his head. He favored her with a nervous smile.

"Yes?"

"Brigadier Abrax has requested your presence."

Nila frowned over toward Abrax. The brigadier had exited her tent and was standing just thirty paces off, staring balefully at the Kez army. Why hadn't she just come over herself? "Of course."

Nila joined Abrax in front of the command tent. "You wished to see me, ma'am?"

"Is it still a secret that you're a Privileged?"

Nila blinked back at her. "I . . . well, I assume so. Bo said that I was still too green for my aura to show in the Else, so the enemy Knacked or Privileged shouldn't know I'm here."

"The enemy has no Privileged. Or," Abrax corrected herself, "the ones they do have amount to very little. None of the mountain throwers of the royal cabal." She turned to Nila suddenly. "Have you told anyone?"

"No."

"Keep it that way. You're to be our trump card."

Nila couldn't help but laugh at that. She stifled it as best she could, but it still leaked out as a giggle.

"Something funny, Privileged?"

Privileged. Being addressed as such sent a shiver down Nila's spine, sobering her instantly. "It's just that I'm only a trainee. I've barely learned to look into the Else, let alone command the elements. I won't be any help at all in a fight."

"You can't do *any* sorcery?" Abrax sounded skeptical.

"I can light my hand on fire. But only when I get very startled or angry."

Abrax turned away, looking slightly disgusted. "We have some Privileged, but they're very weak. They won't do much more damage than a well-placed field gun and they're far more fragile. Borbador told me you were powerful. I'd hoped you'd be of some help."

Bo had said that to Abrax? Why on earth? Nila was untrained, and Bo knew that better than anyone.

"I'm sorry," Nila ventured.

"I didn't realize you were *that* green. Stay back with the baggage. You'll do nothing but get underfoot near the front. And whatever you do, don't attempt any sorcery. You'll likely kill everyone around you. It's unfortunate your bloody master abandoned us. He might have tipped this in our favor." Abrax strode away without another word, barking orders.

Nila stared after her, indignation warring with a sense of helplessness. Bo *had* abandoned her. She knew just enough to know that maybe, with a few months more training, she could have defended herself. But she couldn't be of any use here. She was no better than the rest of the camp followers—part of the luggage. She was back to being with the laundresses and all the rest.

Abrax could go to the pit. If—when—the Kez broke the line, Nila *would* fight. She didn't care if she took the whole baggage train with her.

The baggage and camp were about a quarter of a mile behind the front line. The area had been fortified with hastily dug entrenchments and was guarded by a brigade of Wings of Adom mercenaries stretched out—to Nila's eye—over far too much ground.

The camp followers had been ordered to stay behind when the Wings had marched to General Ket's aid, but even so there had to be several thousand people with the baggage, essential personnel such as wagoners, quartermasters, and the like.

"Shouldn't you be near the front?"

Nila turned to find Inspector Adamat sitting on the ground nearby, looking older and wearier than he had just a few days before.

"Abrax sent me back here. I don't have enough training to be useful."

"Ah. I suppose that's true enough." He smiled as if to soften the comment. "I'm too old to be of any use."

"I've seen infantrymen with ten years or more on you."

"I haven't held a rifle in line since drills at the academy. I'm more likely to stick my bayonet into the man beside me than I am to be of any use up there."

Nila wondered if that were the case. She knew that Adamat had led the charge against Lord Vetas's men. He was more than capable. Perhaps he'd used his age as a pretense to avoid the front. Nila wouldn't have blamed him. Courage, Bo had told her, was overrated.

Adamat certainly didn't look frightened. Just tired. He stared at his feet for a few moments, then raised his head. "They don't have enough men back here to guard the rear."

"I was told an entire brigade."

"The Kez will flank us to the west while General Hilanska hits us from the northeast. I predict this position will be overrun by"— he glanced at his pocket watch—"one o'clock. If we're lucky, we'll be killed outright." He fingered his cane as if he were wondering how much of a fight he had left in him.

"Lucky? I thought it would be preferable to be taken prisoner."

He gave her a skeptical look. "Of course."

If we survive, he'll be sent to a Kez workhouse. And I'll be passed around the infantry until I'm sent to a workhouse as well. Unless an officer catches me first. Then I'll be at his mercy, little more than a slave.

Was that preferable to being killed outright?

Adamat climbed to his feet. The Wings' field artillery had begun to fire, and even at a quarter mile, the sound shook Nila. She remembered the fighting in Adopest between Tamas's men and the royalists and the countless sleepless nights she'd had after escaping. This was going to be so much worse.

"The sound gets to me, too," Adamat said. "Infantrymen might get used to it, but we're just civilians. Artillery is terrifying."

"Like Privileged."

"Yes. Like Privileged." He examined her out of the corner of his eye.

Nila pretended not to notice. *Yes*, she wanted to say, *I am a Privileged. But I can't do anything yet.*

A distant sound caught Nila's ear. It was hard to hear beneath the report of the artillery fire, but she knew it immediately when she turned toward the Kez lines. It was the *rat-tat-tat* of snare drums. The Kez columns, infantry in their tens of thousands, were advancing.

The lump in Nila's throat felt like she had swallowed a carriage. She'd never been this terrified, not even beneath Vetas's threats.

She wondered if Jakob was getting along well with Adamat's children. He was a good boy, still far too young to manage on his own. "Will Faye take care of Jakob after I die?" she asked.

"You won't die," Adamat said halfheartedly. After a pause, he added, "She's not the type to turn out a child."

Nila gave a soft sigh of relief. "I didn't think so, but I don't know her all that well."

Several moments passed as they watched the Kez continue to advance into the onslaught of artillery fire. "How the bloody pit did I end up here?" Adamat muttered.

Nila didn't think it was meant to be heard. What was going on in the old inspector's head? Was he thinking of his children? Or was he trying to think of a way out? Nila knew that's how she should have been thinking. She glanced toward the lazy fields to their northwest. Maybe she could run for it. Hide in some farmer's wheat field until nightfall and then strike out toward Adopest.

It was worth a shot. Wasn't it?

The sight of something moving out there on the plains killed her hasty plans.

"There are soldiers out there," Nila said. Adamat turned and gazed toward the northwest for a few moments, squinting.

"Cavalry." He spit in the dirt and turned toward the closest Wings officer, but it was plain they had already spotted the enemy. A ripple of panic went up among the brigade guarding the camp, and officers had to shout to drown it out.

Adran cavalry. Nila had no idea of their number, but they took her breath away. There must have been thousands. Breastplates glittered in the sun and their Adran-blue jackets and red-striped pants stood out against the tan fields of grain. They must have circled around far to the north and were now blocking the only avenue of retreat.

A Wings colonel sent a messenger running for the front lines. The colonel's face was pale and she gripped her belt with white-knuckled intensity.

Adamat gave a resigned sigh. "I guess that was predictable," he said. "Looks like at least three battalions of cuirassiers."

"Cuirassiers?"

"Heavy cavalry. You can tell by the breastplate. Adran cuirassiers armor their horses as well." Adamat pointed to the Wings' infantry as they fell into lines behind the waist-high breastworks that were their only defense. "They'll break a thin bayonet line like this one without too much problem."

Adamat headed closer to the rear of the camp, where the Wings' infantry were preparing to make their stand. Nila hesitated for a moment and then followed him.

The Wings' colonel gave him a glance as he approached. "Civilians should keep away from the front," she said.

"The front is that way," Adamat said, pointing behind him.

"Tighten up your men, Cronier," the colonel shouted. "If a single man runs, I'll gut him myself!" She looked at Adamat and Nila once more but refrained from commenting.

The Adran cuirassiers drew closer. They were taking their time and it wasn't until they stopped some half mile away that Nila realized they were likely waiting for a signal from General Hilanska. They would charge the rear right as the Kez charged the front.

Looking back to the south, she noted that the Kez were still advancing at a slow, methodical rate. The Wings' artillery left scars throughout their ranks, but it seemed to have no more effect than would scratching a giant. They just kept coming on.

On the hill to their northeast, General Hilanska's infantry suddenly surged forward, advancing at a pace just faster than the Kez.

To the northwest, some three thousand cuirassiers began to advance at a trot.

It seemed to Nila as if she could see her death advancing across those fields. The cuirassiers were really rather splendid, if she considered them without regard to her life. They moved in perfect coordination, the plumes on their horses' heads and the feathers in their steel helmets blowing with the breeze. She wondered if the ground really was shaking, or if it was just her imagination.

"Over there," Adamat said, his voice coming out a dry croak, "to the west. Looks like a battalion of Adran lancers."

She knew that term. More cavalry. Lightly armed.

"They'll swing around and hit our front lines from the west," the Wings' colonel said. She immediately dispatched another messenger to the front, just as the first messenger returned.

The messenger saluted. "Brigadier Abrax orders you to hold your fire."

"Hold my—" The colonel's face turned red. "Hold my fire? What the pit is that supposed to mean? Those cuirassiers will crush us!" She sent the messenger back to the front and fumed silently.

Nila tore her gaze away from the advancing cuirassiers. To the northwest, the Adran artillery batteries suddenly belched flame and smoke, their barrels pointed toward the Wings' encampment. Nila squeezed her eyes shut, remembering the terrible whistling of cannon fire at the royalist barricades, and waited for the horrible sound.

It never came. When she opened her eyes again, she could see the distant figures of the Adran artillerymen busy reloading. "What are they aiming for?" she asked.

Adamat frowned. "I don't know."

Another salvo followed, and Nila strained to see where the cannonballs were landing. The artillery seemed pointed straight at her.

She had no idea how far a cannon would fire, but why would they fire at all unless they were going to hit something?

"I don't think they're firing at anything," the Wings' colonel suddenly said. She sounded surprised by her own outburst. "There's no chance they would overshoot us at that range and..." She fell silent as more of the Adran cannons opened fire.

Nila twisted her head. Was that the sound of muskets? To the south, a low cloud of black smoke hung over the battlefield, and she heard a sudden roar: a hundred thousand voices as the Kez lines charged.

The battle had begun.

It would end soon enough for her. The cuirassiers were still advancing at a trot, but they would charge momentarily. They couldn't be more than a few hundred yards away. She looked down at her right hand and tried to will the fire to come. She had to go down fighting. She couldn't let herself be killed like a commoner. Not now. Not after everything she'd been through.

Her hand began to feel warm, but nothing happened. She concentrated harder. Bo had said she was powerful. Surely she could do something. *Anything!*

A cry went up among the Wings' infantry, and Nila looked up, her concentration broken, to see that the cuirassiers had suddenly changed direction. The whole group had turned west. The Wings' colonel watched with mouth agape as the cuirassiers trotted parallel to the Wings' line, just out of rifle range. The Wings' colonel barked orders, shifting her men to protect that side of the camp.

The Adran cuirassiers continued on, swinging wide of the camp and then even wider of the Wings' front lines.

Nila didn't understand. Were they going to flank the Wings' front line? Then what about the lancers that Adamat had seen? Where the pit were all these cavalry going?

She didn't understand until she caught sight of the Adran artillery. Their crews had stopped firing over the Wings' camp and had readjusted to face south, toward the Kez lines. General Hilanska's Adran infantry swiveled along with the artillery, moving forward to take up positions not *against* the Kez front, but *beside* it.

A messenger on horseback arrived at full gallop and reined in beside the Wings' colonel.

"Orders from Brigadier Abrax!" the messenger gasped. "Swing your men around and prepare to act as auxiliary to the front lines. The Adran attack was a ruse. General Hilanska is no longer in command of the Adran army and they will fight on our side!"

The colonel gave orders to a nearby captain and then grabbed the messenger's horse by the bridle. "Who the pit is in charge, then?"

"Why, Field Marshal Tamas. He has returned."

Nila swayed on her feet, feeling suddenly weak. Tamas was still alive? And he was in command? Maybe, just maybe, she would survive this day.

"Nila," Adamat said kindly, "your arm is on fire."

She looked down to find a blue nimbus of flame surrounding her right hand and engulfing her arm to the elbow. She waved her arm to put it out, and then, experimentally, she touched her thumb and forefinger together. The flame sprang back up around her fist.

To the south, an audible crash rose above the artillery and musket fire, and she looked to see that three battalions of Adran cuirassiers had just slammed into the Kez flank.

CHAPTER
15

Adamat couldn't believe what he'd just heard. Field Marshal Tamas wasn't merely alive, he was *here*?

Tamas must have taken the command from Hilanska. That meant that the Adran forces, including the Wings of Adom, could now present a unified front against the Kez.

Adamat's heart fell as he dwelt upon that thought. The Kez still outnumbered Adro by at least four to one, and now that they battled on the open plains, it would be an easy thing for the Kez to spread their superior numbers and engulf the smaller Adran army.

The bulk of the battle was now hidden in the low cover of black musket smoke, obscuring the southern horizon as if an entire city were afire. To the southwest, Adamat could see the Adran cuirassiers struggling to disengage themselves after a successful charge at the Kez flank. Kez auxiliaries were already advancing at a double march to cut off the cuirassiers' escape.

To Adamat's horror, the auxiliaries continued to fan out, stretching impossibly far beyond the edge of the Wings' lines. The Kez must have been expecting Hilanska to take care of the Wings' flank, and now that the ruse had been betrayed, they had commanded several brigades forward to take care of the job.

And they would do so easily. Even if all those auxiliaries were untrained and unequipped, they more than made up for it in bulk. They would collapse the Wings' right by sheer manpower.

Beside Adamat, Nila had taken to snapping her fingers, igniting her arm and then putting it out again with Privileged sorcery. She had stopped watching the battle and seemed completely enthralled in her own experimentation. He noticed that the Wings' colonel had taken a long step away from her, and he did the same. Nila— by her own admission—didn't have any idea what she was doing, and Adamat didn't care to find out how many charred corpses it took for most Privileged to figure it out.

The Adran cuirassiers finally pulled themselves away from the Kez flank and fled before the advancing auxiliaries. They had left an enormous dent in the side of the Kez infantry, but their own numbers had suffered, and they retreated to the northwest to lick their wounds.

The auxiliaries slowed when they realized they would not catch the cuirassiers and swung around to march against the Wings' flank. Adamat, even with his unskilled eye, could see it would end in disaster. He hoped that Tamas was planning on sending more reinforcements to this side, because it couldn't get much worse.

Adamat swore to himself under his breath. Why had he let that thought enter his head? Of course it could get worse.

It just had.

A brigade of Kez auxiliaries had just broken off from the main body and was marching straight for the camp. Another brigade soon followed, and Adamat realized that nothing but the Wings' colonel and her one brigade of green troops stood between the camp and the Kez.

Even if they managed a strong defense, it would still be a slaughter. The Kez infantry wouldn't turn away at the last moment. They would overrun the camp defenders, kill any followers, loot and burn the camp, and then turn to attack the Wings from behind.

The Wings' colonel gave a rapid succession of orders. Messengers sprinted toward the front, and the companies wheeled from the north to face this new threat.

Adamat drew his cane sword and clutched it tightly in one hand. He immediately felt silly. What would a cane sword do against musketmen with bayonets fixed? He thought to ask the colonel if there was a spare rifle he could use, but she dashed away suddenly, shouting orders at a nearby captain.

That left Adamat alone with Nila. The girl Privileged was still flicking her fingers, sparking blue flames along her arm.

"What on earth are you doing?"

"Trying to get this to work," she answered, not looking up. Another snap of the fingers and the blue flame erupted around her hand. She shook the flames out with a look of frustration.

"Do you think this is the best time for that?"

He noticed that Nila was paying close attention to where she positioned her fingers when she snapped them. Each new try she moved them slightly, and then attempted a quick combination of snaps, rubbing her thumb against first her forefinger, then her middle finger.

"I might not get another chance."

"Well, look," Adamat said. He knew what she was thinking. *Make it work. Save everyone with her newfound sorcery.* But of course she couldn't learn to use her sorcery in just a few moments, and the very idea of the girl trying seemed incredibly absurd. As absurd as him standing here with his cane sword drawn. "We need to get as far toward the back of the camp as we can. Once the fighting starts, we could make a run for the Adran lines. Then we could...Ah!"

A jet of flame shot from Nila's hand and traced a finger of blackened earth across the ground twenty paces away, nearly setting fire to a nearby corporal.

Nila gave a scream—half startled, half victorious. "I've got it!"

"What? You haven't got it," Adamat said. "Do you even know what you did?"

Nila held her off-hand away from herself gingerly, pointing toward an open patch of ground between two nearby tents. She brushed her thumb across her forefinger, then touched it gently to her pinkie. Flame erupted from her dominant hand—not a thin tendril this time, but a gout that seemed to spring up from the ground, setting fire to the grass and rising five or six feet in the air, traveling from her to the spot she'd pointed at as if following a line of lamp oil.

"All right," Adamat said. "I'm impressed." "Terrified" seemed a better word for it, but Adamat didn't think the girl needed to hear that. She didn't know what she was doing. Who knew what an untrained Privileged was capable of? She might be able to set fire to the entire enemy army, but could she keep from doing the same to her allies?

He wondered if he should head toward the Adran lines. If Tamas was back, Adamat would need to report everything that had happened over the last several months. But during a battle wouldn't be the best time.

At least it might get him farther away from the approaching Kez auxiliaries.

"Nila, we should..." He trailed off. The girl was gone. He cast about, then spotted her sprinting, skirts in hand, toward the Wings' rearguard and the Kez auxiliaries beyond them.

What was she doing? She couldn't possibly think she could help. She was just rushing off to get herself killed.

Adamat looked toward the Adran lines. He could make it. The Adran command tent was less than two miles away. He could get there and report to Tamas, and maybe manage to send some help this direction.

The girl wasn't his responsibility. She was Bo's, and Adamat owed Bo nothing.

With a curse, Adamat set off after Nila.

Nila shouldered her way through the line of soldiers preparing to defend the Wings' camp and ignored their yells as she scrambled over the fortifications and ran toward the enemy brigade.

A little voice in the back of her head screamed at her to turn around and run the other way. What the pit was she doing? She was running straight to her death. Even if she could replicate the fire, she couldn't possibly use it to destroy an entire brigade. She might take a few of them with her, but they'd gun her down and trample her body into the mud. She wasn't going to do any good out there.

But she ignored the voice and kept heading toward the enemy.

The voice in her head changed tactics.

You're going to try to kill people. These are human lives you'll be ending. You're not a warrior. You're a laundress. They'll die in an inferno, burned alive, and the screams will haunt you the rest of your life.

But, she argued, *if I do nothing, then the Wings' mercenaries will die. The infantry will be overwhelmed and all their noncombatants will be put to the sword.*

That's what they're paid to do.

Nila slowed, no longer convinced she had the strength to do what was necessary. What would Bo say? Wouldn't he tell her to stop being a coward and learn to act like a Privileged? Hadn't he also said that courage was overrated? Contradictory bastard.

She suspected that in this situation he would tell her she was an untrained bloody fool about to get herself killed.

Nila came to a stop. She was about fifty yards in front of the Wings' lines and the enemy advanced toward her, churning forward like a machine. She could hear the calls of their sergeants and the *thump-thump* of their march in time with the drums.

"Nila!" Adamat snatched her by the arm and pulled her back toward the Wings' lines. "We have to go."

She shook him off, a terrible weight settling in her stomach. It was too late. The Kez were less than a hundred yards off. The Wings would open fire soon, regardless of her presence. She and Adamat would be cut down by the barrage. She'd gotten both of them killed.

"Step back, Inspector," she said. She dropped her skirt and moved forward a couple of paces. She tried to open her body to the Else, the way Bo had showed her, to make the flow of the sorcery come smoothly. Her hands trembled fiercely as she raised them both, with her left hand pointed toward the Kez brigade and her right hand raised above her head. It struck her how theatrical the pose was, and that it was completely unnecessary.

Bo would have approved.

She brushed her thumb across her forefinger and willed the Else to flood the world at her command.

Nothing happened.

She had done it wrong. Her hands shook uncontrollably now. It would be impossible to make the proper connection. Her body had betrayed her, and now she and Adamat would die for it.

Her breath was suddenly squeezed from her, as if she'd been stuck through the stomach and lungs with a lance. A gasp tore itself from her lips and she fought against the dizziness that followed, and when she thought the pain had become unbearable, fire suddenly showered the world.

It spread out from her in a cone like a wave of pestilence, leaving nothing but cinders in its wake. She watched it spread toward the enemy lines and suddenly, without warning, blackness claimed her.

Adamat dashed forward just in time to catch Nila as she fell.

He watched, stunned, as the wall of flame rolled toward, and then over, the Kez brigade. The screams reached him a moment later, but by the time the flame had washed over the advance elements of the Kez infantry, they had already been silenced. Charred skeletons decorated the landscape, twisted horribly from the heat. When the flames finally died, over three-quarters of the brigade had been reduced to ash.

Adamat pulled his gaze away from the spectacle and lifted Nila in both arms. She was a small woman, and were he ten years younger, it would have been easy enough to hurry back to the Wings' lines. As it was, he struggled to trudge back with his burden, feeling every old ache and wound as he did.

Several infantry dashed out to help him get over the earthen barricades. One of them took Nila from him.

"Get her as far away from the fighting as you can," Adamat said, following the soldier back into the camp. They hurried through the tents until they reached the eastern edge of the camp, closest to the Adran lines, and the soldier lay Nila on the ground and sprinted back for the front.

Adamat held a hand over the girl's mouth, and then put a finger to her neck. It took him a few moments, but he was able to find a pulse—albeit a weak one.

He ransacked a nearby soldier's tent for a sleeping pad and blankets and made the girl comfortable. He didn't want to smother her, but it might be a good idea to conceal her, just in case the Kez broke through the enemy lines. Once he'd finished with that, he stole an officer's chair and climbed on top of it to try to get a view of the battle.

A perpetual cloud of powder smoke made it impossible to see anything in the field to the south. The Adran artillery thumped away without rest, and their irregulars were moving into position. It couldn't be going all that well if they needed their irregulars already. It looked as though several companies of Adran infantry had broken away from the front closest to the Wings and were marching double-time to reinforce the Wings' camp.

Adamat was considering Nila's unconscious body, wondering whether he'd have the strength to carry her all the way to the Adran lines and—hopefully—safety, when he turned to the west where Nila had scorched the earth with her sorcery.

The remnants of the brigade she had burned had turned tail and fled without hesitation. From where he was, he could still see them running, and it looked like their own officers were shooting them to try to turn them back.

Good for morale, Adamat imagined.

The Second Brigade was certainly wavering. Their advance had slowed to a crawl and they seemed hesitant to move across the roasted remains of their comrades.

Immense figures—twisted hulks of muscle swathed in black—burst from the Kez lines and raced across the charred plains toward the Wings' infantry. They brandished pistols and forearm-sized knives and they beckoned to the auxiliaries behind them to follow. Wardens, at least twenty of them. They'd tear apart the green Wings infantry all by themselves.

The entire brigade of Kez auxiliaries broke into a charge, trampling blackened skeletons to dust beneath their feet as they leveled their bayonets.

Adamat felt a pang of pity for those poor bastards who would be caught in that stampede.

The first line of Wings infantry opened fire, dropping several of the Wardens and wounding a dozen more. The creatures kept their advance even through the second volley, and then they were over the earthen fortifications and among the Wings troops. They were followed less than a dozen heartbeats later by over four thousand auxiliaries. The wave of tan uniforms scaled the earthworks and slammed into the barricade of red and white.

The entire scene devolved into chaos.

The Wings' soldiers had managed to hold against the initial charge, but already their officers were falling to the Wardens. Cracks formed in their defenses and they would be overwhelmed within minutes.

The Adran reinforcements were coming on quick from the south, but there clearly weren't enough of them, and they wouldn't be here in time to make a difference.

He found a nearby wagon whose driver had fled, and wrapped Nila firmly in several blankets and shoved her beneath the wagon bed, then stacked two empty rifle crates beside it to conceal her presence. He hoped nobody lit the wagon on fire. It wasn't much, but the best he could do on these godforsaken plains.

The Wings' rearguard had held together longer than Adamat expected, but by the time the Adran reinforcements arrived, they were all but spent. The Kez auxiliaries faltered at the initial impact, but their apparent numbers gave them courage and, somewhat chaotically, they wheeled to meet the new threat.

Adamat watched the battle from behind the wagon—no need for heroics from an old investigator—sparing a glance at Nila every so often with the hope that she would regain consciousness.

The battle turned brutal. The Wings' rearguard had been brave but overly young and they had managed to absorb the shock of the initial Kez charge. The Adran reinforcements, while heavily outnumbered, were seasoned veterans. They tore into the Kez auxiliaries without mercy, working in groups to bring down Wardens with their bayonets and keeping their lines firm despite the confusion of the camp tents.

The sky turned dark with clouds of powder smoke, and the air smelled of sulfur, stamped mud, blood, and shit. War cries gave way to wails of the wounded, and the sound made Adamat want to crawl under the wagon with Nila.

The fighting turned desperate as the Adran companies slaughtered auxiliaries by the dozens and Wardens managed to break the Adran lines. The whole affair seemed to be getting dangerously close to Adamat's hiding spot, and then it was suddenly upon him.

An Adran soldier retreated past Adamat's wagon beneath the advancing bayonets of three Kez auxiliaries. The poor soul tripped on a tent line and sprawled on his back, and the three pressed their advantage. They would be on him in a moment's time.

Adamat swore at length as he twisted the head of his cane and drew out the short sword within. He managed to cross the fifteen paces to the nearest of the three Kez without tripping himself and put the blade between the shoulders of the middle one, then turned and stabbed the neck of the second.

The third had already finished scrambling the bowels of the Adran infantryman by the time Adamat finished backstabbing the first two. He turned to Adamat, a look of surprise on his face, and then charged with a wordless scream, his bayonet dripping gore.

It was Adamat's turn to retreat. He scrambled backward as quick as he dared, trying not to end up like the infantryman he'd failed to save. He stumbled once and then turned and full-out ran, hoping that not a soul had seen him do so.

He'd be buggered before he tried to fight a bayonet-armed soldier with nothing more than a cane sword.

The soldier chased him around the wagon twice before he was scared off by a squad of Adran infantry moving in a tight square.

"Old man!" one of the infantrymen yelled. "Get out of the fight!"

What a stupid thing to say. The fight was everywhere. Adamat opened his mouth for a retort but found himself screaming a warning.

A Warden slammed into the squad with the force of a cannonball. Five of the men were knocked off their feet and the rest wheeled to face the creature, jabbing with bayonets that the creature ignored as if they were mere pins. It snatched a rifle from the closest soldier and slammed the butt across another's face with enough force to send teeth and blood flying. It grabbed another of the soldiers by the throat, crushing his windpipe with a casual squeeze and leaving the man to die of suffocation.

It had killed almost half the squad by the time they managed to put the creature down.

Adamat watched as two of the infantrymen put a bayonet through each of the creature's eyes and pinned it to the ground until it stopped struggling. He realized he'd never actually seen one of these creatures before. Even after it should have been long dead its muscles still moved unnaturally beneath its skin and the mouth opened and closed on its own, swollen black tongue lolling out the side of its mouth.

Adamat felt his heart pumping hard after watching the fight, despite not having even engaged the creature. Such strength! Such power! He couldn't imagine the twisted sorcery it took to make one of these things.

His contemplation of the corpse was cut short as a spine-numbing screech cut through the air. Adamat whirled just in time to see a black-clad Warden bound over the wagon, clearing it by a good two feet, and land amid the already reeling squad of Adran soldiers.

It snatched up one man by the ankle and swung him like a club, bashing him into two of the others, then slinging him over one shoulder and through the air.

The lifeless body might have crushed Adamat had he not dove out of the way. He struggled to his feet, one hand searching for his cane sword while the other held the wagon lip to steady himself. He regained his composure in time to witness the Warden slaughter the rest of the squad with a broken bayonet.

The creature turned toward Adamat, giving him his first clear look at it. Once, years ago, Adamat had seen a hairless bear in a traveling circus. This beast more closely resembled that bear than it did a human. It had short black hair and a nasty cut on its cheek, lifting one corner of its mouth into a sneer. It pounded its gnarled fists on the ground like a gorilla and advanced on Adamat.

Adamat grasped desperately for his cane sword or for anything he could use as a weapon.

Not that it would help.

It moved forward slowly, as if suddenly hesitant, squinting at Adamat with brutish suspicion, thick brow furrowed. What the pit was taking so long? Adamat couldn't find a weapon. His hands were shaking so hard he likely couldn't have held one.

End it already, you foul creature.

The beast reached for Adamat's throat and Adamat's eyes fell on its thick, twisted hand. Its right ring finger was missing. A strange detail for Adamat to focus on. But then, men did strange things when they looked death in the eye. Adamat felt his hand touch something—the handle of his cane sword. It had fallen on the wagon. He grasped it and prepared to ram the thing as hard as he could into the Warden's face. It was his only chance.

He tensed, ready to swing.

And felt his heart drop into his stomach. Those dull eyes and the sorcery-twisted skin suddenly looked all too familiar.

"Josep?" Adamat heard himself croak.

The creature leapt back as if it had been burned. It slammed at the ground with both hands, baring its teeth at Adamat.

"Josep, is that you?"

Adamat didn't have a chance to hear if the creature answered. Three Adran soldiers appeared around the edge of the wagon, their bayonets leveled, and charged at the Warden with screams of defiance. It whirled on them, then looked at Adamat, the confusion plain on its face. It took two great bounds toward the soldiers and leapt, clearing all three of them and landing on the other side to break into a sprint toward the Kez lines.

The soldiers hollered their challenges after the Warden, but Adamat could see the relief in their eyes. That was not a fight they would have won.

Adamat heard a thump, then a decidedly unfeminine curse from beneath the wagon. He tore his gaze away from the fleeing Warden and bent over the wagon. "Nila? Are you all right?"

"I'm fine." She lay on her back, rubbing her forehead. "Where am I?"

"I hid you while you were out."

"Oh. Sorry, I fainted. I don't know what came over me."

"You may have saved the entire bloody battle," Adamat said.

There was a pause for a few moments. "Did I kill people?"

"You saved a lot of lives," Adamat said. There was no good response to this. The girl *had* saved a lot of lives. But violence like that always took its toll, both physically and emotionally. It was likely a blessing that she had passed out before the screaming started.

"Thank you," she said quietly. "And now?"

Adamat stood up, surveying the scene. The camp was in shambles. The Warden was nowhere to be seen. Yet the fighting had died down and the only men he saw standing wore Adran blues. "Looks like we've driven them off."

"That's a relief."

"Yes," Adamat said, sinking against the edge of the wagon. "Yes, it is."

What had he just witnessed? That creature might have—should have—killed him without hesitation. And it hadn't. Could it be mere coincidence? The missing finger, the familiar lines of the face, the shape of the jaw that came from Faye's father. Adamat closed his eyes and saw the beast's face in his perfect memory.

Josep.

CHAPTER
16

Nila's entire body tingled.

It felt like stepping out of a springless carriage after going down a particularly long and bumpy road. Her legs were weak and her abdomen warm, and everything she touched seemed to crackle slightly. Her mind was muddled, as if her head were jammed full of wool.

Adamat helped her out from beneath the wagon and she shook her arms, trying to get rid of the tingle.

"Are you sure you're all right?" Adamat asked.

"My body feels like it's been stuffed with bees. Is that normal?"

"No...no, I think not." Adamat's reply was wooden. He watched the retreating Kez auxiliaries, his face slack.

"We won?"

Adamat nodded, but then stopped, as if thinking better of it. "We won that engagement. Barely." He pointed to the south, where dark clouds of powder smoke hung over the battlefield and the thunder of artillery fire continued almost without interruption. "If not for your sorcery, we would have lost the camp. I imagine Bo will be proud."

Distantly, Nila could sense something wrong with Adamat. But she felt a thrill go through her at that, and a cold knot settled in her stomach. *Would* Bo be proud? She could have killed herself. She *should* have killed herself, pulling that kind of stunt. Bo would be furious. *Live to fight another day,* he would have said. *Don't take such risks.*

But did it really matter what he thought? Did she fear some kind of punishment? Or did she fear his disapproval?

None of that mattered now. She could already hear the eerie moans of the wounded as the adrenaline of the battle wore off and men risked calling for aid. "Adamat, we should help."

"Hmm?"

Nila took a hard look at the old investigator. He'd saved her life, carrying her off the battlefield, but he hadn't asked for thanks. He seemed far away, stunned even.

"Were you hit on the head?" she asked.

"No. I don't think so."

"You're sure? We could get a surgeon to look at you."

Adamat patted his chest and arms. "I'm fine. I don't think I was wounded at all, actually."

"Just rest here," Nila said. "I'm going to try to help."

"I don't think that's such a good idea." Adamat shook himself and seemed to come out of his daze.

"There are wounded everywhere," Nila said. "They'll need as much help as can be had." She looked around the camp. Several tents had been set alight to the west and Adran soldiers were doing their best to put out the fires before they spread. Wagoners tried to wrangle their horses and oxen, while surgeons rounded up everyone without a weapon to begin moving bodies.

Nila headed toward where the Wings' Fifth Brigade had met the Kez auxiliaries for the battle. The chaos and clamor only increased as she neared the battle site. When she passed the tents and approached the earthen fortifications, the bodies of wounded and dead of both sides covered the ground like a carpet. The sight of it all nearly made her sick, but the smell was the worst of it. Blood, sulfur, shit, and gore. She'd visited a slaughterhouse once when a cook at the Eldaminse house had been ill. At the time, she'd thought it the most horrific stench she would ever encounter.

This was worse.

The terrible medley of smells was punctuated by the distinct odor of charred flesh. It clung to her nostrils, permeating the silk handkerchief she pressed to her face.

Adamat joined her. He'd lost some of that dazed look in his eyes, and gave her a worried glance.

"It's hard to comprehend, isn't it?" he said.

"Where are all the survivors? Where is the rest of the Wings' Fifth?" Nila hurried over to a man calling out for help, but by the time she reached him, his last breath had rattled from his throat. She backed away from the body.

"Over there," Adamat said, pointing to a small knot of soldiers, many of whom were leaning on their comrades for support. Officers circled the men, separating out the wounded, trying to get the healthy back into columns. Adamat pointed to another group, this one looking even more ragged and disorganized. "And over there. The Kez overwhelmed the entire Fifth before Adran reinforcements arrived. They'll be lucky if more than a thousand are able to still fight."

Three thousand wounded and dead. And that was just among the Wings. The number staggered Nila. That was the entire staff of the Eldaminse household a hundred times over.

Nila caught sight of the colonel of the Wings' Fifth and found herself glad that the woman had survived the battle. She still held her saber in one hand but had lost her hat, and she clutched her other hand to her thigh as she called out orders. Soldiers began to respond to their officers, and gradually the column began to re-form.

"What are they doing?" Nila asked. "Shouldn't they be helping the wounded?"

Adamat leaned wearily on his cane. "They'll round up any Kez prisoners and place a few guards, but everyone else needs to be ready in case of another attack. The battle is still far from decided." He peered toward the smoky southern horizon. "I think."

The idea of having all this slaughter and destruction happen again made Nila's stomach churn—and she'd been unconscious for most of the first fight. She struggled to keep down her breakfast. "What in Kresimir's name is that smell?"

"War," Adamat said.

"But . . . it's like cooked meat!"

Adamat raised his eyebrows at her. "I don't think you . . ."

Nila's gaze rested on the blackened ground off to the southwest. It was an enormous swath, with little more than ash and dirt, and—was that bone? She blinked slowly at the view, remembering her legs pumping beneath her as she ran toward the Kez troops. She recalled the heat of the fire, and the pain and pleasure of the power that had coursed through her before her world had gone dark.

The realization nearly knocked Nila off her feet. That smell of burned flesh had been caused by *her*. She grabbed Adamat by the elbow. "How many did I kill?"

"Nila, you saved many . . ."

"How many did I kill, Inspector?" she demanded. "How many?"

Adamat looked at her with pity, which somehow made it all the worse. "I can't be sure."

"Guess."

"You should let go, Nila," he said, his voice strained.

Nila looked down to find her knuckles white from squeezing

Adamat's arm. She snatched her hand back. "I'm sorry. Please, tell me how many I killed."

"Thirty-five hundred. Maybe more. Maybe less. It looked like you torched the better part of a brigade."

Nila bent over and heaved, emptying the contents of her stomach in one long retch. She heaved once more when she realized she had just vomited all over a dead man's legs. She felt Adamat's hand on her shoulder and let him help her up.

"I can't...I don't even..."

"Stay quiet for now," Adamat said. They started walking, and Nila had no sense of time or space until she looked up to realize they'd left the battlefield and even the Wings' camp behind and were about a third of the way toward the Adran camp.

She dragged a sleeve across her face. "Where are we going?" she sniffed.

Adamat's eyes were fixed firmly on the ground as he walked, and it was several moments before he responded. "To see Field Marshal Tamas."

"We should go back and help."

"You don't need to see that right now," he said sternly.

She wanted to fight him. To pull away and run back to the Wings' camp to help with the dead and the wounded. She deserved to see and smell the results of her power. Was she a coward for not doing so?

"Why the field marshal?" Nila asked.

"Because I need to report to him, regardless of whether or not we win this battle."

"You could have left me behind. I'm not a child. I could help."

Adamat stopped and turned to her. She felt him grab her by the shoulders, and he waited until she finally looked up into his eyes. There was a sort of fatherly, stern caring there. It was painful. Couldn't he see what she was capable of? Didn't that terrify him?

It damn well terrified her.

"Nila, once there's any sort of organization in the Wings' camp, they'll come looking for you. They'll either want you to get to the front and fight for them or they'll realize that you're not in full command of your powers and they'll try to control you. Either way, I couldn't leave you alone back there." Taking her by the arm, Adamat continued walking toward the Adran army.

Nila let herself be dragged along. She breathed in deep—the air was clearer here, between the armies, and the scent of sulfur was almost gone with a northerly wind. But that smell of charred flesh still hung in her nostrils, as if it had been painted on her upper lip.

Adamat produced papers from his jacket to show the Adran pickets, and they soon went around two companies of irregulars waiting for orders and climbed a steep hill to the command tent. Adamat showed his papers once more and asked to see Field Marshal Tamas. One of the guards ducked inside and returned a moment later, nodding them forward.

"Go on in, Inspector. Ma'am."

Nila followed Adamat inside, only just realizing what she was doing. This was Field Marshal Tamas! She had been his personal laundress for months, and even been courted by his bodyguard. *She had seriously considered murdering the field marshal.* There was no way they could know that, could they? What if Olem was here? How would she explain her presence?

She scrambled for some excuse to remain outside, but was ushered in before she could voice any.

It was with some relief that she found the tent devoid of both Field Marshal Tamas and Captain Olem. There were a half-dozen messengers standing at attention along one wall, and a large table laid out with maps, papers, and notes. The biggest map was covered with hundreds of small military models of fifty different sizes and shapes. A young woman in an Adran-blue uniform with black hair and a powder keg pinned to her breast stood over the table—a powder mage and, from the stripes on her shoulder, a captain.

A messenger pushed past Nila and saluted the powder mage. "Two companies of Kez cavalry have broken around the Seventeenth and are pushing toward the Hundred and Second Artillery!"

The woman moved one of the models on the map and then scrambled through piles of notes on the table in front of her for several moments before finding one to her satisfaction. "Send the Seventy-Eighth Irregulars to shore up our eastern flank, and tell General Fylo to throw everything he has at the enemy's left. Those cavalry were the only thing keeping us from taking command of that hill."

The messenger was off like a shot. The woman shuffled several of the notes and then dropped into her seat with a shaky sigh. Her face was drawn and pale, and Nila thought she heard a few quiet curses.

"Captain Vlora, was it?" Adamat asked.

The powder mage gave a curt nod. "Inspector Adamat? The field marshal was hoping you'd turn up sometime today."

"I'm here to report," Adamat said. "Where is the field marshal?"

"He's not here," she responded rather crossly.

The prospect cheered Nila slightly, until she realized the implication. "Where is he?" she asked before she could stop herself.

Vlora peered at her. "You're Bo's apprentice? I take it we have you to thank for torching the Kez auxiliaries?"

"Yes." Nila tried to force a smile, but it felt as limp and cold as a dead fish. She let it slide off.

Vlora was already looking back at Adamat. "The field marshal is gone. He'll be back in a couple of days, if all goes well."

"But we were told..." Adamat started, looking somewhat confused. "I thought he was here."

"He *was*."

"But he's not now."

"Correct."

"But the battle. It looks like we're winning."

"I think we are," Vlora conceded, albeit hesitantly.

"If Field Marshal Tamas isn't here, who is in command? Who is giving orders?"

"Tamas *is* in command," Vlora said, gesturing at the table full of maps and notes. "He fought the entire battle yesterday, on paper, and then headed toward the mountains on personal business."

"You're joking," Adamat said.

"Not at all. And the field marshal was hoping you—both of you—would wait for his return."

CHAPTER 17

Taniel was more than a little surprised to find that Bo had not killed the rest of the Adran infantry.

Thirty-seven soldiers worked to free the rest of their dead and wounded from the results of the rockslide. A rather conspicuous pile of gleaming slag lay a few dozen feet from the bodies that had already been pulled from the rubble. Taniel thought he recognized air rifles, bayonets, and knives, all melted together by preternatural forces.

"You went easy on them," Taniel said.

"I asked very nicely," Bo responded.

"I wish I could have done that." Taniel caught Bo looking at him out of the corner of his eye.

"Well," Bo sniffed. "I'm a little more persuasive than you. Oi! You there, put your back into it! That boulder isn't going to move itself."

Taniel watched two of the soldiers try to move a boulder off a half-crushed body, and attempted to sort out the emotions warring within him. These men had come to kill him. No question about it. Even the rankers knew who they were hunting. Part of him wanted to tell Bo to bury the whole lot along with their crushed comrades. But the blood already on his hands took the sting out of his anger.

"You could help them, you know."

"Not a chance," Bo said.

"I thought as much. Bo?"

"Hmm?"

"What the pit is that?" Taniel pointed down the valley to a brownish-red stain on the canyon wall. It looked like someone had thrown a handful of wet paint against the stones and left it there to dry in the sun.

Bo tugged gently on his gloves. "I made an example of the first one who tried to bayonet me."

And splattered him like a grape. Taniel felt ill. "I was wondering why they were all so cooperative. A little messy, don't you think?"

"I've found that a little messiness is like manure on a field when you're trying to cultivate fear."

Typical Privileged thinking. "Indeed." Taniel watched the prisoners work at extracting the bodies for a few moments before noticing Bo tug at his gloves again. "You're nervous."

"Not really."

Bo tugged on his gloves plenty; most Privileged did that. But he had one leg up on a rock, bouncing it rapidly. He was nervous, even if he didn't want to admit it. "You are. What is it?"

"Nothing, nothing. Don't worry your head about it."

Taniel opened his mouth to argue, but he knew he wouldn't get any further. Not with Bo. "I'll go help Ka-poel," he said. He hurried his way up the narrow path in the canyon wall that led toward the cave where he and Ka-poel had spent the last two weeks. He found Ka-poel just leaving the cave. She had her rucksack slung across her shoulder and had fastened straps from an infantryman's jacket so that she could hang Kresimir's casket from her back.

"I can carry something, if you'd like," Taniel said.

Ka-poel handed him the rest of the rations they'd stolen from the infantrymen.

"Anything else?"

She laid a hand protectively across her rucksack and furrowed her brow. A moment later the frown cleared and she shook her head.

"Pole, I..." Taniel wasn't quite sure what to say. She'd saved his life. Again. And despite the fact that their time in the mountains had been horrible and dangerous, he knew that his chances of being alone with her once they returned to civilization would be slim. There would be fighting to do, reports to give.

Generals to kill.

He realized suddenly that aside from the edge it would have given him in combat, he didn't miss the powder.

Very strange.

They made their way back down to Bo and his prisoners. Bo lay on his back on a flat rock, tossing a pebble up in the air and catching it with one gloved hand. He seemed at ease now, even if he was still watching the soldiers carefully.

"I brought you this," Bo said as they approached, holding out a powder horn that had been concealed in his jacket. "Forgot to give it to you earlier. But if you open that damned thing near me, I swear to Kresimir I will punch you in the face. Just carrying it gives me a rash."

Taniel took the horn and turned it over in his hands. He could sense the powder within—the power that it could give him. It would soothe his aches and injuries, give him strength for the climb down the mountain. "Where'd you get it?"

"Stole it from a Wings infantryman on my way to get you."

"Thanks," Taniel said, looping the strap over his shoulder.

Privileged didn't like black powder. They had allergies to the stuff that made battlefields a nightmare. "Really, Bo. I wish I could repay you."

"You didn't shoot me in the head when your dad told you to. I figured it was my turn to do something nice for you." Bo sat up and jerked a thumb toward the infantry. "We should go. I've given them a stern talking-to. They'll finish their work and bring the bodies back to Adopest."

"A stern talking-to? You threatened them? I can't get four squads of soldiers to listen to *me* when I threaten them."

"You can't pull their veins out of their bodies inch by inch. And if any run, they'll spend the rest of their lives wondering if I'm around the next corner." He barked a laugh. "Best punishment I can think of, really."

"Ah."

Bo's gaze shifted to Ka-poel. "Good to see you again, little sister. Taniel knocked you up yet?"

"You bastard!" Taniel swung halfheartedly for Bo, who stepped deftly out of the way.

"Oh, don't give me that. I knew you were in love with her that day you came for me on South Pike. Little sister, what have you got...oh dear Kresimir above!" Bo backpedaled suddenly, leaping away from Ka-poel with agility Taniel wouldn't have credited him with.

"What's wrong?" Taniel asked.

Bo cowered behind a boulder. He poked his head out from behind it after a few moments. "What the pit is in that box on her back?"

How would Taniel explain this to Bo? There was no possible way he could understand. He opened his mouth, only for Ka-poel to speed through a series of hand motions, pointing at Bo and then touching her finger to her throat, then back to him.

Bo licked his lips while he watched her go through the motions again. "What I just said?"

Ka-poel nodded.

"'What have you got...'?"

Ka-poel made a *get on with it* motion.

"'Oh dear Kresimir above'?" Bo said.

Ka-poel nodded again.

"'Kresimir above'?" Bo confirmed.

One more nod.

"You've got Kresimir in that box?"

Ka-poel gave him a tight smile. To Taniel's shock, it looked as if Bo believed her. Hesitantly, the Privileged worked his way out from behind the boulder. He was pale in the face, and he kept Taniel between himself and Ka-poel as he rejoined them.

"I could have fixed you up with a nice girl," Bo said. "A girl from east Adopest. Someone who doesn't go around keeping gods in boxes."

Taniel took Ka-poel's hand. "Not my type."

"Of course not," Bo said bitterly, tugging at the backs of his gloves. "Now, can we get moving?"

"Are you in a hurry?"

"No," Bo said as he set off at a brisk pace down the canyon. "Well," he called over his shoulder, "yes. A little."

Taniel jogged to catch up. "What is it?"

"Nothing at all. Can the girl get a move on?"

"Her name is Ka-poel."

"Can little sister get a move on? I'm going to need some rest tonight and I would prefer to get it in the valley and not in this bloody canyon."

"When's the last time you slept?"

Bo counted silently on his gloved fingers. "Five days?"

"Pit, Bo, you—"

"That's not really important."

"Then what is?"

"I *may* have left my new apprentice in a war zone. And I killed both my horses getting here in time to save you."

"Wait, wait. You have an apprentice?"

"Very nice girl. The kind I could have set you up with. She has some peculiar powers, and I've grown quite fond of her. She's actually the one who figured out where you were. I wouldn't have left her, except..."

"Yes, yes. You were coming to save me."

"Right."

They continued on in silence for the better part of the afternoon. Taniel forced Bo to slow down so that Ka-poel could keep up, and they worked their way down the canyon. They finally stopped to rest an hour after the sun had left their canyon in shadow. Ka-poel dropped Kresimir's casket on the ground unceremoniously, making Bo wince.

"Tell me about this apprentice," Taniel said as they made a meal of infantry rations.

Bo winced as if he had just cracked a tooth on a piece of hardtack. "How do you people eat this stuff? Blech. My apprentice? Not much to tell, really. Another sorcery slinger. You know."

"You said you were fond of her."

"Did I?" Bo made a show of gnawing on the brick-hard biscuit.

"You slept with her already, didn't you? Isn't there some kind of code of conduct against that type of thing?"

Bo glowered first at Taniel, then rolled his eyes over to Ka-poel, who sat on the ground fiddling with a latch on her rucksack.

"Pole's not my apprentice!" Taniel protested.

Bo rolled his eyes. "I haven't slept with Nila."

"Oh, she has a name now, eh? And you expect me to believe you haven't taken her to bed?"

"...yet."

"I see how it is."

"And I don't think I will."

"Now, that would shock me," Taniel said.

"I'm serious. I like her too much. She's clever, resourceful. And she's going to be far stronger than I ever will."

"Really?" Taniel was skeptical. Bo had once boasted that despite being the youngest Privileged in the Adran Cabal, he was one of the strongest. Tamas had confirmed that boast. For Bo to say something like this…"You're intimidated by her?"

"No," Bo said. "*Julene* was intimidating. And I went to bed with her. Nila is just…"

"You're intimidated because she's a better person than you are."

"Go to the pit," Bo said.

Taniel scowled. He'd just caught sight of something out of the corner of his eye. His breath quickened, and he shifted slightly, trying to look to his left without being obvious about it.

"Well, don't go all silent suddenly," Bo said. "I didn't mean it."

"Quiet." Taniel reached inside his jacket and flicked the cap off of the powder horn. Bo saw the action and stiffened. He checked his gloves.

"What is it?" Bo hissed.

"I saw a flash of Adran blue. A uniform," Taniel said. "Farther down the canyon. About thirty yards."

"Are you sure?"

Taniel reached out with his senses. "Yes. I'm sure." He stood up, and Bo quickly followed, spinning to look down the canyon.

A rock tumbled down from a ledge fifty feet above them, then another on the opposite side of the canyon. An infantryman's forage cap emerged, and Taniel could see the barrel of a rifle. Then another. Then another.

All around them, soldiers appeared on the canyon walls. Taniel stopped counting at twenty-five. "The rest of the infantry company," he said, "the ones camped in the valley. Did you confront them, too?"

"I didn't know there *were* more," Bo said. "The camp I passed had less than a dozen men in it."

Taniel sensed Bo reaching into the Else, and felt sorcery leak into this world. A breeze—touched with sorcery—lapped around Taniel's legs and ruffled his jacket as a dozen more soldiers rounded the bend on the canyon floor, leveling their rifles. "They have gunpowder," he said. "They'll have to come a little closer for me to detonate them."

"No need for that," Bo said.

"What do you mean?"

"Do you recognize that insignia?"

Every one of the men had a patch on his shoulder—a chevron with a powder horn below it. He remembered the same patch on the uniforms of the men who had been guarding him when he awoke from his coma. Someone had told him that they belonged to a special regiment called Riflejacks.

"They're not pointing their guns at you," Bo said.

Riflejacks. That special regiment reported to Field Marshal Tamas's bodyguard.

"Privileged Borbador," a voice called. "If you would please remove your gloves."

Bo's fingers twitched. Taniel could feel his sorcery tightening, like muscles moving beneath the skin. A wave of conflict flashed across Bo's face and he slowly stepped away from Taniel. From up on the ridge and down in the canyon, every rifle followed him. Taniel remembered the gaes that had held Bo, the one that would have forced him to kill Field Marshal Tamas.

"Don't do it, Bo," Taniel said. He could see Bo's arms tense and his fingers wiggle in anticipation. Taniel didn't know what he could do, but this would only end in a great deal of bloodshed if Bo unleashed his sorcery.

Ka-poel suddenly stood up, leaving Kresimir's casket on the ground. She strode around in front of Bo before Taniel could stop her, and held out one hand to him.

"You don't want to stand there, little sister."

Ka-poel thrust her hand at him emphatically, palm up.

"Give her the gloves, Bo. I won't let them kill you," Taniel said. And he wouldn't. He'd kill a hundred of his own countrymen if they came after Bo. He'd die by his friend's side if that was what it meant. He stared hard at Bo until the Privileged gave a barely perceptible nod, acknowledging that he had gotten Taniel's meaning.

Bo lowered his arms. He glared down the canyon as he plucked at the fingers of his gloves and then set them in Ka-poel's outstretched palm. She took the gloves and walked down the canyon until she reached the Adran soldiers. One of the men examined the gloves in her hands and gave a sharp nod, letting her pass.

She reappeared a moment later, and she wasn't alone.

Field Marshal Tamas walked stiffly up the canyon to Taniel. He seemed to have aged ten years in the last few months, and looked more frail than Taniel could ever have imagined him. By his gait, he was hiding a wound. A bad one.

"You look like the pit, Dad," Taniel said.

"You don't look a damned sight better," Tamas said. His back was rigid, and he examined Bo out of the corner of his eye as one might regard a cave lion sitting on one's porch, before he turned back to Taniel. Taniel took a deep breath, trying to calm himself. Last he'd heard, his father was presumed dead, and though there had been cause to consider his survival, Taniel had not had the time to either grieve or rejoice. A torrent of emotions rushed through him, and he struggled to hold them all in check, turning his face into a blank canvas.

"Glad to see you still alive," Taniel said.

The old man's face was impassive. The pinnacle of military discipline.

But for the first time since his mother died, Taniel saw tears shining in his father's eyes. "You too, Captain."

CHAPTER

18

Tamas gave orders to camp in the valley that night.

He put Olem in charge of setting up camp, but made the rounds himself, walking slowly through the tents, waving off salutes, and reminding the men that they had an early morning and a long ride ahead of them and that they should get some rest. When he had finished, he checked on the prisoners, then with the sentries.

"You need some rest, sir."

Tamas jumped. Taniel stood behind him on the banks of the small river that ran down the center of the valley.

"I'm all right," Tamas said.

"You've been fiddling since we stopped to make camp. Losing sleep won't get us back to the front any faster."

Tamas glanced at his son. Taniel looked older. Lean from weeks of hunger, his cheeks gaunt, he still managed to retain a robust physical appearance. He had put on more muscle since the day Tamas had sent him up to South Pike with orders to kill Bo. That seemed like a lifetime ago. What *had* it been? Six months? Perhaps less?

"We should have ridden through the night," Tamas said. He stifled a yawn. "I left at too crucial a time."

Taniel shifted from one leg to the other. "Sorry to be such an inconvenience."

"I didn't…" Tamas turned toward his son, suppressing a frustrated sigh. "That's not what I meant. It's just, the battle. It was a terrible risk to leave it in others' hands."

"You didn't need to come for me."

"Well, I know that now." Tamas chuckled. Even to him it sounded forced. "I should have just left the whole thing to Bo and stayed at the front."

"Indecision isn't becoming of you." Taniel kicked a rock into the river.

Tamas wished he knew what to say. He'd never been a spectacular father, he knew that. But even he could tell that something had changed about Taniel. Something Tamas couldn't quite put his finger on. He could sense the sorcery clinging to him without even opening his third eye, though it was subtle stuff. Supposedly the work of that savage witch Taniel was so fond of. Tamas had his fair share of questions about that girl.

"Bo's not a threat to you anymore," Taniel said. "You don't have to keep him tied up, under guard. Give him back his gloves."

Tamas rubbed at his temples. "It's just until we get back."

"If we get back," Taniel said, "and we need Bo's help against the Kez—which we will get. A little trust will go a long way."

"I'm short on trust right now," Tamas said. He rubbed at the wound that was itching beneath his coat. Only the constant buzz of a powder trance kept the pain away, and only just barely.

"Hilanska," Taniel said.

Tamas cleared his throat to cover his surprise. "How did you know?"

"When Kresimir captured me, he had Hilanska confirm my identity. I know he was the one who sent those bastards." He jerked his chin toward the makeshift stockade in the center of the camp that contained around a hundred and fifty of Hilanska's men.

Tamas considered it for a moment, then unbuttoned his jacket. He lifted his shirt, exposing his flesh to the chill of the night. "Stabbed me right between the ribs."

"Looks bad." Taniel inspected the wound from a respectful distance, aware how much his father's vulnerability meant to him.

"I'm lucky. It was a clean wound. Missed anything important." He let his shirt fall and slowly buttoned up his jacket.

"You need a Privileged to look at it."

"The Deliv king has a few healers with him. I'll get it taken care of when he arrives. It won't kill me before then. Hilanska. That bloody bastard. We've been friends for decades. He was a grooms-man at my wedding. Was privy to all my plans with the coup."

"That's the wound that won't heal," Taniel said quietly.

Tamas didn't trust himself to say anything else, but allowed a nod. When they'd stood for several more minutes, Tamas said, "I could use Mihali. Hah. I can't believe I just said that. Madman chef-god. I don't bloody well know what I'm going to do without him." Tamas felt moisture in the corner of his eyes. They must have been watering from the cold breeze.

"Mihali," Taniel said. "He..."

"You met?" Tamas supposed he shouldn't be surprised. Mihali had his fingers in every pie.

"Yes. He said that I was different now. Thanks in part to Ka-poel's sorcery and in part to my contact with Kresimir."

Tamas remained silent. If Taniel was going to talk, he was going to do it on his own. No amount of prompting would get it out of him.

A few more moments passed, and Taniel said, "Mihali thinks

I'm like Julene now. Or at least the powder mage equivalent of a Predeii."

Tamas ground his teeth at the mention of Julene. So many traitors. So much betrayal. How could Taniel be anything like her? "You can't take anything Mihali said seriously."

"I think he's right," Taniel said. "I barely ate anything up on that mountain, but I wasn't very hungry. I didn't have any powder, but I could still see details at a hundred yards—nothing like with the powder, but my night vision and hearing and smell are all better than they were." He looked at Tamas and his eyes were suddenly red. "I tore the jaw off of a man. Without any powder! I tore out a Warden's rib and killed him with it. Well, that time I did have powder."

"Pit," Tamas breathed.

Taniel snorted. "I know. I'm damn hard to kill, too. I still bleed, but I'm stronger, faster. Kresimir ordered his men to break my arm. They couldn't. I've changed, Dad, and it's terrifying. And Mihali is dead and Ka-poel can't speak, so I can't learn what is happening to me." Taniel stared down at his hands. His voice was raw.

"Taniel," Tamas said. He gripped Taniel's arm in one hand. "Listen to me. Whatever it is that's happening to you, you'll survive it. You're a fighter." *You're my son*, he added silently.

"But what if it's not worth surviving?"

For a moment Taniel wasn't a man but the frightened boy Tamas had held after Erika's death. Tamas grabbed Taniel's shoulders and roughly pulled him into an embrace. "It's always worth surviving, son."

They remained that way for several minutes. Finally, Taniel pulled away and wiped his sleeve across his nose. Tamas let out a shaky breath and hoped Taniel didn't see his own tears.

"Dad."

"Yes?"

"I shot Kresimir in the eye. And then, when he caught me at the old fortress, I punched him in the face."

Tamas stared at his son for a moment, shocked by the absurdity of it all. It started as a twitch deep in his stomach, then he threw back his head and roared with laughter. Taniel joined him a moment later, and they laughed until the tears streamed down their faces and Tamas forced himself to stop because his wound hurt so badly. When they regained their composure, they stared at each other for some time.

"I'm sorry for what I've been," Tamas said. The words hurt to leave him, yet he simultaneously felt a great weight lifted. He watched the side of Taniel's face for some kind of response, but Taniel was suddenly guarded. He turned and Tamas was afraid he'd walk away.

"You have a lot of children," Taniel said, indicating the camp with a wave of his arm. "All your soldiers."

"Only one of them matters."

"They all matter. Dad, can you do me a favor?"

"Of course."

"Forgive Vlora."

Tamas raised his eyebrows. He hadn't known what to expect, but that wasn't it. He ran a hand through his hair, feeling the scar from the bullet that had grazed his skull at the Battle at Kresimir's Fingers. "That might take me a little while."

"Just try."

"I will."

"Thanks. And Dad? Ka-poel is carrying around the effigy of Kresimir on her back. She's the only thing keeping him from killing all of us."

"She's *what*?"

"And there's something else." Taniel drew a shaky breath. "I'm in love with her."

*   *   *

Tamas snuck into the main Adran army camp a day later like a man who'd lost the keys to his own front door.

It wasn't a grand entrance, he reflected, as Olem showed a set of orders to a sentry and Tamas kept the brim of his hat down over his face, hiding behind the lapels of his overcoat. But Tamas didn't need a grand entrance. He needed quite the opposite.

The sentry looked over the paper for a moment, squinting to read it in the pale morning light, her lips moving silently. They were orders that Tamas himself had written, with his own signature at the bottom. When she finished, she handed the paper back to Olem and glanced suspiciously at Tamas. "Looks like everything is in order," she said, waving them past.

Tamas gave a small sigh as they headed into the camp and lost themselves among the tents to throw off any suspicious guards that may have followed. He would have wanted his men to do a more thorough search of strangers—they were trained not to put up with any of this cloak-and-dagger bullshit that officers from the nobility had always seemed to like. But on the other hand, Tamas was glad to get in without being questioned further.

The camp was beginning to stir, the men climbing from their tents, brewing coffee over the coals of their cook fires, laundresses working their way through the camp to return clean uniforms. He and Olem discarded their overcoats and slipped the last hundred yards up to the command tent. Only a few men were about, and those that recognized him shook off their grogginess and snapped salutes.

"Morning, sir."

"Morning."

"Fine bit of work the other day, sir. I meant to congratulate you earlier, but haven't seen you."

"Thank you. Carry on," Tamas said, gesturing a lieutenant back to his breakfast. He leaned over to Olem and whispered, "Well, I assume we won by the fact that the army is still intact."

A captain interrupted him with a salute and a "Good morning." "Congratulations on the victory, sir," the woman said. "Sending the Hundred-and-First up the center like that was inspired work."

Tamas nodded politely, and when they'd passed her, he continued, "And it seems none have been the wiser."

"Well done, sir," Olem said, cracking a smile. He had been in hysterics over the idea of leaving to fetch Taniel, and Tamas might have never done it if Vlora hadn't shouted down Olem's objections. "I suppose you can say you told me so."

"I'll wait for that until I hear the casualty count," Tamas said, stopping to shake hands with two privates who were stirring the coals for their breakfast. He and Olem reached the command tent a moment later and the guards snapped off their salutes, one holding the tent flap while they slipped inside.

The white walls of the tent allowed enough light in for Tamas to see several figures. Vlora, he expected. She lay across several chairs, her boots on the ground beside her, snoring lightly. The others Tamas had not expected. Brigadier Abrax snoozed on a chair beside the door, her hat tipped over her face and chin resting on her chest, while Inspector Adamat mumbled in his sleep from his spot on the ground. Someone else was curled up in the corner, a mess of curly auburn hair spread out over her blanket.

"Captain," Tamas said. No response from Vlora.

Olem leaned over her. "Vlora." He nudged her knee, then gently touched her cheek. She startled awake and blinked groggily at Olem, and then at Tamas.

"Sir," she said, getting to her feet and managing a less-than-snappy salute.

"At ease, Captain," Tamas said. He looked at Abrax. Maybe

they should step outside. He really didn't want to wake her. These things were best done one at a time. "How did everything go?"

Vlora rubbed the sleep from her eyes. "Quite well, sir. The Kez fell for our trap completely. We were able to surprise them with our offensive, while the Wings held off theirs. It was a decisive victory. It went almost exactly as you said."

"Almost?"

"I had to improvise a few times. I've written a full report. It's on your desk."

"I look forward to reading it." *And I better do so soon, if we're to keep up the farce that I was here the entire time giving orders myself.* "Casualties?"

"Fifteen thousand one hundred and seventy-four."

Tamas staggered at the number. So many? That was a fourth of his army, not counting the irregulars. "Pit," he said.

"The regimental breakdown of the losses is also on your desk."

"And the Kez?"

"They've retreated all the way to Fendale."

"Their losses?"

"We can't be entirely sure yet, sir, but we estimate around ninety thousand. We've captured about twenty-five thousand."

Tamas felt some of the tension drain from his body. "That's significant."

"It is, sir. Congratulations."

Tamas allowed himself a deep breath and some hope for this war. "Thank you for staying here."

Vlora looked down at her feet. "It's the least I could do after fighting to have you go after Taniel. I did the best I could."

"I think you were equal to the task."

"Just following your orders. Sir?"

"My mission was successful, Captain, if that is what you're asking."

Vlora gave a none-too-subtle sigh of relief. Tamas wondered what she would feel about Taniel's declaration of love for the savage—for Ka-poel. He had advised that his son keep it under his hat for a while longer, but truth be told, Tamas didn't know what *he* thought of it. Not something he had the luxury to deal with right now. He glanced at the piles of papers on his desk. He would have to scour everything in there to learn the details of the battle. If Vlora had made mistakes, it would be his own fault for leaving her here alone.

"You selfish, foolish prig!"

The voice broke angrily through Tamas's thoughts. He whirled to find Abrax awake and on her feet. She advanced toward him and stopped an arm's length away and thrust a finger out. Tamas felt himself shrink back slightly. She was not a large woman by any means, but with her ire up she could be imposing. She jabbed him in the chest.

"What kind of damned idiocy has gotten into your head, Tamas? How could you do this to us? To me? To your entire army?"

"Do what?" he asked mildly.

She sputtered. "You abandoned us on the eve of a decisive battle. You left a captain in charge of your army and ran off with an entire company of your best soldiers—for what?"

"For my son."

"For one man's life! I thought you were a leader, Tamas."

"I have responsibilities to more than just this country," Tamas said. He could feel his initial fear turning to anger. Part of him understood Abrax's anger, but to harangue him in front of his men? To criticize him for trying, once in his life, to be a good father?

"The country is your *only* responsibility, Tamas. You can't afford to be a father. You gave that up years ago when you decided to overthrow your king."

Tamas's hands shook at his side and he ground his teeth together violently. Everyone in the tent had their eyes locked on Tamas and the Wings' brigadier. Vlora looked shocked by Abrax's outburst, while Olem hovered nearby with a hand on his sword. "I never gave it up," he growled.

Abrax sniffed at him. "You did."

"We won this battle. And you're furious about it?"

"I'm furious that you risked everything. Once battle had joined, I spread the word that you returned. I personally told my officers that you would lead us to victory. Morale soared. They thought you were here, issuing every command yourself. You made a liar out of me."

"Countries rise and fall on bigger lies than that," Tamas said. "And those *were* my orders. I *had* returned, and I *did* give you a victory."

"Semantics!" Abrax spat.

Tamas thrust his finger at the table in the middle of the room, which was covered in his maps and notes. "I fought the entire battle the day before it happened. And we still won." Tamas felt a trickle of sweat go down his spine and hoped that Vlora had, in fact, been honest with how well he'd predicted the battle. "I did all of that in a single afternoon. I fought my way across bloody Kez, through betrayal and death to get back here." Tamas choked as he remembered the night he thought he had lost Gavril, riding hard across the plateau south of Alvation. "I would have won this war already had I not been beset by treachery."

"You're such a bloody genius," Abrax said, her lips twisted in disgust. "You can fight the rest of the war on your own. I'm going to recommend to Lady Winceslav that the Wings of Adom cancel their contract and withdraw our forces. Or what is left of them." Abrax brushed past him and stormed from the tent before Tamas could respond.

Tamas stood in silent shock, until Olem took him by the shoulder. "Sir?"

"I'm all right." He stumbled to a chair and sat down. The exhaustion of months of riding, fighting, desperation, and anxiety seemed to catch up with him all at once and he found that his strength was gone. His eyelids felt weighed down by lead shot. What had he done? If the Wings abandoned him now, could he finish this war?

Someone cleared his throat.

Tamas looked up to find Inspector Adamat holding his hat, looking rather embarrassed to have witnessed the fight between him and Abrax.

"In a moment, Inspector. Vlora, what were the losses to the Wings of Adom?"

Vlora shifted from one foot to the other. She'd not yet put on her boots, Tamas noticed absently. "A little less than twenty thousand."

"Ah, pit. No wonder Abrax was so angry. That's almost half of their forces wounded or killed."

"They took the brunt of the attack, sir. Just like you planned."

"Just like I planned. Of course." His thought had been to let the mercenaries earn their pay. And they had, many times over, it seemed. They weren't his men. They were Abrax's, and she had the right to be furious that Tamas had used them for a millstone. "Inspector. How did the affair with Lord Vetas go? Is your family safe?"

"Lord Vetas is dead," Adamat said. "And thank you for asking, sir. We were able to rescue all but"—he paused to clear his throat—"my oldest son." Adamat looked as weary as Tamas felt. There were large black bags beneath his eyes and the little hair on his balding head was mussed from sleeping on the ground.

"I'm sorry for your loss."

"Thank you, sir. Our expedition against Lord Vetas was a success. We even captured many of his papers and men, but, I'm afraid, it was all in vain. You've been told that Lord Claremonte holds Adopest?"

"That's what I was told. But one thing at a time. We still have to throw the Kez from our lands. Write up a report for me—"

"I have."

"Excellent. I'll read it and we'll talk before the day is over. You're free to roam the camp, but I'd greatly appreciate it if you'd stay close until I know everything I need to about Claremonte."

"I'm afraid I'll be of little help there, sir."

"Every little bit counts. Now I would..." Tamas stopped himself. "Miss, could you come here?"

The girl with the curly red hair slowly stepped away from the corner. At first glance she seemed shy, but upon further examination Tamas recognized wariness, like an animal sniffing the air to identify a friend or foe.

"Nila?" Olem suddenly exclaimed.

"Hello, Captain," the girl said, giving Olem a small smile.

"What are you doing here?"

"You're the laundress!" Tamas blurted out as the memory caught up to him. "The one who disappeared with the Eldaminse boy." He narrowed his eyes. "Where the pit did you get to? And what are you doing here?"

Nila curtsied and then folded her hands behind her back. "Field Marshal," she said, "I did not steal away the Eldaminse boy. Not precisely. We were both captured by Lord Vetas, and escaped when Adamat attacked Vetas's compound. The inspector will corroborate my story."

"Is that so, Inspector?"

Adamat gave a nod, albeit hesitantly. "I don't know the whole of it, sir. But she's an honest girl."

Tamas leaned back. Every vein in his head seemed to throb, and the pain from the wound at his side had surfaced through his powder trance. There was so much that needed to be done. Could he allow himself any rest? He looked cautiously at Vlora and Olem out of the corner of his eye. Olem's brow was furrowed as Vlora regarded the whole affair with a look of bemusement. Tamas wondered if she knew that Olem had courted the girl just a few months ago. But then, the two of them were over, weren't they?

"So she's with you?" he asked Adamat.

"No sir," Adamat said, coughing into one hand.

Tamas raised his eyebrows at the laundress. "Well?"

"I'm Privileged Borbador's apprentice, sir," Nila said with another curtsy.

"You're a Privileged?" Olem asked.

"Yes. Field Marshal, if I may ask? Where is Borbador?"

"Ah," Tamas said. He forced himself to get to his feet. "That's another important matter. Adamat, I understand you were witness to Privileged Borbador ridding himself of his gaes—the one that compelled him to kill me."

"That is true. I saw him remove the gem with my own eyes."

Tamas felt the relief of another small weight being lifted from his shoulders. "Good. Thank you, Inspector. Olem, would you show Nila to her master and release Bo from our custody? They are allowed to leave, but I would be grateful if Borbador would come and see me before he does."

Olem escorted Nila out of the tent, and at a nod from Tamas, Adamat followed them out. Tamas found a seat once again and lowered himself into it with a sigh.

"Sir," Vlora said, "you should get some rest."

Tamas leaned back, pressing one palm to the wound at his side, and closed his eyes. "We have work to do."

"You've earned the rest, sir. If you don't mind me saying so."

"Not quite yet."

"What do you intend to do?"

Tamas opened one eye. Vlora was lacing up her boots. "I'm going to drive the Kez from my country once and for all. I'm going to break their army and then I'm going to break their king. And then we'll see about this army that holds Adopest."

CHAPTER
19

Nila and Olem wound their way through the camp with silence between them, Olem greeting men as he walked, saluting officers, and nodding to infantrymen. Nila was still fuzzy-headed, the smell of an officer's breakfast—ham and eggs, if she wasn't mistaken—made her stomach growl. She had not slept well in two days, her dreams haunted by the screams of the dying, the report of artillery fire, and the smell of burned flesh.

"You understand that it's vital the men think that Tamas was here for the entire battle," Olem said, his voice low.

These were the first words he'd spoken to her since they left the tent. She felt her emotional defenses pull tight, and quickly said, "Of course. I won't say a word." What were they talking about again? Oh yes, Tamas's absence. What did it matter if Tamas had been gone for the battle, if they had won? The mercenary brigadier seemed angry enough about it.

"Thank you." Olem stopped them near the edge of the camp, out of earshot of the closest sentries, and looked off into the pre-dawn darkness. "They should be here anytime now."

"Who?"

"Our expedition. We took two hundred men with us to find the field marshal's son. We found him, Privileged Borbador, and over a hundred prisoners. Once we had secured the prisoners and made sure Taniel was safe, I and the field marshal rode ahead to sneak into the camp to make it look like we've been here the whole time. The rest will be along shortly."

"Won't word get out? If two people know a secret, everyone else does too." Nila remembered a time at the Eldaminse house when one of the maids had been caught sleeping with the head butler—caught by the butler's wife. They'd tried to avoid a scandal by keeping it quiet, but the maid gossiped and the butler was dismissed.

Olem removed a rolling paper from his jacket and began to roll a cigarette. "Of course. Rumors will spread. But as you said, we won the battle and it doesn't really matter now. As long as the Wings don't decide to make an issue of it, it'll stay nothing more than rumor."

He finished rolling his cigarette and held it out to her.

"No thank you."

He nodded and lit it with a match, smoking silently. Nila examined the side of his face and wondered what he had gone through during the last several months. She had thought him dead when she heard about the field marshal being caught behind enemy lines. But here he was, and didn't seem much the worse for the wear—a new scar above one eye, his beard longer.

It was strange to think he had courted her. Had things gone differently, they might have become lovers.

She clung to that bit of nostalgia to silence the voices in the back of her head—the voices of all those men she'd murdered in a wave of fire.

"You've certainly come a long way in life in the last few months," Olem said suddenly.

Nila ducked her head. "And you. I heard someone call you a colonel. Congratulations."

"That's temporary," Olem said.

"Oh? They can do temporary promotions?"

"It's not that. The field marshal wants me to remain a colonel. I just…"

"You don't think you can do it?"

Olem ashed his cigarette and rubbed out the embers with his boot. "It's not for me. But you? A Privileged! That's incredible. I always thought you were more than a laundress." He gave her a smile, and the crack in his façade revealed a deep exhaustion.

"Laundering is a good job," Nila said, somewhat more defensively than she'd meant to. She cleared her throat. "Is that why you courted me? Because you thought I was something more? A spy, perhaps?" Had his interest been fake? She wanted to feel angry at the thought, but found she didn't have the energy.

Olem took a drag on his cigarette and looked her in the eye. "Not a spy." He cleared his throat, then added, "I'm glad you're a Privileged. We'll need you before this is all over."

Need her to do more killing, he meant. The suggestion brought on a wave of nausea. Nila could still see the blackened skeletons, could still smell the smoking human remains.

"Ah. Here they come," Olem said, saving Nila from having to respond. A train of mounted men came into sight over a rise, holding torches and lanterns. They paused before the sentries and were waved on and ten minutes later they reached Nila and Olem.

Olem called to ask how the mission had fared. A major responded that they had succeeded, and a cheer went up among the group. Nila heard one of the sentries call to another.

"Taniel Two-shot is alive! He's come back!"

The word spread like wildfire and Nila couldn't help but smile at the cheers that erupted a few moments later from the camp behind them. Taniel, it seemed, was well loved.

A man rode up to Olem. His hair was dirty, a black beard concealing his weary, pinched face. His skin was a patchwork of bruises and scars. He wore an Adran jacket over his shoulders, a powder keg insignia pinned to it. Taniel Two-shot, Nila presumed. In the saddle behind him was the most striking girl Nila had ever seen.

She was a savage, her pale skin splattered with ashen freckles, her cropped hair red enough to match the torchlight—a far brighter shade than Nila's own auburn curls. While the man gave Nila a curious glance and then looked past her to Olem, the girl caught her gaze and held it for a moment before giving her a wink and a mischievous smile.

The man nodded to Olem, and Olem said, "You better go see your father. You'll want to know he's given orders for Bo to go free."

Taniel gave a relieved sigh and flicked his reins. His companion twisted in her saddle to look back at Nila and Nila watched her in return until they disappeared into the camp.

"So that's the field marshal's son?" she asked.

Olem sucked on his cigarette. "It is."

"And the girl?"

"Ka-poel."

"She's a savage sorceress? I've heard rumors about her."

"Yes." Olem crushed the butt of his cigarette beneath his boot. "She is, as the field marshal put it, something else entirely."

Nila saw Bo a little way down the line. He was surrounded by soldiers, his suit rumpled and his hair disheveled. She wanted to run to see how he'd gotten on, but the sting of being left behind—in a war zone, no less—rooted her feet to the ground.

"Hello, Nila," Bo said jovially as he rode up. He gripped the saddle horn with both hands and it became quickly apparent that they were tied tightly. The two big Adran infantrymen closest to him didn't take their eyes off him. "Hello, Olem."

"Privileged," Olem said with a nod.

"Am I allowed out yet?"

Olem nodded to the men watching Bo, and he was soon dismounted and untied, rubbing the feeling back into his wrists. One of the guards handed him back his gloves, which he took without a fuss, and Bo and Nila were soon left alone.

"Well," Bo said. He put the gloves into his pocket and nodded, as if to himself. "Glad that's over. Where are we bunking down? And I'm famished, let's go—"

Nila put her whole arm behind the slap. She felt the impact all the way to her shoulder and into her frame, and it spun Bo half around again. There was an audible gasp from over a dozen soldiers who had seen it.

Bo held his cheek and stared at her. The thought that she'd just slapped a Privileged with every ounce of her strength made her knees a little weak, but she whispered to herself that she was a Privileged too, now. For good and for ill.

"What the pit was that for?" Bo demanded.

"For leaving me in a war zone."

He rubbed furiously at the side of his face. "I swear I'm going to kill the next person who hits me. You look fine! What the pit are you so mad about?"

"I..." Nila's voice suddenly caught in her throat. The image of charred bits of bone and flesh floated before her eyes, and her fingertips tingled—and not just from the slap. She could still feel the flow of the sorcery through her, the terror and the ecstasy as she became a conduit for destructive forces. Her vision swam.

Bo caught her as she swayed. He led her away from the dismounting soldiers, holding her by the elbow, and when he spoke, the anger in his voice was replaced by concern.

"What happened?"

She shook her head, knowing she must look the fool. Her cheeks would be red, tears streaking down her face. This wasn't how a

Privileged behaved. She felt Bo put a hand on either side of her face as he forced her to look him in the eyes. "What happened?" he asked again.

"I killed them." Her voice sounded so pitiful, and she hated herself for it.

"Come on." Bo took her by the hand. He led them through the camp with his arm around her, shielding her from onlookers as a brother might shield his grieving sister. She remembered him asking questions, and her blubbering out the answers, and soon they were back in her tent. He lit a lantern and hung it from the cross pole. "Tell me," he said.

Nila had managed to regain her composure, and after a few deep breaths she began. "I was back with the baggage and the Kez managed to make a run at us. There were a lot of men—they outnumbered the men guarding the baggage. I was so *angry* that I couldn't do anything. I just kept trying and trying to make the connection." She mimed snapping her fingers, but was sure not to let them touch. "I thought if I could make fire, I could help, and suddenly *I did*. The right gesture and it flowed from me so easily. I ran out in front of the defenders and I just let loose."

"Fire?" Bo asked quietly.

She nodded. "It was like watching a wave roll across the plains. I tried to control it, but it just grew and grew and then I passed out." Nila felt the tears coming again. "When I woke up, the inspector had dragged me to safety. He tried to hide the truth from me, but I saw the scorched plain from afar. I killed them."

Bo produced a flask from his pocket and handed it to Nila. She took several swallows gratefully.

"Passing out is common when you draw too much power and don't properly control it," Bo said. "It's the body's defense against destroying yourself with the Else. How many?"

"How many what?"

"Did you kill."

Nila looked away. "Thousands." When she looked up, she expected her own self-loathing to be apparent on Bo's face. After all, she was a monster, wasn't she? She had murdered so many with just a few gestures.

Instead, Bo's eyebrows were raised. "Bloody good show, girl!"

She punched him in the shoulder.

"Ow. No, I mean it. That's amazing. You saved the entire Wings baggage camp, probably thousands of lives, all by yourself."

She stared at him, uncomprehending. "Can't you see how horrid that is? So many lives gone in an instant! They didn't even get the chance to defend themselves!"

"Nila," Bo said, his expression sobering, "you did an incredible thing. You can't blame yourself for that."

"But I do! Are you so insulated against death? Are you so hard of heart as not to realize what terrible power we hold in our hands?" She held her hands out to him, silently willing him to cut them off. Her cheeks were cold with tears, and suddenly she felt frigid. She began to shiver.

Bo frowned at her for a moment, then sighed. He took the blanket off her cot and pulled it around her shoulders, then moved closer to her. He took her by one hand, stroking her fingers as he spoke softly.

"They made me kill my first when I was fourteen," he said. "Some slave they'd brought in for the purpose—illegal, I know, but legality means very little in a royal cabal. She was probably around seventeen. The olive skin of a Gurlish, with one droopy eye." Bo sniffed. "I refused to kill her four times, and they beat me soundly each time I did. Then, the fifth time, they told me that if I didn't kill her, I would be a dead man myself. I still refused, and they told me that if I didn't kill her, they would slaughter Taniel and Tamas and Vlora. My only friends. Bloody idiot that I was, I believed them. I couldn't let that happen and so when they asked again, I killed the slave girl as quickly as I could."

There was the streak of a tear on Bo's face. He wiped it away when he noticed Nila was looking at him.

"Why would they make you do that?" she asked. The cruelty of it astonished her. To make a fourteen-year-old boy murder in cold blood?

"To harden me. To show me what life in a royal cabal is really like. I tried to run away seven, maybe eight times. They beat me a lot for that. I was the magus's own apprentice and he said he wasn't going to let my talent go to waste just because I was weak-willed. Pit, I hated that man. I did everything I could to make his life miserable: embarrassed him in public, started bedding his own concubines by the time I was sixteen. I even took a shit in his bed once." Bo chuckled. "And every bruise he gave me, every markless, sorcerous torture they inflicted on me, I used to reinforce my hate. I even swore to kill him, but Tamas took care of that for me."

Nila felt hollow inside, her energy and emotions sapped. "Is that what I'm to become? Someone driven by hate and self-loathing?"

"Hey now," Bo said. "I've never been driven by my self-loathing. I keep that locked up tight in the back of my head."

Nila felt the corner of her cheek lift at the joke.

"No," Bo went on. "I don't want you to become that. I want you to learn to wield your power and to follow your conscience. But sometimes, your conscience will require you to kill. That is the life of a Privileged. The burden of such power is to protect your friends and countrymen."

Nila felt herself nodding. She couldn't find any words.

"It'll get easier," Bo said. He gave her a reassuring squeeze. "Don't become callous, though. Don't become like me. You must do your best to prevent that."

She felt his hand move down her side. "Was any of that true?"

"Pardon?"

"Or are you just trying to get in my skirts?"

Bo flinched, and Nila saw immediately she'd said the wrong

thing. It *had* been true. Every word. And she'd just thrown it back in his face—even if it had been in jest.

"I'm sorry," she said. "I didn't mean..."

He smiled crookedly at her. "Nah. That's fair enough. I should go find my tent."

"Don't leave."

He frowned at her, then squeezed her one more time.

Nila fell asleep with her head on his chest, listening to the rhythmic beat of his heart. As she drifted off, the screams echoing in her memory seemed quieter.

Something told her there would be more in the future.

CHAPTER
20

Tamas sifted through mountains of reports on the battle that he had been given credit for winning.

The men had taken to calling it the Battle of Ned's Creek, after the stream that ran down the middle of the battlefield. It seemed, based on camp gossip that excluded any mention of Tamas's four-day disappearance, that Abrax had decided to keep quiet about his absence, despite her anger, and that Olem had managed to keep his Riflejacks silent. For now. Several hundred people knew he had gone to rescue Taniel. Word would get out. But the more time that elapsed until it happened, the better.

Tamas had read Vlora's report three times. He'd also read reports from three generals, five colonels, two captains, and a sergeant. Vlora's was by far the most comprehensive, but the others had filled him in on details that Vlora had either missed or chosen to omit.

He rubbed his eyes and let out a sigh. What he'd give for a bowl of Mihali's squash soup. Or even just a few minutes to chat with him. Mihali, for all his faults, had a way of relaxing Tamas that he hadn't even realized until he'd been told that the god was dead.

Perhaps it was just sentiment.

"Olem!" he shouted. "Olem!"

The tent flap opened and a guard stuck his head inside. Shadows played on his face from Tamas's lantern. "Sorry, sir, it's Olem's off-hours. Is there anything I can do for you?"

"Ah, no. Never mind. I can . . . Wait, what time is it?"

"I think it's around eleven o'clock, sir."

"Thank you. Find Inspector Adamat for me. If he's still awake, have him meet me here in half an hour. Otherwise, let him sleep."

Tamas had read the inspector's report as well. The man deserved his rest.

He climbed to his feet and stretched, only to wince as the pain shot through his gut. Pressing a palm against his wound, Tamas crossed to his desk and rummaged around until he found a plate with the night's dinner. The biscuits were hard, the cheese moldy, and the beef stringy. He choked down half of it before he gave up completely and gathered up a pair of gold bars from his desk, pocketed them, and stepped out into the night.

Somewhere nearby, a soldier was playing her fiddle, singing softly with the tune, her voice carrying over the otherwise quiet camp. Tamas's guards snapped to attention. "At ease," he said. "I'm going for a walk. You can tag along, but give me some quiet."

The guards followed at a respectful distance as he wandered through the camp. He waved away soldiers who tried to stand and salute, and soon the sound of the singing infantrywoman had faded, leaving the night to be punctuated by distant cries and moans that came from the north, where the surgeons had set up hospitals. Fourteen hundred men had lost limbs since the battle, and hundreds more had taken fatal wounds. For the latter, doctors could only give them mala and wait for the inevitable.

After the adrenaline had worn off and medals had been awarded and the glory meted out, only the suffering remained after a battle.

"I should have been here for them. Led them into battle," Tamas muttered.

"Sir?" one of his guards asked.

"Nothing. Have either of you any idea where Captain Vlora has bunked down?"

"No sir," they both answered.

Tamas found Olem's tent not far from his own. Several of the Riflejacks still sat around the fire. One was reading by lamplight, while another whittled at a piece of wood. They all stood when Tamas approached.

"At ease," he said with a sigh. He gestured to Olem's tent. "Just here to see the colonel."

Two of the Riflejacks exchanged looks. A third, a woman of about thirty with blond hair cropped short, cleared her throat. "I think he's asleep," she said.

Tamas squinted at her. "He's a Knacked. He doesn't need sleep." Everyone knew about Olem's Knack. What was she going on about?

"I . . . I think I saw him leave earlier," one of the others said.

Tamas sprinkled a bit of powder on his tongue and headed over to Olem's tent. "Olem, are you . . . ?" The vision in his powder trance allowed him to see the inside as if it were day, despite the lack of lamps. Tamas thought he heard a giggle, and then a curse, and Olem sat up in his cot. He was stripped to the waist.

"Sir?"

Tamas eyed the lump in the cot next to him and couldn't help but crack a smile. Perhaps Olem had reconnected with the pretty laundress. "I'm sorry, I didn't mean to interrupt anything."

"No problem at all, sir."

"I was just looking for Vlora."

Olem cleared his throat. "Er..."

"I'm right here." Vlora sat up in the cot next to Olem and brushed her hair out of her face with one hand.

"Ah," Tamas said. "I, uh, will wait outside."

He retreated to the campfire, where the Riflejacks studiously avoided his gaze. Tamas tapped his foot, trying to think of something to say to Vlora other than "fraternization between ranks."

"Sorry, sir," one of the Riflejacks mumbled. Another one kicked him in the shins.

"It's all right," Tamas said. Part of him wanted to laugh. "I'd expect nothing less from one of them"—he thrust his thumb at his guards—"if *I* had someone in the sack." That brought out a muffled snort from the same Riflejack. He received another kick for it.

Vlora stepped out of Olem's tent a moment later, pulling her jacket on over her half-buttoned shirt. Her boots were still unlaced, and she paused to do them up while Tamas waited, then followed him away from the campfire.

"I'm not sorry, sir," she said when they were out of earshot of Olem and the Riflejacks.

"Hmm? Sorry for what?"

Vlora stiffened and Tamas turned to her with a sigh. "It's life, Vlora. You said that to me yourself. I'm glad you can still find something in each other's arms. I wish I had that same luxury."

"Sir?" Vlora stared back at him openmouthed, and Tamas smothered a small smile. He could still surprise people. That was good to know. Vlora continued, "Do you mean...?"

"I'm not here to reprimand you or anything. I wanted to find you for something else. Fraternization between ranks is still an offense, mind you. But I don't have the energy for that right now."

"Thank you, sir." Vlora regarded him with guarded eyes, as if waiting for the other shoe to drop. "You're giving mixed signals, sir."

"I know. Sorry. I wish life were a little more direct, but I think I've come around since our last talk on this particular subject."

Vlora tilted her head to one side. "Olem thought you promoted him just to keep us from being lovers."

"He did? Huh. Wish I had thought of that. But I didn't. I promoted him because the circumstance called for it and he's one of the few people I can trust completely." He sighed, dismissing the subject with a wave of his hand, fighting the urge to say something else. He still didn't approve of the relationship, but he no longer felt it was his place to say. "Speaking of which, I'm promoting you."

Vlora blinked at him. "I'm sorry?"

"I said I'm promoting you. To colonel, actually. For now, you'll be on special assignment, just like Olem, but I intend on putting you in charge of your own regiment before the end of the war."

"I don't understand. I haven't done anything to deserve that."

"You haven't? Captain—I mean, Colonel—I have spent the last two days poring over reports of the battle and of your actions. They were, in a word, brilliant."

"I was only working with your instructions," Vlora mumbled.

"No battle plan is perfect. Not even mine. Over a dozen critical situations required your response, without my guidance, and you handled each one exactly as I would have. In the case of sending the two companies to relieve the Wings' camp, you did it even better. I would have let them burn, then cleaned up the mess after the chaos died down, which would have been the wrong thing to do."

Tamas hadn't meant to go on, but he found the words tumbling out of him. "These are, of course, extraordinary circumstances. We lost a lot of officers over the last couple of months, and not all of them to death or wounds." Hilanska's betrayal and Ket's thievery and flight still rankled. "There will be hundreds of promotions in the next week, and you won't be the only one to skip ranks. I'd always meant to keep my powder mages as marksmen and soldiers, but I see now that I need to promote those with the talent."

"Andriya should be promoted too."

"He will be, as soon as he arrives with the Deliv king. But

Andriya is too hotheaded. Too vengeful. He's always been better with small groups, which is why he's been in command of the cabal since Sabon. But you've always had a talent for seeing the bigger picture and you proved it the other day."

"Thank you, sir."

Tamas nodded. "This war isn't won yet, Colonel. Don't thank me until it is."

They stood in silence for several minutes, and it was Vlora who spoke first.

"Sir?"

"Yes?"

"May I go?"

"Oh. Oh, yes! Go on. Wait, take these." Tamas put the gold bars into her hand, then folded her fingers over them. He had the sudden urge to bend and kiss her on the forehead gently, a blessing for a daughter, but he stifled it just long enough for her to lunge forward and hug him. Tamas found himself returning the embrace. Then she was off, and Tamas watched her for a moment.

"Uh, sir," a voice said.

Tamas turned to find a secretary waiting nearby. "What is it?"

"Inspector Adamat is waiting for you."

"Ah. Yes. Of course. I'll come right away." He tossed one more glance in Vlora's direction, but she was already gone.

Adamat shifted from one foot to the other and stifled a yawn. It was almost midnight, and there was still no sign of the field marshal. Should he go? Should he wait?

No doubt that Tamas wanted to question him about the series of events that culminated in Vetas's death. It had all been in his report, of course, but a report was never as good as the real thing. Tamas was the kind of man who liked to be thorough. Adamat just hoped he wasn't going to be *too* thorough.

Any questions about Josep, Adamat had already decided, would be evaded as well as possible.

Adamat ran his hand through his hair and scratched at his bald spot. He'd spent countless hours examining that Warden in his mind and he had come to the conclusion that a perfect memory was most certainly a curse. Without it, he may have convinced himself that it was just a trick of the light: That Warden was nothing like his son, and the missing ring finger was simply a coincidence.

But the more Adamat considered the deformed back and twisted but still boyish jaw and the smooth cheeks, he was convinced that his boy had been turned into a Warden.

What had they done to his innocent boy? First a captive, then a powder mage sold into slavery, and now this. Adamat tried to remember everything he knew about Wardens. They were regular men transformed by Kez sorcery into twisted creatures devoid of anything but rudimentary intelligence and brainwashed to obey Kez commanders. These new Black Wardens, created out of powder mages, were only a recent development. Some of the soldiers whispered that they had been created by Kresimir himself, as none of the other Privileged would be powerful enough to twist a powder mage.

What suffering had that caused? What pain had the villainous god forced upon Adamat's son? Adamat replayed the scene in his head over and over again, and examined the eyes of the creature. He expected, upon a closer look, to find anger and sorcery-fueled rage in those eyes.

But there was only fear, of the kind seen in a dumb ox being driven to slaughter.

"Inspector?"

Adamat heard the rustle of the tent flap, wiped hastily at his eyes, and straightened his coat. "Sir, I'm here."

"Inspector, what are you doing standing here in the dark?"

Tamas asked. Adamat could hear the field marshal rummaging about on his desk, then a match was struck and a lantern lit.

"Just waiting. I didn't want to bother anyone."

"We can provide a light, man. I'm sorry to be so rude. I hope I didn't wake you."

Tamas peered closely at Adamat's face and Adamat flinched away. "You did not."

"Pit, you look as bad as I do. Have you been sleeping? Did they get you a proper tent and gear?"

"They did. Thank you."

"I'm sorry to keep you in the camp like this. You understand I've had a lot to catch up with."

"Of course. I do look forward to getting back to my family." *Do I? How will I explain what I have seen—what Josep has become—to Faye?* Adamat realized with a start that he had already considered his son as good as dead. But then, what else could he consider? He'd stared into those eyes in his memory for so long, he knew that the Josep he loved was no more.

"Are you certain everything is all right, Inspector?"

"It is."

Tamas lowered himself into a seat, looking far worse for the wear, and Adamat pulled his mind off his own troubles to examine the field marshal. Troubled by a dozen wounds, or so it seemed, Tamas had aged ten years in the last three months. What little trace of black might have remained in his mustache was gone, and he moved carefully, painfully, favoring his right side.

Adamat had seen that kind of behavior before in men in the Adran police force. Tamas had a knife wound—between the ribs, lucky enough to miss anything vital, but painful as all pit and likely to fester. There were rumors that Hilanska had stabbed Tamas before he fled. They certainly fit.

"Inspector?"

Adamat snapped out of his own thoughts. Tamas had been talk-ing. "I'm very sorry, sir. Could you repeat that?"

Tamas tilted his head to one side, a twitch of anger crossing his face. "I asked if you know why I didn't arrest you after you con-fessed your treachery."

"I don't." Adamat felt a bead of cold sweat on his forehead and his jacket was suddenly too tight. It *was* something he'd asked him-self, though he hadn't dwelt on it. There was too much to do, too much at stake.

"I didn't arrest you because that's what the enemy would have expected." Tamas climbed to his feet and crossed to his desk, pour-ing water into a glass. He didn't offer any to Adamat. "It was a feint, to throw him off your trail. You mentioned in your report that Vetas thought you had been imprisoned."

"So I did," Adamat said, his throat dry. "It worked."

Tamas took a sip of water, watching Adamat with a look that Adamat had seen on men deciding whether to put down a lame dog. "Yes."

"And now?"

"I still hold you responsible for Sabon's death, Inspector," Tamas said. "I had told myself that you would stand trial when all this was over. That you would face the consequences of your actions."

Adamat suddenly felt a fire in his belly. *The consequences? He, who brought me into this whole mess, has the gall to speak to me about consequences? I've faced the consequences of my actions a hundred times over during the last six months.* Adamat had to bite his tongue to hold his peace.

"I had told myself that—right up until the moment I had to choose between leading my men into battle and rescuing my son from being murdered in the wilderness by traitors. You're a good man, Adamat, and you did what you could. There are so few good men left, and I will not send one to the guillotine. But I need your help."

Adamat barely trusted himself to breathe. "*My* help?"

"There is more work to be done."

Adamat felt his chest tighten. *Of course. Always more to do.* What would Faye say to this, were she here with him? She would tell the field marshal to stuff his consequences in his ass and to toss himself into the pit.

"Something funny, Inspector?"

"I was just thinking of what my wife would say if she were here."

"Oh? And what was that?"

"She'd ask, 'What can I do to help, Field Marshal?' So. What can I do to help?" There was nothing else to say. Tamas would expect nothing short of obedience. It was the same arrogance that Adamat had seen for decades among the nobility whom he'd served.

Tamas seemed thrown for a moment. "I see. I still have to finish this war, and when it is done, I'll need to deal with the Brudanian army that holds Adopest. Some kind of contact needs to be made. You shall be my liaison with Lord Claremonte. Find out what he wants. What are his goals? What will make him go away and, if that is not within our reach, discover his secrets and weaknesses and report them to me so I may destroy him and give our country the republic it deserves."

Adamat felt something niggling deep inside his bowels. It felt an awful lot like despair. He'd dealt with the servant Lord Vetas, and now he had to deal with the master, who could only be many times the worse? It would undo him. "I will not put my family in that danger again, Field Marshal. Not for my life."

"Your country needs you."

Adamat wondered if Tamas knew how hollow the words sounded. "You cannot entrust me with this. Not possibly. Lord Claremonte, through his agent, used my family against me once and he will do it again. And if he does that, I will betray you again, I promise you that."

"Your family is no longer in the equation. There is nothing

Claremonte would gain by threatening them. You will be a politician and nothing more."

"He can compel me to give you misinformation."

"You have my guarantee of their safety."

Adamat found himself standing once more. "You cannot make that guarantee! This man is a beast and will use any means necessary to win his twisted game. I have seen his machinations!"

"And that, Inspector, is why I need you so badly. You are the only one who knows anything about him. You are the only one who hates him enough to be ready to destroy him on a moment's notice. Your family will be safe, Adamat. I swear it. You will hear no such guarantees from Claremonte while he holds the city." Tamas took another sip of his water.

"I'm sorry, Field Marshal, but I must refuse."

"You said—"

"I asked what I could do to help. I did not offer to put myself and my family back into harm's way. No, sir, I will not deal with Claremonte. I have already put my family through enough as it is for this cause. I have lost a son!" *And to something far worse than death.*

Tamas frowned down into his cup. "I see."

Adamat realized that his heart was pounding. He'd not expected to come in here and start shouting, but he had to draw the line somewhere. The lives of Tamas's men were in his own hands, and damn him if he thought he could use guilt as leverage against Adamat.

"You'll be going back to Adopest soon?" Tamas asked.

"First thing in the morning," Adamat said. He lowered himself back into his chair. He felt so incredibly old.

"Would a lesser request sway you?"

Adamat cocked an eyebrow, sensing a trap. Tamas had backed off of that far too quickly for one of his kind. "What is it?" He cleared his throat and lowered his voice. "What can I do, sir?"

"Offer Ricard your help in his political campaign. He'll need all the aid he can get—especially from men he trusts. You two are friends, are you not?"

"Ricard is running against Claremonte," Adamat said. The very man Adamat wished to avoid.

Tamas made a calming gesture. "I'm not asking you to get too closely involved. Just give him some help. A kind word. Lend him your talent for memory. Whatever you can spare."

"I'll do what I can," Adamat said after a moment's consideration. "But I don't guarantee anything. I will not get caught up in Claremonte's web again."

Tamas responded with a tight nod. He opened his mouth to say something else, but they were interrupted by a light rap on the tent pole and a messenger putting his head inside. "Sir?"

"What is it?"

"I've a messenger from the king."

"What king? Deliv? They're here already?"

"No, sir. From the Kez. Ipille has sued for peace. He wants to parley."

Adamat's presence was forgotten the moment word came that the Kez wanted to discuss terms of peace. He slunk back to his tent amongst the ensuing round of late-night messengers and sudden meetings and managed just a few hours of restless sleep before his carriage was ready to take him back to Adopest.

He bid his driver to wait for him, and stole through the morning chaos of the camp, working off directions from the field marshal's bodyguard to find one particular tent in a sea of thousands.

He was saved the embarrassment of having to put his head in tent after tent to find Privileged Borbador by spotting the Privileged himself sitting beside a smokeless fire, long-stemmed pipe clutched in his teeth. His jacket was immaculately pressed, his muttonchops trimmed. He looked as dapper as an officer with half a dozen batboys. Adamat wondered how sorcery could be applied to help one's morning routine, and at the same time noted that the fire had no fuel.

"Good morning, Inspector," Bo said softly. He put a finger to his lips and pointed to the tent behind him.

"Good morning, Privileged." Adamat took his hat in his hands and tried not to look nervous.

The Privileged glanced up from his sorcerous fire. "Is there something I can help you with?"

"I..." Adamat cleared his throat. Maybe this wasn't a good idea. Maybe it would be for the best if he just left things alone.

"Yes?"

"It's a sensitive matter."

Bo took out the pipe from between his lips and scowled at the empty bowl. "Haven't had a spare minute to find any pipe tobacco. You wouldn't happen to have any, would you?"

Adamat felt around for his own pipe and pouch, and removed it from his pocket. "Just a little." He gave the rest of the pouch to Bo, who nodded his thanks, taking a moment to pack his pipe and light the bowl from a flame that sprang from his finger. He looked up, meeting Adamat's eyes.

Whatever the Privileged had been pondering when Adamat approached had been tucked away. He now had Bo's full attention, and he wasn't sure he wanted it.

"Does this have to do with your son?" Bo asked.

"It does."

"I promised I would help you get him back. Tamas is trying to recruit me, and that complicates things. But I still plan on holding to my promise."

"I'm returning to Adopest," Adamat said.

Bo watched him carefully, his eyes soft. "Have you given up?" His voice was not unkind.

"Circumstances have changed."

"In what way?"

Adamat licked his lips. It was time to be strong. For himself. For Faye. For Josep. "My son has been turned into a Warden. A Black Warden. I saw him myself at the battle. He would have killed me, but I called his name and he fled."

"Can you be sure?"

"As sure as I can."

Bo seemed to consider this for a moment. "I can't do anything for him. The process of creating a Warden cannot be reversed. The Adran Cabal has tried. And these Black Wardens, even their corpses stink of Kresimir's sorcery. I would likely die trying to counter that."

"I know. I mean, I read a book on Wardens once. Only a few chapters, really, but I know that the process can't be reversed."

"Then why are you here?"

"I wanted to change the terms of our agreement." Adamat thought that Bo might disagree immediately. After all, an agreement was an agreement. He expected Bo to hold to nothing but the letter of it.

"I'm listening," Bo said.

"I want you to find my son. And I want you to kill him."

CHAPTER
21

It took four days to arrange the parley. During the uneasy peace, brigades on both sides were reinforced and allowed to posture, and messengers were exchanged. Two days after finalizing the parley, Tamas found himself in a town just off the southern highway about fifteen miles north of Fendale.

Calling it a town was actually quite generous. There were less than a dozen buildings, the biggest of which, a Kresim chapel, had been appropriated for the purpose of the meeting. There was no sign of the previous occupants of the town. Whether they'd evacuated months ago or been enslaved by the Kez, there was no way of knowing, and it wasn't high on Tamas's list of questions to ask the Kez king.

Riders came and went for the better part of the morning, and Tamas passed his time watching Ipille's retinue where they camped on the other side of the town, about a mile away. Not a lot of the camp was visible—Ipille had set up in a shallow ravine, out of the wind.

And out of sight of any powder mages.

Tamas commented on the fact to Olem, who lifted his looking glass to examine one of Ipille's royal guard standing on a hill overlooking the Kez camp.

"He doesn't trust you, sir," Olem said.

"I can't terribly blame him. I did try to kill him once."

Olem lowered his looking glass and removed a cigarette from the corner of his mouth. "He's tried to have you killed a dozen times, at least."

"True," Tamas said wistfully. "But I've wrapped my fingers around his throat. That's a little different."

"Ah. You ever going to tell me that story?"

"Maybe when I'm drunk someday."

"You don't drink, sir."

"Exactly."

One of Olem's Riflejacks rode up to give his report, and a moment later Olem conferred with Tamas. "Sir, my boys have given the all-clear. The town is empty except for a couple of Ipille's royal guard, and they've scouted everything within half a dozen miles. If it's a trap, Ipille is far cleverer than we give him credit."

"Ipille *is* far cleverer than we give him credit. Fortunately for us, the one skill he lacks is the ability to select for talent. That's why all of his generals and field marshals have only ever been half-competent at best. You've had a few Knacked checking for Privileged and Wardens?"

"No Wardens. And just one fifth-rate Privileged. Supposedly she's the head of the royal cabal now, with everyone stronger dead."

"Tell Vlora to keep the Privileged in her sights, in case she tries something."

"You know, sir," Olem mused, "Ipille is doubtless traveling with a kingly entourage. We've only brought fighting men. We have the superior force. We could..." He imitated a pistol with his thumb and forefinger.

"Don't tempt me." The thought had already occurred to Tamas. Several times. "We're in position to end this war. Kill Ipille, and one of his bloody stupid sons will call for our heads and might even gain sympathy throughout the Nine. Taniel!" Tamas waved his son forward. Taniel looked up from speaking with one of the Riflejacks and waved back. He said a few more words and walked over.

Taniel had cleaned up well since his ordeal in the mountains. He'd shaved, bathed, and been given a new uniform. He bore a dozen more scars than when Tamas had sent him up South Pike Mountain, and there was a patch of white hair around his right ear that Tamas hadn't noticed before. He wore the powder keg pin of a powder mage on his breast, but no rank.

Tamas drummed his fingers on his saddle horn. "I gave you a promotion, you know," he said, eyeing Taniel's empty lapels.

"Technically," Taniel responded, "I'm not one of your soldiers anymore."

"That's rubbish and you know it."

Taniel let his weight fall to his back leg and his hand rested on the butt of one pistol. Even here, surrounded by allies, he adopted the stance of a casual killer. Similar to Olem, but without the bodyguard's watchfulness. Taniel wasn't ready to kill because he needed to. Just... because.

"I made an agreement with Brigadier Abrax. I'm a member of the Wings of Adom."

"And I told you that you never left my service. Your dismissal was orchestrated by a traitor on one side and a war profiteer on the other. No court, military or civilian, would uphold the results of that court-martial."

"Of course, father," Taniel said quietly.

Tamas bristled. They'd had this conversation a dozen times, and each time Taniel made a show of conceding the point. But he still had yet to attach the major's pins to his lapel.

"This could be a trap," Taniel said.

Tamas shook his head. "We've checked."

"It's the real thing? Ipille wants peace?"

"That's what we've been led to believe."

"We could just kill him," Taniel said.

Olem nodded emphatically. "That was my suggestion."

Tamas sighed. No need to dignify that with a response. As much as he wanted Ipille's head on the end of a bayonet, he was acting as a politician now. This had to be done right. And, he reminded himself at the sight of a group of riders cresting the highway a few hundred yards distant, he wasn't doing this himself.

"My lady," Tamas greeted Lady Winceslav when she arrived.

The Lady wore a sharp red riding dress with black boots and rode with a carbine laid across her saddle. She pulled up next to Tamas and looked him up and down.

"Abrax is furious with you."

"I know."

"So am I."

"I assumed as much."

"You're a fool. And you almost lost us this war." Her tone was level, one eyebrow raised as if she were slightly bemused. Despite her outward appearance, Tamas had known the Lady long enough to see that she was quite put out.

"But I didn't," he said.

"You're incorrigible. Hello, Olem. Hello, Taniel."

Olem nodded. Taniel stepped to the Lady's side and kissed her hand. "Good afternoon, my lady."

"I'm glad to see you're still alive. No thanks to this one." She jerked her chin at Tamas, and Tamas forced himself to swallow a biting remark. "Are you sure," she continued, "that you want to remain in the employ of the Adran army? I'll double whatever they're paying you."

Tamas eyed his son for a moment, and Taniel seemed to enjoy the uncomfortable silence that followed. Finally, he said, "My place is here, my lady. For now."

"Pity."

"A word, my lady?" Tamas asked.

They both led their horses off to the side and Tamas leaned over to her. "Will the Wings of Adom continue their support of this battle?"

"I'm having serious doubts as to the mental fortitude of the Adran field marshal," Lady Winceslav said, looking him up and down.

"Oh? And you've made better decisions in the recent past? Shall I bring up a certain scandal among your brigadiers that's only a few months old?"

Lady Winceslav pursed her lips. "Tell me, can you count the number of younger women you've slept with on one hand? On two? How about we include toes?"

"This bickering is unbecoming," Tamas said, giving her a tight smile.

"Is that the best you've got? Where's that famous grin you used to bag them all with?" Lady Winceslav shook her head before he could answer. "I'm here in my capacity as a member of your council. Not as the head of the Wings of Adom. We took impossible losses last week and we haven't yet decided what to do about it." Tamas opened his mouth, but Lady Winceslav leaned close and whispered, "We're going to withdraw. But I won't make that announcement for a couple of days. As far as this parley is concerned, we will provide a unified front."

Tamas's throat was dry. "Thank you," he said back quietly. Louder, "Well. I'll look forward to hearing your answer." He was not happy to hear her decision. If Ipille continued the war, he would need her mercenaries more than ever. But he couldn't make an issue of it now.

Tamas noted that someone else had ridden in just behind Lady Winceslav's escort. He frowned and wheeled his mount toward the approaching rider.

"Nila, was it?"

The laundress-turned-Privileged nodded her head. She kept a white-knuckle grip on the saddle horn, and scowled at the roan stepping nervously beneath her.

"Been riding long?"

"No, actually. This is only my third time."

"I see. You're doing remarkably well, if that's the case."

"Thank you."

"Nila, may I ask what you're doing here?"

"It's Privileged Nila, sir. And yes. I've been sent by Privileged Borbador."

"Have you now, Privileged Nila?"

"Indeed."

"For what?"

"Why, to attend the negotiations."

Tamas blinked at this. "I don't mean to be rude, but you're a laundress who has only recently become a Privileged apprentice. What makes Bo think you belong at a negotiation between nations?"

"He said I should get used to it."

"Did he? Well, you can go back to Bo and tell him that this is not appropriate."

The smile wavered, but to the girl's credit she did not flinch. "I won't do that, sir."

"Even if I order it?"

"With all due respect, I am not under your command, sir."

He could see the nervousness in her eyes now. The slight shake of her hands on the reins. What was this, some kind of test that Bo had put her to? Face down Field Marshal Tamas?

"It is within my power to bar you from the negotiations."

"You can't, sir. I have every right to be here as the representative of the Adran Republic Cabal."

"The what? Taniel!" Tamas whirled his horse and beckoned impatiently for his son. Taniel arrived a moment later. "What the pit is your friend playing at?"

"What friend?"

"Don't act coy with me. Borbador. What is this business about the Adran Republic Cabal?"

Taniel looked at Nila, then at Tamas, suppressing a chuckle. "He's not playing at anything, sir. You've asked him to help with the war effort and he's the last trained Privileged left in Adro. Nila is his apprentice and, from what Bo tells me, she is even stronger than he is. Those two are the Adran Cabal now, and since we're trying to be a republic, he thought it pointless to continue calling it the royal cabal."

Tamas opened his mouth once, then closed it, trying to think of an argument against this that didn't end with him saying "because I say so." He couldn't come up with one. Bo was, technically, still a government Privileged.

"Don't say a bloody word," Tamas said, pointing at Nila. "I'm grateful for what you did at the battle last week and it's earned you my goodwill. But I will not have a former laundress arguing points of politics with the bloody king of Kez."

Nila's ingratiating smile returned. "Of course, Field Marshal. I'm only here as a representative."

Tamas spurred his horse back to Olem. "The laundress is going with us."

"Yes sir. It's almost the appointed time."

Tamas gave a silent prayer of thanks that Olem had accepted the news without comment. "Send a man ahead. Vlora, you have command until I return. If anything happens, kill Ipille's Privileged first, and then Ipille."

"Yes sir."

Tamas led his delegation across the lonely field to the outskirts of the town, where they waited for their messenger to return and tell them that Ipille was already in the chapel. They dismounted and left their horses tied beside one of the small houses, then walked the last hundred yards of the journey.

Two of the Kez royal guard flanked the chapel. Tamas looked them up and down—they wore gold on black, with gray trim. Their feathered, flat-top hats were tipped forward, chin straps hugging their jaws. Dark, unflinching eyes gazed back at Tamas, and he wished he had his powder cabal with him. The Kez royal guard was not to be trifled with. He doubted even Olem's Riflejacks measured up to them.

"I'm here to see your king," Tamas said.

One of them snapped a nod and turned sharply on his heel to open the chapel door. Olem left two men, one for each of the Kez, and then went first, followed by Lady Winceslav and Nila. Three of Tamas's generals, two colonels, and a lawyer who had come along with Lady Winceslav filed inside.

Taniel hung back, a sour look on his face as if he'd swallowed a lime whole.

Tamas waited patiently for Taniel to finally come forward. "It's time to end this," Tamas said.

A muscle jumped in Taniel's jaw. For a moment, Tamas thought his son's discipline would fail him, but ever the soldier, Taniel gave a sharp nod and headed in, leaving Tamas to steel his own emotions before he followed to complete the delegation.

The chapel was poorly lit by a single window on the eastern side. It was one large room, only about twenty feet by thirty. The pews had been stacked along the walls and a large table brought in, covered with a gold cloth and a small feast of fruits and desserts. Candelabras had been lit and artwork hung along the walls—no doubt, additions made by Ipille's retinue to give some semblance of royalty to the place.

A small group of politicians occupied the far end of the table. Field Marshal Goutlit sat on one side with a pair of generals Tamas did not recognize. On the other was a thin woman with delicate, birdlike features in the official tan-and-green robe of the Kez royal cabal. Beside her sat a pale, limp-looking fellow named Duke Regalish—Ipille's closest adviser. A few other noblemen stood along the back wall.

Ipille himself sat at the head of the table.

He'd grown morbidly obese since the last time they had met, the night Tamas had tried to kill him. Once a dapper lion of a man, he sat stuffed into a chair that would have been big enough for a pair of grenadiers. He wore swaths of cloth; thick, bristling furs draped over his shoulders, trimmed with gold, and on his fingers rubies that would make an Arch-Diocel blush.

"Tamas." Ipille's voice sounded like the inside of a bass drum, and his jowls shook when he spoke.

"Ipille."

A chair scraped the stone floor, and Duke Regalish shot to his feet. "You will address his august majesty as 'Your Royal Highness.' He is a king, you common cur, and you will treat him as such."

"Shall I put this dog down?" Olem asked, his hand resting on the hilt of his smallsword.

Tamas let his silence speak for him, letting Regalish stand quivering with indignation until Ipille turned his head toward his adviser. "Sit down, my good duke. Your whimpering will have no effect on Tamas. He is a man of iron. Iron does not bend. It only shatters."

Tamas clasped his hands behind his back and tried to focus through the pain in his side.

Ipille's fat fingers drummed heavily on the oak table as Olem made his way silently around the room. He bent to lift the table-cloth, then strolled around the table, looking over each of the advisers with a studious eye, ignoring their baleful glares.

"What is this, Tamas?"

"Precaution."

"We're here under a flag of truce, are we not?"

"Come now, Your Moribund Majesty. You took your precaution by arriving first. I take mine now."

Ipille's deep chuckle forestalled another outburst from Regalish.

Olem finished his search and gave Tamas a nod, and Tamas gestured to the chairs on his end of the table. "Ipille, I will introduce Lady Winceslav—I believe you've met. My son, Major Taniel Two-shot. Privileged Nila of the Adran Republic Cabal. Members of my senior staff."

"Charmed," the king said. "You know Regalish. I believe you killed his uncle. Some of my advisers back there," he said with a dismissive wave. "Field Marshal Goutlit. Magus Janna." Another of Ipille's deep chuckles. "We're both scraping the bottom of the barrel when it comes to Privileged, are we not? Sad times."

Tamas gestured for his companions to sit, then took his own place at the opposite end of the table from Ipille. "I'd wager on my own companion in a fight."

"Would you? My spies tell me she's an untrained apprentice."

His spies? The royal arrogance showing through. I know he has spies in my army, of course. But for him to admit so is... obscene. "Did they tell you that she cooked the whole of one of your brigades?" Out of the corner of his eye Tamas saw Nila sit up a little straighter, trying to look regal. She was a striking young woman—though the redness on her cheeks marred the image a bit. A little skill and confidence, and she would dominate this kind of negotiation. Bo hadn't sent her as a rebellious insult, Tamas realized, he'd sent her to learn.

"And fainted afterward!" Ipille made a dismissive gesture. "Auxiliaries. I can always get more men. I imagine you're running out. Isn't that right, Lady Winceslav?"

Lady Winceslav gave the king a tight smile and flicked open

a fan, fanning herself gently. "War is equally unkind to all, Your Majesty."

"But especially to those with the fewest troops. Now Tamas, are we going to sit here making veiled insults and threats, or shall we treat together?"

"You have an offer?"

Ipille nodded to Regalish, and the adviser stood, clearing his throat. "This war is costing both our countries millions. By the grace of our lord Kresimir and Ipille II, king of Kez, we extend terms of peace." He paused to clear his throat again. "We will withdraw our forces to Budwiel and the city will be ceded voluntarily to Kez control. Kez will acknowledge the autonomy of the Adran nation, and in exchange will be paid the sum of one hundred million krana as reparations."

Regalish continued for another five minutes on the particulars of their offer, consulting an official-looking document twice on some minor detail. When he'd finished, he cleared his throat once more and returned to his seat.

Tamas put one elbow on the table, resting his chin on his palm, and raised one eyebrow at Ipille.

"You're very amusing people," Lady Winceslav commented.

"You have no chance of winning, Tamas," Ipille rumbled. "I can afford the losses of the past six months. They are a drop in the bucket to our population. You cannot. If nothing else, we will win by attrition."

"Your men have told you that you're now at war with Deliv, correct? The late Duke Nikslaus made a grave error by attacking Alvation with the intention of blaming Adro, and I understand they've invaded you from the north while also sending some sixty thousand reinforcements, which will arrive in just a few days. And *they* still have an entire royal cabal."

Ipille's expression gave nothing away. Regalish leaned close to him to whisper in his ear.

"Where is your one-eyed god, king?" Taniel said suddenly, his voice cutting through Regalish's whispers. "Where are your mighty Privileged and your great armies? Where are your spies and your traitors bought with gold and religion?"

Ipille brushed Regalish aside. "You wish to match yourself against me, boy? You fancy yourself a god-killer? Tell me, did you piss yourself when you looked Kresimir in the face?"

"No. I shot him in the eye."

"Kresimir lives yet."

"Resting peacefully, I'm sure," Taniel sneered.

Tamas flinched. *Watch yourself, Taniel*, he thought. *He only goads you on so you will tell him our secrets.* "That's enough, Major," Tamas said, hating the smug smile in the corner of Ipille's mouth. He removed a paper from his pocket and unfolded it.

"We're prepared to offer generous terms of our own. You will withdraw from Adro completely, relinquishing all your false claims and recognizing our republic with the Nine as witness. You will grant us ten thousand acres of the Amber Expanse. You will agree to a hundred years of peace, again witnessed by every country in the Nine, and you will return every prisoner of war and grant us hostages to guarantee your agreement."

"And in return?"

"I won't slaughter your army like a herd of mad cattle."

Regalish was on his feet again. "You go too far!"

"Sit down, you snake. I treat with your king, not his dogs. In addition to all this, you will hand over Kresimir."

"Kresimir is off the table," Ipille said.

"More like under it," Taniel murmured.

Tamas gestured his son to silence. "Those are our terms."

"Such generosity," Ipille grunted. "Shall I give you my firstborn as well?"

"I already have Beon, though I suppose he's only the thirdborn."

The Kez Privileged swallowed a laugh and received a glare from

Ipille. "Shall I cut off my leg for you, Tamas?" Ipille continued. "Grant you a dukedom? You ask too much."

"Those are our terms," Tamas said.

"And they are intractable?"

"Well. This *is* a negotiation."

The Kez delegation huddled on their side of the room and Tamas took his own advisers close to the chapel doors for privacy.

"You're a terrible negotiator," Lady Winceslav said quietly. " 'This *is* a negotiation?' " she mimicked. "You might as well tell him you'll give up ground."

"I've lost patience in my old age."

"We did not agree on the bit about Kresimir."

"Taniel already let slip that we know Kresimir is comatose," Tamas said with a scathing glance at his son. "And besides, we can take whatever guarantees we want from the Kez. If Kresimir manages to come around, he will destroy us regardless of Kez promises."

"Then what good will having him in our possession do?"

"Our deaths will be that much quicker," Olem suggested.

Tamas glared at his bodyguard. "We can discover how to contain him. Or kill him."

"He won't budge on Kresimir," Nila said. The young woman's voice surprised Tamas.

"Are you skilled in statecraft, young Privileged?" Tamas asked, his irritation leaking through. His side had started to throb, and the conviction with which he'd started the day was waning. Politics was supposed to be an old man's game, yet it wearied Tamas more than war. He preferred the energy and decisiveness of battle to the machinations of bloated monarchs and their council.

"I agree with her," Taniel said.

Of course. "Right. On their demands?"

"We won't pay them a cent," Lady Winceslav said.

"And it's unacceptable that we give them any of our land." Nila again.

"Of course, of course."

The haggling went on through the afternoon. The Kez made offers, and Tamas countered with his own, only to be rejected. The back-and-forth continued for hours, and they retired for lunch and then dinner provided by retainers from their respective camps.

It was two hours after nightfall when they agreed to conclude for the day and meet again in three days' time.

"I must consult with my advisers at greater length," Ipille said. "And discuss the best interests of my people."

"Because you care so highly for their lives and well-being?" Tamas asked.

Ipille gave Tamas a shallow smile. "The crown is a heavy burden to wear."

A little later, Tamas mounted his horse and prepared to ride.

"Shall we make camp nearby tonight?" Olem asked.

Tamas shook his head. "I'd rather be back with the army."

"That's eight miles from here."

Tamas looked first to Winceslav, then to Taniel, and then to Nila. "Your preferences?"

"I'll ride ahead if you camp," Taniel said.

"And I prefer not to be caught out with the Kez royal guard on the prowl," said Lady Winceslav.

It was long past midnight when they neared the Adran camp, and Tamas sagged in his saddle. His side hurt and his head felt like a millstone. These negotiations would be drawn out and exhausting. Their only advantage lay in the fact that Ipille would want to finish them before the Deliv army arrived to tip the scales. Deliv would demand to participate in the negotiations from there on out and it would go worse for the Kez.

Tamas was surprised at how high Taniel rode in his saddle. Eager to get back to his lover, no doubt, and maybe farther from the man who was ultimately responsible for his mother's death. Tamas himself had suppressed thoughts of Erika all day lest he reach across the table and finish the job he'd started with his fingers around Ipille's throat so many years ago. It had been tiring.

"Sir," Olem said, breaking in to Tamas's thoughts. "Something's wrong."

Tamas shook his head to rattle away the sleep. "What is it?"

Olem pointed toward the north. The campfires burned on the horizon and the sky, lit by the cloudless moonlight, hung heavy with smoke.

Too much flame and smoke to be cook fires. And there, on the wind—screams?

"Taniel, wait!" Tamas shouted. But Taniel was already well ahead of them, off at a gallop.

CHAPTER
22

Taniel entered the Adran camp at a full gallop, hurtling past soldiers and camp followers.

The night was full of panicked shouts, punctuated by the screams of the wounded, and the chill air choked with smoke. The flames he had seen from a distance turned out to be fires jumping from tent to tent, burning the trampled grasses and catching everything they could along the way. He passed several bucket brigades working from the nearest streams and soon found himself in a haze of thick smoke near the Eleventh Brigade.

Where his and Ka-poel's tent had been.

He left his horse with the closest soldier and ran deeper into the chaos. Men milled about, faces obscured by blood and ashes. Taniel grabbed one of them.

"What happened?"

"Surprise attack," the man shouted, pulling aside the handkerchief covering his mouth. "They came from the west, at least a dozen Privileged and five thousand men!"

"Who?"

"Kez!"

Taniel shoved the man aside and stumbled toward where he thought his tent had been. Five thousand men? A dozen Privileged? The Kez had no Privileged left of any power, and how could they possibly have gotten close enough to launch a surprise attack? The smoke muddled his senses and the darkness disoriented him. The tents in this area were all gone, all burned to cinders. He plowed onward, knowing he'd have to trust to luck as much as memory to find Ka-poel.

He caught sight of a prone figure in the grass. It wore Adran blues and lay unmoving with a rifle a handbreadth from its outstretched fingers. He spotted another body in the gloom, and then another. All Adran. Some of them were little more than charred skeletons, while others looked as if they'd fallen asleep.

Taniel's head began to pound, and he pulled his shirt up over his nose and mouth to protect him from the smoke. His eyes watered terribly. He opened his third eye and, to his horror, found the world drenched in pastels. Sorcery for certain, then.

Perhaps these pastels were just a sign of Bo fighting back? Taniel dismissed that hope. Not even Bo could unleash this much of the Else in a fight. The colors were everywhere, running parallel to the fire in the grass and splattered across the bodies of the Adran soldiers like paint thrown from a bucket.

Where *was* Bo? Where was Ka-poel? Panic set in and Taniel found himself breathing heavily. He nabbed an Adran soldier by the arm. "Bo?"

The man shook his head.

"Where's Privileged Borbador?"

"I don't know, sir."

As Taniel went on, he found more smoldering bodies strewn

haphazardly about the camp as if the area had been shelled by enemy artillery. Taniel counted more and more dead Kez, and found where the Adran soldiers had put up a valiant resistance. Fifty men, all in a line, their corpses charred beyond recognition and only discernible as Adran by the remnants of the Hrusch rifles clutched in their hands.

"Bo! Ka-poel!"

Taniel tripped and bashed his knee, barely noticing the ashes that blackened his new uniform. He pushed himself up and limped onward, shouting for Ka-poel and Bo. Rescuers soon joined him, putting out any embers and checking bodies.

"Have you seen Privileged Borbador? Or the savage Bone-eye?"

Each soldier shook his head.

Taniel staggered drunkenly through the pandemonium that engulfed the Adran camp. Soldiers pushed past him, and someone collided with his shoulder, nearly knocking him off his feet. He stumbled on, mind in a daze, until he found his father with the Third Brigade, trying to make sense of the chaos.

"Get those fires out!" Tamas shouted. "Olem, I need casualty reports. Who the bloody pit attacked us? How many were there?"

"Kez," Taniel said. "I saw the bodies. There's sorcery marks everywhere. There were at least a few Privileged. Somebody said a dozen Privileged and five thousand men."

Tamas responded, "The damage is bad, but it isn't nearly that bad. Bloody pit. I thought the Kez didn't have any Privileged left. Olem!"

"Yes sir, on it, sir!"

"I can't find Ka-poel," Taniel said.

Tamas whirled. "Olem! Find Ka-poel. I want a dozen men looking for her. Taniel, where's Bo?"

"I can't find him either." Taniel tried to push down the panic that threatened to overwhelm him. His breath came short and his stomach was twisted in a knot of fear. He could still see the pastels of sorcery in the Else floating before his vision and he remembered leaving for the parley at Tamas's insistence. Bo had mussed Ka-poel's hair playfully. "I'll keep an eye on little sister," Bo had said. "Go play politician."

Taniel couldn't stop hyperventilating. His chest felt tight. Beyond Tamas, Bo and Ka-poel were all he had left in this world. To lose them both at once...

"Taniel," Tamas said, putting a hand on Taniel's shoulders even as he kept barking orders to his men. "We'll find her."

"If she's dead, I'll—I don't know. I can't...Bo. She has to be with Bo."

"If she's dead, then we have bigger problems," Tamas said, his voice steady. "If Kresimir escapes whatever enchantment she has him under, we're all dead men."

Taniel grabbed Tamas by the lapels and jerked him around, pulling him close until Tamas's startled visage was just a few inches from his face. "Ka-poel matters more than that bloody god!"

Tamas slapped him across the face, a distant stinging in Taniel's panicked world. "Get ahold of yourself, boy!"

Taniel took a step forward, blinded by rage. He raised one fist, but he and Tamas were suddenly pushed apart.

Bo's apprentice shoved her way between them. "Both of you, stop it!" she said. "Find Ka-poel! Find Bo! We're on the same side!" Her face was a mask of fury and she managed to loom despite being a head shorter than either of them. "Can't you see enough blood has been shed tonight?"

"Get your—" Tamas growled, but his threats were cut short as Nila pointed a finger at him and both her arms were suddenly wreathed in flame. She pointed her other finger at Taniel and looked between them, wide-eyed and wild, as angry as a lioness.

"Kresimir help me, I will set your boots on fire if you don't get your heads together," she snapped.

"Sir!" someone called from out in the darkness. "We've found Privileged Borbador! Come quickly!"

Nila had no time to reflect on the fact that she had just stepped between two of the strongest, most deadly powder mages in the world. She had no time to think of her fire or her anger. Even the men who followed upon her heels barely touched upon her mind.

Bo could be dead.

Once Tamas and Taniel had been pulled apart, a soldier led them all through the smoke and gloom, torch held over his head. Nila stumbled as she ran, her trembling hands betraying her. The burned grass quickly gave way and clods of dirt fouled her already uncertain step. The torchlight played upon the smoke and then upon immense shapes reaching into the night.

Tamas was called away, and he told them to go on ahead and find Bo, then took off at a run after a messenger.

The smoke began to recede and the smell of soil suddenly filled her nostrils as if she had stumbled into a damp root cellar. They stood among immense mounds of mud, scooped from the ground as if with a spade the size of a house. She did not open her third eye—she dared not, for fear of being overwhelmed. She didn't need to. She could sense the sorcery still hanging in the air. Potent sorceries had tilled the ground as easily as a plow might turn a field, and the prospect terrified Nila.

Earth Privileged, Bo had called them. Capable of manipulating solid elements and shaping the very landscape.

Nila was shoved aside as Taniel barreled past her. "Bo? Where is he, damn it? Bo!"

Could he not sense the power that had been unleashed here? To Nila it was as if the ground might close around her at any moment—a trap waiting to be sprung by the unwary. She steadied herself against one of the mounds of earth, trying to catch her breath. Her entire body shook from fear.

"Bo!"

Taniel's certain call drew Nila from within herself and she was running forward before her own fear could stop her once more.

Bo lay half-buried in the dirt. Black rods, each as thick as a man's wrist and three to four feet tall, peppered the ground around him like a small forest, rammed into the ground at an angle, and with what appeared to be great force. The stench of spent sorcery was so thick Nila could barely approach, and the rods steamed in the chill night air.

"Don't touch those!" Bo's shrill, frantic warning came just a moment too late. One unfortunate soldier grasped a rod with both hands and leapt back with a howl, leaving several layers of charred skin on the rod. "Damn it," Bo said weakly. His body trembled and sweat poured down his face. "They're bloody enchanted. Fire and earth, woven together to keep them hot. I don't know how long it'll last, but I'm getting bloody hot in here."

The rods were clustered closely around Bo like a palisade, leaving him trapped and unable to move. She took a torch from one of the soldiers and held it out over Bo to confirm her suspicions. Blood streaked his hands, his Privileged gloves nothing more than shredded ribbons.

"The rods," Nila shouted. "We have to get them out! He can't do it himself. Bring horses and chains."

No one moved and Taniel whirled on the soldiers. "You heard the Privileged. Go!"

Nila ignored them and edged closer to the rods, flinching from the heat. "Breathe, Bo, breathe! Stay with me. Is there anything I can do?"

Bo made a soft mewling sound, then said, "Just hurry with the horses."

"What happened?" Taniel asked. "Where is Ka-poel?"

"Oh, I'm sorry. I thought it was pretty obvious we were bloody well *attacked*!" Bo's voice rose to a crescendo at the end of the sentence.

"Can you move your hands?" Nila asked.

"Barely. Whoever that was, she did a number on me."

"I should have been here."

"You would have been killed."

"Bring a doctor," Taniel shouted. "Where are those horses? You there, get shovels. Dig on that side of the slope. We can try to undermine the rods."

Nila hated that she couldn't do anything. She had no knowledge of air or earth sorcery, the two kinds that would allow her to remove the lances herself. She counted seven of them and tried to focus on the sorcery that caused the heat. She nudged it with her senses, agonizing on the thought that, had she better knowledge of powers, she might be able to at least pick apart the wards. "How long are these rods?"

"I didn't see, as that bitch was ramming them through me," Bo said. "I was too busy trying to kill her back. Kresimir, that hurts and"—he lifted his head toward the men digging downhill from him—"Stop that! The shifting dirt is grinding that thing against me and it hurts like bloody pit."

"One of them's touching you?" Nila asked.

"Uh, yeah. That one down there." Bo waggled his chin. His face was red from the heat. Blood and sweat streamed down his face. "You know, right about where my knee used to be."

Nila suddenly felt sick to her stomach. She had thought that the rods were merely meant to immobilize him, that none of them had actually hit him. But his lower body was buried, obscuring the position of his legs...

"Where are the horses?" Taniel demanded. "Faster now, boys! These damn things are killing him."

"They're not killing me." Bo coughed, flecks of blood on his lips. "They're cooking me. Fine distinction." The quip had no energy.

Nila reached between the rods to touch his hand. She felt his fingers curl around hers. "If I can get your spare gloves onto your hands, will you be able to free yourself?"

"I'm knackered out, and I think a couple of the fingers on my left hand are broken. I couldn't reach into the Else to save myself," Bo said, the sentence ending in a gasp as the rod at his knee suddenly shifted.

"Stop digging!" Taniel bellowed.

Nila heard the jangle of harnesses and chains. "They've got the horses," she whispered to Bo. "You'll be free soon."

Horses were backed into place, chains attached to their harnesses and the chains wrapped around the hot lances. The first was pulled out, with only a few pained squeals from Bo. The second and Nila was able to move closer to him. She leaned in and used her sleeve to wipe the grime from Bo's brow.

He suddenly smiled at her. "How did the parley go?"

"What?"

"The parley? Isn't that where you were?"

"He's in shock," Taniel said. "Where are the damned doctors?"

"Fine, fine," Nila reassured Bo. "You should have been there."

"Had to protect little sister," Bo said. He looked at Taniel and his eyes seemed unfocused. "Did I? Where is she?"

"I don't know!" Taniel said.

"They came for her. That much was obvious. Cut their way through the brigade. She stabbed one of their grenadiers in the eye with her needle. Damn, that girl has spirit."

Another of the lances was jerked out by the horses. The ground shifted and Bo, along with the four lances still surrounding him, slid several inches.

"Who came for her? The Kez?" Taniel demanded. Nila wanted to tell him to back off, but Bo's eyes were now focused, his confusion gone, and he gave a short nod. "Didn't recognize any of their Privileged. Well, I didn't get a good look at the one who stuck me, but her aura seemed familiar. Nothing I can place now. Killed another of them. I think there were two more. The one I killed should be over there somewhere." He made a vague gesture. "Strong lot. I thought you told me all the Kez Privileged were dead."

"They were supposed to be," Taniel growled. "Look, Bo, hang in there. I have to go find Tamas. We have to make sense of what happened."

"Go at it, chap," Bo said, swinging weakly for Taniel's chin with his fist and missing.

Taniel was up and gone a moment later. A fourth lance was now out, and soldiers had managed to dig the dirt from around Bo's legs. He lay on an incline in the dirt, head back, looking almost peaceful. Nila dared a look at his knee.

It was completely destroyed. The lance had gone through flesh and bone like a knife through butter. His pants from the thigh down were cooked away and the flesh of his lower thigh and knee was black and cooked. The smell reminded her of the battlefield when she'd killed all of those soldiers, but Nila forced that out of her mind. She couldn't panic. Not now.

"Is he dead?" a soldier asked.

"No, he's not dead," Nila said, feeling her heart leap. He wasn't, was he? "Bo?"

"Yeah, I'm here." Bo's head came up suddenly. "Any of those damned engineers coming to help?"

"They're still putting fires out," a soldier said.

"Oh. Oh, I see. I'll just lie here and feel myself cook then. Tell them not to rush."

"The horses are doing the trick," Nila said.

"They won't for the one in my leg," Bo said. "That one will be difficult. They'll need levers and math and all sorts of things."

"Go get the engineers," Nila told a pair of corporals. "Now!" When they had gone, she returned to Bo's side. "Bo. Bo? Stay with me!"

"I'm just resting my eyes."

She crouched down beside him and sighed. "Please don't die."

"Not planning on it."

"I don't think most people plan on it."

Bo seemed to consider this. "You are wise beyond your years."

"Shut up."

"All right." He was quiet for a moment, then said pitifully, "This really hurts."

Nila leaned forward and peered at Bo's knee again. She held up one hand and brought fire from the Else to give herself light. The lance was still hot, and his flesh was cracked and cooked like meat that had been roasted over a flame for hours too long. Bo groaned as the soldiers and their horses removed the fifth lance.

"It doesn't hurt as bad as you'd think," Bo said. "After all, the nerves are all dead. But I can feel the heat of it still. Feel it slowly cooking. Pit, I'll be lucky to ever use this leg again."

Lucky? Nila had no experience with battlefield surgery, but as far as she could tell that leg was gone. "We'll get you a healer."

"It'll be a rough job."

"We'll get you the best."

"If you insist. Just tell them to leave a blackened scar. It's more roguish that way. And a pit of a conversation starter."

"Hush, now," Nila said.

"Look, if I stop talking, I'll probably start crying. And I make it a point never to cry in front of women. Especially ones I hope to bed someday."

"Is that so?" Nila climbed to her feet.

"Yes. Makes me look weak. Women can sense weakness. Oh, sure, some women say they want a sensitive man. But no one ever says they want a weak man."

There were just two lances left. The sixth would come out easily enough, but like Bo said, that seventh would be tricky. It couldn't just be dragged out at an angle by a team of horses. It might rip his leg off completely, and the shock might kill him. It had to be pulled up and out, as straight as possible. She looked it over carefully. She had no idea as to the material—some kind of metal, by the looks of it—but sorcery emanated from the thing. Earth sorcery, no doubt. With fire to make it hot, and air to throw it.

Bo kept talking to no one in particular. "By Kresimir, this'll be a conversation starter. I can imagine it now. Some fop in last year's fashion sitting in the tavern, showing a gaggle of women some scar and telling them he got it from a knife fight with a man twice his size. And then, Bam! I lift my pant leg and show them how the strongest Privileged I'd ever seen blasted a lance of sorcery-hewn metal through my kneecap."

"You'll leave out the crying part?"

"I'm not crying, I... What the pit are you doing?"

Nila ignited the fire around her hands. It came as easily as a thought and a twitch of her fingers, and she didn't have time to wonder at that. She tapped the lance hesitantly. When it didn't burn her, she grasped it with both hands, set her foot on the ground beside Bo's leg, and pulled.

His scream almost made her lose her nerve, but she pulled harder, sliding the pole out of his knee like a needle through cloth. It came loose with a jerk and she fell backward, lance in hand, then tossed it away before she hit herself in the face with it.

Bo's body spasmed as he was wracked with sobs. He jerked and screamed, curling on his side and clutching at his blackened ruin of a leg. She threw herself to the ground beside him and took him by the hand. "I'm sorry, I'm sorry! It's out now!"

He wept uncontrollably for a few moments. "All right," he said between sobs. "I'll leave out the crying." And he sagged against her.

Nila checked his pulse with one hand and then let herself slump beside him. He was still alive.

Guilt began to crowd her thoughts. Perhaps if she'd been here, she could have helped. She could have turned that Privileged into a lump of charcoal and... and who was she kidding? She was an apprentice. She would have been killed outright. Bo was very powerful, clever, and trained, and he had only barely survived the battle.

Where were the damned doctors? Wasn't Taniel sending help? Where was he now? Probably going after his savage girl. After all the worry Bo had showed for him, Taniel couldn't just stay here to comfort his friend who might be dying?

She looked down at Bo. He gave out a light whimper when she moved his arm out of the way of the wound. She could *see through his kneecap.*

Her stomach turned at the sight of it. Would he ever be able to walk again? She'd heard of healers who'd regrown whole limbs, but those had just been stories. This kind of damage seemed beyond what anyone could heal, no matter their skill.

She remembered rubbing her fingers together frantically at the Battle of Ned's Creek and hoping and praying for the right combination of sorcery to bring down those men.

And it had worked. She'd killed thousands with a gesture.

Like from the stories.

Bo said that healers were very rare. That they took great skill. But maybe...maybe she could be something other than a killer.

Nila bit her lip and wiggled her thumb. The aether. That's what she needed. She reached out for the Else.

"What the bloody pit do you think you're doing?" Bo batted her outstretched hand weakly to one side. "Are you trying to kill me?"

"I didn't do anything."

"I felt you reaching out for it. Are you mad? I...oh, pit, this hurts. I don't know what's in your head."

"I thought that maybe I could just..." She shrugged.

"You could just heal me? You're bloody mad, woman, and I'll have no talk of that. Remember that the aether is a refined matter that creates and breaks bonds. You're just as likely to make every particle of my body explode as you are to heal me." Bo grimaced and let out a long whimper. "Now, promise me you won't ever try to experiment like that on me. Ever."

"I promise," Nila said, feeling like a scolded schoolgirl.

"Good." Bo let his head fall against the mud.

The crew with the horses moved off, leaving the final lance sticking from the ground, now that Bo was fully free. Three men came out of the night bearing torches. Two were the soldiers who had helped dig Bo out, and the third was a doctor.

"The engineers are coming now," one of the soldiers said.

"Never mind the engineers," Nila told him. "Just help him."

"We need to move him out of this," the doctor said. "Get him to a clean tent and bring me hot and cold water and my instruments."

The soldiers lifted Bo onto a canvas stretcher. Nila walked beside him, holding him by the hand as they moved out of the blasted battlefield. They were nearly out of the swath of destruction when Field Marshal Tamas emerged from the darkness.

"Bo, are you all right?"

Bo eyed Tamas as a man would eye a meal after having just thrown up. His face was scrunched in pain, but his eyes were clear. "I've had better days."

"They've taken Ka-poel. And her package."

"Ah, pit," Bo sighed.

Nila frowned. She didn't know what that meant, but what little color Bo had left in his cheeks was gone.

Tamas said, "We're going back to war. Ipille called us to a truce and then blindsided us. I've had runners just now that our allies are ahead of schedule. The Seventh and the Ninth will be here soon and the Deliv are just behind them. We're marching south first thing in the morning and we're going to throw the Kez from our borders. I mean to destroy Ipille fully for this treachery."

"Sounds good. And Taniel?"

"He wants to—he *must* go after Ka-poel. If they know what she's carrying, we're all dead men."

"Bo, what is he talking about?" Nila asked.

Tamas looked at her. His body sagged from exhaustion and his face was creased with lines of worry and fear. "Not something to discuss in the open, my dear."

Nila seethed. What did he mean by that? Did he not trust her? Did he not trust Bo? She felt Bo's hand on her arm and he whispered, "I'll tell you later." He let out a hiss and suddenly writhed in her arms.

"I'll give you mala for the pain," the doctor said, searching his bag.

"Do you see this?" Bo thrust a finger at his charred leg. "I'm not smoking anything!"

"You're in shock."

"I'm cooking, that's what I am. Get me whiskey. Lots of it."

The doctor looked to Nila as if for some kind of confirmation. Not knowing what else to do, she nodded.

"The Deliv healers will be here within a couple of days," Tamas said. His face was impassive.

"I don't think he should wait that long."

"Get a carriage," Tamas snapped to one of his men. "We'll send him to them."

"I'm going with him," Nila said.

Bo gave Tamas a sudden, wolfish grin. "Get me patched up and me and Tan will go after the savage."

"You're going to the Deliv army," Tamas said sternly. "Taniel has already left. Olem is gathering a squad to send after him. And you, my dear"—he turned his eye toward Nila—"you're staying here."

"What do you mean? I'm not leaving Bo alone."

"He's a grown man." Nila didn't like the dangerous glint in Tamas's eye. "You," he continued, "I'm going to unleash on the Kez."

CHAPTER

23

Taniel rode alone into the night.

He urged his mount as hard as he dared—the horse would have to carry him for as long as it took to catch up with Ka-poel's captors and he couldn't risk riding it into the ground. He stopped frequently for water and once to give the horse long enough to eat. The eastern sky began to grow from black to blue, heralding the morning.

He carried two rifles, four powder horns, three pistols, and enough provisions for two weeks.

The Kez had a seven-hour head start on him, taking the road northwest toward the Black Tar Forest. It was a curious direction, as their main force was to the south, but Taniel thought that they would follow the road into the forest and then turn south, thus avoiding the bulk of Tamas's army that camped on the plain.

Catching them wouldn't be easy. They had planned for this,

after all—a dash into the camp with less than two hundred grenadiers but four Privileged, torching everything in their way until they reached Ka-poel and then immediately retreating. They would have a nearby camp, including spare horses and maybe even more men.

The chain of command left in charge of the Adran forces was still in some confusion after Hilanska's betrayal, and they had not mounted an immediate expedition. Nor should they have. Without powder mages their men would have been torn apart.

And now the Kez would be fleeing with the fear of god in them, knowing that Field Marshal Tamas and his mages would be on their heels.

The sky grew light as Taniel continued on, sleep held at bay with the low buzz of a distant powder trance. The terrain grew more jagged as he neared the mountains, the air warmer as dawn approached, and he worried for his weary horse. He stopped at a farm just off the main road, where a sleepy farmer confirmed that he'd heard a large company of men on horseback pass in the middle of the night.

Despite the reassurance he was on their trail, Taniel began to worry more with every mile. Was Ka-poel even still alive? If they knew about her and about Kresimir, why wouldn't they have killed her outright? *How* did they know about her? What was he going to do once he caught up with them?

The doubt began to work its way deep and to spread. There were too many of them. Even after the damage Bo did to their party—it was doubtless a surprise for them to find a Privileged in the Adran camp—they still had at least three Privileged and fifty men. One Privileged and a squad or two, Taniel could handle. Pit, he could take two Privileged. But three was too many.

It was made all the worse by the knowledge that he'd left his best friend to die alone. No one could survive that kind of damage, not even a powder mage. Bo may be hardier than most Privileged, but he would be dead within a day or two, and Taniel hadn't even said good-bye. He had left in a panic to try to retrieve Ka-poel and he knew he'd regret it for the rest of his life.

He forced the thought out of his mind. There was nothing he could do about it now. He had to save Ka-poel.

Tamas said he would send help, but Taniel knew whoever Tamas sent would move too slowly.

Taniel rode across the farmlands of Adro for another hour before the sun finally rose over the Adsea behind him, illuminating the Charwood Pile Mountains ahead and the Black Tar Forest, which spread out at the mountains' base. At the top of a particularly high rise, he sniffed a pinch of powder and squinted across the fields.

Something moved in the distance.

He took another sniff to sharpen his eyes, increasing the strength of the trance. He could make out a trail of dust from a large group of riders off in the distance. They were at least fifteen miles away and they would be inside the forest within an hour.

He was curious why they had not tried to cut across the plains, but decided that his initial suspicion was correct. Once within the forest, they would turn south at the Counter's Road, taking them to Surkov's Alley and the protection of the Kez army. They would be inside of Kez-held lands within two days, even taking this roundabout way.

Taniel considered cutting across the farmlands to the southwest himself. But there was no good way to do it. Trying to navigate the forest would slow him down and he might miss them entirely. Far better to come up from behind and pick them off one by one from a distance. But even then, could he do it quickly enough before they reached the main army?

He felt the weight of despair in his stomach like lead shot. He wasn't going to be able to get her back. They would kill her and free Kresimir, and then Adro would fall. Mihali—Adom—wasn't here to protect them anymore.

A movement a few miles off caught his eye. He blinked several times to let his eyes refocus, and scanned the horizon. He saw just an old farmstead. Short, with stone walls and a thatched roof. He likely saw the farmer making his morning rounds. Nothing to get excited about.

Taniel was just about to dismiss the farmstead entirely when something new caught his eye. Near the edge of the farmhouse, he made out a uniform of green-on-tan, with a tall black cap with red accents. The man was crouched by the side of the building, staring straight toward Taniel. Without a powder trance, it was unlikely he could even see Taniel.

An ambush. How many men, Taniel couldn't say. He would guess at least a dozen. He opened his third eye and looked again, but was unable to see any sign of a Privileged anywhere near the farmstead. Did they have air rifles? He wished he had asked about that before he left the Adran camp.

Taniel would need to get closer to find out.

He threw his bedroll down and caught an hour of sleep before he continued on, knowing it was his last chance at rest in the near future. Back in the saddle, he crossed the distance of a little over three miles at a trot so that the sun would be just over his shoulder as he approached.

When he was a half mile away, he checked with his third eye again. No Privileged and no Knacked. But these men would be grenadiers—as with Adran grenadiers, they would be bigger, stronger, and better trained than the average soldier.

At a quarter mile, Taniel slid from his saddle and staked out his horse so he could approach on foot. He put two pistols into his belt, fixing the bayonet onto his rifle and holding it across his chest.

He reached out with his senses, looking for powder, and he found it quickly. Powder horns, charges, loaded weapons. He sorted the information in his mind, assessing the arsenal of each man, and guessed there were six grenadiers.

A piss-poor ambush. Likely just meant to slow down pursuers, not stop them entirely.

Either way, these six were not ready for a powder mage. They were in for a damned big surprise...unless one of them had an air rifle. Then *Taniel* was in for a surprise. But nothing he could do for that.

He could sense the first grenadier behind a haystack a hundred and fifty yards away. Taniel took a deep breath, set his rifle to his shoulder, and pulled the trigger. He burned a little powder behind the bullet to make sure it went through the haystack. The crack of his rifle was quickly followed by a scream.

Two grenadiers immediately came around the corner of the farmhouse. Their muskets cracked and powder smoke rose over their heads, but they weren't going to hit anything at this distance. Taniel had already rammed a bullet down the end of his rifle, sans powder, and lifted it to his shoulder. He burned a powder charge in one pocket to propel the bullet and took one of the grenadiers through the eye. The second threw himself back behind the house.

Taniel broke into a sprint toward the farmhouse. He rolled as a grenadier appeared from a nearby ditch. The man's musket belched smoke and Taniel heard the bullet whiz by. Too far to ignite the man's powder, but close enough...

He let go of his rifle as he came out of his roll and drew a pistol. He fired, adjusting the trajectory of the bullet with his mind in the fraction of a second it took to cross the distance and lance the man's heart. The grenadier fell.

Three down, three to go. Taniel's heart sang as he moved, blood pounding in his ears, feeling the rhythm of the battle. A bullet skipped off the ground beside his foot, and he looked to see the grenadier hidden on the roof of the farmhouse. Taniel hesitated between reloading his rifle and drawing his second pistol and decided instead to finish his sprint toward the cover of the house.

Another grenadier rounded the corner of the farmhouse just as Taniel reached it. The soldier raised his musket.

Taniel ignited the grenadier's powder horn and used his mind to warp the blast away from himself.

A slight movement above him was his only warning as the grenadier from the roof leapt down, knife drawn.

Taniel caught the grenadier's knife thrust with the stock of his rifle. He shoved, trying to push him away in order to thrust with his bayonet, but the grenadier grasped the musket with one hand and stabbed again. Taniel was only able to avoid the thrust by throwing himself against the stone wall of the farmhouse.

The grenadier followed through, his face furrowed in anger as he caught Taniel's bayonet under one boot and bent for another jab. Taniel let go of his rifle and snatched the grenadier's wrist, slamming his opposite fist into the man's knee.

The grenadier screamed. Taniel wrenched on his wrist, pulling him down to the ground, and rolled on top of him. He had the grenadier's knife now, and he wrapped one hand around the hilt and slammed it into the grenadier's face.

"Where's Ka-poel? The savage girl! What have you done with her?" Taniel waited a moment, then punched him again. "Tell me!" Why was he doing this? He already knew. What could this bastard possibly tell him? Taniel drew his second pistol and pressed it against the grenadier's forehead. "Is she still alive? Tell me now!"

The grenadier spit blood in his face.

Taniel felt the pistol jerk in his hand, the crack of the blast in his ears, and the grenadier's body beneath him stiffened then sagged. Slowly, he climbed to his feet and tossed the spent pistol aside.

He'd wanted answers. He'd wanted to hear his fears confirmed.

Taniel looked to one side as the sixth and final grenadier came out of his hiding place and advanced, musket leveled. Taniel took a deep breath. Shit. In his excitement, he forgot about the last one.

Too far to ignite the grenadier's powder, and too close for the grenadier to miss him.

A stupid mistake, and it had just gotten him killed.

Taniel flinched away as the grenadier jerked to one side and fell. His musket landed on the hard-packed road with a clatter, and blood seeped from his head to pool on the ground. Taniel took a shaky breath and squinted into the sun, but couldn't make out anything in the glare. His backup must have arrived. No one else was close enough to make that kind of a shot. He would have sensed them.

Tamas must have sent another powder mage. But who? Had the rest of the cabal caught up to Tamas? Had Tamas himself come? Taniel felt some dread in the pit of his stomach, because he thought he knew who it might be.

No use staring into the sun, trying to see who had shot the grenadier. Taniel checked the bodies more closely and found each of the grenadiers dead or very near so. His knife finished the job on two of them. No sense in letting men suffer, and they weren't going to answer questions in their state.

He finished his inspection, checking for other grenadiers he might have missed, and gathered and reloaded his weapons, then walked toward where he'd left his horse. He was just climbing into the saddle as the rest of his hunting party crested the nearest rise. He bent over his saddle, eyes closed, resting as he waited for them to catch up.

"What are you doing here, Captain?" he asked when he heard their hoofbeats come to a stop nearby. He opened his eyes.

Vlora reined in her mount and signaled for the others to stop. "It's 'Colonel,' actually."

"That's quite a promotion." Taniel had known, of course. And she knew he knew. He had called her "Captain" out of spite.

Vlora's cheeks flushed, but she only lifted her chin. "I'm here to help. We're going after those bastards."

"I can't give orders to a colonel," Taniel said. "And I don't think you should lead the expedition." The words came out harsher than Taniel had meant, but he had wanted them to sting. It felt like years had passed, but she'd been his fiancée less than seven months ago, when he found her in the arms of another man. Ka-poel's capture already had him on edge. He wasn't ready to deal with Vlora.

"You've been promoted as well, Colonel," she said, holding out her hand.

He took the colonel's pin and held it up to the light. "First major, then this? I don't deserve it."

"The field marshal feels otherwise. And he needs to fill spots from officer casualties, so..." She trailed off. "You're in command, Colonel."

Taniel pinned the bars to his lapel with some reluctance.

He put Vlora out of his mind to examine the rest of the group. Gavril, the Watchmaster, which was a surprise. Taniel hadn't seen him since he left the South Pike Mountainwatch to pursue Julene and the Kez cabal. In addition to Gavril there were three more powder mages, and a dozen more soldiers wearing the emblem of Olem's Riflejacks. The Seventh and Ninth must have arrived not long after Taniel left, and Tamas had sent his best men.

The despair began to melt away and Taniel felt his resolve harden.

This wasn't a hopeless cause anymore. He could—he would—get Ka-poel back.

CHAPTER
24

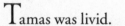amas was livid.

He guided his horse through the Adran camp at a walk, only half listening to Olem as he gave his morning report.

Ipille had betrayed him under a white flag. There were certain rules of war that Tamas found idiotic and others he found snobbish. He would openly flout such rules if it suited him, but the white flag of parley was sacrosanct. It was how peace was made, and for Ipille to have attacked Tamas's camp even while he sat in truce with Tamas was...

Tamas couldn't find words to express his anger.

The remnants of the Seventh and Ninth that had survived their march through Kez had arrived just an hour after Taniel had left. Colonel—now General, as of his arrival at the camp—Arbor had double-marched the men throughout the afternoon and much of the night to arrive far ahead of schedule. Tamas had immediately taken volunteers from among his best men and powder mages and sent them after Taniel, and now the rest of his two best brigades were sleeping off their long march as he tried to decide what to do with them.

Tamas drew up on his reins. Olem had stopped talking. "Go on," he said.

Olem immediately drew a cigarette from his pocket and clenched it with his lips. "You're doing that thing you do, sir." He produced a match and lit his cigarette.

"What thing?"

"Where you pretend you're listening but you're thinking about something else."

"I was not."

Olem puffed on his cigarette. "Whatever you say, sir."

"One of these days I'm going to have you shot for that insubordinate tone, Olem."

"Of course, sir."

"Pit, you're insufferable."

"You did make me a colonel."

"What does that have to do with anything?"

"I've met a lot of colonels, sir. They're all insufferable."

Tamas waved some cigarette smoke away from his face. "What about Arbor? He was a colonel until a few hours ago, and you always seemed to like him."

"Have you played cards with General Arbor, sir?"

"No."

"He's insufferable too. Likable, but insufferable."

"Can one be both?"

"He is."

"Pit. I don't have time for this. What were you telling me before?"

"A report on our powder stores, sir."

"Do we have enough for an extended campaign against the Kez?"

"Yes. Barely. Despite the Brudanians holding Adro, we're still getting shipments from Ricard's businesses. Even more now that General Ket isn't there to skim off the top."

"Good. Then skip the report. Anything else important this morning?"

Olem addressed the stack of notes in his hand. He flipped through them, grumbling to himself. "Beon je Ipille arrived with the Seventh and Ninth. He'd like to meet with you at your convenience."

"It can wait. If I see one of Ipille's spawn right now, I'd probably shoot him in the heart. And I actually *like* Beon. Have all of my promotions gone through?"

"Most of them," Olem said. "All senior officers will be waiting for you in your tent at eight o'clock."

Tamas checked his pocket watch. "We'd better finish this quickly, then."

"Of course, sir." Olem shuffled through his papers and cleared his throat.

"What is it?" Tamas's mind was already drifting back to Ipille. He could feel the bile in the back of his throat, and it wasn't hard to envision putting his bayonet through Ipille's prodigious gut.

"There's one more thing, sir."

"Spit it out!"

"Me, sir."

"What in the Nine are you talking about?"

Olem put his papers away in his saddlebag. "Things are a bit confusing, sir."

"You're my bodyguard, aren't you?"

"Yes sir. That's what's confusing." Olem shifted in his saddle and cleared his throat.

Tamas's patience was wearing thin. "Get to it."

"You made me a colonel. Colonels, traditionally, aren't body-guards or aides-de-camp."

Was this so important that Olem had to bring it up right this instant? Most men don't usually go from sergeant to colonel in the space of eight months, either, but Tamas had promoted Olem nonetheless because it fit his needs. "True," he said.

"I don't think I deserve to be a colonel, sir. I'd like you to demote me."

Tamas stared at Olem. "This? Again?"

"Yes sir. I don't have my own command. Keeping me a colonel but also your bodyguard and aide doesn't make sense. I don't mind the demotion at all."

"You don't mind...? Damn it, Olem. You're going to mind what I tell you to mind. You want a command? You have one now."

"Sir?"

"The Seventh is yours."

Olem's cigarette fell out of his mouth. "But sir! You were going to give the Seventh to Colonel—I mean General—Arbor."

"General Arbor has the First and the Third. They've been humiliated by Ket and Hilanska's treason and he's going to whip them into shape. You will combine the best men from the Seventh and the Ninth to form the new Seventh, which will be called the Marshal's Own Riflejack Brigade."

Olem sat up straight.

Tamas continued. "You don't have a lot of command experience, but you know people. I'll leave it to you to choose your officers. Choose them well, because you're still going to spend most of your time with me."

"Are you certain, sir?"

"Of course."

"You'll need a new bodyguard."

"No, I won't."

"Uh, sir?"

Tamas leaned over to Olem and slapped him on the shoulder. "You're still my bodyguard, and the whole damn Seventh will be too. There's no one else I trust to watch my back."

For once, Olem had no snappy comeback. "Thank you, sir. I'm honored."

"Don't be honored. Just do your job. Now, let's go meet with the senior staff. We have an offensive to plan."

Tamas met his senior officers in his command tent in the center of the camp.

Roughly twenty-five men and women had crammed inside the tent: generals and colonels from most of the brigades. More than half of the faces among them were new officers, recently promoted, and Tamas knew he still had almost a dozen promotions to make before the end of the day. The Wings of Adom brigadiers were conspicuously absent. Lady Winceslav had been true to her word and withdrawn all but a token force from the front lines.

Because of the lack of the mercenaries and the inexperience of his new officers, Tamas knew this conference couldn't wait. The officers—and their men—needed to know where they stood.

Tamas entered through a slit at the back of the tent, hiding his limp and the pain in his side as he quietly took his place at the head of the gathering. Olem was already waiting. He'd spread a few papers on Tamas's desk: casualty figures, regiment strengths, the names of new senior officers. Tamas had gone over all of that hours ago, but it would be good to have something to reference.

He stood behind his desk, hands clasped behind his back, and let his eyes rest at the entrance of the tent.

The seconds ticked by, then turned into minutes. Someone toward the back of the group cleared their throat, and Tamas listened to the shouts of a quartermaster rise over the general din of the camp.

Five minutes passed before one of the new generals raised his hand, false teeth clenched in his fist.

"Yes?" Tamas asked.

General Arbor lowered his hand. "We waiting for someone, sir?"

"We are," Tamas said. "Olem, would you see if our guest has arrived?"

Olem ducked out through the back. Several more minutes passed and Tamas could sense his officers begin to get restless. *What was this about*, he imagined them wondering. Why did he have them waiting here, standing at attention like common infantrymen, when they had work to do?

Tamas decided to let them stew. It shouldn't be longer than a few more minutes now.

Tamas wondered if his Riflejacks had managed to catch up with Taniel yet. It was an unexpected surprise that the Seventh and Ninth had arrived in the middle of the night, but a welcome one. He needed his best veterans more than ever now, and...

The sound of galloping horses cut off his thought. Shouts accompanied the sound—of surprise, but not alarm—from among the soldiers outside. Tamas could sense his senior officers getting nervous at the sound, and was glad to see some of them mimic his stony composure.

Every head in the room turned as the tent flap was swept aside. Olem stepped inside and announced, "His Lordship, King Sulem the Ninth, of Deliv."

A murmur among the officers quickly faded into silence as the Deliv king swept into the command tent. He held his plumed bicorne under one arm and wore a Kelly-green officer's dress uniform, the chest of which was caked in decorations. He was a handsome man with gray hair curled near the scalp, a strong jaw, and white teeth that seemed to shine in contrast with his ebony skin.

Tamas took a deep breath and let it out slowly to calm his nerves. The situation had changed since his last talk with Sulem, and he was not sure if Deliv support would change once they were better informed.

The Deliv king approached and gave Tamas a short nod. Tamas responded in kind, and watched as Sulem turned to survey the assembled officers.

Tamas had been curious how his officers would react to a king in their midst and was pleased to see them all give the same respectful nod as he had. Sulem may be an ally, but Tamas wanted it to be clear to him—and to the rest of the kings of the Nine—that Adrans did not bow and scrape before royalty. If anything, Sulem seemed amused. He did not, however, return their nod.

Sulem took a place beside Tamas, facing the officers.

Olem approached and leaned to whisper in Tamas's ear, "Beon is outside. He's heard an inkling of what's happened and is demanding to see you."

"Restrain him. Gently."

Olem disappeared discreetly out the back of the tent and returned a few moments later. "It's done."

Tamas cleared his throat to get his officers' attention. "Thank you for joining us, Your Majesty," Tamas said. He paused to examine his officers once more. Fine men and women, every one of them. People he could place his confidence in, who would stand beside him against the world. He felt a sudden tightness in his throat, a cloudiness to his vision, and forced himself to choke down the emotion.

"Five days ago, King Ipille of Kez sued for peace. Not a terrible surprise considering the walloping we gave his army at Ned's Creek." There was a round of chuckles, which Tamas let die down on its own. "Just yesterday I met with him to begin peace talks that would end this war once and for all. The talks went better than I had expected and I returned to camp last night optimistic for the first time in five months that the bloodshed would end.

"Optimistic until I saw the flames, that is. As you are no doubt all aware, we were attacked by a contingent of Kez Privileged and grenadiers. The Thirteenth suffered heavy casualties, as did the

Seventy-Fifth Dragoons, which tried to cut off their retreat from our camp. We..." Tamas chewed on his cheek for a moment, forcing down his rage. "Well, you all have the report on the attack. It ends with this: 'We were attacked under a white flag of parley.'"

There was an angry mutter among the officers, and Tamas continued. "This is a sin I will not forgive. This war has been one of defensive battles: Ned's Creek, Shouldercrown, Surkov's Alley, Budwiel. We have suffered betrayal and corruption. We have stood before the might of a sick and petty god. Today, my friends, my brothers and sisters, we go on the offensive."

Tamas paused to think of the foreign army that held Adro, and knew that this was just one of many offensives he would need to rally in the coming days. "Today I march to the enemy camp at Fendale. We will set upon the Kez army like a dog on a rat and we will rid this country of vermin. There will be no quarter given until every Kez cur has been driven from our borders. They have sullied our nation for long enough."

Tamas took another deep breath and clutched his trembling hands behind his back. "Do you march with me?"

A moment of silence followed, and then General Arbor's voice rang clear. "The First and the Third reporting and ready, sir."

"The Seventh is yours," Olem said.

"You have the Nineteenth," General Slarren called from the back.

More voices joined, until every one of the senior staff had given their cry of support. Finally, when the last zealous cheers had died down, King Sulem stepped forward. His gaze swept over the assembled officers and then he turned sharply toward Tamas and drew his sword.

Olem took half a step forward. Tamas's heart leapt to his throat.

Sulem took his sword by the blade and bowed low at the waist, holding the hilt toward Tamas. "You have my sword. You have my pistol. You have my Privileged and artillery. You have my sixty thousand. Our alliance will cause Ipille to quake and the Kez will pay for their crimes."

Tamas couldn't hide his amazement. He knew royalty. He had been honored by the old Iron King of Adro, as well as by the king of Novi. But he had never experienced anything like this before. Reaching out, he took Sulem's sword in hand, then held it over his head.

"I would die for my country. But I'd rather kill for it. Ready your troops. We march!"

CHAPTER

25

Adamat's carriage neared Adopest fifteen days after he'd initially set out south with Privileged Borbador, carrying a warrant for General Ket's arrest.

The city seemed strange to him when viewed from afar. The red of the fall leaves and gold of the fields seemed to hide the brick smokestacks and warehouses of the Factory District, and Adopest seemed less to him than it had been before. It wasn't until he had lost the view and entered into the southern parts of the city that he decided why that was so: The Kresim Cathedral no longer dominated the center of the city, standing like a beacon above most of the other buildings.

Adamat noted the wreckage of a dozen churches as his carriage wound through the southern suburbs and then through the Factory District and headed north toward his home. It was four o'clock, the autumn sun already well on its way to the western horizon, when he was dropped at his front door, and he had worked himself into a fury over Claremonte's men having destroyed all the churches in Adopest.

What right had they? This was not their city. Not their country. And yet no one had opposed them when they pulled the priests from their chapels and murdered them in the streets; when Claremonte's Privileged had torn down the churches with sorcery, laying waste to every brick.

An illness had settled in Adamat's gut and he had the horrible feeling that he should have accepted Tamas's mission to rid the city of Claremonte. *Someone* had to fight against the bastard.

Cane and hat in hand, Adamat carried his bag up his front steps and set it against the door. He bowed his head. None of that now. Claremonte was in the past. Vetas was in the past. This was the present and now he had to tell Faye about Josep.

He remained there for several moments, trying to find the right words, when the sound reached him—or rather, the lack of it. No voices. No children shouting or playing. No feet on the wood floors. He raised his head and peered in at the front window, but the shades were drawn. Where was his family?

His hands shook as he tried to turn the doorknob, but it was locked. He reached into his pocket for the key, only to have it drop from his stiff fingers.

He bent to retrieve the key and heard the scrape of the lock, and the door opened. He looked up.

"Adamat? You're home, how wonderful!"

Adamat breathed a sigh of relief, feeling his knees wobble. "Hello, Margy."

The foreman of the biggest textile mill in Adro was a strong woman in her forties with graying hair and a pair of spectacles perched on her thin nose. "Do come in, I was just keeping Faye company for the afternoon. She said she didn't expect you for... well, for some time."

"Who's there?" Adamat heard Faye call from the sitting room.

"I am," Adamat responded weakly.

"Oh, hold on!"

Adamat came inside and put down his bag and hung his hat and cane by the door. Faye came out of the sitting room and put her hands on Adamat's shoulders. He leaned forward to kiss her on the cheek, and he couldn't help but see the look of hope as she smiled at him, and then the cloud that passed over her face when he closed the door behind him.

He gave a slight shake of his head.

"Margy," Faye said, "I'm so sorry to do this, but..."

"Oh, now, don't be like that. I should get home to my girls anyway. You should be with your husband."

"I'll stop the cab," Adamat said. He went back out into the street and shouted for his carriage to return. A few minutes later and Margy was climbing inside with her umbrella.

Adamat forced a smile and waved as the carriage drove off. Beside him, Faye did the same, and he wondered at her ability to face the world with a stiff spine after all she had been through. They went back inside.

"Margy was telling me she's going to run for treasurer of her district in the new elections this fall."

"Where are the children?" Adamat asked.

Faye let herself fall against the wall in the hallway. Adamat touched the plaster beside her, noting how it didn't match the rest. She'd had someone come and fix the hole there, from where Sou-Smith had put an assassin's head through plaster and brick.

"Ricard offered to hire a governess for them full-time," Faye said. "I took him up on it. They're off for a walk in the park right now and they'll be back for dinner in a couple of hours."

"Is that safe?"

Faye made a quiet noise that seemed halfway between a sigh and a sob, but did not respond.

"That was very kind of him," Adamat added. They stood in the hallway in silence for several minutes. "I should never have answered that bloody summons," he finally said. "I would never have gotten involved with this entire thing and—"

"Is Josep dead?" Faye asked.

Adamat tried to work moisture into his mouth. When that failed, he gave a small nod. Better that she not know. It would break her. To know Josep dead was one thing, but to know that he had been twisted by hideous Privileged sorcery into some . . . *creature* . . .

Better that *no one* ever know.

Faye stared at the floor. She went back into the sitting room and a moment later Adamat heard her muffled sobs. He closed his eyes. How had his life come to this?

He took two steps up the stairs, bag in hand, when he turned and went into the sitting room. Faye perched on the edge of one of the chairs, a half-empty cup of tea on the table beside her. Adamat knelt on the floor behind her and put his hands on her arms. He soon found himself weeping as well.

Adamat wept until the collar of his shirt was wet and he felt like he had no more tears to give. His legs were both asleep and Faye had composed herself some time ago and now stared unseeing at the far wall of the sitting room. He kissed her on the forehead and extricated himself from her desperate embrace, brushing the dampness from his face with one sleeve and clearing his throat.

She looked up at him, a sad smile on her lips, and he again wondered at her strength to deal with all of this. To hide her own fears and sorrow and anger, to put on a happy face for him and the children just a handful of weeks after the end of her own ordeals—it was incredible.

"I worry for you," he said.

"I'm stronger than you think."

"I know. But I still worry."

She took his hand and kissed his knuckles. "Worry for yourself."

"Field Marshal Tamas has returned. He won a great victory against the Kez." *Without even being there, though I don't think Tamas wants that to be common knowledge.*

Faye scowled. "And he's asked you to do something more for him, hasn't he?"

"He did," Adamat admitted.

"No! You are done with that man and his revolution!"

"Be still," Adamat said. "I told him I would not help him any further."

"Good."

"I did..."

"You did what? What? You stupid oaf!"

"I did promise to help Ricard with his election. Not much. I won't get too involved. I'm not doing this for Tamas, by the way. I'm doing it for Ricard. I owe it to him for helping me get you back."

Faye stuck her chin out at him. "Owe it or not, if you even walk into his office you'll get involved. I know him. And I know you."

"So I shouldn't do anything?"

"You should be here with your family. Ricard will understand." She kissed his hand again. "Don't take any jobs for a while. Let's just leave the country. We can take the children and go to Novi. We have the money Borbador gave us."

Adamat wanted to. He really did. Part of him said he would be a coward to do it—he would be running away. But another part told him it was the smart thing to do. The best thing for his family. "I can't just abandon Ricard," he said.

"But you can abandon your family?"

"I'm not...I..." Why couldn't she understand? She and the children meant everything to him, but he had obligations. To Ricard. To Adro.

Faye pushed his hand away. "Fine. Do what you want. You always think you know best."

Her next words were drowned out by a knock on the door. "Are you expecting someone?" he asked.

Faye shook her head. "The children would come in through the back, but they shouldn't be here for an hour yet."

Adamat approached the front window slowly and moved the curtain aside with one finger. When he saw who it was, he ran to the door and threw it open.

SouSmith stood on his front step, hat in hand, a scowl marring his battered face. The old boxer gave Adamat a nod, then an "Evening, ma'am" to Faye.

"Come in, come in," Adamat said. "I just arrived home. I was going to come see you tomorrow."

SouSmith shook his head at the invitation.

"What is it?" Adamat asked.

"There's been a bombing," he grunted.

Adamat felt his heart skip a beat and his palms begin to sweat. "What? Where?"

"The Holy Warriors of Labor."

Ricard's headquarters. A flurry of questions ran through Adamat's head and they all jumbled up, causing him to feel tongue-tied. He looked at Faye.

"Go," Faye urged.

Adamat snatched his hat and cane and followed SouSmith out the door to the waiting carriage.

Adamat eyed the light street traffic and silently urged the carriage faster. "Is Ricard hurt?" he asked.

SouSmith shrugged.

"How about his secretary, Fell?"

Another shrug.

"Damn it, man, do you know anything?"

SouSmith shook his head. "Was in Forswitch when I heard."

"So you weren't there?"

"Just thought you'd want to know. Was on my way past."

"Well, thanks for that," Adamat said. "What were you doing in Forswitch?"

"Helping my brother."

"The butcher?"

A nod. SouSmith cracked his knuckles and peered out the window. "Carrying meat. Big hogs, one on each shoulder."

"Been boxing lately?"

SouSmith kept his gaze on the street outside. His only answer was a small shake of the head.

Adamat frowned. It had been nine weeks to the day since they attacked Lord Vetas's lair, capturing Vetas and rescuing Faye. He had released SouSmith from his employ a few days later, what with the danger passed. It seemed strange that SouSmith had had no matches since then. He was old, sure, but he hadn't lost his edge. Why wouldn't the Proprietor put him in the ring? Unless...

"Has the Proprietor suspended all of the boxing?"

"Yeah."

"Because of the eunuch's death?" An event that had occurred during Vetas's capture. In fact, Vetas himself had killed the eunuch during Faye's rescue.

"Still looking for a new second," SouSmith said.

"I see." The Proprietor was the head of the criminal underworld in Adro, and the eunuch had been the face of his operations for at least eighteen years. It had to be stirring up plenty with the eunuch gone. After all, only five people in the world knew the Proprietor's true identity, counting the Proprietor himself.

And Adamat.

Adamat cleared his throat. "I might have some work for you soon," he said, though he immediately regretted it. Hiring Sou-Smith meant that he *needed* a bodyguard. And needing a bodyguard meant he was going to get involved with things he knew he shouldn't. But someone had tried to kill Ricard.

SouSmith raised one eyebrow. "Hmm."

For the tight-lipped boxer, it was an enthusiastic response.

Night had fallen, the street lanterns were being lit, and most of the shops were closed by the time they neared Ricard's headquarters. The evening traffic was blocked, so Adamat paid the driver, and he and SouSmith walked the rest of the way. Adamat peered into the hazy darkness to try to see what damage Ricard's old warehouse had taken.

Two of the windows high up on the second floor had blown out, and the front door had been taken off its hinges in order to maneuver stretchers through. The brickwork appeared unhurt, and in fact the new mural on the side of the building with Ricard's face and election slogan of "Unity and Labor" was barely scratched. A prison carriage—empty—blocked traffic in the street, and a dozen police officers milled about, speaking with onlookers and each other. Torches had been posted to supplement the light from the streetlamps.

One of the officers stepped up to Adamat. "Sorry, sir, no one's allowed in or out, on the commissioner's orders."

"I'm Inspector Adamat. Is Ricard all right?"

Another officer looked up from his interview of a scantily clad serving girl—one of Ricard's hostesses. "Hey, Picadal, you can let Adamat through. The commissioner will want to see him."

"The commissioner is here in person?"

"Yes. Says it's a high-profile attack, what with Ricard being a candidate for First Minister."

Adamat was waved past. When he turned to SouSmith, he found the big boxer lagging behind. "Come on," Adamat said.

"I'll wait here."

"What is it? Oh, never mind. Suit yourself." Adamat headed

inside, where he paused to take in the building for a moment, logging every detail in his perfect memory for future perusal.

While the building was, indeed, an old warehouse, Ricard had gutted the entire thing and improved it with paint, red curtains, gold candelabras, crystal chandeliers, and busts of philosophers. The headquarters of the Noble Warriors of Labor had enough gold trim to make a duke blush. Most of the building was one large room, with offices for business in the very back.

It didn't take an experienced investigator to see that the explosion had come from the back of the warehouse. For one thing, the offices no longer existed. Blackened wreckage was all that remained of those rooms and, in fact, the better part of the rear wall of the warehouse. The parts of the interior that hadn't been caught in the explosion had been subsequently damaged by fire. Only the very front of the great room had escaped the worst of the blast.

Adamat was stunned by the destruction. There could easily have been a full barrel of gunpowder hidden inside one of those rooms, or beneath them, in order to cause such damage. No mean feat in a building with this much traffic during all times of day.

Policemen picked through the wreckage alongside some of the union men, trying to save scraps of important documents and pieces of furniture. There was no sign of Ricard. Adamat suppressed his rising panic and turned to one of the policemen.

"Have you seen Ricard Tumblar?"

"Around the side."

A side door, completely intact despite the damage to the rest of the building, led out into an alleyway, where Adamat was relieved to find Ricard sitting with his back to the building next door. The union boss had his head in his hands. A little farther down the alleyway, Fell was talking quietly with the commissioner of police. The whole alley was lit by a pair of large lanterns outside the side door.

"Ricard," Adamat said gently, squatting next to his friend.

Ricard looked up, his eyes a little distant. "Eh?" he asked, far too loudly. "Oh, Adamat, thank Adom you're here."

"Are you all right?"

"What? Oh, I can't hear a damned word in this ear. Here, come around over here."

Adamat moved to Ricard's other side. "Are you all right?"

"Yes, yes. Just a little frazzled, that's all." He made a vague gesture toward the warehouse. "I've lost...well, everything. Thousands of documents gone. Millions in banknotes. Darilo."

"Please tell me you're insured."

"For some of it. Not enough."

"Union documents."

"Yes."

"You've made copies? Please tell me you've made copies."

"Yes, yes."

"Then you haven't lost everything. Who is Darilo?"

"My bartender. Poor man. I sent him into my office to grab a coat for Cheris, and then..." He stared absently at the wall of his warehouse. "He's been with me for over a decade. I went to his wedding. I had to send word to his wife. I'll go see her myself tomorrow." He finally looked over at Adamat. "Only fourteen people were killed in the explosion and it's a bloody miracle. There were nearly two hundred of us in there for a party. The heads of the goldsmiths' and millers' unions are dead. The head of the street cleaners' union is having his leg amputated as we speak. I've lost half of my hearing. Cheris was hit in the shoulder by flying debris. It's just..." He trailed off.

"You're alive. That's what matters."

"But the campaign..."

"You'll recover."

Ricard met Adamat's eyes for the first time and Adamat realized that Ricard was still in shock. "Several of my friends were in there. Relationships. Money. Time. Resources. All of them lost because of some damn bomb. Who the bloody pit would have done this?"

Claremonte seemed the likely answer, of course. Ricard's competition in the campaign for First Minister was not a man to trifle with. He would not hesitate to kill hundreds, maybe thousands, to reach his goals. Adamat knew from firsthand dealing with his lackey, Lord Vetas.

"The police will find out."

Ricard suddenly took Adamat by the collar. "I want you to find out. Bloody police. They won't get anything done."

"Shh!" Adamat tried making a significant glance toward the police commissioner, who was standing a dozen feet away. Ricard was talking very loudly.

"Don't shush me! I'll pay you anything, Adamat. Just find out who did this!"

"Calm down, Ricard. I'll help. Of course I will." It wasn't even a choice. Ricard had helped him and Faye with so much over the years. And now, against his will, Adamat was being dragged back into the fray.

CHAPTER

26

Taniel and his group of Riflejacks and powder mages entered the Black Tar Forest under the cover of darkness the next evening. Wary of ambushes, they pressed on along the road with two men out front at all times, ready to spring any traps.

Taniel felt a pressure in the depth of his chest that urged him forward. They had not yet come across a small, broken, freckled body left to rot alongside the road. Ka-poel might still be alive. She had to be. Otherwise they would have killed her during their raid on the Adran camp and been done with the whole affair. They must *need* her alive, and that prospect scared him almost as much as finding her dead.

When he caught these Kez dogs, he would put a bullet through every last Privileged's brains. He would garrote the grenadiers with their own bootlaces. The rage pushed him onward, while a voice in the back of his head warned that he was pushing too hard.

He ignored it. What if the Privileged couldn't kill her? Perhaps she shielded herself with the same sorcery that she used to shield him, and they would be forced to keep her prisoner until they managed to unwind her wards.

She was not impervious to pain. What kind of tortures would they inflict on her?

He had to get her back.

"Taniel!"

Vlora's voice snapped through his thoughts like the sting of a wasp.

"What is it?"

"We have to stop."

"Already?" He blinked moisture into his eyes, dry from staring into the wind as they rode. "Gavril, call the halt. We'll rotate men." It was their practice these last two days to ride with the two far ahead watching for traps, and to rotate those two every hour. Gavril put his fingers to his mouth and gave a shrill whistle, calling the vanguard back toward them.

"No," Vlora said, drawing her horse closer and lowering her voice. "We have to stop for the night. It's a miracle none of the horses have fallen in the dark. The men are exhausted."

"Dark? There's still plenty of light to see."

Gavril said a few words to the men and brought his horse stepping toward them. "You're running a damned powder trance," he said. "And you've been running it too long. Can't tell the night from the day."

"What are you talking about?" Taniel rubbed his eyes and for the first time felt the tension in his shoulders, the ache in his legs. Perhaps it was past dark. "The sun must have just gone down."

"It's almost midnight," Vlora said softly.

There was concern in her eyes, and it made Taniel angry. Why did she care? He thought to tell her off and keep the men moving, but a glance around the group found them all bleary-eyed and stiff.

"We'll camp here," he said. "Norrine and Flerrier, take first watch. I'll take second. Vlora and Doll, you take third. We move again at dawn." He dismounted, putting his horse between him and Vlora, glad to hear her trot off. He'd assigned only powder mages to watch, a technique he'd learned from his father for smaller missions. Though the mages were ranking officers, they needed less sleep than the regular soldiers.

It was twenty minutes before he'd finished rubbing down his horse. He made his camp a little ways from the rest of the men and built a small fire using dry branches, igniting it with a flash of powder. He held his hands to the flames, trying to work the ache from his fingers, regretting the three days straight of clutching his reins.

The pressure still pushed on the inside of his rib cage, like some kind of wild animal clawing to be free. His own exhaustion was but a shadow in the back of his mind and he had doubts that he would get any sleep until Ka-poel was free.

"Norrine and Doll made a quick sweep," Gavril said, emerging silently from the darkness of the forest and dropping down beside Taniel. "No one lying in wait down the road. It's safe to make a fire." He glanced wryly at the flames over which Taniel still held his hands.

Taniel's throat was suddenly dry. Pit, what would Tamas say about this? Taniel was supposed to be in command. He should have seen to the scouts, checked with the sentries, then told the men whether they could make their own fires. "Thanks," he croaked.

"Don't mention it." Gavril shifted around until he was comfortable, his back up against a tree trunk, and produced a flask from his vest pocket. "Drink?"

"No."

Gavril took a sip. "You eaten yet today?"

"Of course." Taniel couldn't recall. The last dozen hours seemed like a distant memory, a barely remembered dream.

Gavril produced a paper-wrapped parcel and tossed it into Taniel's lap. Marching rations, by the look of it.

"I'm fine," Taniel said, handing it back.

"Eat, you stubborn bastard. By Adom, who the pit you think you are? Your father?"

Taniel bit back a reply and unwrapped the dried beef and biscuits. He was halfway through the meal when he realized that the big Watchmaster had elicited exactly the response he wanted with the comment about Tamas. Taniel sniffed and tried to pretend he hadn't just been manipulated. "You don't know anything about my father."

Gavril made a choking sound and rolled onto his side, coughing. "Oh pit, I just snorted Fatrastan rum up my nose."

"What was that about?" Taniel demanded. He had a vague memory of someone mentioning that Gavril had served with Tamas, but though that conversation may have happened just months ago, it felt like years.

"I said I accidentally snorted rum."

"No, I mean when I said, 'You don't know anything about my father.'"

"Nothing, nothing. Some other time."

Gavril fell silent and Taniel chewed on the road rations, swallowing mechanically, the hard biscuits having no flavor. Gavril was watching him eat. The effect was rather unnerving, especially from such a bear of a man. "Did you want some?" Taniel asked.

"Ate hours ago," Gavril said, taking another sip at his flask. His gaze shifted to the small fire.

Taniel finished the meal and fumbled about for his canteen. Gavril offered his flask again and Taniel took it. The rum burned the back of his throat, leaving a slightly sweet aftertaste. "Where'd you get that scar?"

Gavril's eyebrows rose for a moment, then he looked down to his uncovered wrist. A pink line stretched across his broad forearm and ended on the back of his hand. He shook the sleeve of his jacket down to cover it. "You're too hard on your old man," he said.

"Excuse me?"

"He's a tough old bastard, but he has tried to be a good father."

"That's really none of your damn business." Taniel felt the color rise in his cheeks.

Gavril held up his hands in peace. "Sorry, sorry. Just making an observation."

They sat in silence for several minutes while Taniel let his anger cool. The pleasant feeling of a full belly made his eyelids droop and he reached for the hope that maybe he would actually get some rest.

"You were on campaign with him?" Taniel asked. "In Kez? Caught behind the lines?"

"Aye," Gavril said.

"Was it bad?"

Gavril was silent for several moments. Taniel watched the side of his face, realizing only now that Gavril weighed at least two stone less than he had all those months ago on South Pike. There was a new scar on his right cheek, faded in a way that spoke of healing sorcery, and the hint of healed bruises around both eyes.

"It was," Gavril finally answered. "Killing the horses for food. Being dogged by Kez cuirassiers. Gathering up powder and food from the men so we could ration it back out wisely. I had to shoot a man because it was found he had stolen two weeks' worth of rations."

It sounded like stories Taniel had heard from his father about the Gurlish campaigns. Except those were decades ago, half a world away. This had just happened in the very heart of the Nine. "Tamas put you in command?"

Gavril shrugged his big shoulders. "Sure. He needed someone like me. You see the worst of humanity up on the Mountainwatch. Convicts and debtors, thieves and fools. Pit, *you* remember. Not Adro's finest, by a long stretch. If I could keep that lot in line, I could keep Tamas's infantry going with one hand and manage the scouts and cavalry with the other."

"You'd never boast about it, though," Taniel said with a snort.

"A boast is something you have to back up with your fist." Gavril raised one ham-sized hand. "I could let the results do the talking, there." His sleeve fell, revealing once again the long scar. Gavril examined it for a moment, then said, "I got this from the Kez. They were wearing Adran blues and I was ranging too far ahead of the main army. They caught me, beat the shit out of me, and took me to Alvation. That's where they really went to work on me."

He raised his shirt to show several other scars across his belly. "Snapped my wrist when I wouldn't give them the information they wanted. The bone sheared clear through the skin. God, I haven't screamed like that since my leg was run over by a wagon as a boy."

"Alvation?" Taniel asked. He'd spent just a little time with Olem, Tamas's bodyguard, on their way to the parley, and Olem had told him some things about the Seventh and Ninth's disastrous trek through Kez and Deliv. "This just happened?"

"The Deliv Privileged healers are good at their craft. I told them to leave the scars. Gives me more stories to tell." He paused. "I heard about Bo. If they can get him to the Deliv healers in time, he'll come out practically unharmed."

Not with his leg practically burned off, he wouldn't. And that was a big "if." Taniel felt his voice catch in his throat. "Don't you blame Tamas?"

"For what?" Gavril belched loudly and took another swig from his flask.

"For getting you caught by the Kez. You were tortured."

"Let's get one thing straight," Gavril said, a darkness passing across his face. "The only one who got me caught by the Kez was me. And when I did, Tamas came for me. He pushed his men through the pit and made a deal with an old, spurned lover to get me back. Boy, I've spurned a few lovers, and let me tell you, making good with one of them can be harder than moving a mountain. Especially for a man as proud as Tamas."

Taniel was surprised at the outburst. He opened his mouth, but Gavril cut him off.

"I've blamed Tamas for a lot of things in my lifetime. He's guilty of some of them, but as far as the very worst—well, I'll just say he's innocent. Besides, getting caught by the Kez allowed me one thing I thought I'd never get the chance to do."

"What's that?"

"I spit in the face of the man who murdered my sister."

The crack of a twig brought Taniel's attention around to a shape in the darkness. Squinting at it, he realized that his powder trance was starting to wear off. A moment later, Vlora stepped into the firelight.

"Can I have a minute, Gavril?" she asked quietly.

Gavril gave a mighty sigh and climbed to his feet. "Have to take a piss anyway," he muttered, lumbering off into the darkness.

Vlora did not take Gavril's place, instead settling opposite Taniel across the small fire. Taniel stared into the flames. He could feel her gaze upon him, prickling the back of his mind like a sixth sense. The feeling brought back memories of thin sheets and shadowed bedrooms, and he felt his cheeks begin to warm in spite of himself.

He took a twig and poked at the fire. "What do you want?"

"To talk," she answered softly.

"Well," he grunted, "go ahead."

"I . . ."

"Why are you here?" Taniel demanded, cutting her off. The urge to be off, riding fast after Ka-poel, had finally found its outlet, and his words came out much louder than intended. Heads were raised at the other small campfires. "Why," he asked, tempering his voice, "do you insist on haunting me?"

"Haunting you?" Vlora was taken aback. "I'm here to help you."

"Why? Did Tamas send you? No, I think not. He would have wanted you for the next battle with the Kez. You and I are his best marksmen and he wouldn't have sent you away at a critical time like this."

"I asked to come."

Taniel leaned forward until he felt the heat of the fire on his face. "Why?" Were those unshed tears in her eyes? It didn't matter. He needed an answer. Everything else in his small world seemed unimportant suddenly. "We've been friends since we were kids. We were lovers. You pulled out my heart and tossed it on the ground." He gestured violently. "Sprinkled some salt on it and cooked it over a fire!" He thought he heard a chuckle from the woods, but he paid it no heed. "Why are you mocking me like this?"

Vlora's face seemed to melt and re-form, the sorrow dripping off and being replaced by steely-eyed determination. Her jaw clenched and her cheeks seemed to tighten, and he could sense the fight in her the way an old sailor can sense a coming storm.

"You think I wanted to be left alone for two years? Until that night you found me, I'd never had a lover but you. Bo kissed me once, when we were young, but I didn't let it go farther than that."

"He what?" Taniel felt like he was riding a horse that had just thrown a shoe.

She talked over his agitation. "I took no other lover, but I heard the rumors. Taniel Two-shot. Hero of the Fatrastan War for Independence. Killing Kez Privileged left and right. Wooing hundreds of women. Tended night and day by a little savage sorceress."

"I was never unfaithful."

"That's not what I heard."

"Lies! I saw you in the arms of another man. With my own eyes!"

"I'm sorry!"

Taniel surged forward, carried halfway across the fire by his own fury, then pulled up short. "What?"

Vlora's nostrils flared. "That's the third time I've tried to tell you. It was a horrid mistake. You going to Fatrasta. Me taking that prig to bed. Mistake after mistake after mistake."

Taniel returned slowly to his sleeping roll. There was a part of him that wanted to rush to her, take her in his arms and comfort her, but he knew that would make things more...complicated. They were done and nothing would change that. He had Ka-poel still. *If she was still alive.*

She thinks I'm lying. The thought hit him like a bolt of lightning from a clear sky. *She thinks Ka-poel and I have been lovers for these last two years.* "Vlora," he said. The name seemed foreign on his lips, as he'd refused to say it for so many months. "Me and Ka-poel. It's just been recently, it..." He trailed off. "I just need to get her back."

"We'll get her back," Vlora said.

Was it her way of apology? Some kind of self-sacrifice? "Why?" He had to know.

"Because she still loves you, you daft tit." Gavril's voice came out of the darkness to Taniel's left, and Taniel realized it had been his laugh he heard earlier. Taniel surged to his feet, reaching for his sword, swearing to cut the big man in two.

Vlora was faster. She leapt into the darkness and dragged Gavril back to the fire, throwing him to the ground like a child, though he was twice her size. Her jaw was set in anger.

Gavril squirmed on the ground, and it took a moment to realize that he was laughing so hard that tears streamed down his face. Vlora planted a boot in Gavril's ribs, eliciting a single "Oof" and then another chorus of laughs. "What's so funny, you fat bastard?" She grabbed him by the hair, lifting him to his knees, and his laughter suddenly ceased. A dangerous glint entered his eyes.

"Vlora…" Taniel stepped forward, ready to throw himself between them.

"You like putting your nose in someone else's business, do you?" Vlora said in Gavril's ear. "Well, how's this: Taniel, this hairy ass is your uncle. He didn't tell you on South Pike because he was too ashamed of being the Mountainwatch drunk, and he doesn't tell you now because…well, I don't know." She kicked Gavril in the small of the back and stormed into the darkness.

Gavril caught himself over the small fire and deftly rolled to his feet. He wiped the tears of laughter from the corner of his eyes and watched Vlora go, then turned to Taniel. Catching Taniel's gaze, he gave a sheepish grin and held out his flask. "Drink?"

"My bloody uncle?" Taniel asked.

Gavril bowed at the waist. "Jakola of Pensbrook, at your service, nephew."

CHAPTER 27

Adamat shuddered at the memory of the last time he had been to Skyline Palace. It had been in the middle of the night over six months ago when Field Marshal Tamas summoned him in order to investigate the last words of members of the Adran royal cabal. The gardens of the great palace had been dark and unguarded, and instilled him with a deep sense of unease that flowed through him even now.

Though, he acknowledged to himself, his unease this morning was likely of a different sort.

Lord Claremonte was the late Lord Vetas's employer. And anyone who employed such a monster would surely be a monster himself. Every fiber of Adamat's being told him to turn around and run, to return home and lock his door and never take a job in the city again—and bugger Ricard and Tamas and Claremonte and everyone else involved in this deadly dance.

But he'd made a promise to Ricard, so he straightened his jacket and dusted off the brim of his hat.

Most of the gardens had become overgrown, untended over the summer, and dozens of sentries in the colors of the Brudania-Gurla Trading Company were posted about the grounds. Adamat's carriage traveled up the front drive, past the immense, silver-plated doors and along the front of the palace until they rounded one corner and proceeded to the servants' entrance.

Adamat emerged from his carriage just as three policemen and the commissioner of police stepped out of theirs. The commissioner tipped her hat to Adamat and then strode up to a rather ordinary set of double doors and rapped twice.

The door opened a crack. Words were exchanged, and then the commissioner headed inside, with her officers on her tail. Adamat followed.

"Keep close," Adamat said to SouSmith as the big man emerged from the carriage behind him. "I don't trust Claremonte in the least." He jogged to catch up with the commissioner. "What the pit is Claremonte doing here?" he asked.

"Running for First Minister," Commissioner Hewi replied, straight-faced. Hewi—a sharp-eyed, soft-spoken woman with light-brown hair curled tightly beneath a small hat—was wearing a loose-fitting day dress that managed to look both utilitarian and elegant at the same time. She had been appointed by the Iron King not long before his death and had, from the rumors, been one of the first people informed of the coup. Upon hearing that the Iron King's son was to be executed, her words had famously been, "It's about damn time."

"I meant *here*. In the palace."

"He's rented the space from the city," Hewi said. "Housing his troops and Privileged here."

"And we just let him rent it?"

"The Reeve agreed to it, from what I hear," Hewi said. "Better than letting it sit empty. Claremonte's paying an astronomical fee for use of the building and grounds, and the city needs the money."

"I'm surprised Tamas didn't have the place burned down," Adamat said.

"I'm not. It's part of our cultural heritage. Over four hundred years old. Many of the walls and ceilings are works of art in and of themselves. I think Tamas knows better than to destroy all that out of spite."

Adamat conceded to himself that the commissioner had a point. He noted that even the walls of the cavernous kitchens, as they passed through them, were covered in bright murals.

"Still," Hewi added, "Tamas had most of the art and furniture removed to the national gallery. Some of it was sold to pay off debts, from what I heard. The rest will be put on display for the public. Laudable, I think."

"Though it would have been far safer to destroy every vestige of the nobility."

"Right. Seems Tamas is something more than simply pragmatic. Who would have thought?"

They left the kitchens and went up the servants' stairs to the main floor. Adamat had heard that the passageways behind the palace were a labyrinth all to themselves, but this was his first time experiencing them. They ducked around so many corners, led by one of Claremonte's servants, that Adamat imagined that men without his Knack could very well get lost. He frequently stopped to urge SouSmith along so that the boxer didn't get distracted gazing at all the art.

They passed by dozens of rooms, each one seemingly bigger than the last, with more ornate gold-work trim and colorful frescoes. Marble-faced fireplaces took up entire walls in some rooms. Curtains were drawn in most of them, casting the rooms into shadow, and what little furniture was left had been covered in white sheets to keep the dust off.

The servant stepped aside suddenly and gestured to a doorway.

Hewi and her officers went inside. Adamat paused momentarily, wondering if there was any significance to Claremonte's having them use the servants' halls and entrances instead of the immense, echoing hallways and full-length doors. Letting them know they were beneath him, perhaps?

Adamat glanced at SouSmith to reassure himself and then went in.

"Welcome, welcome!" Claremonte's voice bounced off the vaulted ceilings. The room was about thirty feet by forty. Unlike the others they'd passed, this one was decorated entirely in silver— metallic paint on the walls, ornate silver-plated trim. Even the dual fireplaces were a marbling of light and dark gray that matched the walls. On the ceiling was a mural showing some ancient hero making a deal with a two-faced celestial being.

Brude. Fitting that Claremonte would pick a room watched over by Brudania's two-faced patron saint.

Claremonte wore a fine robe over silk pajamas, though it was well past nine in the morning. He lounged lazily in a wingback chair beside one of the windows overlooking the garden and held a cup in one hand, newspaper in the other. He stood as they approached, repeating his welcome.

"I'm sorry I'm not yet dressed, Commissioner. It was a late night last night, working on a campaign speech for a meeting I'm having this afternoon with the Society for City Gardens."

Hewi extended a hand. "Thank you for allowing us to come by on such short notice."

"No trouble at all. Oh, Inspector Adamat. Good morning to you, sir."

"Good morning," Adamat said stiffly. He felt a drop of sweat snake its way down the nape of his neck.

"How are your lovely wife and children?"

Adamat forced a tight-lipped smile. This had been a terrible mistake.

"I wasn't aware you knew the inspector," Hewi said. "Or that you've met his family!"

"The inspector was among those who greeted me upon my arrival to the city," Claremonte said, a magnanimous smile on his lips. "And I only know his wife by reputation."

To other men, Claremonte's smile may have been gracious. To Adamat, it seemed full of mockery. Claremonte extended his hand to Adamat.

"Pardon if I don't shake," Adamat managed.

"Of course." The words were almost a purr. "Hewi—may I call you Hewi? Hewi, I can only assume that you've come to ask me about the unfortunate incident with Ricard Tumblar yesterday."

"That's true," the commissioner said.

"I want to assure you that I had nothing to do with it." Claremonte moved back to his chair by the window and dropped gracefully into it, sending his robe fluttering. "Can I offer any of you some breakfast? Eggs? Coffee? Biscuits?"

"Nothing, thank you," Hewi said. "You understand that we'll need to look into your records? This case will be very high-profile and you are running against Mr. Tumblar for First Minister of Adro. You have the means and the motive."

"I understand. Your men are welcome to my records and to question my employees. As long, of course, as it does not interfere with my campaign."

"We'll do our best to keep the investigation discreet."

"Many thanks."

Adamat let his eyes search the room once more, trying to find anything he had missed—and trying to get his emotions under control. No good inspector could allow himself to be ruled by emotion.

There were three other chairs aside from the one Claremonte sat in, but he hadn't offered his guests a seat. The sun blazed through the window, casting long shadows on the floor and inside wall and making it hard to look directly at Claremonte. Strategic placement, or happy coincidence?

Something about that bothered Adamat. He couldn't quite place what it was.

Strategic placement, Adamat decided. A man like Claremonte didn't do things by accident. Which meant his pajamas were meant to say something as well. Presenting casual indifference? Disrespect?

"Lord Claremonte," Adamat said, interrupting something Claremonte had been saying. "Can you give us any reason why you *wouldn't* want Ricard dead?"

Claremonte seemed taken aback. "Why, several. For one, attacking Mr. Tumblar and failing to kill him will only raise his public sympathy."

"Or expose your opponent's weakness."

"Perhaps, but he's very well liked. For another thing, if he had been killed, his Second Minister would have stepped forward to run in his place. And I have no desire to run against a war hero like Taniel Two-shot. Not with all these rumors going around that he's killed a god and what other nonsense. He's got a cult of worship among the people almost as deep as his father's."

But *would* he step up, Adamat wondered. He decided not to voice the question, lest it give Claremonte any ideas. "So you think you have the best shot of winning with Ricard alive?"

"Yes. Alive, and in one piece." Claremonte shook his head sadly. "Regardless of who is to blame, some of the public will surely blame me. I would rather the whole event never have happened. I'm in a very good place right now—public perception is high and supporters are flocking to me in droves. I've just landed an incredible endorsement. The election is just over a month away, and anything like this bombing that could destabilize public perception can only work against me."

"May I ask who will be endorsing you?"

"You'll find out with the rest of Adro in a few weeks. He's my trump card, if you don't mind the saying. I don't want to let out the word too early."

"I see. I'm sorry to have interrupted, Commissioner," Adamat said, lapsing into silence.

Hewi examined Adamat for a moment and then turned back to Claremonte, asking him a series of standard questions. Adamat was pleased to hear her go a little harder on him than she would have before Manhouch's removal. He had heard from his friends still with the police that investigations were so incredibly easier now that kowtowing to the nobility wasn't a standard part of the job.

Adamat listened to the questions for several minutes before slipping out the front of the room and into the grand hallway of the north wing of Skyline Palace. He needed to clear his head. Something in that room bothered him. It lurked on the edge of his awareness, tantalizingly out of reach.

He strolled down the hallway, listening to the click of his cane and the heavy footfalls of SouSmith following along behind him. Aside from those sounds, the hall was absolutely silent. Strange, what with most of Claremonte's five thousand men stationed on the grounds. He would have thought there to be more activity.

A small sound caught his attention. He followed it, head turned, past three empty sitting rooms and into a fourth, where a series of small scratching noises proved to come from fifty pens all writing at once. A salon had been turned into a clerks' office. Several dozen men sat at desks set up in the room, working studiously while a monitor moved up and down the aisles, occasionally bending to whisper to one of the clerks.

Adamat continued to explore the wing of the palace. He found two more rooms filled with Claremonte's employees and another with printing equipment. The presses were all cold and empty, but they must have been used recently, as the room had been lined with cotton batting to keep down the sound. Thousands of newspapers were hung to dry on lines up in the vaulted ceiling.

Printing his own paper, in addition to the presses he'd bought from Ricard's competitors. Smart. "Claremonte seems very confident," Adamat commented, his words echoing down the hall.

"Yeah," SouSmith rumbled. "Too confident."

"I don't like it. Have you heard anything about this endorsement?"

SouSmith shook his head. "People talk. Some like him. Some hate him. Nothing certain."

Well, that wasn't much help. Adamat drummed his fingers on the head of his cane. "Did anything seem strange about Claremonte himself?"

SouSmith shrugged. "Seems nice enough." He cracked his knuckles, the sound echoing down the hallway, and a dark look passed over his face. Lord Vetas had killed SouSmith's nephew, and SouSmith wasn't ever going to let that go. Adamat realized suddenly that bringing the big boxer here may not have been the best idea.

Of course, if he put Claremonte's head through a wall, it would certainly make life a lot easier for everyone.

"There's just something…" Adamat trailed off as they returned to the silver sitting room. Claremonte's manservant eyed him and SouSmith suspiciously, but didn't ask where they had been.

"Ah, there you are," Hewi said. "We were just leaving, Inspector." She made an impatient gesture toward the door with her hat.

"Pardon me, Commissioner," Claremonte said, "but could I speak with Adamat alone?"

Hewi gave a nod and stepped outside. Adamat felt his heart suddenly beat a little faster. Alone? With Claremonte? The temptation to brain him over the head with his cane might prove too much. He nodded to SouSmith, and a moment later he was alone with Lord Claremonte.

"Inspector," Claremonte said. "I hope that any past unpleasantness that you may think occurred between us can remain in the past."

Adamat bit his tongue. *Your man kidnapped my wife and family!*

Abused them in unspeakable ways, and caused the death of my son! I'll see you dead. "As you say," he said, remembering one of the phrases he used to use when caught in an awkward conversation with a nobleman.

"Don't waste your time with me, Inspector. I didn't try to kill Mr. Tumblar. I don't know who did. I would offer my help with the investigation, but I don't think you'd accept it."

"We'll see," Adamat said, matching Claremonte's condescending tone. "Thank you for the advice."

Claremonte quickly rose from his seat and crossed the room to stand beside Adamat. The sun shone just behind him, surrounding Claremonte with a glowing halo and forcing Adamat to look away. "If I wanted Mr. Tumblar dead, Adamat," Claremonte said, his voice barely above a whisper, "then he'd be dead."

"Or else your men cocked up the job."

Claremonte snorted. "Indeed. You're a very suspicious man, Inspector. Be sure it doesn't put you in an early grave." Claremonte turned away, his back to Adamat, and Adamat was sorely tempted to take a swing at him. One well-placed strike with his cane could paralyze the man—Adamat was sure he'd then be able to strangle him before anyone returned to the room.

Instead, he tried to come up with some witty retort. When none was forthcoming, he joined Hewi, SouSmith, and Hewi's officers in the servants' halls.

"What did he want?" Hewi asked.

"Nothing important," Adamat murmured.

They were led back out through the maze of corridors and servants' doors to the side of the palace and Adamat got inside his carriage. It rocked heavily when SouSmith climbed in beside him. Adamat rapped on the ceiling with his cane, but the carriage didn't move.

"Inspector," Hewi said, coming to the window. "You should steer clear of Claremonte."

I should. But I won't. "I have work to do, Commissioner. With all due respect."

"And with all due respect, steer clear. Claremonte isn't the man we want."

"How do you know?"

Hewi tipped her hat back and leaned into the carriage. She glanced at SouSmith, then gestured for Adamat to step outside. He followed her a dozen paces from the carriage. "One of the officers I had with me is a Knacked," she said in a low voice. "We keep it quiet, because he's very hard to see in the Else if you have the third eye."

"What is his Knack?" Adamat asked.

"Swear to keep this quiet?"

Adamat nodded.

"He can hear lies. He knows when a man is telling the truth or a fib. It's one of our secret weapons, and if it ever got out, the Proprietor would doubtless have him killed."

Adamat whistled. "With good reason." He'd heard of Knackeds like that. One of the most valuable Knacks in the world, and very rare. Adamat wanted to ask what the man was doing working for a police force in Adopest when he could be some king's truthsayer and living like, well, a king. But that would have to wait.

"And you're saying that Claremonte didn't lie?"

"Not a word of it. Fudged a little bit when he said we could have access to all his employees, but that's no surprise. A man like that has secrets. But he didn't order Ricard killed."

Adamat bid farewell to the commissioner and returned to his carriage, dropping into his seat with a sigh.

"Somethin' important?" SouSmith asked.

"Claremonte isn't our man."

"Hmm."

"My thought exactly. I don't even bloody well know where to start if it's not Claremonte." The carriage was soon rolling, and

Adamat slowly went through the list of Ricard's known enemies in his head. "We'll have to go see Ricard. I have to find out if Claremonte has as good a chance at winning as he seems to think. Maybe we'll have a..." Adamat trailed off, a thought entering his mind.

"What?"

"We need to go to the library, too. It'll have to wait until tomorrow, but... Pit!"

SouSmith cocked an eyebrow at him. "Yeah?"

"I just figured out what was bothering me so much about that room. Claremonte was sitting in the window, with the morning sun at his back."

"And?"

"And he didn't cast a shadow."

CHAPTER

28

Field Marshal Tamas!"

The voice echoed up the line and made Tamas's shoulders tighten with recognition. He could hear the approaching rhythm of hoofbeats and the occasional curse of the infantrymen as a man rode up the lines too closely. A glance beside him showed Olem turned in his saddle—not, as some might think, to look toward the rider, but to see which soldiers he'd show the back of his hand later that night.

This was no time to tolerate any show of disrespect, even to Adro's enemies.

"Good afternoon, Beon," Tamas said as the rider came abreast of him.

"Field Marshal," Beon said. The third in line for the Kez throne looked well. His wounds had healed nicely, thanks to the Deliv

Privileged, and his cheeks were fuller now from weeks of inaction and enjoying Sulem's hospitality. "I must speak with you."

"It appears you already are," Tamas commented. The wound in his side still itched despite Sulem's healers and he imagined he could still feel the sharp pain deep in his flesh, though whether that was real or was due to the sting of an old friend's betrayal, he did not know.

Beon had a boyish face despite being in his late twenties—the effects of cabal sorcery meant to keep the royal family looking young—and Tamas thought that the pale scars from the Battle at Kresimir's Fingers helped make him look more serious. He removed his hat and mopped at his forehead. "In private, if possible."

Tamas exchanged a look with Olem. The bodyguard gave a slight smirk.

"There's not a lot of privacy on the march, Sir Prince," Tamas said.

"This is a serious matter," Beon insisted. "I have . . ."—he checked himself, glancing toward the nearby marching infantry, and lowered his voice—"I have learned that you sent away my father's messengers. Without even hearing them!"

"Someone's tongue has been wagging, Olem."

"I'll see to it, sir," Olem said gravely.

Beon stiffened. "I don't make use of spies, but I do have ears, sir! Your men talk to each other loudly and I need only but listen to find out what's going on in the camp."

"You disapprove? I find letting my men gossip is easier and more beneficial than the Kez way—silence enforced by fear. Keeps up the morale."

"You evade my meaning."

"The messengers? It's true. I have nothing to say to them and nothing to hear from them. You know what your father did."

"But *did* he do it?" Beon demanded. "Can you be certain?"

"I have the bodies of thirty-seven grenadiers in Kez uniforms, carrying Kez muskets, bayonets, swords, and powder. They have Kez coins in their purses and they wear boots made in the south of Kez. That's fairly damning evidence."

"I would agree, sir, but..."

"But what?" Tamas felt his ire returning. He respected Beon. He even liked him, as much as he could like a member of the Kez royal family. He was a talented cuirassier and had a sharp mind. Tamas had not thought him so naïve.

Beon plowed on before Tamas could continue. "But I don't think my father would have done this. Why did they go west instead of south? If they were my father's men, they would have bolted straight for the Kez lines after such a daring attack."

"They went west because they hit the rear of the camp and it was easier and faster to take the western road and skirt brigades than it would have been to fight through them. And you don't think he would have done this? Your father, who authorized the sacking of Alvation in order to turn Deliv against Adro? Your father, who by your own admission is just as likely to have you executed for your failure to stop me as he is to welcome you, his son, back from a harrowing campaign?" Tamas shook his head. "Explain it to me. And use small words, for I fear I'm not as nimble-minded as you on this matter."

Beon scowled at Tamas, and Tamas was reminded of Ipille's famous temper. Would Beon reach over and strike him for that? And would Olem shoot him the moment he did? Part of him wanted to find out. But this wasn't the time. "This isn't Kez," Tamas said softly. "And you decided to march with me instead of with the Deliv. You will be accorded respect, but your royalty means little here, son of Ipille."

"Not even my father would break a flag of truce," Beon said after a moment, chewing on his words as if he hoped to convince himself of their truth.

"I think he would. I know he did. You can go see the bodies

of those grenadiers yourself, if you like. They're in some wagons back near the rear of the column. I intend on flinging them at your father's feet before I fling *him* in a dungeon and ransom him back to Kez for all the krana in your damned country."

Beon drew himself up, fingers tightening on the hilt of a cavalry saber that wasn't there. "You go too far."

"Sir," Olem said quietly. Tamas tore his gaze away from Beon long enough to look at his bodyguard. Olem held his cigarette to his lips with one hand, gazing over his fingertips calmly at Tamas.

Tamas felt his anger slip. "Perhaps you're right," he said to Beon.

"Then see his messengers!" Beon said. "You can avoid more bloodshed."

"No, no. You're not right about your father. You're right that I went too far and I apologize for that. Your father attacked us under a flag of truce—likely unaware that the Deliv were as close as they were. He will pay for that crime, though I suspect it is his people who will pay the price and not he himself. Further bloodshed is unavoidable."

There was something that bothered Tamas. Ipille *must* have known that the Deliv forces were on their way. He must know that Deliv had already invaded Kez from the northwest. Why would he dare such a raid against the Adran camp?

Each time he pondered it, he came to the same conclusion: Ipille had somehow learned of Ka-poel and her power over Kresimir and had gambled everything on her capture. Perhaps even now he was learning how to bring Kresimir out of his slumber so that the god could destroy everything in his path. Had Ipille grown so desperate? The stories Taniel had told Tamas about the night he stole Kresimir's bloody bedsheets had made Tamas's skin crawl. How could even Ipille want anything to do with such a creature as this mad god?

Tamas wondered briefly if the Deliv royal cabal would be able to put up any kind of fight in the face of such power.

This wasn't information Tamas was about to relay to Beon. Instead, he said, "Your father's messengers are a delaying tactic. He will try to put me off as long as possible while he brings up fresh troops from Kez. I will not allow that to happen."

Beon relented and stared at his saddle horn in contemplation. Tamas welcomed the silence, hoping that Beon would remain that way, and wondered how Taniel had reacted to his sending Vlora and Gavril to help. It had been a difficult decision—one that might drive Taniel to distraction, but Tamas hoped that Taniel's drive to save his savage lover would force him to work with Vlora. There was no deadlier pair in the powder cabal than those two, save Taniel and Tamas himself.

Maybe Gavril could keep their heads level.

Olem drew Tamas's attention to a messenger galloping down the lines. She wore the blue-and-silver uniform of an Adran dragoon. The woman was covered in sweat and dust, and Tamas noted blood on her silver collar. She reined in ahead of him and saluted.

"Corporal Salli reporting, sir, of the Seventy-Ninth Dragoons. Sir, a moment to catch my breath, sir!"

"Granted," Tamas said, exchanging a glance with Olem. The Seventy-Ninth were supposed to be scouting the western plains. Had the Kez Privileged from the other night tried to cut across the plains and run into his dragoons? "General Beon, if you would excuse me." Tamas waited until the Kez prince had fallen back out of earshot, then said, "Are you wounded, soldier?"

A quizzical look crossed her face, then she touched her collar. "Oh, this? Not my blood, sir. Belongs to some Kez cuirassier."

Olem brought his mount up next to hers and offered his canteen, which she took gratefully, draining half in one go and splashing a little on her face and neck before handing it back. "Thank you, sir."

"Your report?" Olem asked.

"We were attacked a little north of Gillsfellow by Kez cuirassiers. We outnumbered them two to one, but they managed to surprise us, and took their toll before we were able to recover and win the day."

"How many did you lose?" Tamas asked.

"A hundred and twenty-seven dead, three hundred and twelve wounded. We killed one hundred and seventy-one of the enemy and captured twice that many, most of whom are wounded."

"Could be worse, I suppose."

"It is, sir. We lost Colonel Davis."

Tamas swore. Colonel Davis was a capable cavalry commander, if a little shortsighted at times. "Gillsfellow is north of us. Damn it, how did they get behind us? And what the pit are they doing so far north?"

Corporal Salli shook her head. "Not sure, sir. I passed two companies of our dragoons on my way to give a report. The Thirty-Sixth has been badly mauled, and their major has lost all his messengers. Gave me a report for you." She handed the report to Olem. "I also spotted more Kez in the distance, about eight miles northwest of here. Looked like dragoons, at least a regiment of them."

Tamas took the report and glanced over it before handing it to Olem. "Get some rest, Corporal. I'll have orders ready for the Seventy-Ninth in a quarter of an hour."

The messenger saluted and rode on down the line. Tamas swore again under his breath. "I can't afford to lose any more senior officers. Find out if there's anyone worth promoting among the Seventy-Ninth. If not, find a replacement from that list I gave you earlier."

"Yes sir," Olem said.

"Also, send messengers to our dragoon regiments. Let them know that Ipille is trying to win superiority of the plains. He must have sent all his remaining cavalry north the day after the parley.

They should keep their eyes out for traps. He's trying to distract us and I won't let that happen. Send a messenger to Sulem and see if he can spare a couple thousand dragoons to reinforce our own." Tamas tried to make sense of everything in his head. The battle would have taken place not far south of where Taniel was chasing those Kez Privileged. Perhaps the Kez cavalry were screening for the retreating grenadiers.

"Our cuirassiers, sir?"

"They're too slow out in the open. I'm keeping them in reserve for when we meet the Kez lines. If Ipille wastes all his cavalry in a bid for the plains, he'll have nothing to counter ours when it comes to the real battle."

"But they'll be behind us, sir."

"And cut off from communication with the main army. A fact we can use to our advantage. See if Sulem has any riding Privileged."

"Oh, that'll be a nasty surprise for Ipille's cavalry. Excellent thinking, sir."

"Looks like another one coming in, sir." Olem nodded up the line to where a horseman had just crested a hilltop and was coming down toward them along the road.

"Shit. What is it this time?"

The messenger was one of Tamas's own—a ranger from the vanguard. "Sir," he said before he'd come to a stop.

"Tell me we're getting close to the enemy camp."

The messenger grimaced. "We are, sir. A little under four miles."

"But?"

"But they're gone, sir. They've up and fled. They left this morning, marching double-time."

Tamas felt as if a cold hand had reached into his gut. He dismissed the messenger and sat brooding in his saddle.

"Sir? Isn't that a good thing?" Olem asked.

"No," Tamas said. "It's as I suspected: Ipille is pulling back, resorting to delaying actions. He just needs to keep us off of him long enough to awaken Kresimir, and then he'll kill us all."

"What do we do, sir?"

"We press on, and hope Taniel catches up to his savage Bone-eye in time."

"And if he doesn't?"

"Then we're all dead men anyway, and I intend on taking Ipille with me when we go."

CHAPTER

29

W hy didn't you tell me?" Taniel asked.

He rode alongside Gavril on the western road, trying desperately not to think about Vlora. She still loved him, Gavril had claimed, and she had not denied it. The revelation had been a shock—something that Taniel hadn't even considered. She'd bedded another man, hadn't she? That meant that she no longer wanted him, didn't it? Feelings he'd spent the last six months trying to bury were suddenly bubbling to the surface. Until last night the whole situation had been cut-and-dried. He'd dealt with it and moved on, only to find that he'd never had the facts straight in the first place.

It was confusing and it made him want to shoot something.

The big man beside him sat slumped, looking half-asleep and almost ready to fall out of his saddle. It was a misleading posture.

He was watching the road, and he read the wear of hooves in the mud like a scholar might read a long-dead language.

"Eh?" he rumbled. "Oh, you mean back on South Pike?"

"Yes."

"I was drunk."

"You sobered up pretty quick."

"Well, that's the odd thing. I kinda assumed you knew."

Taniel peered more closely at the big Watchmaster. "What?"

"It didn't actually occur to me that Tamas wouldn't tell you that I was your uncle. Not for a while, anyway, and when it did, there wasn't a good time to tell you. We were in the middle of a rather violent siege, after all. And I thought he probably had a reason for not telling you that the South Pike Mountainwatch drunkard was your uncle."

Taniel couldn't help but feel some indignation at that. "So you weren't going to actually tell me? I've thought—for years—that Tamas was the only close family I had left."

"Really?" Gavril straightened in his saddle. "You know, every time I think I've come to terms with the shit your father does, I find out about something like this. He didn't even mention me?"

"I have vague memories," Taniel said. "Of being told *about* my uncles. Nothing more. No names."

Gavril grunted and tugged gently on his reins. "I've been a fairly reprehensible drunk since your mother died. Maybe Tamas didn't want me to meet you. Or maybe the memories of another family were too much for him." He snorted to show what he thought of that.

"Too much? I don't think the man has emotions."

"You'd be surprised. Your other uncle was Camenir, my little brother. He was just a boy, not much older than you when we went after Ipille. He's buried in Kez." Gavril held up his hand for a halt and pointed at the ground. "Riders. Around sixty came through here yesterday. They rested here. If memory serves, we're getting pretty close to the Counter's Road, the north-south highway. We'll want to slow our pace, prepare for anything. If there's going to be another ambush, it'll be soon."

Taniel stowed the questions he wanted to ask Gavril in the back of his mind and tried to ignore the surge of confused emotion caused by the sight of Vlora coming back down the road toward them. She had been on scouting duty with one of the Riflejacks. He could tell by the urgency with which she leaned forward in the saddle that she had found something.

"We're about a half mile from the intersection," she said as she reached them. "And the grenadiers have laid a trap."

"How do you know?" Gavril asked the question before Taniel could.

"They're waiting about a little under two miles to the south, flanking the road. I got just close enough to sense the powder and get a feel for their positioning and came back."

Taniel asked, "Any Privileged?"

"None that I could see with my third eye."

"Perfect. Their Privileged must have left them behind to deal with us. We have the advantage because we know their positioning. We can turn their trap back on them."

"Better than that," Vlora said. "I can just detonate all their powder. Take out the whole lot in one go. Few enough powder mages can do it at a distance."

"Few enough? There's just you."

Vlora gave him a grin. "So they won't be expecting it."

"They might have Ka-poel."

"Not if the Privileged aren't there," Gavril said. "They'll have taken her on ahead if they know what she's carrying."

Of course. They would keep her close as they fled. But...but what if they didn't? Vlora could detonate all their powder, killing her right along with the grenadiers. "I can't risk it."

"Can she be seen in the Else?" Vlora asked.

"She has the glow. It's hard to tell, for most."

"But *you* can tell?"

"Yes."

"Then come with me. The two of us can get close enough, make sure she's not there. You can put a bullet through any Privileged they may have and I'll detonate the powder. Our Riflejacks can stay back half a mile and come in to mop everything up."

Taniel checked his pistols to be sure they were loaded. "That'll work."

They continued on until they reached the T-intersection, where their highway ended in the Counter's Road. Vlora stayed out front with the scouts, and Taniel hung back with Gavril. He wanted to ask the big Watchmaster about his mother, but his mouth didn't seem to want to form the words. Vlora was still in love with him, his own lover was still held captive by the Kez, and they were about to ride straight into half a company of grenadiers.

"Taniel," Gavril said, bringing him back to the present. "Bad news."

"What is it?"

"Someone's ridden north, here at the intersection."

"What do you mean?"

Gavril dismounted and spent a few moments examining the ground of the intersection, mumbling quietly to himself. "Eight, maybe ten split off from the main group. They're heading north. Everyone else went south."

"Can you be sure?" Taniel asked, feeling a sudden fear. What if the Kez had planned a second ambush? Taniel's company would turn south along the road and try to spring the first trap while a second group of them came down from behind. He reached out with his senses, pushing them to their limit to try to feel something else out there—Ka-poel, a Privileged, powder. There was nothing.

"Not completely, no," Gavril said. "It could be travelers. It could be Adran patrols, unaware that the Kez are even in this part of Adro. Pit, it could be Mountainwatchers, down from the peaks to cut wood or get supplies."

Of course they weren't going north. That would be preposterous. There was nothing to the north but Adro for hundreds of miles. They could try the high passes for Deliv, but the Deliv were on the warpath after Alvation. No Kez would make it through their lands alive.

"Norrine," Taniel said.

The powder mage drew her horse over to Taniel and saluted. "Sir?"

"You're the best rider of this bunch and you've got sharp eyes. Go with Gavril. The two of you move north and try to sniff out a Kez trap. Vlora and I will go south and slaughter the grenadiers. It'll be up to you two to tell us if the Kez have come in behind us. Flerrier, Doll, and the Riflejacks will take the road and be ready to guard our rear."

"Yes sir."

Gavril gave a slow nod. "It's risky, splitting like this. But it's the best way to keep them from getting the drop on us."

"Get to it, then." Taniel looked around the gathered soldiers and mages. "We have Kez to kill."

Taniel dismounted and handed his reins to one of the Riflejacks, then collected his pistols, rifle, and sword. Vlora followed him, and together they crept through the forest, flanking the road on the east side by a few hundred yards. It would allow them to avoid any trickery on the part of the Kez and to sneak up on the grenadiers from the side—they wouldn't expect mages in hot pursuit to slow down long enough for this.

Not that it was slowing them too much. He and Vlora could move through the trees more quietly than most, and they both burned powder trances, which made them move and think faster.

Taniel could hear every crack of twigs and creak of trees in the forest for two hundred paces. It was a cacophony of information, but part of his training as a mage had been to filter that information into what were the animal noises of the forest and what was the movement of men.

Taniel found himself relieved that their mission required silence and the clear focus of moving quietly in the woods. He couldn't afford to let Vlora distract him now. He was able to push those thoughts to the back of his mind, where they haunted him like a half-seen shadow.

He knew they would be back.

He let Vlora take point. Less than half an hour later she raised a fist, signaling a halt, and crouched down into the underbrush. Taniel crept to her side.

"We're about a half mile out," she said.

"Very close."

"That's about the farthest I dare try the detonation, and I have a clear sense of them all. They're flanking the road from high vantage points." She touched her temple and was silent for a moment, her eyes looking unfocused. "I'd guess as many as sixty of them."

"Sounds right," Taniel said. "Any Privileged?"

"No. I don't sense your savage girl, either. You'd better check for her."

Taniel took a sniff of powder, trying to ignore the way Vlora had said "your savage girl" and the accusation in her tone. He opened his third eye, steadying himself with one hand on the rough bark of a tree, and studied the Kez trap.

He focused on the area where he could sense the black powder and squinted into the trees, looking for the familiar dim glow of pastel color in the Else that indicated Ka-poel's presence. The strength of her glow was somewhere between a Knacked and a Privileged, but several shades darker in color, which made her more difficult to see.

Several minutes passed before he let his third eye drop. He put his forehead against the back of his hand for a moment, fighting down his nausea. When he'd recovered, he said, "No sign of her. Does it seem odd to you that they have no Knacked?"

"Now that you mention it..." Vlora's eyes were fixed on the Kez position. "Maybe they had one or two and they were killed in the attack on our camp."

Taniel brushed off the niggling doubt he felt in the back of his head. "Probably right. Are you ready?"

"Yes." Vlora moved several feet forward to crouch behind a fallen tree. Putting her back to the hollow trunk, she set her rifle across her knees and closed her eyes. Taniel saw a smile touch her lips and then felt her reaching out with her senses.

He felt the series of explosions rippling through his mage senses. A moment later and he heard angry bangs going off like a fusillade on a battlefield.

"Go," Vlora said.

Taniel hopped the fallen tree and was sprinting through the forest, rifle held at the ready, eyes sharp for the green-and-tan uniforms of the Kez grenadiers. He heard Vlora fall in behind and to his right. Dry leaves crunched under his feet and branches whipped his arms and face. This wasn't about stealth now but about catching any survivors before they could recover.

They would be confused and disoriented from the explosions— more than likely wounded—and thinking that a whole brigade of Adran troops were about to fall on them. Taniel had to reach their position quickly and take them captive or kill them before they realized they were only facing two powder mages.

He reached the top of a hill and paused to get his bearings. "Where?" he gasped.

"Next rise!" Vlora didn't pause, racing past him and taking point. She had already fixed her bayonet. Taniel cursed and fixed his own as he chased after her.

He skidded to a stop near the top of the next rise and ducked behind a tree. He could see Vlora up ahead. She had slung her rifle over her shoulder and drawn a pistol. Slowly, she stood up.

Taniel waited for her signal to move forward and strained for the sounds of the wounded and dying. Nothing. Even with his powder-enhanced senses the forest was utterly still. No birds, no animals. Had Vlora's powder ignition killed every single one of the grenadiers outright? That didn't seem possible.

The moments stretched on while Vlora stood silently, and Taniel finally lost all patience. He dashed to her side, rifle ready.

The scene on the hillside below them stopped him dead in his tracks. He could see the road from this vantage, and the evidence of powder detonations all along this hill and the hillside on the opposite side of the road. Black stains marked the trees, leaves smoldered, fallen branches burned, and the scent of the spent powder hung in the air like a fog. The ground was pockmarked with small craters.

But the only victims were the trees themselves and a couple of unfortunate squirrels.

Taniel lifted his rifle further and spun around. His eyes scanned the surrounding forest, looking for a trap within a trap. Not a creature stirred.

"I don't understand," Vlora said. "Is this some kind of distraction? Something to slow us down?"

A nearby motion caught Taniel's eye. Upon closer examination he found it to be the leather strap of a powder horn, the ends burned off, but the leather itself surprisingly unharmed. It swung from a branch gently, as if mocking them. Taniel felt his heart thundering in his chest as he tried to discover not how they'd been tricked, but why.

"Do you hear something?" Vlora asked.

Taniel cocked his head to the wind and waited for the sound to reach his ears. It didn't take long.

"Screams," Taniel said. He was already running for the road as he said it. The screams were coming from the north. From the Riflejacks they'd left behind.

This wasn't the entire trap.

Taniel raced down the hard-packed dirt tracks of the western highway.

He could hear Vlora's pounding feet behind him as he tore a powder charge from his belt pouch and stuffed it in his mouth, feeling the grit of the black powder in his gums. In his haste he dropped several charges, but he didn't have time to stop for them.

The trick was so simple. So obvious. They knew that Tamas would send powder mages after them. The mage would sense the trap, approach with caution, and then be ambushed from the rear. Or, in this case, he'd be separated from his men entirely. He had fallen for it without hesitation!

It took him and Vlora less than two minutes to cross the mile between the false ambush and where their men waited on the road, but even that was too late.

He took in the scene as he rounded a bend: Sixty or more Kez grenadiers, armed with pikes and heavy sabers, their kits stripped of black powder, had fallen upon the Riflejacks. Bodies of men and horses littered the road and surrounding woods, and though less than fifteen Kez grenadiers remained on their feet, the Riflejacks, along with Doll and Flerrier, had been slaughtered.

Taniel put on a burst of speed, ready to close with the surviving Kez, but he felt a pair of hands on his side and he was thrown from the road and into a dry streambed.

He landed with an *oof* and Vlora on top of him.

"What...?" he started.

"Shh."

He fell silent for long enough for her to poke her head from the streambed. "What the pit was that?" he hissed.

"Our men are down," she said. "No sense in rushing in like fools."

Taniel collected his hat. "Within minutes they're going to figure out that there were more than two powder mages in the group and come looking for us."

"Give me a moment, I'm thinking."

Taniel gripped his rifle. "We don't have a moment. Gavril and Norrine, remember? They'll have heard the screams as well as us."

"Shit."

Taniel slapped her on the shoulder. "Go on. Back across the road. Take that hill over there and hit them on my signal."

"All right." Vlora retreated along the streambed, back to the bend in the road, before crossing over. Taniel gave her thirty seconds and then made off at a crouching run.

He circled behind a knoll some forty paces from the road. His eyes, accustomed to forest tracking in Fatrasta, saw the signs of the grenadiers immediately. They had hid behind this very knoll, waiting for the Riflejacks to cross their path, then descended upon them—probably from both sides, considering their lack of muskets. They needn't have worried about cross fire.

He reached the top of the knoll and hunkered down beside a tree with a clear view of the road. The grenadiers had rounded up three bloody, wounded Riflejacks and were questioning them aggressively, while their comrades tended to their own wounded.

Taniel loaded his rifle with two bullets and looked for the stripes of the grenadier commander, a captain. It was the man doing the questioning, and as Taniel watched, he leaned over and casually slit the throat of one of the Riflejacks.

Taniel's bullets caught the grenadier captain in the right temple, and a sergeant, likely his second-in-command, in the stomach. Before Taniel could load more bullets, the grenadiers sprang into action. They readied their pikes and kicked rifles and powder horns away from them. These men were trained for fighting powder mages.

One ill-timed kick lost a grenadier his leg as the powder detonated. Taniel grinned, reloading his rifle as the Kez scrambled for cover. His next double-shot hit only one of his targets, taking the woman down with a gut shot. He heard one of the grenadiers shout in a language that was most definitely not Kez.

Was that Brudanian? Why would Kez soldiers be shouting in Brudanian? Taniel didn't have time to think about it. Ten big Kez soldiers leapt from their cover and rushed Taniel's knoll. None noticed as one of their number was gunned down from behind.

Taniel didn't have time to finish loading another shot. He leapt to his feet, throwing another powder charge into his mouth and blocking the thrust of a pike with his rifle barrel. He was forced back, unable to counterattack due to the closeness of the trees, and helpless to do anything but watch the grenadiers flank him.

He let go of his rifle and leapt to the side as the soldier's momentum carried him forward. Taniel drew his belt knife and rammed it between the grenadier's ribs, thrusting the man aside and taking his pike, whirling to block the thrust of a saber.

He dispatched two more, taking a heavy cut above his brow that poured blood into his eye before Vlora joined the fight. She whirled through the remaining grenadiers with her short sword and a powder trance, giving her a huge advantage in speed in the close quarters, cutting down every remaining man in moments. By the time Taniel had wiped the blood from his face, the fight was over.

Winded and half-blinded, Taniel turned toward the sound of hoofbeats pounding up the road. He snatched up his rifle and loaded it, ready for the worst.

Gavril's and Norrine's horses stopped short of the slaughter, refusing to go any farther. Taniel could hear Gavril's curses from the woods.

"Taniel!" Gavril yelled.

"Here," he called back, already jogging toward the road.

"It was a damned trick," Taniel said. "The powder was set a mile down the road, laid out like men lying in wait, and the grenadiers hiding here in the woods."

Gavril swung from his horse while Vlora ran to free the two surviving Riflejacks.

"Sorry, sir," one of the Riflejacks said to Taniel, wincing as Vlora helped him to his feet. "Came out of the woods like ghosts. Flerrier and Doll fought like the pit, but we were overwhelmed after our first volley. The pikes did in our horses without trouble."

Gavril put down one of the frightened, thrashing horses with his pistol, while Norrine gave Taniel stitches on his brow. "Gather their survivors," Taniel ordered. "I want to find out what the pit they know." His head spun and he was still trying to make sense of it all. The trap had been perfect, and he'd walked right into it. It made him furious to see those Adran soldiers—*his* soldiers—lying dead in the road. There was no one to blame but himself.

There were twenty-three surviving grenadiers, and Taniel could tell at a glance that most of them would be dead of their wounds by morning. His own two surviving Riflejacks might survive if they could avoid infection, having gotten off with a dozen light wounds between the two of them. The Riflejacks' horses—and Taniel's and Vlora's—were either dead or had thrown their riders and fled.

Taniel climbed to his feet after Norrine finished his stitches. He'd had time to catch his breath and let the pain and anger simmer. He had to come up with a plan now. They'd lost valuable time, and they'd lost their advantage of five powder mages.

Norrine knelt beside one of the Kez grenadiers, removing her own needle and silk thread.

"No, don't," Taniel said. "They're not getting any help until they tell us what the game is." He walked up and down the line of grenadiers, now stripped of their jackets and with their hands tied behind their backs with their own belts. Gavril stood over them, arms crossed, teeth set. He did not look like a man to cross right then.

"How about it?" Taniel asked. "First man who tells me how many men your Privileged master has left will be the first man to get medical treatment."

Some of the soldiers stared at their feet. Others stared at him dumbly. A few of them moaned from the pain and one was weeping and holding his bloody side.

Taniel repeated his offer in Kez. The soldiers glanced at each other but did not answer. "Any of you speak Brudanian? I don't know more than a few words."

"I do." Gavril said, then rattled off a few sentences. The men seemed to perk up at this, and one of them answered. Gavril switched to Adran. "He says it's just three Privileged, six grenadiers, and the savage."

"Why the pit would they be speaking Brudanian?" Taniel asked, though he already knew the answer.

"Because they're Brudanian," Vlora said. "Like the army that's holding Adopest right now."

Gavril said, "Norrine and I followed fresh tracks, nine sets, north. We only turned back when we heard the fighting. They're taking your girl to Adopest."

"Bastards have pulled one over on our whole damn army," Taniel said. "Tamas is fighting the wrong war."

CHAPTER
30

Nila worked her way through the Adran and then the Deliv camps, slowly gathering her courage to approach the Deliv cabal.

She had not expected them to arrive so soon. Tamas had insisted she stay close in case he needed her magic—whatever good it could do him, considering she still couldn't consistently pull sorcery from the Else—and hadn't let her accompany Bo to the Privileged healers. He'd said Bo could be gone for too long to risk losing both of his Privileged for a possible fight.

But just two days later the Kez cabal had arrived. Had it been some kind of a trick to separate her and Bo? Or just a miscommunication?

Perhaps she was just being overly cautious.

Bo would be proud.

She threaded her way through Deliv soldiers, who watched her closely but kept their distance. She wore a blue dress too fine for a laundress but not fashionable enough for a lady, and she had done her hair in a borrowed mirror. She was just wondering why no one had asked for her credentials, when a dark-skinned Deliv slid up beside her.

She recognized the stripes of a captain on his lapels. He was a handsome man, quite tall with slender shoulders. He grinned at her. "Going somewhere, my lady?"

"Yes, thank you." She could feel his hand hovering just behind the small of her back.

"Can I help you find where you're going?" His hand brushed her ass gently. She turned toward him, a welcoming smile on her face, and punched him in the nose.

He reeled back with a high-pitched squeal, fumbling at his face. "Aii! Pit, woman!" Surprise turned to anger, which quickly progressed to fury. He wiped his nose with one sleeve, looking down at the trickle of blood on his cuff, then reached for his belt. "You made a mistake, lass."

Nila realized that mistake just after her knuckles connected with his nose. She was in a foreign camp—she had no companion or chaperone, and she didn't know the least thing about Deliv social mores. What's more, this man had the stripes of a captain on his lapel. This wasn't the Adran army—he was most likely a nobleman and could cause all sorts of trouble for her.

"No," she said, advancing as her mind raced. Nothing to do now but follow through. "I'll teach you a lesson, you ingrate. I'm looking for the Deliv cabal. If you touch me again, I'll put that hand so far up your ass, you'll be able to scratch your own nose."

The Deliv captain retreated several feet. He visually searched her up and down, glancing repeatedly at her bare hands, looking for evidence that she was a Privileged. She could see his mind working for several moments, as if he was weighing his odds. Finally, he said in a nasally tone, "They're sequestered just to the east."

"Thank you."

She turned her back on him though every instinct told her not to, and began heading in the indicated direction. This was another part to play, she reminded herself. No more dangerous than the parts she played for Lord Vetas. She was a lady, a Privileged, and she had to demand respect.

"Watch yourself, lass," the Deliv's voice called to her.

She wanted to make a rude gesture, but she thought perhaps that was beneath the dignity of a Privileged.

The Deliv cabal, it turned out, was not hard to spot. Immense tents of white and Kelly-green rose just beyond the next rise. While not as high as the tent belonging to the Deliv king, these were far wider and more numerous, with dozens of chambers seemingly interconnected by cloaked avenues to keep the Privileged's comings and goings shielded from common eyes. The whole area was cordoned off from the rest of the camp by a fine green ribbon tied at intervals to tall wooden posts. Each post was covered in Deliv script and arcane symbols, which Bo had taught Nila enough to recognize as wards—and the warnings that accompanied them.

She followed the ribbon around to the south until she found an opening. Deliv cabal guards—immense men with broad shoulders, gleaming breastplates, and spiked helmets—stood at attention with muskets shouldered.

She stepped between them, only to find her way immediately blocked by those muskets.

"Step back," one of the guards said in heavily accented Adran, the words laced with menace.

She did.

Neither of them so much as looked at her. Glancing from guard to guard, she extended one foot slightly, only to watch the tips of their musket barrels slide back across her path. It seemed like something out of a comedy play.

"I'm looking for Privileged Borbador," she said, pulling her foot back.

Neither of the men responded.

"He's an Adran Privileged. He was taken to your healers just two nights ago."

Again, nothing.

"I'm here from Field Marshal Tamas. This is an important query," Nila ventured. If invocation of Tamas's name meant anything to the cabal guards, they didn't show it. "Is there someone I should see?" A cold sweat broke out on the back of Nila's neck. Did these men even know who Bo was? Had Bo reached the Kez cabal alive? The possibility that he had died on the way crept into her mind and she felt a rising panic.

What did she have to do to be allowed admittance to the cabal? She needed answers. Maybe if she set fire to their shoes, they wouldn't be able to ignore her any longer.

A quick glance at the polished bayonets of the guards, and she imagined that setting their shoes on fire would be a quick path to a disemboweling. She raised her hands. A demonstration of some kind seemed to be in order. There was nothing else for her to do. She still didn't know how to wield her powers. Without Bo she might as well go back to being a washerwoman.

"What do you want?"

Nila nearly jumped out of her skin. A woman had approached from behind one of the guards. Her caramel skin was lighter than most of the Deliv and her face was long but beautiful, with high cheekbones and a narrow chin. Her spine was straight, her head held high, and her hands were clasped at her waist, clothed in runed Privileged gloves.

"Make it quick," the woman said impatiently before Nila could answer. She didn't look at Nila's face, but rather over her head, as if Nila herself was worth little more than a cursory glance.

"My name is Nila. I'm looking for Privileged Borbador."

"He's not seeing anyone."

Nila swallowed, her throat dry. "I'm..." She stopped herself, a warning dancing across the back of her mind. "*Careful with any*

Privileged," Bo had said, not long after discovering that Nila didn't require gloves for her sorcery. "*They detest change. Any change could bring the upset of their unrivaled power among the Nine. If a member of a rival cabal discovers your unique ability before you've learned to defend yourself, you may wind up being cut apart by Privileged surgeons in a dank room somewhere.*"

"I need to see him," Nila finished.

"You his whore?"

She nearly choked on this. "Excuse me?"

The woman's eyes narrowed and she seemed to look at Nila for the first time. "Bo's been letting himself slip. Your skin's too pale and you're too short. By Kresimir, his tastes have gotten worse."

"I'm here from Field Marshal Tamas," Nila said, biting her tongue. "I need an update on Privileged Borbador."

"Don't lie to me, wench. One of Tamas's men was here an hour ago. Pit, you must be new. Bo's always liked the clingy types more than he should. He's still alive, if that's what you're asking. If he still wants you, he'll find you in a couple of weeks. If he doesn't, you won't hear from him again. I suggest you go spread your legs for some Adran officer to occupy your time."

Nila was near bursting. How could this woman, Privileged though she was, speak to her in such a manner? Even when she was nothing more than a laundress, the lord and the lady of the house had never been so contemptuous, and Lady Eldaminse had *hated* her.

The Privileged waved one gloved hand in dismissal. "If you come around here anymore, I'll make sure he never sees you again." There was no malice or threat in her tone of voice. It was just a statement, as casual as a cook might speak of cutting up a chicken. She turned around and strode off without another word, leaving Nila looking for something, anything, to say to her back.

Nila's hands clenched and unclenched behind her back, and she snatched them to her sides before she caught her dress on fire. She took a step forward, only to find two muskets blocking her path again.

"You should go," one of the guards said, a note of sympathy in his voice.

Nila whirled on the ball of her foot and stalked away, wondering if she had the power in her to set fire to the whole damned cabal pavilion before they knew what was happening. A "whore," that Privileged had called her! Spreading her legs for an Adran noble? She could feel the blue flames dancing on her fingertips, and balled her hands into fists.

That's what the wards are for, dummy. She could hear Bo's voice in the back of her head. A lick of flame summoned from the Else, directed at that cabal camp, and all the pit would come crashing down on her head.

On a whim, Nila changed course and worked her way around the cordoned cabal camp. Perhaps she should have told the woman that she was Bo's apprentice—that she was a Privileged, not some commoner to be treated like trash. Maybe she would have gotten a little more respect.

Then again, that woman shouldn't treat anyone like that.

Nila caught sight of a break in the Privileged's tents and saw the smokeless flames rising from a fire pit. A guard eyed her inquisitive glances but said nothing as she stood on her toes and looked for some sign of Bo. There were a few Privileged and two or three times as many cabal soldiers in their heavy armor, carrying heavy pikes and sabers. She wondered that there weren't more muskets, then remembered Bo mentioning that most Privileged were allergic to black powder and avoided it when possible.

She felt a smile touch her lips as she caught sight of white skin among the various shades of black and brown. There was Bo, sitting next to the fire, staring disconnectedly into the flames. He looked very pale but otherwise unharmed. Nila took a breath, a shout on the tip of her tongue, but it caught in her throat as the

Deliv Privileged—the same one who had dismissed her so rudely—emerged from a nearby pavilion and approached Bo.

He said something to her, but she just shook her head, then stepped over to him and pressed her lips to his. He didn't resist or protest—his cheeks flushed and he was soon kissing her back. She traced a finger down his chest and her hand dipped lower . . .

Nila was halfway back to the Adran camp before she had another rational thought, and she was already at Tamas's command tent before she knew where she was going.

Field Marshal Tamas stood outside the front of his command tent, eyes shielded from the sun, and examined a pair of maps laid out on the dirt in front of him, the edges held down by several fist-sized rocks. A couple of his officers muttered as she approached, but no one stopped her.

"What happened to your dress?" Olem asked.

She looked down. It looked like she'd been smeared with soot. The bottom half of her dress had two black streaks, as if ink had dripped off her hands. She could smell singed cotton. "Nothing," she snapped. "When are we leaving?"

Tamas snorted, bending down over his maps, but didn't say anything.

"We're camped here for the night," Olem said. "We'll leave in the morning."

"Oh. Right. When will we meet the Kez on the field?"

"Sooner than you may wish," Tamas muttered, barely loud enough for her to hear.

"What's that supposed to mean?"

"Nila," Olem said, a note of warning in his voice.

"It's all right, Olem," Tamas said, still not looking up from his maps. "She's learning how to be a real Privileged, and the insolence goes with it. It means, Privileged Nila, that you are woefully under-prepared for what I'm going to ask you to do."

"What's that?"

"Slaughter thousands of Kez soldiers. Burn them like tinder. Listen to their screams as they wither beneath your sorcery."

Nila balked at that. "Why do you say I'm unprepared? I did it once, didn't I?" Nila *was* unprepared. She had blocked that battle out of her mind so thoroughly that she'd almost forgotten it, and she felt a wave of nausea at the memory.

"Because that's what Bo said," Olem interrupted.

"You've seen him?"

"An hour ago. He's still alive, but he's in no state to fight. He asked me to give you a warning—stay away from the Deliv cabal. We're to keep your presence a secret until it's absolutely necessary."

Nila remembered that Deliv Privileged kissing Bo, her hand reaching between Bo's legs. "I'm sure he did," she said.

Tamas finally looked up, but it was only to exchange a glance with Olem.

"Another messenger coming in, sir," Olem said.

"Of course." Tamas gave a weary sigh.

A Deliv in his Kelly-green uniform rounded the tent on horseback, barely reining in before his mount trampled Tamas's maps. "Sir," the messenger panted. "We've been attacked!"

"The Deliv camp?"

"The baggage train," he said.

Tamas leapt into his tent and returned, buckling his sword to his belt. "Rouse the troops!" he called to Olem.

"Sir, they're already gone," the messenger said.

"What do you mean?"

"They hit and left before we could mount a defense."

"The baggage train?" Nila asked. A glance from Tamas urged caution. The Deliv weren't supposed to know about her. She took a deep breath, fighting the anger and sense of helplessness that threatened to overwhelm her.

"Yes, ma'am," the messenger said.

"How the pit did Kez dragoons get behind us?" Tamas demanded. "They shouldn't be . . . Pit, is that sorcery?"

Nila looked to see what had caught Tamas's eye. To their northwest, light flashed along the horizon like the sun reflecting off a dozen mirrors. She opened her third eye, slowly so as not to let it overwhelm her, and saw the splashes of pastel color whirling in the distance, fighting something—a strange darkness, the likes of which she had not yet seen in the Else. It seemed to swallow all light that touched it, moving like an inky cloud upon the horizon.

Something about that darkness touched a nerve in Nila's subconscious and she felt sick with fear.

Doubt crossed Tamas's face. Had he seen it too?

"Our people are giving chase, sir," the messenger said. "King Sulem has requested your presence."

"He better have a damned good explanation. Your people were supposed to be backing up my dragoons to prevent this very thing from happening."

Nila caught Tamas's quick glance. "Stay here," he said quietly. "But be ready for anything." Then he was gone, yelling for his horse, Olem close on his heels.

Be ready for anything, he'd said.

That's a little vague. She looked to the northwest. The flashes of light were now gone, but a chill crept up her spine as she remembered that darkness with which they had warred.

CHAPTER
31

Tamas could feel his anger begin to ebb as he arrived at King Sulem's tent.

The Deliv messenger escorted him up to the royal guards, then excused himself and returned to the camp, while Tamas and Olem were admitted immediately. Tamas paused once to look toward the west, where he'd last seen flashes of sorcery, but all signs of the battle had faded. He could still sense that sorcery-swallowing darkness in the Else like a bad taste in his mouth.

King Sulem's tent was not all that different from Tamas's own, if perhaps a bit more spacious. The king was not an ostentatious man. His luxuries were limited to fine furs, hardwood chairs, and an intricately carved desk in one corner. His sleeping and dressing chambers were closed off from the main room, and a bodyguard stood in each corner, both inside and outside the tent, their bayonets fixed.

Sulem sat cross-legged on a fine cushion in the middle of the floor, reading glasses perched on his nose and what looked to be some kind of report in his hands. Tamas noted the two Privileged in the room—Magus Doranth, head of Sulem's royal cabal, was a colossus of a man, a head taller than Tamas, with skin as black as night, jade rings on his fingers, and black hair tied in a thick knot behind his neck. He stood beside his king, arms folded, and glared at Tamas.

Privileged Vivia seemed Doranth's opposite in every manner. Her skin was the color of coffee with cream and she had blue eyes, hinting at ancestry that was not fully Deliv. She had a long, slender face that gave her a queenly visage, and she managed to lounge on one of the hardwood chairs in the corner. From what Tamas knew of the Deliv cabal, these were the two major players—and they disliked each other immensely.

"Vivia," Olem whispered in Tamas's ear, "is the one who's seeing to Bo. They go quite a ways back."

Tamas bowed. "King Sulem. Privileged," he said, addressing the group.

"Magus," Doranth corrected in a low, rumbling voice.

"Is a magus not a Privileged?" Tamas asked.

"You hold the rank of field marshal. Would you rather I call you 'king-killer'?"

"Oh, let it go." Sulem waved a hand at his cabal head. "We can prattle on all day about honorifics. We have a problem."

"I understand that to be the case," Tamas said. He had not been offered a seat, so he clasped his hands behind his back and looked down at the Deliv monarch, who seemed unbothered by Tamas's looming over him. It was not the king who spoke.

"For the past two days, our baggage train has been ravaged by Kez dragoons," Vivia said. Her tone was clipped, and she examined Tamas not with the hostility of Doranth but with a certain amount of wariness.

Tamas swore inwardly. The Deliv baggage train was not just supplying the Deliv but was also providing food, surgeons, and ammunition for the Adran army—items his men were running dangerously low on. "I've sent my cavalry onto the plains, and last I heard, you had sent three thousand of your own as reinforcements. Are they not getting the job done?" Tamas hadn't had a report in twelve hours; not something that would normally have concerned him, but now he was nervous. He had thought his men would have little trouble mopping up the Kez cavalry who had slipped up north of them.

"Our people have had a few losses," Doranth said.

"A few?" Vivia said, her tone rising in disbelief. "You have a strange definition of 'few,' Magus."

Doranth bared his teeth at Vivia. "You'll be quiet until you're addressed."

"No, I will not be quiet." Vivia rose from her seat, smoothing the front of her Deliv uniform with one hand. "Not while you run this cabal into the ground." She turned to Tamas. "We fielded six thousand dragoons and cuirassiers forty-eight hours ago. We have less than twenty-seven hundred left."

Tamas reeled at this information. The Deliv weren't known for stellar cavalry, but instead for their finely trained infantry. But that didn't mean their cavalry were worthless. Far from it. How could this be possible?

"Not only that," she continued, talking over Doranth's rumbled warning, "but we've lost eight Privileged in those two days."

"Eight Privileged!" Tamas couldn't contain his outburst. "How?"

"This is none of the powder mage's business," Doranth said to Vivia, advancing on her quickly. Vivia made a warding motion with her hand, though neither of them wore their gloves.

"Sit down!" Sulem's voice cut through the commotion. Both Vivia and Doranth returned to their places. The king sighed, like a schoolteacher taxed to his limit by unruly students. "The Kez dragoons have a magebreaker. A very, very powerful one. He can null the sorcery of my Privileged even at a distance, and his dragoons are better than any of the cavalry my generals have faced in Gurla. They've managed a raid against the main camp each of the last two nights, each time assassinating at least one Privileged."

"No magebreaker is that good," Tamas said.

"He has those blasted Black Wardens."

Tamas thought he detected a hint of desperation in Doranth's voice. It had not occurred to him that the Black Wardens would be that terrifying to a Privileged, but it made sense. Wardens had been created by the Kez cabal to hunt powder mages. Black Wardens had been made *from* powder mages. It couldn't get much worse than that.

"Then go after him," Tamas said. "I'll bring up my cuirassiers and we'll perform a sweep of the western plains and crush him together." He fought down frustration even as he spoke. Ipille was outmaneuvering him. He had betrayed a flag of truce, moved his cavalry into position during the ensuing confusion, and now all he had to do was kill time until they could awake Kresimir. They were doing a damned good job of it.

Sulem climbed slowly to his feet and set his report on his desk. He removed his reading glasses, then gave Doranth a long look. The Deliv cabal head lifted his chin, and some silent communication passed between them. "Out," Sulem finally said.

"My Liege..."

"Out," Sulem said again.

Doranth left, his wide shoulder hitting Tamas on his way past.

"You, too," Sulem said to Vivia. The Privileged woman bowed to her king and retreated after the cabal head.

Tamas searched Sulem's face. Something was going on here, something under the surface. It wouldn't bode well for either him or his men.

"My generals are terrified," Sulem finally said. "This phantom of a dragoon has them jumping at shadows. They've never lost so many cavalry in so little time. He's quick, he has perfect timing, and his ability to nullify the sorcery of my Privileged has everyone in the army on edge. 'The Kez Wolf.'"

Tamas wasn't sure whether to be more impressed by this Kez magebreaker or by the fact that the Deliv had managed to keep all of this a secret from him the past two days. After all, they were supposed to be working *with* Tamas. His own limitations had forced him to trust the Deliv entirely.

"In just two days, this magebreaker has shattered the confidence of my cavalry."

"Losing over half their number will do that," Olem commented quietly.

The king examined Olem for a moment, as if wondering why a commoner would address him in such a manner, then snorted laughter. "My Privileged will not send out any more riders. They absolutely refuse. You may have seen that battle on the horizon?"

"Yes," Tamas said.

"That was five of my Privileged letting loose on a raid by the Kez Wolf, just to drive him away from our baggage."

"Pit."

"Exactly what I thought." The king drummed his fingers on his desk. "Those five Privileged barely killed three-score Kez dragoons. The rest of the company escaped. My generals won't pursue. They fear a trap."

Tamas watched Sulem for several moments. Normally so serene, the Deliv king seemed uncharacteristically agitated. "We can't stop to track him down," he said. "We have to march for Budwiel. We can't delay."

"And let this brigand dog our heels?"

Tamas almost told him about Ka-poel and Kresimir. Sulem needed to know why Tamas was so desperate to march on Budwiel. But it wasn't a tale he cared to explain, nor one that lent itself to believability. "I'll deal with the Kez dragoons."

"I..." Sulem spread his hands.

"I will deal with it." Tamas understood that Sulem was not about to call his own men cowards. Sulem's generals had rarely, if ever, experienced a battle in which they couldn't rely on the power of their Privileged. Tamas had been training his men, and himself, to do so for decades—even when there *was* an Adran Cabal.

Tamas left the king's tent. It was well past noon, his army was poised to march for the rest of the day, and he knew he had to do something about this immediately. "Olem, I..." He paused. Doranth stood nearby, his big arms crossed, face livid.

Tamas found himself less and less inclined to exercise restraint. He crossed to the Deliv magus. "All the power at your fingertips and you'll let a single magebreaker shut you down?"

Doranth opened his mouth.

"No," Tamas said. "No excuses. This is war, not some stupid bloody political game. If you can't win it with the tools you have, you make new tools. Something you damned Privileged will never understand."

"You're a fool."

"And you're a coward."

Doranth unfolded his arms to reveal he had put on his gloves. He threw his arms wide, like a bear ready to swipe, a snarl on his lips.

Tamas stepped inside Doranth's guard, even as Olem drew his pistol. He stared up at the towering magus. "No," he said. "Not a good idea. I may be an old man, but I'm running a mighty powder trance right now and I'll twist your balls off before you can twitch a finger. You might be able to kill me before I can end you, but you'll die squealing a moment later. Remember what I did to the Adran Cabal."

Doranth's arms shook with fury. Moments passed, and Tamas could feel the sweat rolling down his back and wondered idly if he really could take the magus with him. He *was* getting old. His reflexes weren't what they once were.

Doranth lowered his arms and tugged his gloves off. "I will kill you, Powder Mage."

"I'll probably be long dead before you get the chance." Tamas stepped away. "Let's go, Olem."

It wasn't until they were out of the Deliv camp that Tamas allowed himself a relieved sigh. "Pit," Tamas said, wiping his brow, "I should not threaten allied Privileged."

"I thought it was an interesting tactical choice," Olem said.

"And I thought you were around to keep me from doing stupid things."

"You looked in control from where I was standing."

"Then why did you draw your pistol?"

Olem shrugged. "Just in case."

"You're a man to inspire confidence."

"I try."

Tamas could sense a plan forming in his head. "Find me Beon je Ipille. And that Privileged girl. Meet me in my tent in twenty minutes."

"His name," Beon said, "is Saseram."

Tamas watched Beon through narrowed eyes. He'd undone his jacket, as his tent felt warm and muggy despite the cool breeze out-side. There was an ache deep in his bones, and he wondered how many years it had been since he last had a drink. "That's a Gurlish name."

"That's because he *is* Gurlish," Beon responded.

"A Gurlish cavalryman, fighting for the Kez? That seems a stretch." Tamas glanced at Olem, who had raised a skeptical eye-brow. Nila stood beside him, looking uncertain of herself. She'd changed out of her scorched dress and now wore a white daydress with a violet scarf.

"He changed sides during the third campaign—it was his defection that allowed us to take Delfiss. This was all when I was very young, of course. All I know is what I've heard from father."

"I've always wondered about Delfiss. So he's a magebreaker?"

Beon smoothed the front of his uniform. "Well, I didn't want to give up any state secrets, but if you already know—yes. That was a condition of his defection. He was once a very powerful Gurlish Privileged. My father wasn't interested in allowing a foreign Privileged the run of his army. The way he tells it, Saseram agreed almost too quickly. He willed away his Privileged powers and became a magebreaker."

"Magebreakers are former Privileged who are able to nullify sorcery," Tamas said to Nila, who was looking more than a little lost. "Most of them had little power to start with, and that's reflected in how close a proximity they must be to stop magic. I hired one once. He was fairly weak and had to be within spitting distance to stop sorcery. A powerful Privileged turned magebreaker can stop quite a bit more."

Beon glanced toward her. "May I ask who this is?"

"So he's a Gurlish Wolf rather than a Kez. Why have I not heard of this man?" Tamas asked, ignoring the question.

Beon's eyes lingered on Nila for a moment. "Because he changed his name when he entered Kez service."

"And who was he before that?" The Gurlish Wars had been a bloody series of campaigns half a world away involving most countries in the Nine. Tamas could think of half a dozen powerful Gurlish Privileged who had died or disappeared under mysterious circumstances.

Beon smiled in response, and glanced at Nila, but Tamas shook his head. He wasn't about to reveal Nila's identity over this. Not just to sate his own curiosity. "Anyway," Beon continued, "he's been rotting in some border town for the last fifteen years. He's a bloody good cavalryman, maybe even better than me—and an expert in guerrilla warfare. I imagine that you'll have a very hard time catching him indeed."

Tamas didn't have time for this. A few hours ago, he had been ready to order his men to march through the night so he could catch the Kez forces at Auberdel. Now he discovered that his allies—fifty thousand strong, including a third of a royal cabal—had been cowed by a single regiment of Kez cavalry.

"Thank you, Beon."

The Kez nobleman seemed to know he was being dismissed. He stood, brushing his hands together, eyeing Nila. She met his gaze, and Tamas chuckled inwardly. He had known that there would be a day when the Adran Cabal would need to be rebuilt. He had secretly hoped it would be long after his death. But he could do a lot worse than having Borbador and Nila as its foundation.

With Beon gone, Tamas climbed to his feet and rebuttoned his jacket. "Olem, have you created a cavalry regiment for your Rifle-jacks yet?"

"Yes sir. Six hundred dragoons and three hundred cuirassiers."

"Excellent. Take another five hundred cuirassiers—the Fifteenth won't miss them—and hunt this Gurlish magebreaker down."

Olem straightened. "Sir!"

"You wanted a command, Olem. You've got it now. Don't let me down."

"I won't, sir!" Olem grinned proudly, his shoulders squared.

"And Privileged Nila."

Nila swallowed hard, but she met Tamas's eye. He held his hands behind his back so that she couldn't see his nervousness, and wondered if he was making the right decision.

"You're going with Olem. Burn those bastards to the ground."

He had the brief satisfaction of her eyes growing wide before he strode out into the sunlight to let his men know they would be leaving at first light.

CHAPTER
32

A few hours into her ride, as her legs began to cramp and her ass began to hurt worse than anything she'd ever felt, Nila wondered if Tamas would have allowed her to say no.

Perhaps he might have, if it had occurred to her to refuse. She had her doubts. It seemed likely that few people told Tamas no. This was the same man who had slaughtered the Adran royal cabal in their sleep and then guillotined his own king. One didn't say no to a man like that. Instead of refusing what sounded like a horribly dangerous mission, she had asked him to give a hastily written note to Privileged Borbador. Tamas had seemed slightly put off by the request, but Nila didn't know who else in the camp she could have asked, and in the end, Tamas agreed.

She had an ever-growing notion that this expedition was a terrible idea and that it would end with her corpse lying in some farmer's field. The darkness on the horizon that sorcery could not penetrate, the darkness that had tied her stomach in knots, had been a magebreaker, and she was now riding toward him.

"What the pit good am I going to do?" she asked, trying not to let the pain come through in her tone. *Back straight. Act like the Privileged you want to be.*

Olem stood in his stirrups, looking annoyingly at ease in the saddle, his eyes scanning the horizon. "The idea," he said, "is that we go straight for the throat. We identify and kill the magebreaker and then you unleash your sorcery on his cavalry."

Behind them, a trail of dust rose over thirteen hundred Adran cavalry. They were a stunning sight, she had to admit. The uniforms of the dragoons were dirty and rumpled from the road, but their swords were held straight and their carbines laid across their saddle horns, while the breastplates of the cuirassiers shone in the setting sunlight. She now wore a uniform that matched the dragoons—Adran blues with silver trim and red cuffs, and pants, which were so much better for riding than a dress.

"Didn't the Deliv already think of that?"

"Likely," Olem said.

"And they failed."

"We'll just have to succeed where they failed."

"Are you going to get me killed?"

Olem stroked his beard and lowered himself back into his saddle. She wondered briefly how her life would be different if she had let him court her and had given up on her obsession to protect Jakob Eldaminse. Would she still be just Nila the laundress, another soldier's lover, toiling with the rest of the camp followers? Or would she have been captured along with so many others when Budwiel fell, and now be either dead or enslaved?

"I'll try not to," Olem said. He began to roll a cigarette. "If—when—we catch these bastards, I want you to stay near the middle of the column, where it's safest." He paused to lick his rolling paper. "To be honest, nowhere is safest in a cavalry skirmish, but that'll have to do. The magebreaker will have heard about the Battle of Ned's Creek, but if we're lucky, he won't suspect that we have a Privileged with us."

And he won't see my glow in the Else because of my limited experience, Nila finished silently. "What if I can't do sorcery?"

"Keep your head down."

"Easy for you to say. You have a sword."

"And a pistol and carbine," Olem said.

"You're very reassuring."

"That's what Tamas says, strangely enough."

"Tamas? Are you on a first-name basis with the field marshal?"

Olem grunted. "That was inappropriate of me. Sorry. Nerves are a bit frayed. I've ridden with cavalry before, even been in a few skirmishes, but this is my first command."

"Oh, now that *is* reassuring."

Olem flinched, and Nila wished she could take it back. "You'll do fine."

"Thanks, mother," he said. "Don't worry, I'm leaving the heavy lifting to my officers. If I do one thing well, it's pick good men. If I don't do fine, at least they will."

"You should give yourself more credit."

"Should I?" Olem put the rolled cigarette to his lips, then checked the carbine holstered to his saddle.

"Yes."

"*You* didn't."

Nila jerked back. What was that supposed to mean? "Now wait a moment."

He held up a hand. "Ancient history," he said. "Forget I said a word."

She scowled at him while he called over one of his officers and gave the order to stake camp. When the man had ridden away, Olem ashed his cigarette.

"I didn't mean to hurt you," Nila said.

"Oh?"

"I had my reasons," she continued. Jakob had needed her protection. She hadn't trusted Tamas at that time, and then she had been carried away by Lord Vetas and caught up in Bo's battles. She wanted to tell him all of that, but she hardly knew where to begin. "I really did like you."

"Well, that's a nice consolation prize."

"Don't be such a dense ass." Nila's voice rose. "I wanted to be with you, but I said no because I knew I had to protect Jakob." Her jaw snapped shut, and she blinked at him for several moments, not able to believe she had just said that.

"Oh," Olem said, both eyebrows now raised, his head cocked back in surprise.

Nila brushed some dirt from her uniform. "It's just... I'm sorry. Part of me wishes I had said yes, but as you said—ancient history."

Olem remained silent for several minutes, watching his men dismount and set up a picket line for the horses, readying the area for a campsite. When the silence was approaching the point of madness for Nila, he finally crushed his cigarette on his saddle horn and flicked the butt into the long grass. "I'll have one of the boys find you some good stones that we can warm in the fire. It'll help the ass-ache."

"Excuse me?"

"Hot stones, wrapped in the leather. You put them between your legs and all the fiddly bits downstairs won't hurt as much in the morning."

Nila decided she'd liked Olem more when he was being bashful back in Adopest. This seemed entirely too... forward. "Thank you."

Olem merely nodded a reply. His eyes were on something on the horizon.

"What is it?" she asked.

Olem removed the looking glass from his saddlebag and held it to his eye. Nila squinted to the west and thought, beneath the glare of the half-set sun, that she could see a rider. She heard a sharp intake of breath, and Olem lowered his looking glass.

"Pack it up, boys!" he yelled over his shoulder. "Kez to the west!"

The speed of it all made Nila's head swim. Within five minutes the whole regiment was back in the saddle, the thunder of their hooves ringing in Nila's ears and the adrenaline of the chase drowning out the pain from a day's worth of riding.

Olem ordered out dozens of scouts and formed his men with the bulk of the cuirassiers in the middle and the dragoons on the wings as they crested the hill in the waning light of dusk.

Nila could see the distant speck of the Kez rider galloping across the plains.

"Is there anything you can do?" Olem asked.

"What? I mean, no, what *could* I do? He's too far for Privileged sorcery, even if I was confident I could hit him at all."

He gave a stiff nod and ordered his men to advance, all while eyeing the scouts fanning out across the plains ahead of them. She could see the indecision in his eyes—was this an opportunity or a trap?

They proceeded on the trail of the Kez rider. Nila watched as the dragoons on their right flank swept up and over a hill to the north, out of sight, and their left flank proceeded along a matching arc a quarter of a mile out past a distant wheat field. She felt cold, apprehensive of the disappearance of those five hundred cavalry. What if it *was* a trap? Would they return in time?

The sun had nearly set by the time the cuirassiers crested a short hillock to look down suddenly into a steep valley cut into the hills. Less than a mile distant, Nila could see the flickering of campfires and groups of picketed horses.

"We've found the enemy camp!" a breathless scout told Olem.

"I can see that." Olem gazed through his looking glass, a look of consternation on his face.

"Could it be a trap?" Nila asked.

"They're scrambling like a kicked anthill down there," Olem said. "It could be a trap...but we may have gotten lucky. Form up!" he bellowed. "Three lines, flanking formation!"

The cuirassiers split into three equal wedges. One of them took the north side of the valley while the second went straight down the middle. Nila's wedge, with Olem at the head, rode along the southern lip. As they drew closer, Nila could see the Kez begin to ride out in waves from the camp—it was no desperate flight, but an organized withdrawal.

"Faster, damn it!" Olem yelled. He had his head cocked to the wind, and Nila could hear the distant call of bugles from the north and south. "We're in the clear, we've got these bastards!"

Nila tried to swallow her terror as her mount kept up with the galloping horde. Down in the valley, she could see their center wedge sweep through the Kez camp.

The valley was not long. Less than a half mile later, it ended in a narrow, steep hill that brought the Kez cavalry back onto the plains. Nila thought the hill would slow them down, but was shocked to see the whole regiment fly up it without a stumble.

Olem's cuirassiers were a quarter of a mile behind the Kez cavalry and it was clear even to Nila's eyes that they were far too slow to catch them. The cuirassiers were weighed down by their armor and heavier weaponry, while it appeared the Kez cavalry had lighter weapons and no armor, and had been forced to leave behind bedrolls and supplies when they fled their camp.

Up ahead, Nila could see the plains begin to roll steadily, flat fields of wheat disappearing into a myriad of hills cast in darkness by the sun setting behind the mountains. The Kez would reach those hills soon, and something about those shadows made her shiver.

She could hear Olem swearing at the top of his lungs. He bent over his mount, urging him faster, and Nila wondered briefly how easy it would be for one of these horses to lose its footing and stumble, taking out the entire line behind it. Up ahead something caught her eye, and she couldn't help the cheer that escaped her lips as Adran dragoons suddenly burst into view from the north.

They were almost on top of the Kez cavalry. She heard the crack of gunpowder as pistols were fired. Nila expected to see a milling confusion as the Adrans and Kez locked in battle, but the dragoons turned sharply to follow—they hadn't been able to cut off the Kez retreat.

Olem suddenly grabbed Nila's reins and the two of them pulled out in front of the rest of the cuirassiers. "Fire," he shouted. "Now!"

Fire? Sorcery! Nila's mind went blank of all Bo's lessons and her fingers felt numb. The Kez were too far away! How could she possibly get any of them?

Raising her hands, she rolled her eyes back and tried to focus on the Else, plucking with two fingers to bring fire racing down on the wind toward the retreating cavalry. To her surprise, flames appeared in the air several hundred yards away, swirling patterns in the sky above the Kez. She moved her off-hand too much and the flames suddenly slammed into the ground, showering the area with sparks. Her hands were shaking too hard, her concentration too unsteady.

Slowly, she managed to get her fire under control and send it blazing onward. Olem's dragoons had split to give the fire an avenue. She felt her heart hammering in her chest as the flames closed in on their prey, surging forward like a wave out of the pit itself. This was her! She had the power to catch them and stop them. She struggled to keep control, shoving the flames farther forward.

An inky blackness seemed to reach out of the shadows of the hills and Nila's fire suddenly went out. The suddenness of it caught her off guard and nearly sent her tumbling from her saddle. She felt a cold hand brush at the very edge of her awareness, and then it was gone.

"Call them back!" Olem said.

A bugle played frantically over Nila's shoulder and she saw the dragoons slowly pull up. She reined her mount in, wrestling with the excited horse until Olem snatched her reins from her hands and managed to calm the beast.

"Why did you call them back?" Nila asked, trying to shake the fear she felt from that blackness.

"Because I'm not following this Gurlish Wolf into Brude's Hideaway at night."

"My fire..."

"The magebreaker was there. I saw his influence in the Else."

Nila took a shaky breath. "What's Brude's Hideaway?"

"A bloody labyrinth of hills and valleys that stretch from here all the way through the western forest to the Charwood Pile." Olem leaned from his saddle to spit. "Damn it! We had luck on our side for once—they barely saw us coming—and we lost our chance."

Nila watched him for a moment, listening absently to the curses of the other cuirassiers. No one was happy about this development. "We're going in there, aren't we?"

Olem nodded. "Yes, but not until we have daylight on our side."

Nila wanted to tell him how terrible an idea she thought that was. She'd heard Beon je Ipille's description of this Gurlish Wolf. Olem had told her about the conversation with the Deliv magus. Going into those hills against the magebreaker was going to get them all killed.

She bit back her words and thought about Bo telling her to act like a Privileged. She felt a flare of jealousy with the memory of that Deliv Privileged leaning over to kiss Bo, and said, "At first light, then. We'll go in after the bastard."

CHAPTER

33

Two mornings after the bombing, Ricard had moved his entire base of operations for the election from the destroyed shell of the Holy Warriors of Labor headquarters to a posh hotel in the middle of Adopest.

Located just a few blocks from Elections Square, the Kinnen Hotel was one of the few buildings in the center of the city that had escaped looting by the riots after Manhouch's execution, damage in the royalist uprising, as well as severe structural harm from the earthquake in the spring. It was a squat fortress of a building only three stories tall, but with a footprint that encompassed an entire city block.

It also belonged to Ricard Tumblar, a fact that Adamat thought had something to do with why it had not been harmed by the riots—it would have been very well guarded by union muscle.

And it was still well guarded, it seemed. Each of the entrances was watched by no fewer than four union men. There were marksmen on the roof and armed laborers in the street. Adamat had to show his credentials three times before he reached the grand foyer of the hotel, and even then he could feel eyes on his back as he made his way to the east wing of the second floor.

He was admitted in to see Ricard after showing his papers yet again.

The union boss sat with his feet on his desk, chair tilted back, a cigar clenched between his teeth and a cold compress against his left temple. "No, I don't care how much it costs," Ricard was saying to a clerk, his voice just a little too loud. "Buy up every bolt of silk in the city and...oh, Adamat!" Ricard waved cigar smoke from his face and shooed the clerk out of the room with a single jerk of his chin.

"You're buying silk, now?"

"A little economic warfare," Ricard said, relishing his cigar smoke. "We've word that Claremonte has already promised the textile union he'll lower the import price of raw silk if elected. And he can't do that if I control everything in the city stores and keep an eye on what he brings in over the mountains."

"The textile union?" Adamat slid into a chair, feeling far too grateful to be sitting for a man his age. "Isn't that your territory?"

"The union head was killed in the blast last night," Ricard said. "We'll be fighting over a new one for months, and in the meantime Claremonte is going to try to sway their support. And yes, it is my territory. I won't let him take it."

"I still think you should use your emergency powers to appoint a new textile union head right away." The voice startled Adamat and he stood, looking toward where the voice seemed to come from—a window, where a woman perched beside the curtain with her arm in a sling and a glass of wine in her right hand. She was staring down at the street outside.

She was about fifty with rounded cheeks and severe, almond-shaped eyes. She wore a purple dress with black trim. She gave Adamat a quick look up and down.

"I'm sorry, ma'am, I didn't see you there." He ran through the catalog of names and faces in his memory.

She raised her wineglass slightly. "Cheris, the—"

"Head of the bankers' union," Adamat finished. "We met briefly a couple of months ago."

"I apologize, I don't remember." She set her wineglass down just long enough to adjust the strap on her sling.

"I'm Inspector Adamat."

"Oh, yes! The Knacked who can't forget. Ricard has spoken of you a great deal over the years. I should have remembered you. I do apologize. The things you've gone through in the last few months . . ." She trailed off, clucking her tongue sadly.

Adamat shot Ricard a glance. What was he doing telling this woman—or anyone, for that matter—about his problems?

Ricard gave him an apologetic shrug. "Do you have any leads on the bombing yesterday?"

"Should we talk about that in private?"

"Cheris was with me last night. A beam from the ceiling fell and broke her arm right after the explosion. She'll want to know about this as much as I."

But can she be trusted? "You look awfully well for having survived such a catastrophe," Adamat said.

Cheris blushed slightly. "If you must know, I've had a little mala today—for the pain—and more than a little wine." She gave what Adamat suspected had been meant to be a soft laugh, but it came out as a loud giggle.

"Of course. It's to be expected." Adamat returned to his seat.

"Did you go with the police yesterday?" Ricard asked.

"Yes."

"And? Do you think it was Claremonte? It was Claremonte, wasn't it? The bastard. I'll tear him limb from limb, I'll—"

"It wasn't Claremonte," Adamat said.

Ricard leapt to his feet and instantly began to pace. "What do you mean? Can you be sure?"

"I'm quite certain," Adamat said.

Lady Cheris interjected, "But how?"

"Believe me, ma'am. It wasn't Claremonte."

"I'll believe you when I know how you can be certain," Cheris said. "He has the means and the motive. He almost certainly ordered it done."

"Bah." Ricard stopped his pacing just long enough to fetch and light another cigar. "If Adamat says it's not Claremonte, then it's not Claremonte. But who?"

"I don't know yet. I've only just begun my investigation. You have enemies, don't you?"

"No," Ricard said, sounding somewhat offended. "I make friends. It's what I do best. Friends are far more useful than enemies."

Adamat gave Ricard a long look.

"Well, maybe. All right, yes. I have enemies. But not an over-abundance of them."

"Any of them who would want you killed?"

"I don't know if any of them hate me *that* much. Perhaps some of the other union bosses. One or two of them have been angling for my job for the last couple of years."

"Who?"

"Jak Long, the head of the blacksmiths' union. Lady Hether, the head of the street cleaners' union."

"She died in the bombing," Cheris said quietly.

"Oh. Right." Ricard stabbed his finger into the air. "The gun-smiths of Hrusch Avenue might have had something to do with it. They certainly know gunpowder, and they don't like that I've been trying to unionize them."

"Do you have candidates for a new textile union head?" Adamat asked, voicing a sudden thought before it slipped his mind.

"Of course. I can't stand any of them."

"And you have the power to just appoint one?"

"Technically. In an emergency. It would make a lot of people very angry, though."

"There's a foreman in the textile mill off of Vines Avenue. Her name is Margy. Very intelligent. Might shake things up a little if you appointed her."

"An unknown," Cheris said. "Intriguing."

"It's just a thought. She's politically conservative, vocal about her opinions, but not a troublemaker. She has no love of Tamas or the council, but there's no chance that she'd back Claremonte. Not after he leveled all of the churches in the city."

"Fell!" Ricard yelled. "Fell, where are you, damn it!"

The woman appeared in the doorway before he finished his sentence. She gave a slight bow at the waist. "You called, sir?"

"Look into a woman named Margy. See if she'd make a good candidate for the head of the textile union as an appointee. She's a foreman in the mill in . . ."

"On Vines Avenue," Adamat supplied.

"Yes. On Vines."

"Yes sir. Good afternoon, Inspector."

"Good afternoon, Fell."

"I'll send a man over, sir," Fell said to Ricard.

"Do it quietly. I don't want anyone getting wind of this."

The grandfather clock on the far side of the room suddenly chimed twice. Lady Cheris removed a pocket watch from the folds of her dress and checked it, then approached Ricard, kissing him lightly on the cheek. "I have to go."

"Come by tonight?"

"Of course."

She bid Adamat a good afternoon and left quickly. Ricard moved over to her spot by the window, his fist under his chin. "What was that?" Adamat asked.

"What was what?"

"The kiss. Are you two . . . ?"

Ricard flashed him a tight grin. "Perhaps a little."

"I remember you mentioning that she hated you."

"It's an alliance of convenience. For both of us."

"So she doesn't hate you?"

"Oh, she does. And I hate her back. We've been on-and-off lovers for the last fifteen years. You know how it goes. Passion, politics."

"And you've never told me?"

"A man has to have *some* secrets."

"You've been married to various wives for much of that time."

Ricard gave a noncommittal shrug. "Cheris is very smart. And ambitious. That's attractive to me. And my money and ambition are attractive to her. It's a match made in the pit. We'll be back to trying to kill each other after this whole thing is over."

"Interesting choice of words."

"What? Oh. I know what you're thinking," Ricard said. "Cheris didn't try to have me killed. She'd have nothing to gain from it. She's not in my will and most of the other union bosses hate her. Without my support she'd be out of the union within a year."

"I see." Adamat wasn't convinced. He'd have to go through his memories later and try to sort out anything he knew about Cheris—or anything Ricard had mentioned about her. If the two had been lovers for that long, they had certainly hid it well. It reminded Adamat that boisterous and loud though Ricard could be, he also had a talent for subtlety that most people missed.

"Something good has come about from this whole affair with Claremonte," Ricard said.

"Oh?"

"Apparently I have the support of the religious right."

Adamat couldn't help but bark a laugh. "Is that a draft in the room, or has the pit frozen over?"

"Cigar?" Ricard offered after a quiet laugh. "Glass of wine?" Without waiting for an answer, he shouted for Fell again.

The undersecretary appeared once more in the door, a bottle of wine already in one hand and two glasses in the other. "Ahead of you, sir."

"Adamat, have I told you that I couldn't live without this woman?"

Fell poured two glasses and handed one to Adamat, who swirled it around and took a sip. He eyed the undersecretary cautiously. Assistant, political liaison, seductress, bodyguard, assassin. Trained at the most exclusive finishing school in the world, Ricard had said. Somewhere between a slave and an indentured servant, Fell was the most capable person Ricard had brought onto his staff in... well... ever.

Could she have betrayed him?

Adamat pushed the thought away. Ricard had let Fell completely into his confidence. If she wanted to kill him, she could have done so any number of ways. She could have killed or destroyed him several times over in the last few months. Unless she had something more long-term in mind...

"Ricard."

"Yes?"

"Can Claremonte really win?"

"What? Of course not. He's a foreigner. He destroyed historic public property. The man is a menace."

"Seriously, Ricard."

Ricard returned to his pacing, wine in one hand and cigar in the other. He paused on the opposite side of the room and drained the rest of the glass in one long draught.

This wasn't going anywhere. Adamat turned to Fell, who had slipped into a chair along the back wall of the suite. She had one foot tucked under her and the opposite knee pulled up to her chest—no mean feat in a black tailored suit. "Can Claremonte win?" he asked her.

She glanced at Ricard, then said, "He has a good chance. He has managed to gain a remarkable amount of support in just the last few weeks—much of it had already been arranged through intermediaries."

"Lord Vetas?" Adamat asked, the very name making his skin crawl.

"Some," Fell admitted. "That's what he'd been in town doing, after all. Paving the way for Claremonte. When we took Vetas, we got a list of names of people he'd bribed, cajoled, and threatened into backing Claremonte. Some of them we've been able to turn. Others are still in his pocket."

"But it's worse than we thought."

"Much worse," Fell said. "Several of the prominent gunsmiths have backed him and—coincidentally—the Brudania-Gurla Trading Company has signed countless new contracts for Hrusch rifles. Dozens of big merchants are campaigning for him and will not even see our people. We think they fear the Trading Company and the power they have over shipping. His public approval is high because of his perceived protection of the city."

"I saw that in the newspaper the other day," Adamat said. "He claims that the Kez haven't dared attack the city ever since his army arrived. No word about Field Marshal Tamas or the Adran army."

"Of course," Ricard said. "This is politics, after all."

Adamat let out a disbelieving sigh. "He could win...and a foreigner would hold the highest position in our country. You realize that Tamas would never let that happen."

"He can't stop it."

"Have you met Tamas? He would storm the city and kill Claremonte himself. I don't see how we could dissuade him."

"This will be the first election in the history of Adro," Fell said. "If Tamas disrupts that, he will destroy everything we've worked for."

Ricard said, "We'll have to deal with that when we come to it. In the meantime, we still have a murderer at large."

"You're worried he'll try again?" Adamat asked. "You've certainly tightened security."

"Of course I am. I don't have hearing in one ear because of whoever planted that bomb, and several of my top union bosses are dead or injured. They'll try again, or I'm a shoemaker." Ricard gave Adamat a fraught look, and Adamat realized how incredibly desperate his friend had become. He put on his airs, but the attempt on his life had shaken him deeply. And he was really worried that Claremonte would win the election.

"We have another problem," Ricard said quietly.

"Another?" Adamat tried not to sound too tired. He failed.

Ricard hesitated a moment.

"Go on," Adamat said. "Tell me."

"Charlemund has escaped."

"Excuse me?" The former Arch-Diocel of Adro was not only a traitor but a formidable killer. "I thought he was in a coma."

"He was," Fell said. "We think that Taniel Two-shot's savage Bone-eye put him in that coma in order to bring Taniel back. Some kind of magical exchange. Whatever it was, it wore off. We had Charlemund hidden, tied down. His body was guarded at all times. He escaped and disappeared without a trace. We still haven't figured out how."

"Sweet Kresimir," Adamat swore.

"He got away about three weeks ago," Ricard said. "Cut his ropes and knocked out his guards and just walked off. We've had people quietly combing the city for him ever since."

"No sign of him?"

"None at all. Like he vanished into thin air."

Adamat nodded tiredly. "I'll keep my ear to the ground. I'm going to go down to the ruins of your headquarters. They're still sealed off, correct?"

"Yes," Fell said. "We asked the police to keep everyone out, and we have one or two of our own men down there keeping an eye out."

"Good. I'm going to see if the police missed anything. Do you think I could borrow you for a couple of hours, Fell?"

Fell looked to Ricard, who nodded. "Go ahead. I hope you can find something."

"As do I."

"Thanks for your help," Ricard said. "You don't know how much it means to me to have someone I can trust doing the footwork. I would send Fell out, but she's running my whole campaign. This investigation could take months."

"You sure you can spare her at all?"

"For a few hours. We need to find out who did this."

"I'll work on that," Adamat said. "You work on winning the election. Because if you don't, Field Marshal Tamas is going to start another war, and this one will have Adopest right in the center of it."

CHAPTER
34

The blasted remains of the union headquarters looked somehow worse in the light of day. Walls that the other night had appeared unharmed were revealed to be blackened with soot, the plaster cracked and chipped. Sometime during the last two days the rest of the roof had caved in.

Adamat nodded to the uniformed police officer standing guard at the street and entered the ruin through the still-standing front door.

Ricard's men had protected the building from looters and picked through the wreckage for everything of value to the union. Papers, artwork, furniture, everything but the building materials themselves had been removed, and Ricard said even those would be torn down and dumped or recycled within days so they could start the process of rebuilding.

"Bloody mess," SouSmith commented from behind Adamat.

Adamat shoved at a piece of fallen roof. When it became clear he wouldn't be able to move it, he climbed on and over it until he was able to get back on his feet near the center of the great room. To his surprise, no one had shut off the pumps to the fountain in the middle of the grand hall. It was still running, practically undamaged, creating a strange sort of serenity in the midst of all the destruction.

SouSmith paused to reach into the fountain and pull out a silver ten-krana coin. He balanced it on his thick thumb and flicked it in the air, catching it with his other hand. "Don't know what you're gonna find," he rumbled.

"Me neither," Adamat said. He was beginning to think he'd wasted his time in coming here. Two days since the blast and the whole thing had been trampled over by Ricard's men and the police. What little evidence that might have pointed toward the culprit was long gone by now. Only investigative instinct kept him from leaving this place behind to go find some breakfast.

He worked his way through the rubble until he reached the back of the building. "I'm shocked more people weren't killed," he said.

"How many?" SouSmith asked.

"Thirteen casualties," Adamat said. "Another twenty-seven injured. There were three hundred people here the other night. It could have been much worse." At the rear of the building Adamat entered what used to be the hallway leading to Ricard's office. The office was a total loss. It didn't take a professional to tell that this had been the epicenter of the blast. All four walls were gone, the desk was nothing more than splinters, and the floor had all but caved in.

Adamat heard the scrape of boots in the rubble and turned to see Fell approaching from the way they'd come. SouSmith tipped his hat to the undersecretary but remained silent, eyeing her with obvious suspicion.

"The police said the powder barrel was under his desk," she said.

Adamat looked over the room once more. Yes, that seemed right.

He stepped carefully into the room, testing the floor with every step, half expecting what was left of it to collapse beneath him. He could see the dark of the basement beneath the remaining tiles. He crossed to the middle of the room and envisioned how it had been set up, using his mind's eye to examine the memory of Ricard's office. He held his hands about where the desk would be, and imagined sitting at the desk.

There was something wrong about this.

"What else did they tell you?" Adamat asked. He hadn't gotten the chance to speak with the chief inspector yet, but had a lunchtime appointment for that very purpose. It would be useful to get two different perspectives on this.

Fell kicked idly at a piece of masonry and pulled a pipe out of her pocket. She set the stem on the corner of her lip and struck a match. After puffing it to life, she said, "That there were two bombs."

"Two?" That was a surprise. "Where was the second?"

"In the basement."

There was no evidence of the second bomb until they reached the cellar stairs. The door to the cellar was gone and there was less left of the stairs than there had been of Ricard's office. The marble floor was cracked and seemed to crumble beneath their feet. One of Ricard's men had left a ladder there so they could access the basement. Adamat climbed down into the dark.

The cellar was of the kind found beneath old manors: a vaulted ceiling with thick, stone arches. Adamat could feel the crunch of glass beneath his feet. He could make out a stone alcove behind where the stairs used to be and black scorch marks along the wall.

"Shall we come down?" Fell asked.

Adamat answered by climbing back up the ladder and joining her and SouSmith in the ruin. "The bombs were set off by a quick-burning fuse, correct?"

"That's what the police think," Fell said. "They think that the culprit waited until the offices were all clear, came in through the back, and quickly placed two black powder kegs, rolled the fuse out into the alley behind the building, lit it, and ran."

Adamat took a deep breath of Fell's pipe smoke and drummed his fingers on his stomach. "Do you know anything about a person not having a shadow?"

"What does that have to do with the investigation?"

"Nothing. Just curious."

Fell considered this for a moment. "Doesn't sound familiar."

"A pity." He let out a sigh and returned to the matter at hand. "I can make three easy assumptions of the assassin. Whoever did this was just hired muscle. They were hired by someone who knew Ricard well. And they didn't want to kill everyone in the building."

"How do you determine that?"

"One: The kinds of people who want to kill Ricard won't dirty their own hands. Two: They dropped the first barrel under Ricard's desk. Ricard loves his parties, but he likes to stay relaxed by slipping out about halfway through the night for a quick dalliance with whatever young lady happens to be handy."

Fell gave a quick nod, the corners of her mouth turning up slightly at that. "But why the second barrel?" she asked. "The floors were reinforced because of the way Ricard had had this place built. They should have placed the barrel in the middle of the cellar, where the blast could have killed the people standing above it."

"Why did Ricard build the cellar that way?"

"So he had 'someplace evocative to take his guests to pick out wine,'" Fell said, slipping into a startlingly accurate impression of Ricard. She let the impression drop and Adamat could see the realization hit.

"He loves to show off his wine collection," Adamat said. "For a party like the one last night, the assassin had a very good chance of catching Ricard either in his office or in the cellar. Those two spots would allow for the best chance of killing Ricard without killing everyone else in the building."

SouSmith flipped his silver coin in the air and caught it coming back down. "Doesn't help us."

"It does help us," Adamat disagreed, "if only a little. The person would have to know Ricard fairly well to know those two items. Or else they had an inside source who does. Regardless, it lets us narrow in on the few dozen people who knew Ricard best, rather than spend our time combing through the whole of Adopest."

Something else was bothering Adamat, and he couldn't quite place it. The explosion was . . . off in a way that he couldn't grasp.

He left SouSmith and Fell near the cellar stairs and went back to Ricard's office. Tracing the blast patterns on the floor and remnants of the wall, he worked his way carefully around the room and then into the hallway. Once he was satisfied with that, he borrowed a lantern from the policeman in the street and descended into the basement, where he traced out the blast pattern and examined the walls.

The whole process took about an hour. Fell sifted through the bits of papers remaining in Ricard's office and SouSmith idly flipped his coin. When Adamat finished, he went to Ricard's office and cleared his throat.

Fell looked up from the floor, her eyebrows raised.

"The blasts were far too big for the size of the barrels," Adamat announced.

Fell scoffed. "You couldn't possibly know that just by looking."

Adamat tapped the side of his head. "Perfect memory. It makes eyeballing measurements much easier. I've seen my fair share of explosions and I don't have to be a scientist in these matters to see that the destructions caused by the barrels downstairs and at Ricard's desk were far more thorough than would have fit in those two places."

"Could it have been a powder mage?"

"Perhaps. It would explain the other thing I realized."

"Which was?"

"I thought the barrel had been placed under the basement stairs. But it wasn't. It was right in the middle of the basement hall, where anyone could have stumbled over it."

"That makes sense if they were trying to do this quickly."

"It's...too quick. Ricard has dozens of servants. Maybe fifty or sixty on the night of one of his parties. The chances of both his office and the basement being empty are incredibly slim." He paused to examine the outside wall of the office and then went back to the basement stairs, noting the long hallway leading to the basement. He did some mental math, then returned to Fell and SouSmith. "Someone could have thrown the explosion. It would require two people working together, but that's not out of the question."

"A grenado," SouSmith said.

"Like a grenado, yes. But much more powerful."

"We're going back to a powder mage," Fell said. "One of Ricard's enemies could be employing a foreign powder mage. I've heard of mercenary mages."

"As have I. But no, I think not. As I understand it, mages are limited by the power of the black powder they use. They could warp a small blast to allow them to kill more people, but not enough to cause this much destruction to the whole building."

"Some kind of refined black powder could do it. Something that packs more of a punch than the traditional kind."

"It would," Adamat said slowly. "And I think it's the best lead we have. Tell Ricard I'll be looking into a few places."

"Good luck," Fell said. "And don't get yourself killed."

Adopest University had seen better days.

Adamat's cane tapped on the cobbles as he made his way through the myriad of stone buildings that made up the university. This was the same walk he'd taken just six months ago on the day of

Field Marshal Tamas's coup and Manhouch's execution. Now the brown and orange of fall filled the trees, and the world seemed a little older. But that wasn't the only difference.

The center of the university looked like a battleground. The western façade of Banashir's Hall was missing and the old clock tower that had once dominated the skyline was no more than a squat ruin, looking bare in the fall weather. It had been knocked over by sorcery in a battle between two Privileged and had landed on the once-mighty glass atrium—the pride of the university. Entire buildings were roped off, sitting idle while the university sought to raise money for their rebuilding.

The scene acutely reminded him of both the destruction at the union headquarters and the aftermath of the earthquake that had occurred four months ago. Adamat knew that Tamas had meant well with his coup, and this destruction was not all a result of his actions, but Adopest had taken a horrible beating since that fateful day.

Adamat took to the stairs in the rear entrance of the administration building and paused when he realized he was alone.

He retraced his steps to find SouSmith staring at the destruction in the quad outside of Banashir's Hall. The earth had been cut up as if with an enormous plow, great mounds and furrows that would take a hundred men several weeks to even out. Adamat wondered why the university hadn't yet restored the fields, but he realized they likely lacked the funding.

"What's wrong?" Adamat asked.

SouSmith held the silver krana coin he'd taken from the union headquarters. He flicked it in the air and caught it. "Thinking."

"About?"

The old boxer didn't respond as he flipped the coin several more times, catching it each time without looking. "That Privileged I punched."

"When you were a kid?"

He nodded and let out a sigh.

"Lucky he didn't do something like this"—Adamat gestured to the destruction—"to your insides."

"Yup."

"Just proves that they can be hurt. That they're fallible. No one's perfect, even the people with the power to do this kind of thing."

"More scary," SouSmith grunted. He stuffed his hands in his pockets and trudged along in the same direction Adamat had been going.

Adamat had heard that the administration building had taken significant damage during the Privileged battle. Inside, it was clear where they'd focused their reconstruction efforts. Sections of the north wall and the roof were all new. The art that had once lined the main hall—of vice-chancellors in the history of the university—had been taken down or destroyed.

He passed the office of Vice-Chancellor Prime Lektor and paused just long enough to note there was dust on the handle. He rapped on the next door.

"Come," a muffled voice responded.

Adamat entered the tidy office of the assistant to the vice-chancellor. Uskan sat behind his desk, book open flat before him, glasses perched on the end of his nose. He looked up from his reading and gave Adamat a tight smile. "Good afternoon."

"Hello, my friend," Adamat said. "Thank you for seeing me at such short notice."

"Of course." Uskan sat up and brushed the hair from his brow. "Anything for a government official."

"It's not like that," Adamat said, feeling his heart skip a beat. Uskan hadn't offered him a place to sit. His manner was forced, and his eyes were not trusting. Adamat knew his friend was politically conservative, but...

"It's not? So they're not calling you Tamas's hound?"

"Not within earshot, anyway," Adamat said. "I thought you knew I was working for Tamas."

"Tamas's reign has brought nothing but ruin to the university," Uskan said. "The last time you were here, you told me you were involved, but not that you were running errands for our new dictator."

"He's not a dictator," Adamat said.

"Oh?"

Adamat dropped into the chair in front of Uskan's desk. He didn't have the energy for this. "Tamas is reported dead, anyway." He eyed Uskan, gauging his reaction to see if word had reached him yet of Tamas's return. "It's all in the past."

"And because of him we'll have no future."

"I don't want to talk politics with you. I just hoped you'd answer a few questions."

"As I said, anything for a government stooge."

"Uskan!"

"Adamat, I will help you, but I will not be happy about it!"

Adamat drummed his fingers on Uskan's desk. "Where's the vice-chancellor?"

"Away. Tamas put him in charge of the eastern front after South Pike erupted. Why, I have no idea. The man's a scholar, not a warrior. And we desperately need him here helping us rebuild the university. Tamas has—had—taken it upon himself to ruin Adopest University and—"

Adamat cut him off. "He sent him because the vice-chancellor is a Privileged."

"You're joking." Uskan seemed to find this genuinely funny, but his dry chuckle trailed off after a moment.

"I saw his gloves on Saint Adom's Day," Adamat said. "He's a Privileged and even you, locked in here with your books, will have heard he's one of Tamas's councillors. You trust *him*, don't you?"

"Of course! I've known Prime Lektor for most of my life."

"And how much money have the Holy Warriors of Labor donated to the university since the midsummer?"

"What does that have to—"

"Just answer the question."

"Several million krana. They're the only ones who have really given us any support."

"Well, right now I'm on a case for Ricard Tumblar, the head of the union, who is another one of Tamas's councillors. Give Tamas a little credit. He's trying to do good by all of us. Don't blame everything on him. You have to look beyond your books, Uskan. If Tamas hadn't been caught beyond enemy lines, I suspect he would have paid a little more attention to the disaster here." Adamat would have liked to think so anyway. Was he saying all this to convince Uskan, or himself?

Uskan raised his nose indignantly. "You speak as if he's still alive."

"He is. I've seen him myself."

"You just told me he was dead. And now that he is alive. What am I supposed to believe?"

"I only said that it was 'reported' he was dead."

"To try to trick me into—" Uskan stopped himself with a frustrated sigh. "There's no need for any of this. What was it you needed to know?"

"Do you know anything about why a person might not have a shadow?"

Uskan blinked at Adamat for several moments. "What? Well, no. I've never heard of that before."

"That's too bad." Adamat tried not to let his disappointment show. Another dead end. Adamat had hoped Uskan, of all people, might have heard something in all his studies. "Could it be a side effect of being a Knacked or a Privileged? I know you've made a hobby of sorcery studies."

Uskan rested his chin in the palm of his hand and stared at something above Adamat's head. After several moments he finally said, "No. Nothing at all."

Adamat hoped that his old friend was not withholding information just out of spite. "Anything in any of the books on sorcery in your library?"

"Many of those were destroyed or vandalized before you came looking after your last mystery. You're welcome to look, but I doubt you'll find anything. I can let you into the library, but I don't have the time to help you look."

"Thank you, but I'm here on more important business, to be honest. I'm curious if you've heard about anyone experimenting with black powder."

"In what way?"

"Refining it. Creating something better, more destructive. More explosive."

Uskan tapped a finger on his chin. "Now, that I can help you with."

Adamat perked up. A lead? "Oh?"

"There's a chemical company out on the west side of the city. They make and import gunpowder for the Adran army, and they employ several chemists who make powder of various consistencies and burning temperatures. Very important for artillery, bombs, and all that. I heard earlier this summer that they were working on something called 'blasting oil.' Something they want to use in mining."

"Do you remember their name?"

"The Flerring Powder Company."

"Excellent." Adamat got to his feet. This was exactly what he was looking for.

"There's something else," Uskan said.

Adamat paused, concerned by the sudden bleakness of Uskan's voice. "What is it, my friend?"

Uskan stared at his fingers for several moments before answering. "The vice-chancellor—Prime Lektor—has fled the country."

"He *what*?"

"He fled. I caught him here about three weeks ago, collecting things from his office. He cleaned everything out, sold his home in the countryside, and left. He told me that I should flee too."

"Why on earth would he do that?"

"He said that Adom was dead. Kresimir was coming back and with him something worse. And that we'd all burn for Tamas's mistakes." Uskan rubbed his sleeve across his eyes. "The man was my idol, Adamat. I've known him for decades and he's been calm, unflappable Prime. But when I saw him that night, he looked like a madman on the verge of hysterics. He left me here, alone. He said I was the new vice-chancellor if I wanted to be, but told me I'd be dead within months if I decided to stay."

"Uskan, I'm sorry."

Uskan sniffed and wiped his eyes once more, sitting up straight. "Nothing to be sorry for. You're right, I need to look beyond my books. I've been rather fraught since the battle on the campus, but I thought we'd rebuild. I figured Prime would help us create everything anew. And now he's gone."

"Is there anything I can do for you?"

"If Tamas is still alive…well, put in a good word for the university."

"Of course."

Adamat rounded the desk to put a hand on Uskan's shoulder. "You're right, you know. I shouldn't have gotten involved in any of this. It's hurt the people I love in so many ways."

"I don't think it's your fault," Uskan said.

"Thank you for that."

SouSmith, still leaning on the door frame of the tiny office, cleared his throat.

"Yes," Adamat said. "Well, I should get going."

"Wait."

Adamat stopped just outside the office and turned back to Uskan.

"You should check a private library," Uskan said. "Someone who will have books not accessible to us or to the Public Archives."

"I'm open to suggestions."

"Charlemund's manor," Uskan said. "The Arch-Diocel had an enormous library before he was arrested. It's meant to be split between Adopest University, the Public Archives, and Jileman University, but we haven't had the time to work on it."

"And it's at his manor still?"

"Under guard, I think. But not inaccessible to someone with friends in high places." Uskan gave him a lopsided smile.

"I'll look into it. Thank you very much."

Out in the hallway, SouSmith fell in beside Adamat as they headed back toward their carriage. "Anything?" he asked.

"I have two leads now," Adamat said. "We'll sniff it out. I know we will."

"What was that about the vice-chancellor?"

"He fled the country, apparently." Adamat fiddled with the head of his cane. "I'm curious what he knows that we don't."

CHAPTER
35

Tamas sat brooding in a cloth folding chair in front of the tent his soldiers had set up for him to take his lunch.

His last report from Olem arrived twenty-four hours ago, letting him know that they were going into Brude's Hideaway to hunt the Gurlish magebreaker and his Kez cavalry. Tamas couldn't help but glance to the northwest, wondering why Olem hadn't sent his morning report. Two a day, Tamas had ordered. It was vital that he be kept abreast of the situation on the western plains if he was to proceed against the Kez armies to his south.

The messenger's horse may have thrown a shoe, or he might have been sent off a few hours late. Tamas chewed on the inside of his cheek. Olem may have been defeated in battle, for all he knew. Whether it was a portent of ill or not, he didn't like the lag in communication.

"Olem!" he shouted.

"Olem's not here, sir." Andriya, one of Tamas's powder mages, appeared from inside his tent. He was a tall man with scraggly blond hair and a pockmarked face.

"Bloody pit." Tamas rubbed at his temples. "How many times is that?"

"Seventeen in the last four days."

"Sorry. Habit, I suppose. Damn bodyguard has been with me less than a year and I'm already doing that."

Andriya picked at his teeth with one fingernail and turned to spit. "Funny, sir, but when Cenka died and you got Olem to replace him, you never confused the two."

"Surely I must have."

Andriya shrugged. "Maybe. That's fine, I never liked Cenka anyway."

"You don't like anyone."

"I liked Erika," Andriya said after a moment of introspection.

"My late wife saved you from the hangman's noose in Kez. I certainly hope you liked her."

"It wasn't just that," Andriya said. "She had a certain"—he made a rolling motion with one hand—"something about her."

"I know," Tamas said quietly.

If Andriya noticed Tamas's discomfort, he didn't show it. He leaned on his rifle and began to pick at his nails again. "Messenger coming in, sir."

Tamas stood up and stretched, trying not to look too eager. Had Olem's man finally arrived? Tamas needed to know what was going on at his flank. He couldn't meet the Kez infantry in battle with that Gurlish Wolf at his heels.

Tamas's heart fell. The messenger coming in was not one of Olem's. He was an outrider, a scout with the Second Brigade, keeping track of the Kez movements to the south. Someone was following the scout. As they drew closer, Tamas could see it was a woman in a gray woolen dress and a tan apron. Tamas knew that uniform. It was the clothing given to camp followers in the Kez army.

The scout said something to the woman and she stopped a ways off while the scout approached. He saluted. "Sir. Found this woman early this morning making her way toward our camp. She said she has news, and it's urgent."

"And you brought her to me?" Did chain of command mean nothing in this army anymore?

"She wouldn't talk to anyone else. She had the right passwords."

"Passwords?"

"I'm one of your spies, you daft man," the woman said in Kez, her voice husky, her tone impatient.

Andriya let out a laugh. Tamas silenced him with a glance and looked at his other bodyguards. Andriya seemed to be the only one present who spoke Kez, other than Tamas himself. The rest hadn't understood her. "Let her through."

The woman approached. She looked about thirty, with raven hair, brown eyes, and hollow cheeks—she could have fit in anywhere in the Kez countryside. Her dress was well kept but covered in stains, her knees and elbows caked with mud, likely from crouching in the long grasses on her flight from the Kez camp.

"Would you like to clean up?"

"No time, but I could damn well use a drink." Her switch to Adran was so flawless that Tamas wondered if he'd imagined her speaking Kez a moment ago.

"Get her some water," he told Andriya.

"Wine."

Tamas rolled his eyes but nodded. "All right. I didn't know we had any spies left in the Kez army."

"There are few enough," she said. "There was a purge about seven weeks ago. Like someone gave them a Kresimir-damned list of names. It was pure luck that I didn't get nabbed as well. I haven't been able to use any of our normal channels to send reports— you've gotten nothing from me for weeks and for that I'm sorry."

Tamas put his hands behind his back and gave a sharp nod.

"Glad you made it out alive." Inside, he was seething. General Hilanska, no doubt. When this whole thing was over, he was going to drop Hilanska into the deepest part of the Adsea and see how long he could swim with that one arm. "What's so urgent that you had to leave your cover?"

The woman took an offered wineskin from Andriya and drained half of it before answering. "Aside from the intelligence I haven't been able to pass on for the last month? I slept with General Fulicote last night. You know who he is?"

Tamas nodded. One of Ipille's many infantry commanders. As far as Kez command went, he was a decent commander. He'd commanded a brigade in the Gurlish Wars twenty years ago.

"Then you know he's a teetotaler, like you. Well, last night he was piss drunk."

"Why?"

"Ipille has ordered the entire Grand Army to make a stand at the mouth of Surkov's Alley."

"So? That doesn't seem like an unreasonable order."

"So?" the woman retorted, before draining the rest of the wineskin. "So Ipille doesn't think he can win. He's been with the army for the last two months and now he's turning tail and running back to Kez. General Fulicote and all the rest have been ordered on what they know is a suicide mission. Ipille told them that any man who runs from the battle will be caught and publicly flayed."

"Do you have proof of this?"

The woman removed a letter from her bodice and smoothed it against her skirt before handing it to Tamas. It bore the royal seal of the Kez king, hastily broken by a clumsy thumb. Tamas opened the letter and skimmed the contents. Ipille was ordering his men to make a stand, but the final threat at the end allowed Tamas to read between the lines, just as General Fulicote and this spy had done: The Kez army wasn't meant as anything more than cannon fodder to slow down Tamas and the Deliv.

Tamas returned to his chair, deep in thought. "What could he possibly gain by this?" he muttered.

"The Kez have all been asking the same thing of you since you attacked after the parley."

Tamas was up on his feet again. "*That* was Ipille. He broke that parley."

"That's not what his officers think. I've managed to spend the night with four senior Kez officers since then and not a single one of them thinks Ipille actually broke the parley. They're convinced that you and the Deliv fabricated the whole thing so you could push into Kez and try to dethrone Ipille."

"I would do no such thing." Tamas shook his head. Why was he explaining himself to a spy? A niggle of doubt had entered his mind. If Ipille hadn't launched the attack on his men during the parley in order to kidnap Ka-poel, then who had?

He didn't have time to wonder. If Ipille was fleeing and throwing his whole army away, that meant he had some kind of plan. Whether he meant to force Ka-poel to awaken Kresimir or he planned to retreat to his capital and spend the winter raising levies and trying to forge alliances among the Nine, it didn't matter. Tamas needed to end this quickly.

"Report to General Arbor, he'll see that you get somewhere to rest," he said over his shoulder. "Andriya, get my horse!" He ran into his tent and sorted through his maps until he found one of southern Adro.

Thirty minutes later he strode into Sulem's command tent. The Deliv king was surrounded by half a dozen members of his royal cabal and five of his generals. "We need to speak," Tamas said.

Sulem shushed the angry mutters of his generals and cabal with a raised hand. "Everyone out," he said.

They were alone within moments. "Do you read Kez?" Tamas asked.

"Yes."

Tamas handed him Ipille's orders to his general. Sulem read the letter twice and examined the seal. "May I have my Privileged check the authenticity?"

"By all means."

"Vivia!" Sulem called. The caramel-skinned Privileged arrived a moment later and took the letter with a few words of instruction before disappearing.

Tamas began to pace the tent, his mind racing. Royal seals always had the faint touch of sorcery to them, much like a ward. It allowed generals in the field to check for authenticity. Tamas had been able to sense it himself, but Sulem needed to be convinced as well.

"These are the words of a desperate man," Sulem said. "You should be pleased."

"He's trying to buy time. He knows that we won't advance into Kez while the snows fall."

"So what if he does? My armies have by now ravaged the Amber Expanse. They shall retreat to Alvation for the winter and sharpen their bayonets. Come spring we will crush whatever resistance the Kez have left."

Tamas paused in his pacing. He still did not want to explain to Sulem about Kresimir and Ka-poel. Nor did he think that Sulem cared much for the fact that a Brudanian army held Adopest. "He may be able to forge alliances. If Starland or Novi decides to enter the war on their side, this war will last for ages."

"Novi wouldn't dare," Sulem said with a wave of his hand.

One flap of the tent parted as Vivia returned. She handed Sulem the letter. "It's Ipille's," she said, and slipped back out the way she had come.

Tamas advanced to the table in the middle of Sulem's tent and pushed several maps and correspondence out of the way, laying his own map of southern Adro down and rubbing it smooth. "I will not allow this war to last any longer."

"You have a plan?" Sulem approached the table curiously.

"The Kez will likely gather here and prepare for our approach," Tamas said, pointing to the northern entrance to Surkov's Alley. "They're less than half a day ahead of us. I propose that we march double-time into the night tonight and all day tomorrow and catch them unawares."

The Kez king frowned at that. "You mean to stop them before they can secure a defensive position at Surkov's Alley?"

Tamas smiled. "I mean to do much more than that."

CHAPTER
36

When Adamat told his carriage driver to take him to the Flerring Powder Company on the west side of Adopest, he hadn't expected them to head well outside of the city and into the countryside.

He and SouSmith climbed out of their carriage at about three o'clock in the afternoon the day after their visit to Uskan and paused to examine their surroundings. The chemical company was at the end of a dirt track several miles off the main highway. It appeared to be a collection of over two dozen buildings of various sizes spread out at distant intervals across a wide field. A creek ran through the center of the complex, providing power to a single mill.

Near the river, set apart from the rest of the buildings by some several hundred yards, Adamat noted a black smudge of dirt that looked like it had once been the foundation for yet another building.

The perils of making gunpowder.

Adamat headed toward the largest of the buildings.

He was stopped just outside the building by a woman holding a blunderbuss. She stood half a head taller than Adamat and had the shoulders of a boxer. Long brown hair half covered her eyes, and she leaned against the building door. She pointed the weapon lazily at his feet.

"Can I help you?"

Adamat noticed the cudgel hanging from her belt and wondered if she was the only guard. He didn't think that likely. Companies like this needed manpower to keep their secrets safe from competitors. "I'm looking for Flerring the Elder," Adamat said.

"Do you have an appointment?"

"I don't."

"What do you want?"

"I need to discuss a matter of some urgency."

"And that is?"

"I should probably speak with Flerring himself."

The woman tilted her head to one side. "I'll see if he's available. Whom can I tell him is here?"

"Inspector Adamat."

"You here from the state?"

"Yes."

"Then go away until you've made an appointment. Or come back when you've got more goons. We're not rolling over for your idiot regulations."

Idiot regulations? "You think I'm a government inspector?"

"That's what you just said."

Adamat let out a chuckle and smoothed the front of his jacket with one hand. "No, no. I'm not that kind of inspector. I'm investigating a murder attempt."

"And that knowledge is supposed to get you inside?" The woman

looked him over skeptically and raised the barrel of her blunderbuss by half an inch.

"I think we got off on the wrong foot," Adamat said, putting
both hands out in a calming gesture. "I need to speak with Flerring
about his blasting oil."

The blunderbuss was raised until it was pointed at Adamat's
chest. "Well, then you're definitely not coming in."

SouSmith stepped forward suddenly, putting himself between
Adamat and the gun. "Lower the weapon," he rumbled.

"I don't care how big you are, I don't—"

"Put. It. Down." SouSmith took a step forward.

"SouSmith, it's okay, we don't need to escalate this further."

The woman suddenly lowered her blunderbuss. "Did you just
say SouSmith? As in the boxer?"

"That's me." The words came out of SouSmith in a growl.
"Problem?"

Her face split into a grin. "Uncle SouSmith! It's me, Little
Flerring. My dad's Flerring the Fist."

SouSmith's fists slowly uncurled. "This is *that* Flerring?" He
snorted. "You're all grown up, Little."

She grinned back at him. "Been, what, ten years? People grow up
in that time. I haven't seen any of the old crew since Dad moved us
out here to start the powder company."

"Never took Flerring for a chemist," SouSmith said.

"Mom does most of the headwork. Dad does the mixing—well,
he did anyway. Lost both his hands in an explosion two years ago.
He oversees a dozen mixers now and runs the place while Mom is
in Fatrasta."

Adamat stepped up beside SouSmith and leaned on his cane.
"Do you think we could see your father?"

"You're not bringing us trouble, are you, SouSmith?"

SouSmith looked at Adamat, and Adamat drummed his fingers

on his cane. Impossible to tell. If Flerring made the blasting oil, he could very well be complicit in the attempt on Ricard's life. Not that they had to know that. Adamat shook his head. "Just chasing a lead. You probably won't hear from us after today."

Flerring gave a nod and opened one of the double doors that led into the building. "Careful what you touch," she said, "We don't keep a lot of powder in the main building, but you can never be too careful."

They entered what looked to have once been an immense stable capable of housing almost a hundred head of horses. The stalls were filled with raw materials, their doors marked in white chalk telling what was stored inside. They passed dozens of them filled with barrels and boxes of sulfur, saltpeter, charcoal, glycerol, nitric acid. Everything was packed in sawdust and straw, which was strewn all about the place.

"This looks incredibly unsafe," Adamat commented.

"We keep everything separate," Little Flerring said. "None of the ingredients are particularly dangerous on their own."

"Lots of straw. Seems an immense fire risk."

"No flames allowed within fifty feet of the building. We do all our work during the light of the day."

Adamat noticed she had left her blunderbuss outside. It *did* seem they were quite careful. "What can you tell me about blasting oil?"

"I'll let Dad do that," she said, pausing beside one of the stalls. She gestured inside to a makeshift office.

An old man sat at an all-too-small desk in one corner. He was bent over with age, his hair gone gray, but he still had shoulders half a hand wider than SouSmith's. The outer-stall wall had been given a large window, and the man hunched over a book. Adamat instantly noted the man's hands—or, that is, the lack thereof. Immense arms now ended in iron caps. One had a dual hook for grasping, and the other a flat piece of steel in the shape of a paddle.

"Dad, you've got guests," Little Flerring shouted. "Dad!" She gave SouSmith and Adamat an apologetic look. "He's very hard of hearing."

"Eh?" The big man turned toward them. At the sight of strangers he got to his feet, and Adamat almost took a step back. Flerring the Elder—Flerring the Fist—was immense. He towered over Adamat and made even SouSmith look regular-sized. The left side of his face was burned and scarred, making it look lopsided when he smiled. "Is that SouSmith?" he asked loudly.

"Fist," SouSmith said, nodding.

"Fist?" Flerring shook his handless arms at SouSmith. "Not so much anymore." He gave a long, almost mechanical chortle.

The two big men made their greetings and Adamat introduced himself. Flerring the Elder led the whole group around the corner to part of the barn where the stalls had been removed and a comfortable sitting area installed, including several sofas, armchairs, and the entrance to an ice cellar, into which Little Flerring disappeared, only to emerge a moment later with a bottle. She poured them all chilled wine while her father talked.

"Blasting oil," the big man said, shaking his head. "It was our first big discovery. We've done well over the years, creating specialized powder for the Adran army and the Brudania-Gurla Trading Company, but blasting oil was going to make us stupid rich."

Adamat sat up at the mention of Claremonte's company. "You do business with the Trading Company?"

"Everyone does," Flerring said. "And you're naïve to think they don't. The company is our biggest source of saltpeter. We have other sources, of course, but they control just about all the import business. Where was I? Oh, yes. Blasting oil."

"Can you tell me about it?"

"Eh?"

Adamat repeated his question loudly.

"It's a liquid mix of..."—Flerring paused—"Well, I'm not gonna give out trade secrets."

"I understand," Adamat said sympathetically. "What can you tell me without giving up too much? Does it explode similarly to gunpowder?"

"It's a high-velocity explosive. Far more destructive than gunpowder. It doesn't take much, either. A glass ball or tube of the stuff no bigger than my stub here"—Flerring wagged one arm—"is enough to crack stone. We planned on revolutionizing the mining industry with it. Just didn't work out in the end."

It didn't take an inspector to see an awfully significant gap between "going to make us rich" and "didn't work out." "What happened?" Adamat asked.

"We had a chemist named Borin on our payroll," Flerring said. "Nice lad, very smart. I'd thought about trying to marry him to Little here."

Little Flerring made a face as she handed her father a wineglass. "That wouldn't have happened, Dad, and you know it."

"Thought about it, is all I said, hon." He hooked the wineglass deftly and took a sip. "Anyway, Borin came up with the blasting-oil recipe about two years ago. Spent every waking moment since working to stabilize it. It was too volatile, you see. Killed two of our mixers in an accident early on. It explodes by shock rather than by flame, which makes it damn near impossible to transport."

Shock. Now that was an interesting tidbit. Adamat thought about his theory that the explosives had been thrown into Ricard's headquarters. "So you haven't sold any?"

"Of course not! You think I'm in the business of blowing up my customers? I've learned my lesson with explosives." Flerring gestured to his scarred face with the metal paddle fixed to his left hand. "That's why we fired Borin, actually. He wanted to see the blasting oil put to practical use, so he sold a couple samples to a mining company."

"So he *did* sell it!"

"Yeah. Little found out, and we agreed we couldn't trust him anymore. We drew up a contract that let us keep a percentage of the profits if he wound up selling the formula to another company and we parted on good terms. That was only about two weeks ago."

Adamat was on the edge of his seat now. He had something solid. Someplace to take this investigation. If Borin still had his formula and had sold it to Ricard's attempted murderers, he could track them down. "Can you point me to him? I need to speak with Borin."

Flerring exchanged a glance with his daughter. "He's over there," he said, waving his hook vaguely to his right. "And over there. And there."

Little Flerring chuckled in an exasperated manner. "That's unkind, Dad."

"Look, I tell all my mixers and chemists that if they blow themselves up, it's their own damn fault."

"Don't make sport out of the dead, Dad."

Adamat felt his heart fall. "Borin's dead?"

"Very. About as dead as a man can be this side of angering a Privileged. Best as we can guess, he was packing up his samples of blasting oil and dropped one at his foot. You might have seen that grease spot over by the river on your way in?"

"Yes."

"That used to be a very sturdy stone building. It's where our chemists worked. That building was built to survive any size explosion. It could have lasted through an artillery bombardment. Took out Borin and all of our ongoing experiments. There weren't even pieces of Borin left after that, and we're still finding bits of stone everywhere we walk."

Adamat leaned back in his seat and let out a sigh. "I'm sorry for your loss."

Flerring shrugged. "It set us back, but our people keep good notes. It destroyed every bit of the blasting oil we had left, which I think is a damned blessing."

"Dad…"

"Don't you 'Dad' me." Flerring shook his head at his daughter and turned to Adamat. "I've put a stop to all research on the blasting oil. Burned all but one copy of the notes, and only I know where the last copy is. Infernal stuff isn't going to get us all killed while I'm still alive. Once I'm dead, my girl here is welcome to blow herself up as quick as she wants. But not before that."

A dead end. Dead as Borin. There was no way to know if Flerring was telling the truth about any of this without the chemist to corroborate. Maybe Flerring killed Borin to cover his tracks. Adamat could bring in a dozen officers and tear the place apart, but that was the last thing he had time for. And SouSmith might not forgive him.

"Do you happen to know who Borin sold the stuff to?"

Flerring scratched his head with his hook. "A mining company. Do you know, hon?"

"There's a receipt somewhere," Little Flerring said. "I'll see if I can find it."

She disappeared for a few minutes, during which time Flerring and SouSmith talked about their boxing days. Adamat couldn't help but be amazed at how vigorous the boxer-turned-powder-maker was, despite his injuries.

His daughter returned holding a scrap of paper and handed it to Adamat. "The Underhill Mining Coalition," she said.

Adamat paused as he reached for the paper and let his hand fall. "You sure?"

"Yes."

"I'll remember it, thank you."

Little Flerring shrugged and put the paper in her pocket.

"This mining company. You didn't happen to meet their representative, did you?" Adamat felt his heart begin to race.

"No. Borin did business with them behind our back. We wouldn't have agreed to the sale otherwise."

"Did Borin happen to tell you *why* they needed it?"

"They were looking for high-powered explosives," Little Flerring said as if it were obvious.

This wasn't helping at all. "But did they come to him or did he go to them?"

"Oh. They came to him."

"That's all we need to know. Thank you," Adamat said, getting to his feet. "I think it's time we go. I appreciate your help a great deal."

"Didn't think we were much help," Little Flerring said. "If you track down the samples Borin sold, let me know. I'd prefer they were destroyed."

"You were a great deal of help. And don't worry, I'll tell you." Adamat shook hands with Little Flerring, then tentatively grasped the Fist's offered hook. A few minutes later and he and SouSmith were back in their carriage headed toward Adopest.

"Good to see him," SouSmith rumbled.

Adamat barely heard him, deep in thought. "Yes, I'm sure."

"Been a long time. Girl's grown up."

"Oh? You thinking of settling down, SouSmith?"

SouSmith chuckled. "Too young for me." He paused. Then, "Why such a hurry?"

Adamat drummed his fingers on the head of his cane excitedly. "Because the Underhill Mining Coalition isn't a mining company," he said.

"Don't follow."

"They're a club. A group of thieves and smugglers who call themselves businessmen. They meet to drink and play cards at an exclusive—and hidden—location in Adopest. Most people know them as the Underhill Society and I happen to be friends with one of their members."

"Who's that?"

"Ricard Tumblar."

*   *   *

Nila and Olem hunted the Kez cavalry through the gorges and hills of Brude's Hideaway for three days. On the first day a low cloud cover descended over the area, obscuring the peaks of the Charwood Pile to the west, and on the second day a heavy fog rolled in. Nila wondered if the fog had some kind of sorcery behind it, but neither she nor Olem could sense anything amiss in the Else.

It was just bad luck.

Nila couldn't see the ends of their cuirassier lines as they swept the ridges and bends of the highlands. The sun was obscured and the whole world seemed gray.

She stood in her stirrups the third day, wondering how any man or woman could possibly stay in the saddle for hours at a time, let alone several days. *Everything* below her waist hurt, and most of the things above it. Her knuckles were sore from gripping the reins and her spine ached from the jolt of her horse's stride. Her head spun from hour after hour of trying to maintain her vision of the Else, attempting to spot anything in the fog. Olem told her to drink more water.

Olem sat beside her at the top of a small hill looking to the south—or maybe the north, she couldn't really be sure, with no point of reference. There was a white chasm at their feet where the earth dipped beneath the fog, and she couldn't tell if this was merely a divot in the landscape or a valley a mile long.

"The good news," Olem said, puffing on a cigarette, "is that the fog screws with them as much as it does with us. They're left reading the ground and listening for echoes in the murk, same as us."

Nila sniffed. He'd become progressively more optimistic as the hours rolled past. He seemed to hold the opinion that every minute they spent circling the Gurlish Wolf in the fog was another minute he wasn't abusing the flanks of Tamas's army. Which, she supposed, was true, if the Gurlish Wolf hadn't slipped past them and was back on the plain already, attacking the Adran army.

"They have an advantage over us," Nila said.

"Oh?"

"They can smell your cigarette smoke from farther away than we can see them."

Olem took the cigarette from his mouth and stared at it sourly before putting it out on his ash-stained saddle horn and tossing it into the damp grass. "Damn it."

They sat in silence for several minutes before Nila said, "How do they communicate in this?"

"Pit if I know. I haven't heard a trumpet since the fog descended, so it's not that."

"Maybe they have a Knacked?"

"Maybe," Olem mused. "Someone with very precise hearing. A few years back I heard a story about a pair of Knacked twins that could communicate over a hundred miles just using their minds. That kind of thing is rarer than a Privileged healer, I'd imagine." He drew his tobacco and rolling papers from his breast pocket, stared at them for a moment, then put them back with a sigh. "No, I imagine they've done the smart thing and hunkered down in one of these valleys to wait out the fog."

Nila studied the ground beneath their feet, looking at the horseshoe prints in the mud—horseshoes marked by a Kez blacksmith. The tracks led into the gully below them. The Kez had split up after being run from their camp three days before. Their tracks seemed to lead everywhere, crisscrossing and doubling back without any clear path to follow.

And like a hound looking for a scent, Olem had patiently been following every one of those trails. He kept his formations tight, his scouts plentiful, and never stumbled blindly into one of the fog-concealed valleys.

It all seemed very professional to Nila, but she wouldn't have had any idea as to any of this if Olem hadn't been explaining it to her along the way.

"You're picking this stuff up quickly," Olem said.

"What stuff?"

"All this." He tapped the pocket where he kept his tobacco. "Cigarette smoke. Something I didn't think of, but a Kez cavalryman would. Good call."

Nila ducked her head. "Thank you."

"A fighting Privileged," Olem said. "Six months ago, if I had to guess what extraordinary thing you'd become, I would not have guessed that."

Nila knew it was meant to be a compliment, but it niggled at her all the same. "You don't think I'm capable?"

"You've shown yourself to be capable."

"But you wouldn't have thought that."

"That's not quite what I meant."

"And what did you mean, Colonel Olem?"

Olem removed the rolling paper from his pocket and was about to sprinkle tobacco on the center before he made a face and put it back. "Privileged are born to it. You were a laundress. No offense, but it didn't seem like something on your horizon."

Nila opened her mouth, ready to take the argument further, then decided against it. What was she doing, arguing like this? Olem was right, of course. A Privileged? Her? It was laughably unlikely.

"If you don't mind me saying," Olem said, "you've been on edge. More than just a chafed ass."

Nila let out what she had wanted to be a dismissive laugh, but it came out as just this side of hysterical. "You could say that."

"The field marshal has a habit of using the hottest fire to temper soft metal," Olem said. "I'm not sure if he should have sent you."

"I'm soft metal, am I? No. It's not that. Well. It is that. But so many more things. I've never ridden before and my body hurts so badly I want to cry every moment. I'm untested, barely trained. This infernal fog!" Her voice rose a little too high and a nearby cuirassier glanced at her.

Olem sat unmoved, listening for several moments before he said, "At least you know your failings."

"Oh, thanks."

"Really. I mean it. I've met dozens of officers who think their immaculate mustache can move the world. Not knowing one's weaknesses gets people killed."

Nila shook her head and gave a short laugh, relieved to hear this one sounding a little less desperate. "Little do they know that an immaculate beard is what it takes."

Olem grinned at her. "Right you are." His hand was halfway toward his rolling papers again before he swore under his breath.

"Are you with anyone?" Nila asked, the question leaving her lips before she could stop herself.

Olem glanced up in surprise. "Huh? Well..." He rubbed the back of his neck. "Kind of. It's a tenuous thing."

Nila was surprised to find herself hurt by his answer. She had turned him down, after all, and that was months ago. Maybe she had hoped he would pine for her a little longer. "Another soldier?"

"Yeah."

"What's she like?"

"Long legs. Black hair. Very good at what she does."

"Oh? And what does she do?" She felt a smile tug at the corner of her mouth when Olem's cheeks turned red.

"She's a powder mage."

Nila gave a low whistle. "You don't settle, do you?"

"Never have," Olem said, giving her a lingering glance. She opened her mouth, but forgot her response immediately when Olem held up a hand. "Do you hear that?" he whispered.

Up and down the line, cuirassiers grew alert. Nila strained her ears to listen, but couldn't hear anything. "What is it?"

Olem put one hand on the stock of his carbine. "I thought I heard a horse down there."

They remained in silence for several minutes, during which Nila barely allowed herself to breathe. The fear and anxiety all returned in those precious minutes of waiting, and she could feel her heart hammering against her chest like a bird trying to escape its cage.

A shadow appeared in the fog down in the gully. Nila thought her heart would burst at any moment, until she saw Olem relax, his finger edging away from the trigger of his carbine.

"It's one of ours," a cuirassier said. "Looks like Ganley."

A horse came out of the fog carrying a blue-uniformed rider. Olem called out a greeting, and Nila sat back in her saddle, trying to find a comfortable spot on which to sit. There wasn't one. She closed her eyes, trying to reach the meditative state that Bo had taught her—a place between this world and the Else, where she could let her worries fade.

She had yet to reach it.

When her eyes opened again, she found that she'd slipped past her target and gone into the Else—here at least, she sighed to herself, the fog couldn't penetrate. The hills rolled on in the distance, and she could see that the gully before them was indeed a deep one, extending thirty feet down and on into thick brush in the distance. Hundreds of small flames danced before her eyes like fireflies.

Several things happened at once. First, she screamed. Second, the returning scout, Ganley, fell from his horse, his bloody throat grinning up at them all from the ground, and third, those hundreds of fireflies suddenly shot forward and the rumble of hooves brought Nila out of the Else and into the real world, where horses seemed to erupt from the mist, ridden by Kez cavalry in their green-on-tan uniforms.

Olem's carbine went off, causing a ringing in Nila's ears. A dozen other shots were fired before the Kez cavalry were suddenly upon them.

Nila felt a Kez mount ram her own, sending the creature reeling to the side. She sawed at the reins and nearly fell out of her saddle, when a sword flashed in front of her eyes. The cuff of a blue uniform sprang into her vision as Olem countered a stroke meant for her neck. She heard him grunt, swear, then he was gone.

A Kez dragoon leaned into Nila from the side, and she'd barely got her hands up before the guard of his saber cracked into the side of her head. Vision swimming, she latched onto the man's arm, pulling him closer, and put her fingers around his throat.

She willed the fire from the Else, pouring her anger and energy in behind it, and waited for the man's head to wither like a burned mushroom.

Nothing happened.

Panic seized her. She pushed herself closer to the dragoon, feeling his breath upon her neck, grasping for the Else. It was still there, she could still sense it at her fingertips, but nothing was happening.

The guard of his saber hit her again. She reeled, unable to grasp her sorcery, yet knowing if she let go, she would die with a split head. She dug her fingernails into his throat and tore. The man suddenly disengaged, cursing angrily in Kez and holding his bloody throat.

Nila remembered the pistol Olem had given her. She grasped for the butt, her hands shaking, and leveled it at the dragoon.

A grin flashed across his face, and the last thing she felt was a tug on the back of her head and the whole world going upside down.

CHAPTER 37

"Three days," Adamat said as he was led into Ricard's office in the Kinnen Hotel. "It took me three days to get an appointment to see not you but your undersecretary! What the pit is going on here, Ricard? I thought you wanted me working quickly."

Adamat came up short. Ricard sat slumped behind his desk, hair frayed, jacket discarded in one corner, a pair of reading glasses perched on his nose and a newspaper in one hand.

"Pit," Adamat said. "It looks like you haven't slept in three days."

Ricard stifled a yawn. "Five, I think. Well. I've caught some naps. Here and there. Fell," he shouted.

"Right here, sir." Adamat exchanged a glance with Fell, who was standing right beside him.

Ricard squinted over his glasses. "So you are. Fell, tell the boys out front to let Adamat in to see me immediately no matter what."

Fell cleared her throat. "No matter what, sir?"

"Unless I'm indisposed. Kresimir's balls, that's obvious. Look, Adamat, I'm sorry. I've quadrupled the security since the bombing, and you know how it is with logistics like this. Orders get crossed, people can't see me. It's a nightmare. You should have just come by my home."

"I did. Several times. You weren't there."

"Sir," Fell said. "You haven't left this office for two days. You haven't been home since before the bombing."

Ricard scratched his head. "That's right. Oh well. Wine?"

"It's nine o'clock in the morning." Adamat took a seat opposite Ricard.

"Coffee?"

"Yes, please."

"Fell, have someone get us coffee. And put a little whiskey in mine."

"That's awful, Ricard," Adamat said.

"I've had worse." Ricard hiccupped and pounded twice on his chest with one fist. "Now then, what can you tell me about the bombing?"

"The bombing was done with something called 'blasting oil,'" Adamat said. "It took some time, but I was able to track down the manufacturer."

"Who was it?"

"The Flerring Powder Company."

"Never heard of them," Ricard growled. "And when I'm done with them, no one ever will. I'll see them out of business! I'll destroy everything they—"

Adamat cut him off. "That's quite unnecessary."

"What do you mean?"

"I interviewed the owner and his daughter. The blasting oil wasn't ready for sale. It's too unstable. One of their chemists sold a sample of it behind their backs and they canned him for it."

"I see. This chemist?"

"Blew himself up the day after they fired him."

"Convenient."

"Perhaps. Whether it was an accident or not, Flerring insisted that he wouldn't have sold the stuff himself, and I believe him."

"Where does that leave us? The owner claiming innocence and the chemist dead? I don't like it."

"They told me who their chemist sold the sample to."

A young man entered the room carrying a silver platter with two cups and a pot of coffee. When the drinks were served and the man had left, Ricard leaned forward. "Who bought it?"

"The Underhill Mining Coalition."

Ricard made a strangled noise and spit some of his coffee out down the front of his shirt. "Pardon?"

"The Underhill Mining Coalition," Adamat repeated. "Which, if my memory serves, is a front for the Underhill Society. The name they use when one of the members wants to buy something with funds that can't be easily traced."

"*If memory serves.*" Ricard scrunched up his face and mimicked Adamat in a high voice. "Bloody Knacked and your bloody memory. You can't be certain."

"It's the only lead I have."

"Perhaps you got the explosive wrong. Maybe it was something else."

"I put the time to good use while I was waiting for my appointment with Fell," Adamat said, removing a paper from his pocket. "I employed Flerring the Younger, the heir to the Flerring Powder Company, as an expert in my investigation. She examined the union headquarters and has given me written evidence that the explosion was indeed caused by blasting oil, and that the oil was purchased by the Underhill Mining Coalition."

"How the pit did you get her to sign that?"

Adamat coughed into his hand. "I swore that we wouldn't prosecute her or her company."

"You're a bastard."

"If we need a scapegoat, the dead chemist is as good as any. But we don't need a scapegoat. We just need the location of the Underhill Society."

Ricard sprang to his feet. "Absolutely not."

"Why is that?"

"What's the point of a secret society if it's not secret anymore?"

"They tried to kill you."

"They? More likely just one or two of the members." Ricard cursed under his breath. "I rose up through their ranks. I've been friends with those men and women for the last twenty years. I've given every one of them good jobs, business opportunities. Pit, I've kept three of them out of jail."

"How many members are there?"

"There are—" Ricard's mouth snapped shut. "I'm not supposed to talk about it at all. Secret society, remember?"

"I think they waived their right to secrecy when they decided to use the society as their front while trying to kill you. Are any of them particularly stupid?"

"It's not as stupid as you think. Less than fifty people in Adopest even know that the Underhill Society exists. Giving the name to some small powder company means absolutely nothing, and let's be honest—we only know it was this blasting oil because of you. The police didn't notice anything different about the explosion." Ricard slumped back in his chair and drained his cup of coffee. He bent over suddenly, his face twisted in a grimace.

"Are you all right?"

"That coffee was really hot." Ricard recovered and went on. "I can't do it. I can't betray them like this."

"They betrayed you."

"One or two of them. Maybe! Pit."

"I understand this is hard for you, Ricard." Adamat leaned across the desk. "They'll try again, though."

"How can you be certain? You said they only had a sample."

"After examining the union headquarters, Flerring the Younger said she thought two explosions weren't big enough for them to have used all the blasting oil. They may still have enough blasting oil to make several more bombs."

"Well, pit."

"If you can give me the names of one or two of the society members you suspect, I can trail them. I would need some men to help me, but we might be able to find out where they keep the blasting oil or their next target."

"I know where they're keeping it," Ricard said miserably.

"Where?"

"At the Society building."

"They're keeping an unstable explosive at the Underhill Society? How stupid are they?"

"Not as stupid as you think."

"You have to tell me where it is."

Instead, Ricard turned and shouted for Fell. When she appeared at the door, he said, "Get together five of my most discreet men."

"When?"

"As quickly as possible. Within the hour."

"Yes sir. What is it for, sir?"

"We have to search the basement of this building for a powerful explosive."

Adamat was astonished at how quickly Fell prepared the operation.

At Fell's insistence, Ricard left the building—ostensibly to meet Cheris for an early lunch—and several of his most valuable lieutenants were suddenly called away. Within thirty minutes, two men and three women had gathered in an empty hotel room. Adamat could only assume they were union members who had earned Ricard's trust but not yet been given any duties of importance.

Adamat stood near the window of the hotel room. Two of the women sat on the bed, and a third near the door, while both men had their backs to the wall. Everyone watched intently as Fell entered the room and closed the door behind her.

She began quietly, "What we say at this meeting does not leave this room, understand?"

The gathered group exchanged looks before giving their unanimous consent. Some of them glanced at Adamat and he wondered if any of them knew who he was. He recognized three of the faces by happenstance, but didn't know any of their names.

"There is a strong chance that someone has placed a bomb beneath this building," Fell said. To their credit, none of them headed for the door. "The perpetrator does not know that we know, and we are going to search the premises quickly and quietly until we find it. We will start with the basement and work our way up. Before any of you ask, this is not a volunteer assignment. If one of you leaves the building before I say so, you will never find work in this country again."

Adamat noted that one of the men had started to sweat violently. Fear? Or guilt? The woman by the door swallowed hard.

"That being said," Fell went on, letting a smile touch her lips, "once we find and dispose of the bomb, each of you will find yourself well rewarded. You'll receive promotions within the union and a not-insignificant amount of money. Inspector Adamat and I will lead the search. Questions? Yes, Draily?"

The woman by the door lowered her hand. "I don't know a damn thing about bombs. How am I going to help with all this?"

Adamat cut in before Fell could respond. "No one knows anything about this kind of bomb," he said. "It's not gunpowder, but something called blasting oil. It does not respond to flame but rather to concussion, which means that our search needs to be very, very careful. Handle everything gently and, for Adom's sake, do not drop anything!"

"Then what the pit are we looking for?" the sweating man asked, his voice strained.

"I don't know," Adamat admitted. "A container of some sort. The blasting oil was sold in ten clear glass vials, stoppered at the top with corks. Our suspect may have transferred the oil to a new container, or it may still be in those same vials. We'll make a thorough examination of any liquid on the premises."

"Does this have anything to do with the bombing at the union headquarters?" one of the women on the bed asked.

"Possibly," Adamat said. They didn't need to know anything more than that. "Any other questions?"

A round of headshaking.

"Good," Fell said. "And again, be damned careful! If you find anything suspicious, let Inspector Adamat know immediately. Don't make a scene. We want to do this as quietly as possible. Now, everyone to the basement."

Adamat stepped over to Fell as they all filed out of the room. "The brunette," Adamat said.

"Little Will?"

"Yes. Something about all this was making him nervous as pit. Grab him and put him under guard."

Fell gave a quick affirmative and left the room quickly after Will. Adamat passed them in the hall, Fell with her hand on Will's shoulder and Will's collar soaked with sweat. Adamat followed the rest of the group down to the cellar. Lanterns were handed out quickly, and voices talked in hushed tones. Adamat held his lantern high and gripped his cane tightly. A tingle went down his spine as he descended into the damp stone basement.

The four union workers looked to him when they reached the bottom, and he realized that Fell had not yet come down. He was seized by sudden suspicion. If even one of them was in on this bomb plot, they might make a go at him. He found himself sizing each of them up, planning the best way to defend himself.

A few moments passed before he realized they were still watching him.

"Well, get to it."

"Uh, sir," Draily said. "Look."

Adamat shook the fear from his head and stepped forward. They stood in a long, arched hallway with walls of stone, and off the hallway to the right were a dozen niches that extended out beneath the hotel. At the far end of the hall was a low, heavy door.

Draily was pointing into the first niche. Adamat held his lantern inside and squinted. "Nothing but wine," he said.

She rolled her eyes. "Is it?"

"Oh." Realization set in. Of course. Any of these wine bottles could be the bomb or bombs he was looking for. It would be the best place to hide something like that—in plain sight. Adamat tapped his fingers on his stomach, then said, "Search everything else. I'll check the wine."

The rest of the group moved on to the other niches, and Adamat began to inspect the wine. At first glance he estimated upward of two thousand bottles here, and Adamat wondered if this was the other part of Ricard's wine collection or whether the hotel was just this well stocked.

Adamat removed his jacket and hung it from a peg on the wall, rolling his sleeves up. He began examining each wine bottle, starting at the top row. They came in every variety; some were slender, dark-brown bottles, while others were fat green bottles with long necks.

He looked for consistency; the thickness of the dust, how the labels were positioned, as well as the size and shape of the bottle itself. He felt a growing despair as he went—if the blasting oil had been hidden inside a wine bottle, it might be impossible to find. A hotel such as this went through wine at an alarming rate. Some of the bottles had been here for months or years, and those were easy to tell from the layer of dust, but there were still at least eighty bottles that had been handled recently.

"You think our bomber is that devious?" Fell's voice said from the hallway.

Adamat didn't look up from his examination. "They'd have to be an idiot not to see the opportunity," Adamat said. "I don't know how to go about this without opening four dozen bottles to check their contents."

"A last resort, I think," Fell said. "You know how Ricard is about his wine."

"Would he rather drink a glass of blasting oil?"

"I'll have to point that out to him." She paused, then, "You're certain it's here?"

"Ricard was certain," Adamat said. "That's all I have to go on."

"He may be wrong."

"A possibility, sure," Adamat said. "But if he's right..."

"Not worth the risk. That man you pointed out, Will?"

"Anything?" Adamat stopped his search long enough to look hopefully toward Fell. If they'd just happened upon a conspirator, they might get a lucky break. Investigative science practically depended on lucky breaks.

"Just nervous," Fell said. "His father worked for a powder company and was killed in a blast two years ago. Will's terrified of explosions. I should have remembered it earlier. Poor man pissed himself when I wouldn't let him leave the building."

Adamat returned his attention to the wine bottles. "A pity."

He heard a jingle of keys, and Fell said, "Mark where you are and come with me. I'll set a man to make sure the wine isn't disturbed. We need to search the Underhill Room."

"Oh?" Adamat made a mental note of the wine cellar and followed Fell down the hallway to the thick door at the end of the basement. She unlocked it and pulled it open, the strain of her shoulders testifying to the weight.

Inside, Adamat was surprised to find another long corridor. He held his lantern high and glanced back at Fell.

"Go on."

He crept down the hall slowly, still clutching his cane, and he wondered briefly how much he trusted Fell. Her loyalty was supposed to be to Ricard for the duration of her contract. But what if that was all a lie? Could she have planned the bombing? She could kill him down here without a problem, then hide the body and tell Ricard he had left. Adamat's mind whirred through a dozen possible motives and all the reasons why he was wrong. By the time he reached the end of the hall, he was no less wary, and all the more certain that he wouldn't stand even the faintest chance against Fell in a fight.

His lantern created eerie shadows in the large, square room at the end of the hall. Fell squeezed past him to light candelabras along all four walls until the entire room had been illuminated. It looked like any of the hundreds of gentleman's clubs in Adopest— the walls were covered in velvet and the candelabras were polished brass. There was seating for at least a dozen people in the form of divans and couches, and the center of the room held a velvet-lined card table with room for six.

There was a dumbwaiter in one corner, likely leading up to the kitchen, and a smaller, private stock of wine as well as an untapped keg. A fireplace sat at either end of the room, though upon closer examination they appeared to be wood-burning stoves with stone façades.

"So this is the Underhill Society?"

Fell finished lighting the candelabras and blew out her lantern. "Yes."

"Has it been here the whole time?" Adamat remembered hearing about the Underhill Society for the first time over thirteen years ago and knew it was much older than that. Ricard had owned the hotel for only six.

"Only since Ricard bought the hotel. He hasn't told me where they met before that."

Adamat pointed back down the hallway. "Are they..."

"They can come search the room. It shouldn't take long. Just don't mention the...well, you know."

Fell's searchers finished their assigned niches and then moved into the larger room, checked every nook and cranny thoroughly and without comment as to the room's purpose. Adamat returned to the wine cellar, resuming his examination of the bottles.

Frustration continued to mount. Every bit of instinct told him that the blasting oil should be hidden among the wine. It was too good a spot for any henchman with half a wit, and if the perpetrator had a whole wit, the oil would have been bottled carefully and put in among the less-used wines. Adamat cursed under his breath and tried to recall the latest fashionable wines among Ricard's friends and associates—those would be the easiest to rule out.

The searchers moved up to the next floor, and Adamat only barely noted their passing.

It must have been almost an hour later when he heard someone on the basement stairs. He noted Fell's soft footfalls.

"Any progress upstairs?" he asked.

Fell set her lantern on a wine barrel in one corner. "None. It's a large hotel and with only four men it's a slow business. Progress here?"

"I've narrowed it down to a possibility of three dozen bottles," Adamat said.

"Are you sure you're putting your energy in the right place? After all, I'd think it would be obvious if any of the wine here had been uncorked."

"Certainly. But they could have done it off-site and brought the wine here." Adamat sighed and returned a bottle to its place. "I should have asked Ricard if any of his guests have brought him new wine recently."

"Everyone does," Fell said.

Adamat eyed the shelves where he'd sorted the most probable

bottles. "Have him make a list for me. The only way to know for certain is to open every bottle. Or, more safely, to take the whole lot out of the city and throw it off a high cliff."

"Ricard would be . . . cross. He already lost his collection beneath the old headquarters. You know how he feels about his wine."

"The captain of the hotel will already gut me for destroying whatever system he had in place down here. Might as well infuriate Ricard as well. Get someone to help me carry these upstairs." He rubbed at his temples. "Pit, how am I going to get this out of the city? From everything Flerring told me, it's a terrible idea to transport the stuff by carriage. Too bumpy."

"Ma'am?" a voice called down the basement stairs.

Fell stepped into the basement hall and called back. "Yes?"

"I think we've found something."

Adamat was on his feet in moments. He followed Fell up the stairs, where Draily waited. The woman led them both into the kitchen and stopped beside the silver cabinet. "Had to get the captain to open it up for me." She opened one of the doors and knelt in front of it. "You'll want to look yourselves. I don't really want to reach in there."

Adamat lay on the wood floor beside the silver cabinet and took Fell's lantern.

On the bottom shelf, behind the silver serving platters, was a wooden crate. It held glass vials with corks in the top and each one was filled with a clear liquid. Adamat suddenly felt his heart hammering in his ears.

"Bloody pit," he said.

"It's there?"

"Yes."

Fell gave an audible sigh of relief.

"Fetch Flerring the Younger," Adamat said. "Probably best to have one of her professionals deal with the stuff. Post a heavy guard on this room, but try to do it quietly. And get me the kitchen staff. I want every single one of them here for questioning by this evening."

Fell barked orders to her people. Adamat felt her hand on his arm. "Excellent work, Inspector."

"Don't thank me yet," Adamat said, still lying on the floor, unable to take his eyes off the innocuous-looking bottles of blasting oil.

"Why?"

"There are two bottles missing."

CHAPTER
38

Tamas crept through the riverside rushes, knee-deep in the cold water of the Addown River.

He had one pistol in his belt, the other held with the barrel pointed skyward, and the sword at his side leaving a slight furrow against the current of the river. The night was crisp, his breath visible to his powder-enhanced senses. Somewhere off to his left, a fish jumped in the water, and he heard Andriya start behind him.

"Shh," Tamas said quietly. "Don't get twitchy on me."

Tamas was ready to reprimand him for a smart remark, but Andriya behaved himself. They pushed forward, frogs going silent at their advance but no sign of alarm in the fortress up ahead of them.

Fortress, Tamas reflected, was a stretch. The stone building was only two stories tall, with a twelve-foot wall that stretched from the riverside a hundred feet to the main highway. The whole thing was little more than an inspection station where government officers could check both carts on the road and barges in the water for contraband and tax dodgers heading between Adopest and Budwiel.

Before the revolution, it would have been staffed by just eight to ten servants of the crown. The Kez, when they swept past this point, had reinforced the whole building. Small-caliber cannons had been mounted along the wall and a sixteen-pound artillery piece had been placed on the end of the stone wharf that stuck out into the Addown. Tamas guessed that they'd left no less than a forty-man garrison.

Tamas approached the base of the wharf, his eyes on the top of the inspection station. Torches lit the wall, and he could see the bobbing of a bayonet that betrayed the presence of a guard.

Something touched his arm and Tamas stopped, looking back. Andriya pointed into the rushes, and after a moment Tamas could see a nest where a yearling goose eyed him angrily.

He waded deeper into the water to avoid the nest, then shoved his pistol in his belt and tightened his sword against his thigh. He reached up until he could feel the stone ledge above him, and with a quick motion he was up on the wharf.

Tamas drew his belt knife and padded toward the artillery piece sitting at the end. A Kez sentry leaned against it, his soft snores reaching Tamas's ears. He stiffened as Tamas's knife took him between the ribs and a moment later his body lay behind the cannon. Tamas looked back toward the inspection station just in time to see Andriya, silent as a gliding owl, slip over the battlements above the second story. Tamas heard a pain-filled grunt and had to remind his hammering heart that he could hear far better than the guards inside.

He stole through the door to the inspection station. The garrison, if he remembered, correctly, would be on the second floor. He paused at the foot of the stairwell, a sound catching his ear, and went back past the door to the wharf.

Four Kez soldiers were playing dice in the tiny mess hall by the light of a single lantern. Tamas eyed them through a slit in the door. They were intent upon their game and likely a little drunk. He decided to take care of the sleeping ones upstairs first.

He was just about to step away when the door suddenly pushed open, nearly hitting him in the face. He leapt back, and a fifth guard stared at him in surprise.

Tamas slammed his knife into the man's throat and drove him backward into the room, shoving him across the main table. The other four guards jumped to their feet, shouting and scrambling for weapons. Tamas was faster. He pulled his knife hand back and dragged it across a second guard's throat before leaving it in the heart of a third. He leapt the table in a single bound, the powder trance singing in his veins. His foot came down on the bench opposite and he barely had time to swear as it gave way beneath him.

He stumbled upon landing and threw himself into a roll, tumbling across the room. He came up beside the fourth guard just as the man turned on him with a pistol. Tamas reached out with his senses and fizzled the ignition of the powder as the hammer came down. He wrenched the pistol out of the man's hand and slammed the butt into the guard's face hard enough to hear his skull crack.

The fifth guard ran for the door. Tamas drew his boot knife and threw, flat-handed. The knife hit her just beneath the shoulder blade. She let out a yell, stumbled, and reached back for the hilt. Tamas crossed the room and broke her neck.

He scrambled for both of his knives and took up a position beside the door. The silence was deafening. Where were the reinforcements? Where were the sleeping guards?

A single pair of boots sounded on the stone stairwell. Tamas hazarded a glance, only to see Andriya appear. The man was covered in blood, but by the looks of him none of it was his own. "You're making too much noise," Andriya said.

Tamas let out a soft sigh of relief, cleaned his knives, and led

Andriya back upstairs. They passed the bunk room, where Tamas could hear a soft death rattle.

"Take care of that," he said.

On the roof, two sentries lay in pools of their own blood, and Tamas shielded his eyes from the flickering torches and surveyed Surkov's Alley to his south. To his surprise, he saw nothing—no fires, no camping companies of Kez reserves. In the distance, he could see the torches of Midway Keep, and far beyond that the glittering lights of Budwiel.

The entire Kez army was now to his north.

He snatched one of the torches and waved it twice. Within moments the ground to the north of the inspection station was writhing with the dark figures of Adran soldiers as they flooded forward. He was joined a moment later by Andriya.

"Didn't we do this once before?" Andriya asked. "Going behind the enemy's lines? I seem to remember it didn't end so well."

Tamas glanced toward Andriya. Somehow, he had gotten even more blood on him. Olem, he reflected, might not be as good a killer as Andriya, but he was far better company. "You should change your uniform."

"I don't have a spare."

"That was shortsighted."

Andriya licked a bit of blood off the tip of one finger, a not entirely human smile playing upon his lips. "We climb the walls of Budwiel tomorrow. I want the bloody Kez to know what's coming for them when they see me."

"If you insist." There was no "sir" when Andriya had his blood up like this. Killing Kez was his favorite thing in this world. "Just stand upwind from me."

Tamas turned to watch more of his army emerge from the darkness. The vanguard had surrounded the inspection station now, and on the road he could see the long, dark snake of his army marching forward through the dark. On the river to his right, several cargo barges moved into view, cutting quietly through the water, loaded down with heavy artillery.

"The Kez army be damned," Tamas said. "Nothing will stop me now."

Nila's first instinct after regaining consciousness was to scream.

She nearly bit her tongue in half to keep herself from doing so. Her hands were bound behind her back and her eyes opened on nothing but darkness. Fear threatened to swallow her whole, adrenaline tearing through her veins and overwhelming the stiffness of her limbs and the saddle soreness at her very core.

She slipped into the place between the real world and the Else almost instinctually—in fact, it was several minutes before she realized what she had done. Her breathing was calm, her heart no longer fluttering. The world floated before her in a translucent haze. Bo had described this as a good place to be calm and to think, but had warned her that her brain would not receive the information that it needed to analyze the world around it. Sounds were muted, and even the feel of the ground beneath her legs seemed distant.

Cautiously, she let herself leave that place, sinking back into the real world. With it came all of the pain and aches of being alive and she couldn't help but let out a slight whimper.

A nighttime camp came into focus around her. She could hear low voices, the crackling of a nearby fire, and the soft whinny of horses off in the darkness. She lay on her side, her left arm numb, and the smell of vomit stung her nostrils. A trail of crust along the corner of her mouth told her that the vomit was hers.

Blinking the tears of pain out of the corners of her eyes, she realized she was staring into a bruised, blood-caked face. The man lay on his side, facing her. He had been stripped to the waist and she could see thick black stripes on his bare shoulders and arms—he'd been whipped and beaten until he was raw. His hands were bound behind his back. The inhumanity of it made Nila want to recoil in horror.

She didn't dare. If she moved, they would know she was awake and she might be given similar treatment. If she was lucky.

Her heart began to race again, the calm she had attained slipping away from her like grains of sand through her fingers. She could feel her arms trembling and then . . .

She recognized the man lying beside her.

It was Olem.

She bit back a curse. Was he still alive? "Olem," she whispered, her own pain forgotten. "Olem!"

His eyes opened far too slowly for Nila's liking. It took several moments before she could see the recognition in them. His short beard was matted to his face with blood, but she could see the corner of his mouth twitch upward.

"Glad to see you awake." He coughed.

"What the pit did they do to you?" she hissed.

"Just asked some questions."

"They beat you senseless!"

"They didn't like the answers."

She wanted to ask him if she was next, but it seemed insensitive. "Barbarians."

"Yeah." Olem shifted slightly, grunting in pain. "Pit, that hurts."

"They have to give you medicine. I'll shout until they do. How can they do this to a prisoner of war?"

"Shh," he said. "Don't say a word. Keep still for as long as you can. Most of them are asleep. They won't bother you till morning."

Her calm was completely gone now. "And if I wake them?"

"I don't know. The commanding officer is the Gurlish Wolf. He'll do just about anything. The rest of them aren't much better."

"I'll burn this whole camp down."

Olem gave a slight shake of his head, grimacing as he did so. "They don't know you're a Privileged."

"Really?"

"No gloves, remember? I told them you were my secretary."

Nila tried to find that place between reality and the Else again, but had no success. She couldn't believe it had gone so wrong. One minute they'd been alone, and the next these Kez had erupted from the fog to kill them all. "We're finished. Did they wipe us all out?"

Olem's eyes had closed and for a moment she thought he had passed out. Then, "No. They hadn't expected us to all be in close formation. It was heavy fighting for a while, then I got separated from the rest of the regiment. Been listening. They captured fifteen or twenty of us, killed a few dozen more, but the rest of the boys are still out there."

"There's hope, then?"

Olem didn't respond to that. "Been listening," he repeated. "They plan on sending my head back to Tamas. Probably with you. Best chance for you to get away from this."

"No!" she said, a little too loudly. When no one seemed to take notice, she went on. "They wouldn't!"

"They're spreading fear and doubt. Trying to get Tamas off of Ipille's trail. My head seems like a solid idea."

"We'll make a run for it," Nila said. "We'll slip out in the middle of the night. We can—"

Olem was shaking his head again. "Too dangerous. They'd just kill you too. This is the best way. That's why I told them who I was."

"Olem." Her voice cracked, and she cleared her throat. "Olem, don't say that."

"Is all right," he slurred. She could see his head droop. He was passing out.

"Olem, stay with me!"

There was no response. Nila tried to wake him several more times, and short of a cold bucket of water she didn't think anything would do it. She prayed silently that he wouldn't die right then and there.

She rolled over on her back and took stock of her surroundings. Forms around the nearby campfires snored in their bedrolls, and she could no longer hear any talking. She and Olem appeared to be unguarded, and that seemed odd to her. It took several moments of considering this to realize that they had no need of personal guards. He was beaten to within an inch of his life, and she was a mere secretary, and unconscious to boot.

She reached out and touched the Else. She could feel the sting of fire on her chafed wrists as her bonds melted away beneath her sorcery. A brief hint of burning hemp touched her nostrils and she was free.

Cautiously, slowly, she got to her feet. She checked Olem's pulse—he was still alive, thank Adom—and then she began to walk quickly through the camp. No one paid her any mind. No one was awake to do so, and if they were, the still-thick fog obscured their vision. A few minutes later and she was past the last campfire.

She literally tripped over the first sentry. He lay in a thicket, musket on his chest, gently dozing until her foot hit him. He shot awake, a startled exclamation on his lips. She could see the outline of his face in the darkness. She saw his eyes take in her blue uniform and then his mouth open to yell a warning.

Her hand shot forward, taking him by the throat.

She would not allow Olem to die for her safety. She would not allow herself to be beaten and humiliated and used by foreign savages.

Blue fire shimmered and she felt his flesh give way beneath her fingers. She squeezed, feeling the melted flesh and warm, sizzling blood between her fingers. Her fingers wrapped around his spine and even that seemed to slide away, leaving the man's head to roll down a hill and farther into the thicket.

Nila was up and running a moment later. She didn't have time to think about the murder. It was just one more on top of the count-less she'd committed over the past few weeks. She had to flee. The Kez magebreaker might have sensed her sorcery—he could be on her trail in minutes.

She navigated the hills with the use of her third eye, fighting down nausea. Between the darkness and the fog, her regular vision would be useless. She ran, forcing herself forward though each step made her want to scream in agony. Her thighs hurt from riding, her body from a night with her arms tied. Tears rolled down her cheeks from the pain, and her stomach pitched like she had been at sea for weeks.

Hours passed. She stopped on every hilltop to listen for pursuit, but no sound followed her. She ran blindly—she would be hopeless at getting her bearings in the misty darkness. She knew that, for now, she had to get as far away from the Kez as possible. Though every hilltop looked the same to her in the Else, she attempted to memorize each one, tearing up grass or piling rocks whenever she could. She hoped that in the light of day she would be able to lead the Adran cavalry back the way she'd come.

It was Olem's only chance.

The earliest light of morning tinged the mist. Nila could no lon-ger open her third eye. Exhaustion flooded her senses and it was all she could do to keep stumbling through the dew-soaked grass. Her uniform was ripped and sodden, her boots full of water. She clutched her arms to her chest, shivering violently.

She stopped to rest at the bottom of one of the countless ravines she had traversed. Her fingers stiff, she used what was left of her strength to coax a nimbus of flame from the Else. Kez pursuers be damned, she *had* to get warm! The flame sheathed her hands, then her arms, and she felt a dull warmth work its way into her bones. Her shivering slowly subsided. Steam rose from her clothes, and with a startled curse she realized that the flame now covered her whole body.

It winked out, leaving her standing at the bottom of the ravine, the world once again cold and wet. She wanted nothing more than to lie down in the muck and sleep. The Kez be damned. Field Marshal Tamas be damned.

A vision of Olem's face, his beard matted with blood and his flesh torn to ribbons, sprang into her mind. That was all it took for her to begin to climb the side of the ravine.

The rising sun began to burn away the mist. If the fog cleared, she could get her bearings. She would head east in the hope that the rest of the Riflejacks were looking for the Kez camp to save Olem. It was risky, if the Kez were, in turn, looking for her. But she had no choice.

It was not long after her rest that she caught a distant sound on the wind. The neigh of a horse, perhaps? The peaks and valleys of Brude's Hideaway played tricks on her ears, and she struggled on to the next rise, where she stopped to listen, peering into the thinning morning fog.

She thought she heard a shout. Whether Kez or Adran, she did not know. It was impossible to get a bearing on the sound. *Please*, she thought, *please be Adran*. She strained, head tilted to the side, until she heard it again.

The sound came from behind her. She began to move again, heading cautiously onward. An Adran scouting party could have gotten behind her. After all, she didn't know north from south right now. She could be heading just about any direction.

Another shout. Nila's senses pricked at the sound and a chill went down her spine. It hadn't been quite intelligible, but that sounded Kez.

The clop of hooves on stone reached her ears. She had crossed a series of flat rocks a while back, hadn't she? Those hooves were following her, and the shouts were getting closer.

She broke into a sprint, calling up every ounce of her energy for the run. They were on her trail now and when they found her, they would run her down like a tired dog in the street. A glance over her shoulder showed men on horseback less than two hundred yards behind her.

Leaping across a streambed, Nila scaled a steep escarpment and threw herself down the other side, tumbling head over heels down a hill. She was back up a moment later, ready to run, when the sight of a mounted figure brought her up short.

The figure was less than ten paces away. It sat silently, the fog barely seeming to touch it, the rider's body cloaked against the weather. Steam rose from the horse's nostrils, indicating it had just made a hard ride.

She was cut off. The Kez had her now. Nila stiffened and waited for the figure to draw his or her pistol and fire.

"Why do you run?"

The voice startled her and she nearly fell. It was speaking in Adran. A male voice. "What?"

The figure slapped his saddle horn angrily. "Why do you run?" he demanded.

Horses rounded the far side of the escarpment thirty paces to Nila's left. There were a dozen of them, coming hard, and she saw carbines raised to fire.

"Bo?" she asked, breathless.

"You aren't a fox, fleeing before the hounds! You are a goddess of fire to these ants."

What was Bo doing here? How had he found her? "The mage-breaker is chasing…" Nila ran toward him. The two of them might have a chance of escaping on his horse.

"He's not with them. You should have stopped to check. Turn and defend yourself. Show them what you are!" Bo's voice rose to a bellow at the end. Nila stared at him, astonishment freezing her in her tracks.

The crack of a carbine snapped through her thoughts and she found herself whirling in response. She made a flinging motion with her off-hand and fire like liquid gold spewed from her fingertips. The flames crossed the space in the blink of an eye and cut through men and horses like a bullet through paper. Black powder exploded on contact with the flames, and a single cry of dismay reached her ears before the entire party was gone, reduced to a black, smoking skid on hissing soil.

Nila stared at the spot for several moments, trying to process what she'd just done. There had been no thought, no concentration. She'd just killed a dozen men and horses purely by instinct. The air hung heavy with acrid black smoke and the smell of burned meat.

"Well done."

"I..." She turned to look up at Bo and could instantly see that something was wrong. He slumped in his saddle, his face pale and sweat on his brow. He swayed back and forth, knuckles white on the saddle horn. "Never run from a fight you can win. By the saints, you're going to be powerful. I've never seen such...beauty." His words were labored and breathless.

"What are you doing here? Are you all right?" Nila rushed to his side and put a hand on his leg, from which she immediately recoiled. She had touched something hard and thin, and when she reached forward to lift his pant leg, she found not flesh, but a wooden prosthetic where his calf had once been.

He didn't seem to notice. "I got your...note." He fumbled at his jacket pocket and removed a creased paper. It fluttered from his fingers and he made a weak attempt at catching it.

Nila snatched it out of the air, barely remembering the angry words she'd scribbled down before riding off with Olem. All thoughts of the charred remains behind her were gone. Memories of the way she'd been treated by the Deliv Privileged were shoved aside. "Bo. What's wrong?"

"Nothing, nothing." He frowned at the paper now in her hand. "I've...I didn't think...it proper...my apprentice off on her... own." His words were halting and disjointed.

"Bo?"

He waved away her concern, and promptly slid from his saddle. She threw herself beneath him and they both went down in a heap beside the horse. She looked up in horror at the prosthetic still stuck in the stirrup, and the empty pant leg beneath his knee.

"Sorry," he said. "Feeling a bit fuzzy."

Nila felt tears in her eyes. Bo was her only hope of getting away, and here he was, crippled and sickly. How would they be able to find the Adran cavalry and return to rescue Olem? She briefly considered leaving him here and taking his horse, but that could very well be the death of him, and she couldn't do that. Not after he'd brought himself out here to find her.

Bo's eyes were closed and she could see his chest rising and falling slowly. It hurt her deeply to see him like this, so vulnerable after everything he had done for her. She fought back her tears, angry at herself. This was the kind of weakness he despised, wasn't it?

"That's enough of that," Bo whispered. His eyes remained closed. "You're safe now."

"You're not, you bloody idiot!"

"Oh, I'll be...fine."

Nila held him close and knew she had to act soon. She could only save one of them—Bo or Olem. And Olem might already be dead.

"Where are the Adran cavalry?" she asked.

"I got a bit ahead of them," Bo said, seemingly able to keep his sentences coherent only when he whispered. "I rode hard when I saw your sorcery in the Else."

"Ahead of them?"

"They'll be along...ah. There they are."

Nila raised her head. The creaking of saddles and the jostling of weaponry suddenly reached her, and from the depth of the fog emerged hundreds of cuirassiers, their breastplates beaded with morning dew, carbines resting across their saddles.

Bo gave a groan and rolled out of her arms. He snatched the prosthetic from the stirrup and rolled up his pant leg. She caught sight of a leather harness attached to the healed, but ruined remnants of his knee. He strapped the prosthetic to the harness. Nila got to her feet, drying her cheeks, and helped Bo up and, at his insistence, back in the saddle.

A cuirassier rode forward holding the reins to Nila's horse. "Privileged Nila," he said, his voice booming in the quiet of the morning. "Thank Adom we found you."

"Indeed," was the only reply she could manage. Her knees felt like jelly beneath her, but she knew that this morning wasn't over. She took the reins, never having thought she'd be so relieved to see a horse. Raising her voice, she said, "They have Colonel Olem. He couldn't escape with me because they had flogged him half to death."

An angry mutter spread through the cuirassiers. "Can you lead us to their camp?" one of them asked.

Nila closed her eyes, trying to picture every rise and valley she'd crossed in her desperate flight. It was a jumbled haze in her memory, but she knew the Kez cavalry that had chased her would leave a trail more easily followed.

"Yes. Let's go."

CHAPTER
39

I never thought I'd see the day when I assaulted one of my own cities."

Tamas stared at the walls of Budwiel. The city sat in the narrowest spot in Surkov's Alley, flanked on either side by the immense, sheer cliffs called the Gates of Wasal. There was no way into the city but over those formidable granite walls, each stone protected by sorcery as old as the city itself. If not for what he now knew to be Hilanska's treachery, the same walls on the south side of the city would have withstood months of bombardment by the Kez army.

And now Tamas had to take the city in a single day.

General Arbor eyed the city, leaning on his heavy cavalry saber the way a gentleman might lean on a cane. The ancient general looked older than ever, but there was an excited fire in his eyes. He flexed his jaw, popping his false teeth out into one hand. "Aye. It'll be a pit of a fight."

"Ipille has lined the walls with his personal guard," Tamas said. "They'll fight tooth and nail for their king. Once we breach the city walls, every street will be a bloodbath."

"I can give you some good news on that," Arbor said. "I've dug up Ket and Hilanska's spy reports, and if they're to be believed, the Kez have left few enough of our people inside unmolested. Most were slaughtered in the initial attack and the rest have been sold as slaves."

"That's the worst good news I've ever heard." Tamas wanted to spit, but he knew it wouldn't remove the bad taste in his mouth.

Arbor gave him a toothless grin. "Just trying to say that there's no harm in shelling the city! You have to look at the bright side of these things, sir."

"You're not making me feel any better."

Doubt assaulted Tamas on all sides. Where was Taniel? There hadn't been word or sign of him yet. If he had succeeded in his task of rescuing Ka-poel, Tamas would have heard by now. He didn't want to think of the alternatives.

Around Tamas, his camp swirled with motion. Artillery that they had sent south on the Addown River was being moved into position as earthen fortifications went up. Ladders and hooks, spare ammunition, and fresh rifles were all being unloaded from the barges. Tents had been pitched, and his tired men were taking shifts to get a couple hours' rest before the attack.

Last night they had taken Midway Keep, making enough noise to draw Ipille's personal guard out of Budwiel and into a half-dozen skirmishes throughout the earliest hours of the morning. The guard had slowed him down by a couple of hours before they retreated into the city, and now their silver conical helmets lined the tops of the walls three men deep.

A puff of smoke rose over the walls and a moment later Tamas heard the report of cannon fire. The ball slammed into the earth several hundred yards in front of Tamas's foremost artillery pieces.

Arbor gave a mirthless chuckle. "Those walls aren't designed to hold heavy cannon. They won't be able to shoot back at us with anything bigger than short-range six-pounders."

"I'm more worried about the grapeshot when we assault the walls," Tamas replied. "More's the pity that we don't have time to wait them out. We're going to have to charge straight into their teeth."

"Really?" Arbor held his false teeth at arm's length and picked something out from between them. "I'm all for a good charge, but we won't hope to put a scratch in that wall today, not if we had fifty more cannon than we do. And, uh, no offense meant, sir, but sending twenty thousand men over those walls will be just about the stupidest thing I've ever seen you do."

"I'm a desperate man, Arbor." He glanced over his shoulder, craning his head to look back up Surkov's Alley. He wondered if the main Kez army had grown wise to his plan and were coming up fast behind him. Sulem was to have joined them in battle yesterday afternoon to keep them from marching back down to pinion Tamas against the walls of Budwiel. If the Kez had escaped the Deliv, this would end in disaster. "Come with me."

Arbor followed him from their vantage point down toward the largest artillery battery, Andriya shadowing them the whole way. Tamas's newest bodyguard was coated in dry blood and smelled like a slaughterhouse. Anyone else but one of his powder mages, and Tamas would have had the man forcibly washed. This afternoon, though, he needed Andriya's gun and blade.

"Colonel Silvia," Tamas called, catching the attention of one of the artillery crews. Silvia was a middle-aged woman with brown, short-cropped hair and a mouselike face stained with black powder. The cuffs of her uniform were almost black with the stuff as well. Tamas had to go all the way down to a captain to find an experienced artilleryman that hadn't been a friend or student of General Hilanska, and Silvia had in a single day found herself a colonel in command of Tamas's bombardment.

"Sir!" She stood, snapping a salute.

"You almost ready?"

"Getting there, sir. A few more mortars to move into position and then we'll start the bombardment on your order. We'll sweep the walls and just behind them with the mortars and focus direct fire on the main gate."

"Cancel that. You have a spyglass?"

"Yes sir." She produced a spyglass from her kit and snapped it open, then waited for Tamas's instruction.

"Go about three hundred yards to the east of the main gate. Do you see a pattern of discolored stones? They look almost like a face. It's very faint."

"I don't...wait, I see it. Adom, looks like a grinning skull."

"Fire a pattern of straight shot right at the nose. Hit, wait seven counts, hit, wait two counts, hit, and wait another four. It might take you a few tries."

Silvia had lowered her spyglass to look curiously at Tamas. "Sir?"

"What is that?" General Arbor asked. "Some kind of combination?"

"In a manner of speaking. The royal cabal that wove the wards into that wall so many hundreds of years ago left a backup plan in case Budwiel ever fell to the Kez and we were forced to take it back. Do this, and that section of the wall will be vulnerable to our cannon fire."

"And how the bloody pit do you know that?" Arbor asked.

Tamas snorted. "I was the Iron King's favorite, Arbor. It came with some perks." *And if this doesn't work,* he reminded himself silently, *I'll look like a complete idiot.*

"When do you want me to start, sir?" Silvia asked.

"Begin your shelling of the main gate as soon as you're ready. Have a grouping of cannons standing by to wait for my signal to fire at that particular spot. We won't be ready to attack for at least an hour."

Tamas strode back to his command tent, Arbor at his side. "Sir, what happens if Ipille has already fled toward his capital?" Arbor asked.

"Then we'll hunt him down like a bloody dog," Tamas said with a confidence he didn't feel. Ipille might have left two days ago. He could be so far ahead as to make it impossible to catch him. It was a risk Tamas was willing to take.

"Keep everyone working," Tamas said as he reached his tent. "And keep formations loose. I don't want the Kez to suspect that we'll assault today until the very last minute." He slapped Arbor on the shoulder, and the general saluted him, false teeth still in one hand.

Tamas ducked inside and let himself sag against the main tent post, squeezing his eyes shut. His nerves were raw, his body strung out from too much powder and too little sleep, and the effort of hiding his exhaustion from the men. "One more day, Tamas," he muttered to himself. "It'll either all be over tonight or you'll be dead at the foot of Budwiel's walls."

"That's why most commanders don't lead the charge themselves."

Tamas drew his sword and whirled toward the voice. Gavril sat on Tamas's cot, his whole body caked with road dust, the sleeve of one arm sliced through and stiff with dried blood.

"Bloody pit," Tamas said, sheathing his sword. "That's about the closest I've ever come to a heart attack. What the pit are you doing here? Where's Taniel? Get out of my bed."

Gavril threw up both hands but made no motion to stand. "I'm resting. I just rode all the way down the Counter's Road, dodging Kez patrols. Reached the Deliv camp a few hours after you left and commandeered a canoe and paddled the whole way here on the Addown."

Tamas paced his tent. He had planned to plug his ears with wax and catch a few hours of sleep before the attack, while his artillery scattered Ipille's men from the walls. No chance of that now. "And Taniel? The girl? Where are they? Spit it out, man!"

"Taniel's alive, Vlora too and Norrine. We lost everyone else in an ambush."

"And the savage?"

"No sign of Ka-poel. When I left, we still hadn't caught up to the Privileged."

"Then what are you doing here?" Had Taniel followed the Kez Privileged down here and slipped inside Budwiel? Had he been captured by Kez patrols? Tamas found himself growing more nervous every moment Gavril didn't speak.

"You should probably sit down," Gavril said.

"I'll sit when I damn well feel like sitting!"

"The Kez didn't break the parley. It was the Brudanians in disguise."

Tamas stumbled to his chair and fell into it. "No," he said, the word coming out as a gasp.

"Afraid so. Captured a couple grenadiers in the fight. Imagine our surprise when not one of them speaks a word of Kez. What's more, they weren't heading south. They were heading north, going far out and around to avoid any of our people between the army and Adopest. Vlora and Taniel are on their trail now, but we suspect they're going to meet up with the rest of the Brudanians in Adro. Are you all right?"

Tamas stared at his brother-in-law for several moments, his mouth hanging open. How could this have happened? He had been played like a fool. The Kez hadn't broken the parley. *He had.* Blinded so thoroughly by his own righteous anger, he had ignored Ipille's pleas for another meeting and dismissed the Kez messengers.

He was too old for this. Too proud, too angry. He had made mistakes in his time—even the best officer did—but the magnitude of this...

"You couldn't have known," Gavril said quietly.

"No." Tamas let out a mirthless laugh. "I've become what I most despise. Am I nothing more than a warmonger, Gavril? Another dictator with an army and a grudge? You know, that's what the old tales say that the Nine was like back before Kresimir came. They were just a collection of squabbling warlords."

"It's not like that."

Tamas went on. "I see a vision of the future, revolutions spreading out across the lands as people pull down their monarchs. The strongest men, unordained by saints or gods, rise to the top and carve out their own petty empires. Men and women die by the millions and all the progress that our world has made in the last thousand years is lost in the dust of time. All because of me."

Tamas held his fingers in front of his face, watching them tremble.

"I think you give yourself too much credit."

The vision floating before Tamas's eyes slowly faded and he felt older than time itself. Every muscle ached, every bone remembered its old breaks and bruises.

The thump of artillery brought Tamas back to the present. "Are you wounded?"

Gavril glanced at his blood-soaked sleeve. "Just a scratch. I gave myself stitches while I rode."

"You should have them redone. Probably looks like they were made by a blind monkey."

"Poked myself a few times, but they're straight and the wound is clean. You forget I've spent far more time in the saddle than you."

"Mostly running from jealous husbands."

"Some of them were very dangerous. Oh, I forgot to tell you. The Deliv have engaged the main Kez force, but I passed a column in the middle of the night."

"Kez?"

"Yes. Coming for you. Didn't look like more than a few thousand—they're far more worried about the Deliv infantry—but it'll be enough to put you in a damned tight spot."

"How far?"

"A couple hours."

"You should have probably mentioned this earlier."

Gavril yawned. "It was a long night."

"You hear any news about Olem?"

"No," Gavril said. "Should I have?"

"He's chasing Kez cavalry that got behind us up north. Never mind that. Andriya!" Tamas shouted.

The powder mage put his head in the tent. "Sir?"

"Tell Arbor we have company coming up behind us. He has forty-five minutes until we assault the walls, and we'll only have time for one attack."

"Yes sir!" Andriya left to find Arbor, looking as giddy as a schoolboy.

"There's something wrong with that boy's head," Gavril said.

"You know, he's one of the ones Erika saved. A year before she was..."

"That doesn't explain the blood all over him."

"He revels in killing his former countrymen. Perhaps a little too much, but people like that have their uses. For instance, there are few soldiers I would want more clearing the way for me as we go through the breach or over that wall."

Gavril ran his fingers gingerly over his shoulder. "I don't think you should take part in the attack," he said.

"I always have."

"You're not a young man anymore."

"Don't I know it." Tamas shook his head. "Some men lead from the back. I prefer to do it from the front."

"It just takes one lucky musket ball. One thrust of a bayonet."

"That knowledge has never stopped me before."

"When will your luck run out?"

Tamas extended a hand. "Maybe today. Maybe never. Help me up. I have another king to kill."

"I thought you just meant to capture him." Gavril helped Tamas climb to his feet.

Tamas grimaced. "I will. Wishful thinking, I suppose. I'll be out in a minute."

Gavril went on ahead. Once he was alone, Tamas leaned over, hands on his knees, and took several deep breaths. He'd made a horrid mistake. Many of them over the course of this short war, now that he paused to look back. Too many. Misplaced trust. Bad timing. This final misstep with the Kez—it needed to be his last. When it was all over, he had to put down his pistol and walk away, or else everything he had fought for would be for naught and his vision would come true.

Straightening, Tamas adjusted his sword and checked his pocket to be sure he had enough powder charges, then marched out into the sun.

It was time.

CHAPTER 40

Adamat's questioning of the kitchen staff revealed two important things:

The first was that Ricard's security was not nearly as good as he claimed it was. The second was that a man named Denni of Rhodigas had left the blasting oil behind the silver over two weeks ago. He told one of the scullery maids that they were bottles of imported vodka specifically for Ricard's next birthday and gave her a fifty-krana note to keep quiet about the "surprise."

The poor girl had broken down weeping when Fell told her what, exactly, the bottles were. It was enough to convince Adamat that she wasn't in on the plot, though he still told Fell to have her watched for a few days.

Adamat knew Denni, but only by reputation. He was a jack-of-all-trades—a con man, muscle-for-hire, thief, and smuggler. He lacked both ambition and vision, and while he had helped Ricard set up the first union, he had not wanted the responsibility of actually running anything.

"He's really not a bad guy," Ricard repeated for the third time in as many hours.

Adamat leaned against the cold brick wall of the basement Underhill Society secret room, clutching his cane in one hand, the head already twisted so he could withdraw his sword swiftly. The candelabras were lit, a deck of cards laid on the table, and cold drinks set out. Everything was prepared as it should be for the society, in addition to hiding two of Ricard's enforcers in the basement niches and placing SouSmith innocuously near the front door of the hotel.

"He tried to kill you," Adamat replied.

Ricard sat behind the card table, fiddling with a corkscrew. "He might not have known."

"Oh?" Adamat rolled his eyes. "That you, the head of the union, would have been at a union function in your own headquarters when he threw a bomb into your office? Or maybe he threw the second bomb, the one that landed beside your wine collection, where you spend plenty of time."

"He might not have thrown the bombs at all," Ricard said. "He might have bought them for someone else."

Fell sat beside Ricard, chewing thoughtfully on a handful of cashews. "That's what we mean to find out."

Adamat felt for Ricard. He really did. The members of the Underhill Society had been his closest friends and allies for over twenty years and secrecy was part of the mystique of their business cabal. Betraying something like that was very difficult.

But it had to be done.

"He's late," Adamat said, checking his pocket watch.

"He's always late," Ricard responded.

"You've delayed the others?" The only way to get Denni to come in was to hold Ricard's regular weekly meeting. Everything had to seem completely normal. That required invitations to everyone else in the society.

"Yes," Fell said. "They'll all be at least a half hour late. Denni isn't usually more than ten minutes behind schedule."

"And you're sure he'll come?"

"I'm sure," Ricard said. "He doesn't get a lot of work these days. Lots of time on his hands."

"Unless he suspects something," Adamat muttered.

"He was here last week," Fell said.

Ricard asked, rubbing at his bald spot, "Is this really necessary? I could just talk to him."

"You're being naïve, Ricard," Adamat said.

Ricard picked beneath his fingernails with the corkscrew and gave an exasperated sigh. "All right, all right. Maybe I am. Get on with it, damn it. Look at me, bullied around by my own hirelings."

"If I was just another hireling, I would have turned down the job," Adamat said sharply. "I am here as your friend. Understand?" He opened his mouth to continue, his ire raised by Ricard's unwillingness to do what was necessary, but the sound of footsteps on the basement stairs caught his attention. It was a heavy tread and it came down the hallway without hesitation. He tightened his hand on his cane.

Denni of Rhodigas was a little shorter than Adamat but built like a strongbox with broad shoulders, thick arms, and very little body fat. He wore a brown tailored suit and held a top hat in one hand and a cane in the other. His curly black hair was cropped above his ears. His eyes went to Fell, sitting beside Ricard, and he frowned. Then he saw Adamat waiting over by the wall.

"Denni," Adamat said. "We have some questions for you."

Adamat threw himself out of the way as Denni leapt forward, swinging his cane like a truncheon. He raised his own cane, ready to deflect another attack, but it had only been a feint. Denni was already gone, sprinting back up the hallway.

"Now!" Adamat cried. He set upon Denni's heels, with Fell right behind him. By the dim light of the basement hall he caught a glimpse of a struggle. "Careful!" he said. "He might have—" There was a spark, and he was deafened by the sudden blast of a pistol going off in the confined space.

One of Ricard's enforcers collapsed. By the time Adamat reached the scuffle, the second enforcer was reeling beneath the butt of Denni's pistol. He stumbled backward and tripped, falling into the hotel's wine collection. The roar of a hundred glass bottles smashing to the floor at once seemed distant in Adamat's deafened ears.

Adamat swung his cane, but only managed to strike air, as Denni was already on his way up the stairs. Adamat was pushed aside by Fell, who he scrambled to follow.

Adamat rushed through the halls of the hotel, then the kitchen and the pantry, and then out a back door into the alley behind the building, barely catching glimpses of Fell's back as she chased Denni. He passed another of Ricard's enforcers lying in the alley behind the hotel, clutching at a fresh knife wound. Adamat was already breathing hard, his heart pounding, when he reached the main road.

The avenue was not crowded at this time of the evening, but there was enough traffic to worry Adamat that Denni might have the extra bottle of blasting oil on his person. He tried to search his memory as he ran, picturing Denni as he came into the Society room. Had there been a bulge in his jacket pocket? One at his belt as well? That explained the pistol, but the other one could be anything—his knife, another pistol, or the bottle of blasting oil.

He caught sight of Denni sprinting down the thoroughfare,

cane in hand, his hat dropped somewhere along the way. Fell was close behind him, but not gaining quickly enough.

Adamat cut across the street as Denni ducked into an alleyway, running parallel to Denni's escape route until he reached the next street. He rounded the corner a moment later, his lungs burning, and ran toward the next alleyway.

Denni appeared from that alley a moment later. He swung around, heading straight toward Adamat.

"Stop!" Adamat shouted. He drew his cane sword and planted himself in Denni's path.

Denni didn't even slow down. He raised his cane and swung with his powerful shoulders, forcing Adamat to parry the blow or risk being brained about the head. Adamat felt the cane sword wrenched from his fingers and saw it clatter off down the cobbles. Denni planted a shoulder in his chest, and Adamat felt like he'd been hit by a charging horse. He was flung to the ground with enough force to rattle his bones.

He rolled onto his hands and knees, spitting blood and cursing. He looked up, expecting to see Denni disappearing down the street.

But Denni had stopped and turned toward Adamat, just twenty paces away. Adamat's heart leapt into his throat as Denni pulled a stoppered glass vial from his pocket. He didn't have time to think as Denni flung the vial at him and turned to sprint away.

Adamat threw his arms up over his face. The whole world seemed to slow to a crawl, every regret and mistake flashing before his eyes as the blasting oil arched toward him. He'd seen the power of the stuff. There wouldn't be enough left of him to scrape off the cobbles, and he found himself grimly hoping that Denni had misjudged the distance and was still within the blast radius.

There was a flash of movement as Fell sped past him. She reached out one hand and snatched the blasting oil out of the air. She pivoted on one leg, spinning, and went to her knee, setting the blasting oil carefully on the cobbles before Adamat's eyes. A moment later she was off again, chasing after Denni.

Adamat's hands trembled, but he snatched up the blasting oil lest a passerby accidentally kick it. He wondered how the pit the stuff hadn't gone off during the scuffle and chase, and chastised himself for ever doubting Fell.

"I thought you said he wouldn't be armed!" Adamat said as Ricard rounded the corner behind him, huffing and puffing.

Ricard gasped out, "He wasn't supposed to be."

"He either got tipped off or he was planning on finishing the job tonight. Hold this." Adamat put the vial in Ricard's outstretched hand. "Don't drop it!" He grabbed his cane sword and set off in pursuit of Fell, hoping that Denni didn't have the other missing bottle on his person.

He sprinted down the road, listening for sounds of the chase over his own labored breathing. He caught sight of Fell as she raced across a side street. Adamat followed, then crossed another road and ran into a shoe shop. Shoes lay on the floor, shelves tipped over by Denni in his rush to get away. An old cordwainer crouched behind his workbench and let out a startled moan as Adamat tore through the front room, down the hall, and out into the alley.

He entered the dimly lit alleyway just in time to see Fell corner Denni at a dead end. Denni whirled toward her, his spent pistol held by the barrel. When he saw Adamat, he lunged at Fell, likely hoping to take her down before Adamat could help.

The first swing went wide. Fell leapt, catlike, to one side and jabbed Denni in the throat with one hand. The blow would have sent any other man to the ground, windpipe collapsed, but Denni seemed to shrug it off and swung his pistol again.

"We need him to talk!" Adamat shouted, his voice echoing down the alley.

Fell caught the falling pistol butt with one hand, dropping to one knee beneath the force of the blow. Her fist shot out once again, slamming Denni hard in the balls before she got to her feet and closed the gap between them, her hand clawlike on his throat. She ducked, slipping beneath one arm, and came up behind Denni, stiletto in her hand, pressed against his cheek just below the eye.

Denni froze.

The whole fight occurred in the time it took Adamat to reach them. He slowed to a walk, and his heart felt near to bursting. He had to put a hand against the alley wall to support himself.

When he'd finally recovered, he stood up and straightened his jacket, stepping up to Denni with his cane sword in hand. "You have a lot of explaining to do. Where is the last vial of blasting oil?" Adamat asked.

"I don't know. I don't have it."

"Who has it? Who hired you to bomb the union headquarters?"

Denni sniffed, putting up a tough façade.

"The easy way gets your ass thrown in a cell. The hard way, and she carves out one of your eyes, and then we break your kneecaps."

Denni choked, then inhaled slightly as Fell pressed the stiletto harder against his cheek. "It was Cheris!"

"Excuse me?" Adamat lowered the tip of his cane sword.

"Cheris, the head of the bankers' union! She sent me to buy the blasting oil. She had me hire men to throw those bombs into Ricard's office, and she told me to kill him tonight at the Society meeting."

"That was easy," Fell said. The tip of her knife didn't leave Denni's cheek.

"Bloody pit! Bring him with! Ricard," Adamat said as the union boss entered the alley from the cordwainer's back door. "Get the police. We have to move quickly."

CHAPTER
41

Nila felt exhausted. Her head drooped and she had to wrap the reins around her hands to keep them from slipping from stiff fingers as she rode. Every inch of her body throbbed from the pain of running and riding, and she wanted nothing more than to lie down in the grass, wet though it was with morning dew, and sleep.

But she knew that if she did that, Olem would die.

If he wasn't dead already.

Bo looked worse than she felt. He seemed to have gained a second wind, head up and eyes alert, but she could see the rings under his eyes and the grimace that he tried to hide as he was jostled in his saddle.

"Your leg," she said quietly as they rode just behind the vanguard of the Riflejack cavalry. The scouts were up ahead, following the trail her Kez pursuers had left.

Bo slouched in his saddle. "What about it?"

"They couldn't..."

"No, they couldn't. The flesh was too damaged at the knee. Healers can work miracles, but there's a limit to what they can do. If they *had* managed it, I'd be two inches shorter on the left side and unable to bend my leg."

Nila imagined Bo strutting down the street, jerking along like a marionette, trying to look casual. She swallowed an inappropriate laugh, covering her mouth, and tried to play it off as Bo glared at her. When he finally looked away, he said, "Yeah, that would have been kind of funny."

"I'm so sorry, Bo."

"Don't be. I'm lucky to have everything above the knee. Let's just get this over with so I can get out of this bloody saddle. Are we getting close?"

Nila looked around. "It all looks the same in the fog," she said, then pointed to a scuff in the dirt on a hilltop. "That's one of my marks."

"All right." Bo took a flask from his pocket and took a swig.

"Should you be drinking before a fight?"

"Better I drink now than pass out from the pain halfway through the battle."

They rode on in silence until word was passed quietly back that they were to halt. One of the scouts approached Nila and Bo, and tipped his hat. "We have them, Privileged. They're camped in a valley over the next hill."

"Carry on," Bo said.

"Do you want me to stay close?" Nila asked.

"Any other time I would say yes," Bo said with a tired but flirtatious smirk. "But not this time. The magebreaker might know about you by now. He might not. Regardless, he's gonna think there's only one Privileged with the cavalry. If we stay well apart, he might not be able to cover us both with his nullifying sorcery. Remember, air in front of you to stop bullets. Keep your fire to a short distance, lest you blast our own people. A fight like this requires deft execution, not brute force."

The cavalry split into two groups and created a horseshoe-shaped formation around the valley in which the Kez had camped. Nila could smell cook fires now, and she thought she heard muffled voices in the fog. Her wedge of cavalry formed up and she was assigned an escort of two heavily armed cuirassiers to keep her safe.

Nila tried to steady her breathing as she waited for the signal. She didn't have the training for this kind of fight. She didn't have the training for *any* kind of fight. All she knew how to do was unleash herself, and even then it only seemed to work half the time.

She didn't have time to panic any longer. A horn was blown and the cavalry leapt forward, charging the Kez camp. They swept down into the valley, swords at the ready, and thundered in among the tents and fire rings.

Nila resisted the urge to summon fire to surround her hands—not only would she burn through her reins but she would work best with the element of surprise here.

She heard the clash of swords and the fire of muskets and carbines, while her own wedge of the cavalry continued forward unopposed. One man beside her commented on the lack of resistance, but they surged on, spurred by the sounds of the clash up ahead.

She recognized this bit of the camp. She remembered sneaking through it last night on her flight out. Somewhere nearby was the poor sentry whose neck she had burned through.

She saw the body of an Adran soldier lying in the mud. "Olem!" she shouted, digging in with her heels. Her horse jumped forward, nearly throwing her. She drew close enough to realize that the body did not belong to Olem. But the man's head was near slashed from his shoulders, fresh blood pouring from his neck. She saw another body in a similar state, then another. The Kez were killing their prisoners.

A Kez soldier emerged from the fog standing above the kneeling figure of an Adran soldier. She recognized the scourged shoulders and the blood-caked beard of the kneeling man.

The Kez soldier's sword flashed.

Nila reacted out of panic and instinct, her fingers twitching, and her fire took the Kez soldier's head off as cleanly as a cannonball. The Kez's body fell, and slowly, tiredly, Olem raised his head.

Nila fought to gain control of her horse as her bodyguards clashed with several other Kez soldiers on foot. When she had calmed the animal, she slid from the saddle and threw herself to the ground beside Olem. He had fallen from his knees to his side. She cut his bonds, only for him to wrench the gag from his own mouth.

"Behind you, you fools!" he bellowed.

Entangled with the few Kez remaining on foot, the Adran cavalry struggled to turn back toward the sudden charge coming up behind them. The bulk of the Kez dragoons slammed into their flank with a thunderous concussion, cutting their way through Adran cuirassiers that had only moments ago held the upper hand.

Nila stretched out one hand, her flames consuming a horse and rider heading straight toward her. Startled by her own precision, she turned and repeated the gesture, searing through another Kez dragoon.

"A sword!" Olem yelled, though one of his arms hung uselessly at his side. He caught a weapon tossed by one of his cuirassiers and spun to deflect the swing of a Kez dragoon. The dragoon roared past and spun to charge forward again, intent on plowing Olem beneath the hooves of his mount, but one of Nila's bodyguards came at him from behind, slicing neatly through the base of his neck.

Nila helped Olem get back to his feet.

"Ignore me," he said. "Keep up the fire!"

She flung a ball of flame the size of an ox, consuming the closest Kez dragoon, and then felt a blackness touch the corner of her mind.

Fear seized her as the flames dancing on her fingertips went out. The magebreaker.

She could sense his influence grow around her, and when she reached for the Else once more, there was nothing to touch. Panic rose in her chest, threatening to overwhelm her. She could not fight with a sword or shoot a pistol. Her one strength was now gone.

She couldn't pinpoint the location of the magebreaker. Her preternatural senses failing her completely, she threw herself back toward her horse, hauling herself into the saddle, knowing that her options were now limited to fleeing.

There was a flash of lightning in the air behind her, and she turned in time to hear two large explosions somewhere in the fog. She had forgotten about Bo. If the magebreaker was here, if she could keep him distracted, maybe Bo would be able to end this single-handed.

A man screamed out of the fog astride the biggest, fastest horse she'd ever seen. He was clothed in black furs and brown leather, swinging an immense, curved sword. He galloped toward her, blade flashing through the throat of one of Nila's bodyguards, and then he was past.

Nila raised her hands, only to remember she had no sorcery to throw at him. "He's going for Bo!" she shouted. "After him!"

Not stopping to see if Olem's cuirassiers were following, she urged her mount toward where she'd seen the flashes of sorcery.

The Kez camp was now a field of bodies of the dead and the wounded, Kez and Adran alike. Horses galloped through the fog riderless, and unseated cuirassiers and dragoons stumbled about, locking in combat when they came across one another.

Nila felt completely vulnerable in the fog and suddenly realized again how helpless she was. Should she try to help Bo now? Or would she just get herself killed?

It was too late to wonder. She came out of the densest fog and upon a string of sorcery-made corpses. Horses and men alike lay dead, murdered by spikes of dripping ice.

She saw Bo, still astride his horse, reins in his teeth to leave both hands free, frost clinging to his sideburns. He twisted in his saddle toward a charging group of Kez dragoons, and wind slammed into the lot of them, sending horses and men tumbling and screaming, carried off into the swirling mist.

Something moved in the fog behind Bo. At first she thought it was a riderless horse, running terrified and confused. But the creature stalked forward with an implacable gait and the shadow became something more like a man. It was large and twisted, fury etched on its mangled face as it crept up behind him. She had only seen Wardens from a distance. Close up, it was all the more terrifying.

"Bo!" Nila shouted.

Bo swung around as the Warden leapt. His fingers twitched, and the creature was suddenly impaled upon icicles as long as spears. The Warden snapped the icicles off at its chest, blood and water dripping behind it as it loped forward, seemingly unaffected. Bo's fingers twitched again and the creature was thrown backward as easily as a leaf, screaming angrily into the gust of sorcery-fueled wind.

It managed to land on its feet, and Nila waited for Bo to finish the creature off as it resumed its charge toward him. But his attention was grabbed by the sudden arrival of more Kez dragoons. They raced toward him from the side, only for their horses to stumble against his sorcery. Bo swayed in the saddle, looking like he was ready to fall at any moment. He was too tired to continue this fight, and she could sense the dark presence of the magebreaker. Any second now Bo wouldn't be able to use his sorcery at all.

Nila snatched at a rock on the ground and flung it at the charging Warden. The rock skipped off its shoulder and it skidded to a halt, its massive misshapen head turning toward her. Her breath caught in her throat at the sight of its malevolent, beady eyes. The Warden bellowed and charged straight at her, head lowered like an angry bull.

Nila backed up, then turned to run. What could she do? The creature would tear her limb from limb. It would kill her and then it would kill Bo, and all she had fought for would be for nothing. The sound of its heavy footsteps pounded behind her and she spun to meet her death face-on.

Panic, anger, and desperation snatched at the Else through the ribbon of darkness that was the magebreaker's influence. Nila tugged at the Else, forcing the tiniest blast of fire into the world and shoving it like a spike through the Warden's eye.

The Warden stumbled and fell, a smoking black hole through its head.

Nila's breath was dashed from her as she was suddenly flung to the ground. She hit hard, rolling to absorb the impact but feeling her arm twist unnaturally beneath her. The magebreaker charged past her, sweeping toward Bo. Bo raised his hands, face twisted in anger, but his sorcery sputtered and failed and only his sudden jerk at the reins carried him out of the way of the magebreaker's heavy scimitar. The Gurlish rider disappeared into the fog.

Nila struggled to her feet, checking her arm, thankful that it was not broken, and ran toward Bo. "Quick," she said. "We have to go. We can't fight him."

Bo seemed to agree. He urged his horse toward her, reaching out one hand.

Out of the corner of her eye, Nila saw the magebreaker's charge.

The Gurlish Wolf was pounding straight for her on his charger, his scimitar swinging, and she could do nothing about it. She opened her mouth to scream.

Bo's horse hit the bigger Gurlish stallion on the shoulder. Both horses bucked and reared, throwing their riders and flailing and neighing in panic.

Nila ran toward Bo as he struggled to sit up. She could see his prosthetic still in the stirrup, and as he tried to roll onto his front, the magebreaker had already regained his footing and was sprinting toward Bo, sword at the ready.

Nila felt the tears in the corners of her eyes. She strained at the blackness that cut her off from her sorcery, reaching through the inky depths for the Else. She had pushed through it once and she had to do it again.

It was there. She could feel it, seemingly just beyond her reach. She clawed for the Else and it felt as if it were there at her fingertips.

The magebreaker's shirt burst into flames. He threw himself to the ground, rolling to put them out, his face a mixture of confusion and rage. Nila strode forward. The Else slipped from her fingers and she drew up, trying desperately to reach it. The magebreaker whirled on her now, sword held in both hands, and she scrambled to recover the Else.

She threw herself out of the way of the first swipe. Flames sputtered in front of her hands, singeing the magebreaker's arms. It put him off long enough for her to scramble away, but in only a moment he was after her again.

Out of the corner of her eye she could see Bo crawling toward her, helpless to stand without his leg, and his prosthetic still stuck in the stirrup.

The magebreaker swung, missing Nila's face by inches. In her haste to get away she fell to the ground, trying to grab once more at the Else. It would not come to her. The sudden blast of a pistol from just a dozen feet away made her jump.

The magebreaker tripped and slumped to the ground. He writhed for a few moments, blood pouring from his mouth and nose, and then did not stir.

Bo sat on the ground, good leg tangled in his empty pant leg, suit dirty and hair disheveled. "Pit, I hate gunpowder," he said, tossing the smoking pistol off to one side with a grunt. "Did you happen to see if that Warden was missing a ring finger?"

CHAPTER

42

This is suicide, you know."

Tamas gave his brother-in-law a sidelong glance. Gavril had cleaned up quickly, and now wore a cuirassier's coat with the stars of a lieutenant colonel at his lapels. He'd taken the promotion without so much as a "thank you," and Tamas suspected that as soon as this was all over, Gavril would disappear back to the Mountainwatch. "Your confidence is a little underwhelming."

"It's not that," Gavril said, fixing a heavy saber to his belt. "I just think you should have someone else lead the attack."

Adran mortars rained down on the city, and cannons hammered at the main gate. It seemed that for every member of Ipille's bodyguard that the mortars swept from the gate, two would cram themselves at the top, and Tamas wondered if Ipille had an infinite number of them.

"Are you worried about me?" Tamas said.

"More worried about me. I'm not as lithe as I once was."

"You don't have to come," Tamas said.

"If I let you die, Erika will come back and haunt me for the rest of my days. I'm convinced of it."

"I didn't know you were afraid of ghosts."

Gavril shrugged. "Looks like the gate is not an original," he said, gesturing toward the city.

The mighty blackwood doors that sealed the main gate of the city had splintered under the withering cannon fire, and Tamas could see through the wreckage that the portcullis had fared little better. The ancient sorcery that protected the wall had not, it seemed, been replaced when the doors had. He could hear the artillery commander calling for heavier, slower shot to finish the job. "As soon as that door is clear, we go," Tamas said.

All around him his men were coming to the line, grouping by company, spurred on by the snares of their drummer boys. Officers on horseback rode up and down those lines, yelling to their men, sabers waving above them.

"Breastplate!" Tamas said. A pair of boys ran to Tamas and fitted him with a cuirassier breastplate. Another brought his horse, and then his helmet, which Tamas took in place of his bicorne. "It's been a long time since I've stormed a city."

Gavril nodded, looking on sourly. "I can't remember the last time I saw you wearing armor. Mine doesn't fit anymore."

Tamas jabbed a finger into Gavril's stomach. "Lose some weight before the next campaign." Truth be told, Tamas's barely fit him. He wasn't about to let Gavril know.

"I'm not coming to the next campaign."

Pray to Adom that I'm not either, Tamas thought.

The boys finished their job and Tamas climbed onto his horse, then reached down for his ivory-handled pistols, which he thrust in his belt with a thought for Taniel. The boys handed him his sword and carbine. "General Arbor!"

General Arbor reined in beside Tamas, popping out his false teeth and stowing them in a saddlebag before snapping a salute. Arbor had ten years on Tamas and was no powder mage, yet seemed twice as sprightly. Tamas wondered how he did it. "Yes sir! The boys are ready, sir," he shouted above the cannon fire.

"Good." He glanced toward Budwiel's main gate. The door had been smashed nearly to pieces after the latest attack, and the portcullis was a mangled jumble of metal. Ipille's soldiers weren't even trying to mend the gate. "Two minutes!"

Gavril climbed into his saddle and glanced down at Andriya. The powder mage held his bayoneted rifle in one hand, the other hand grasping his belt casually. "Is he not riding?"

"Horses don't like me, and I don't like them." Andriya took a pinch of powder from his breast pocket and snorted it.

"You could bathe," Gavril suggested.

Andriya touched his blood-crusted uniform and laughed.

"He'll keep up," Tamas said.

"If you say so. You, boy, give me the flag!"

One of the groomsmen ran forward with the Adran flag, a crimson background with the teardrop of the Adsea sitting before the mountains. He handed it to Gavril.

"Where's Beon?" Tamas asked. "Andriya, do you know where Beon is?"

Andriya gestured vaguely to the space behind Tamas's command tent. Standing with a view of the battle, Ipille's favorite son stood between two guards, his hat shading his eyes, jaw tight as he gazed at Budwiel. Tamas rode over to him.

"Why am I here, Field Marshal?" Beon demanded. "What damned deed do you have planned?"

"What, you think I'm going to threaten you?"

Beon did not respond.

"Tell me truly," Tamas said, "if I put you in a noose and told your father to throw down his sword or I'd hang you, would he do it?"

"No."

"I thought not. You're here because your father's royal guard will not surrender unless ordered to by a member of the royal family."

"You think they would listen to me? You think I'd tell them to in the first place?" Beon demanded, chin raised.

"They'll listen to you if Ipille is dead."

Beon paled.

"Or," Tamas continued, "if he's fled. If I win the day—if I truly take Budwiel and further fighting will do the Kez no good—I want you to tell your men to stand down. Will you do that?"

Beon didn't answer.

Tamas tugged gently on his reins, edging his mount toward Beon. "This doesn't have to be any bloodier than it will be. A fight through the city, building to building, is not going to do anyone any good. If I fail, you'll likely be rescued and you can dance on my corpse."

"I'd rather not. I have more respect for you than that."

"I believe you."

"Very well, Field Marshal. If you clearly win the day, I will order them to stand down—though I can't guarantee they'll listen. But how long do you have? How long until the Grand Army comes up behind you? It will take you more than one assault to capture those walls."

"It better not," Tamas muttered, nodding to the guard to take Beon away. He held his sword over his head and pointed it at General Arbor. The general dismounted, true to his preference, as a boy took his horse away. Arbor ran ahead of his infantry, shaking his sword and bellowing to his men. They shouted back, bayonets thrusting in the air once, twice, three times.

The snares rolled out a beat and the ground shook beneath the feet of the Adran army.

Seventeen thousand infantry began the march toward Budwiel's walls. Less than three minutes later they were within range of the few light cannon left to the Kez, and Tamas watched the first rifts open in his columns. Not a man among them wavered, and they continued on, bayonets glimmering in the sunlight.

"That's a beautiful sight," Gavril said.

"It is."

"Sir!" a voice yelled. It was Silvia, the artillery commander. "I need more time. That portcullis will slow you down."

"You don't have it," Tamas said. "Make me an opening! I want a gap in that wall opened when my men are two hundred yards from it."

Tamas expected her to argue, but she returned to her gun crews, a slew of curses and orders on her lips.

Tamas turned in the saddle. Behind him, three hundred cuirassiers stood ready in their stirrups. Breastplates were polished, helmets donned, and carbines loaded. Each of them was armed with a long lance to reach over the bayonets of the Kez infantry. Their horses wore breastplates and side skirts, the heaviest armor still used by the Adran army.

"Men of the Thirty-Seventh!" he shouted. "That gate is the mouth of the very pit itself. I'm riding through it. Are you with me?"

A roar answered him as their swords were drawn and thumped against their breastplates in a terrible clamor. Tamas grinned at them. "Forward!"

The cuirassiers sheathed their swords and grasped their lances, and at Tamas's signal they rushed forward. Tamas had left behind fewer than a thousand men in his camp; gun crews, grooms, support. Everything he had he now poured at the walls of Budwiel.

He prayed his men wouldn't break.

With a sea of lances at his back, Tamas rode through the advancing companies of blue-uniformed Adran infantry. He kept his eyes on the spot on the wall—the one he'd told Silvia about. His heart thumped with the beat of the snare drums as the first cannonball suddenly slammed into one of the off-color stones. He counted the time in his head until the second ball hit, and then his heart lurched with the strike of the third.

Nothing happened. "Bloody pit!" he yelled.

The Kez on the walls lowered their muskets and he could see one of their officers stand up on the fortifications and raise his sword.

On the ground beside Tamas, Andriya kept pace with the horses with little apparent effort, his eyes gleaming from a powder trance. He shouldered his rifle in one smooth motion, not stopping even for a moment, and pulled the trigger. Tamas looked toward the walls, trying to see Andriya's target—only to bark a laugh as the officer on the parapets plummeted to the ground.

A cloud of smoke rose from the wall a few moments later as the royal guard opened fire. Rows of Adran soldiers went down beneath the volley.

Tamas drew closer and closer. A second series of cannonballs hit the wall in the weak section, and still nothing happened. His men neared the base of the wall, the foremost companies much depleted, and he could see them preparing hooks and ladders for the assault. At the gate, the very last splinters of the blackwood doors had been knocked asunder and the portcullis had been reduced to jagged edges. The entrance yawned like a mouth full of broken, black teeth. Tamas focused his gaze on that. This battle was in motion, and for victory or ruin he could do nothing but ride forward with the tide.

Tamas threw his hands up as a sudden wind tore against him, snatching the breath from his lungs. He sheathed his sword and raised his carbine, looking for a Privileged upon the walls, but was startled to feel something push at him from the Else.

Was this some kind of trick? Another of Ipille's traps? Tamas opened his third eye and immediately felt the shock travel through his fingertips and into his very core.

The array of colors in the Else that indicated the ancient wards holding the wall together *writhed*. Like a carriage spring pulled into a straight line, they seemed to grow taut, and then with a snap that nearly blew him out of his saddle, the whole thing burst open.

He dropped his third eye, expecting to see the world in ruin, the wall a pile of rubble and his infantry scattered, but no one seemed affected by the blast, and the wall was still whole.

"Did you feel that?" he shouted to Gavril.

"Feel what? You almost fell off your horse."

Tamas picked out a few infantrymen whom he knew to be Knacked and noted that several had stumbled—one had even fallen. Whatever had just happened, it had affected only those with sorcerous power. He looked to his side to see Andriya still keeping pace on foot, but the powder mage was shaking his head like a confused animal.

Tamas's attention was brought back to the wall as the next round of straight shot pounded the ancient stone to dust. Green-and-tan-clad bodies tumbled from the heights, and chips of rock took down his soldiers on the front lines. Without the sorcery to protect it, the wall was but porcelain to the modern artillery. Silvia's cannon all seemed to open on that one spot, and within seconds there was a rubble-strewn path through the wall.

Adran infantry rushed the breach, and that was the last Tamas saw of his front lines as the gatehouse loomed before him.

"Set lances!" he bellowed.

Lances fell into place and a dozen cuirassiers streamed around him to take point. Beside him, Gavril drew his sword, and as one, the whole company thundered through the shattered gate and into the maw of Kez bayonets beyond.

Tamas's world became chaos. The sound of screaming horses mixed with the frightened yells of men, and the clash of steel on steel filled his ears. The first rank of Kez bayonets was down, but another moved forward to fill its place. The small courtyard beyond the gatehouse became a butcher's pit of bayonets and lances. He felt a bayonet slash at his breastplate and turned to shoot a Kez soldier in the face with his carbine. In one motion, Tamas holstered the carbine and drew his sword.

A hole appeared in the wall of bayonets. Tamas urged his horse through and then turned against the Kez formation from the side. One Kez soldier turned to face him, and another, and then another, and within moments the Kez ranks were in disarray.

Tamas pressed forward—there were hundreds more cavalry behind him and they wouldn't do any good in the courtyard. With the bayonet line broken he was able to push through in moments, and soon he was in the street.

The avenue behind the wall was jammed with Kez soldiers. They streamed up to reinforce the walls, shoved forward to fill the gaps, and dozens were already charging toward him. He reached out with his senses and detonated powder among the front rank, blowing them to pieces, letting his sorcery do the work.

There were too many, forced forward by the weight of their own comrades behind them. Even with his sorcery and cavalry, they wouldn't be able to make a big enough corridor for the infantry to follow.

"Sir," a cuirassier shouted, "our men are wavering!"

Tamas sheathed his sword. "Damn it! Gavril, give me the flag!"

Gavril paused to unlatch the flag from his saddle, his sword spattered with gore. He threw it overhand and Tamas caught it, leaping from his horse. "Andriya, make me a path!"

Andriya disemboweled a Kez infantryman and sprinted toward the nearest stairs up to the wall. His rifle was spent and probably useless, covered in blood, and he used the bayonet as a spear as he battled his way up the stairs.

Tamas followed in his path, kicking the dead and dying off the stairs in Andriya's wake. They entered the second floor of the gatehouse and fought their way through the soldiers within. A moment later they were out in the sun.

The scene took Tamas's breath away. His thousands were

churning forward, their bayonets bristling, and the tops of the walls swarmed with the green-on-tan coats of the Kez infantry. His men came over the wall in their hundreds, but he could see the ranks at the base of the wall wavering. His men would break if they weren't spurred on.

Tamas tore the Kez flag from its holder above the gates and flung it from the heights. It arched downward and toward the embattled armies like a spear. He watched it fall until a Kez grenadier, easily twice his size, charged at him with an indecipherable war cry. Tamas slammed the end of his flagpole into the grenadier's chin, toppling the Kez, before raising it high above his head and waving it. A shout resounded among the infantry on the ground and he saw them surge forward with renewed vigor.

"Take this!" Tamas said to an Adran infantryman as he climbed over the wall. "Don't let it drop while you still draw breath."

"Yes sir!"

Tamas leapt to the grenadier whom he had beaten down and grabbed the man by the hair, dragging him backward into the second floor of the gatehouse.

"Where's Ipille?" Tamas shouted in Kez.

The grenadier spit in his face and drew his boot knife. Empowered by his powder trance, Tamas lifted him bodily with one hand and snatched his wrist with the other, feeling the bones snap beneath his palm. He slammed the grenadier into the wall hard enough to bring dust down from the rafters.

"Where is your king?"

The grenadier screamed and swung a fist. Tamas caught it, twisting the grenadier and tossing him down the gatehouse stairs. He ducked back out into the sunlight to find the flag still waving and more of his men pouring over the wall.

It wouldn't be enough.

"Andriya, find out where Ipille is!" Tamas bounded back down the stairs and leapt into his saddle. "Lances!"

Most of the cuirassiers had fought their way past the courtyard and into the street. Tamas counted over a dozen empty saddles, but there were still plenty on their mounts. Tamas fought his way to them, his eye on the current of the fight. He watched the ebb and flow of the Kez infantry, an experienced eye pulling the pattern out of the chaos. He saw them advance, back off, then advance again.

"Formation!"

As the Kez infantry fell back, his cavalry regrouped, pulling tight into formation, lances at the ready. Gavril fell in beside Tamas. "We need to capture Ipille. We won't be able to take these walls."

"We will take these walls if I have to do it myself. Lances, wheel left!"

Only about a third of his cavalry still had their lances. They moved to the middle of the formation while the rest took the sides, fighting off the advancing infantry with their heavy sabers.

"Charge!"

The whole group surged forward, slamming into the disorganized crowd of infantry. Even without the lances, there was more to work with in the open avenue. Infantry went down beneath the armored breast of Tamas's horse and he leaned forward in the saddle, swinging his saber.

A bullet took the cuirassier to Tamas's right out of his saddle. Another fell with a strangled cry to the enemy bayonets. Their charge ground to a halt after just a hundred paces, but Tamas could see that it was enough.

The breach farther on down the wall seethed with blue uniforms. His own infantry fought their way in, heavy grenadiers at the front. Tamas's charge had grabbed the Kez's attention so that his men could take the opening, and like a dam that had formed a crack, the whole tide of the battle broke.

Tamas felt a knock against his breastplate and suddenly his world turned upside down. He threw himself away from his falling horse, rolled beneath the hooves of another, and struggled to his feet, numbness in one leg.

He raised his sword in time to fend off the stroke of a Kez officer. He parried twice and lunged forward for the kill, but his leg gave out beneath him and he tumbled forward, the officer's sword crashing against his helmet. He raised his sword to fend off another thrust, but a bayonet erupted from the officer's stomach and the body was thrust aside.

"On your feet, sir!" Andriya snatched Tamas under the arm and helped him up. "There's more to kill!"

Tamas took the opportunity to check himself. A deep gash ran along his left thigh—it would be a bad one—and his breastplate bore no fewer than five deep scratches that would otherwise have seen him killed.

"You move too slowly in that thing," Andriya said.

"That's just because I'm getting old. The king?"

"He's holding court in the Kresim Cathedral. As far as these men know, he's still there."

Tamas made his way through the fighting, shielded on one side by Andriya and by the avenue shops on the other. He limped to a high stoop and pulled himself up to survey the battle. It could still go either way—more Kez poured in from the side streets and they still held key sections of the wall. They would make Tamas's men pay in blood for every inch.

Several of Tamas's cuirassiers, led by Gavril, found him on the stoop. "Can you ride?" Gavril asked. Both he and his mount had taken a score of cuts, and his calf was soaked with blood, but he seemed ready to keep fighting.

"I can." Tamas extended his hand, and Gavril pulled him up into the saddle behind him. "Kresim Cathedral," Tamas shouted into Gavril's ear. "We have to end this now!"

"Up the main thoroughfare?"

"No, take that street there." Tamas pointed down the avenue to one of the side streets that seemed to have emptied of all its Kez reinforcements. He waved his sword. "Lances! To me!"

They had to fight through two half-built barricades as they made their way toward the center of the city, but it was clear that the barricades were not properly manned, merely someplace for the Kez infantry to fall back to. Tamas's cavalry numbered less than thirty now, and every man who fell would be one less he could use to storm Ipille's final stand.

They emerged from one of the side streets into the cathedral plaza. While the Budwiel cathedral was not nearly as large as its recently destroyed cousin in Adopest, it was still a breathtaking building. Four spires rose above the tallest buildings in the city, framing a bronze dome and magnificent, fortresslike walls.

The plaza was empty. Tamas called a halt, sensing a trap.

He slid down from his spot behind Gavril and put a whole powder charge into his mouth, letting it dissolve, paper and all, on his tongue. He drew a pistol from his belt, checked to see if it was still loaded, and gestured for his men to proceed cautiously.

Their hoofbeats echoed like snares on the plaza flagstone, and the fighting at the wall seemed muted and distant now. Tamas had expected the toughest resistance here, where Ipille would have centered his best and bravest men, but the cathedral seemed all but abandoned. Tamas swept it with his third eye and there were no final Privileged or Knacked lying in wait.

"Something's not right," Gavril said, his voice overly loud in the empty square.

Tamas checked his second pistol. His leg burned, even through his deep powder trance, and he was forced to limp. "They may have fled."

They approached the main doors. One of the pair of double doors was open a crack. Tamas peeked through. He could see nothing but the stone walls of the cathedral entrance hall. His men dismounted, securing their horses, and Tamas nodded to Andriya. "Five men," he said.

Andriya called out names. The soldiers took position around the door, then threw it open and leapt inside. Their feet echoed in the recesses of the building as they charged through the entrance hall and into the nave. Tamas held his breath, waiting for the crack of rifles and the shouts of fighting men, his muscles tensed to lead the rest of his men inside.

Silence.

"The bastard ran," Tamas said, shoving his pistol back into his belt.

"Sounds like it," Gavril agreed.

"Didn't even have the guts to tell his personal guard." Tamas kicked the wall and immediately regretted it. He swore under his breath and listened to the sound of his cuirassiers' footsteps as they cleared the room inside. "Let's go."

He limped into the entrance hall only to come within a pace of colliding with Andriya.

"Sir," Andriya said, his face pale. "You should see this."

Tamas exchanged a glance with Gavril. Anything that had Andriya worried couldn't be good.

He saw the first body as he came around the corner. One of Ipille's elite—green-on-tan uniform with gilded trim and a gray undercoat. The woman's sword was half-drawn, and she'd been shot in the heart from close range. The next two bodies were mere feet apart, two more of Ipille's elite locked in battle, knives buried in *each other.*

Tamas entered the nave, his eyes brushing past the immense columns that marched down the center of the room to hold the dome aloft, looking at the battlefield lain out before him. Well over a hundred of Ipille's elite lay dead or dying. He even caught sight of two dead Wardens. He opened his third eye, but there wasn't a hint of sorcery in the room.

"What the pit happened?" Gavril said.

Tamas pointed toward the front of the nave. "I bet he knows."

Using his sheathed sword as a cane, with one pistol in his other hand, Tamas limped his way toward the Diocel's chair at the front of the room. In the chair sat Ipille, his immense bulk overflowing the armrests. He was pinned in place by a small sword with a jeweled hilt, and the marble floor around the chair was slick with his blood. At the foot of the dais sat a haggard-looking man in his early forties, chin in hand, staring blankly at Tamas.

He wore the uniform of a Kez general, and his resemblance to the fat corpse in the chair was plain. After all, he was Ipille's oldest son.

The prince stood as Tamas drew near, and presented his sword hilt-first. Tamas came to a halt and gazed at the sword. He suddenly felt very tired. "Florian je Ipille. It appears you have committed a coup."

Florian seemed to flinch away from the corpse just over his shoulder. "I have done my duty as the crown prince. I have freed my people of a war they could not win. On behalf of the Kez nation, I surrender my sword to Field Marshal Tamas."

Tamas put away his pistol and took Florian's sword, holding it up to the light. "This is Ipille's sword."

"It is the king's sword. I am now king."

Tamas wondered what Kez law would say to that. Or Florian's younger brother, Beon. He wasn't familiar with the finer points of Kez succession, especially when it came to coups. This had all the ingredients of a Kez civil war all over it. But that wasn't Tamas's concern. "You ask for terms?"

"That the Kez people be treated fairly in a court of their sister nations. That Adro and Deliv immediately cease their attacks on the Kez army, both within and without our borders."

"I have two immediate conditions for your surrender, in addition to those that will come later."

"Name them."

"That you order your men to stand down."

"Lororlia!" Florian shouted. "Are you still alive?" A figure emerged from the recesses of the nave, a Kez woman with black hair and hawkish eyes, wearing the uniform of a Kez colonel. She walked with a pronounced limp and clutched at her arm.

"Yes, my lord?"

"Send word to our officers. Our men are to stand down at once."

Lororlia looked to Tamas and he thought he saw a spark of defiance there. "Yes, my lord." She limped off.

Tamas turned to Gavril. "Send one of our cuirassiers back to the front. Tell our men to accept the surrender of the Kez immediately and to withdraw outside the city walls—all except the infantry of the Seventh. They're to begin the disarmament of the Kez army." Tamas glanced at Florian and saw a smile at the corner of his lips. He suspected that there was more to this coup than a means to end the war. "And," he added in a lowered voice, "get Beon somewhere safe. Put him under heavy guard. I don't want him getting a knife in the back. Pit, you better go yourself."

Gavril strode from the room, taking several of the cuirassiers with him.

"What else?" Florian asked.

"Surrender the body of the god Kresimir."

Florian's eyebrows went up. "Bah. It's in the Diocel's chambers over there. Take it. He has brought us nothing but sorrow."

"Secure that body, Andriya," Tamas ordered. "Don't touch it."

"Is that all?"

Tamas straightened and held Florian's sword at arm's length. "Florian je Ipille, I accept your surrender on behalf of the Adran and Deliv alliance. May Adom smile upon the end of this bloody war."

CHAPTER

43

Taniel and Vlora each rode three horses to collapsing as they followed the Brudanian Privileged up the Counter's Road and east toward Adopest.

They ate up the miles, and Taniel knew they must be gaining on their quarry as they drew closer and closer to the city. His body shuddered from exhaustion, while his mind was a chaotic knot of fear, anger, and hope. There were not many miles left, and if Adopest was in the hands of the Brudanians as Vlora had said, they needed to catch up to Ka-poel and her captors before they entered the city.

They continued on, no words between them, until they rode over a hill and saw Adopest resting on the tip of the Adsea in the distance. Taniel's mind buzzed from a powder trance, his body sagging beneath days without sleep.

They had had to leave Gavril and Norrine behind. Gavril had gone south to try to warn Tamas about the Brudanian trickery, while Norrine had stayed with their couple of wounded to oversee the Brudanian prisoners. Taniel had not wanted to abandon her, but he knew that he and Vlora would travel the fastest alone.

"There," Vlora said.

Taniel shook his head to clear his vision and focused on a party just outside the city limits. There were nine riders, and even at a distance he could tell by the overcoat, hat, and small frame that one was Ka-poel. They left a dust cloud behind them as they hurried for the anonymous streets of the city, and Taniel's hopes of catching them before they reached the city walls were dashed.

He did not reply to Vlora, but leaned over the neck of his horse, urging it forward.

They reached the edge of High Talien on Adopest's west side less than an hour later. Taniel could feel panic rising in his chest as the midmorning crowds closed in around him, his horse foaming at the mouth, sides shuddering. The Brudanians were gone, and along with them the chances of getting Ka-poel back.

"Taniel." He heard Vlora's voice as if far in the distance. "Taniel, we won't find them now."

He whirled on her. "I will. I will find them, the bastards. If I have to kill every Brudanian I cross, I will get Ka-poel back."

"Well, you're going to have a good start of it."

Taniel's mouth opened but he could find no reply. People were staring at them and their near-dead horses. He followed Vlora's gaze off to his left. Brudanian soldiers flooded onto the street ahead of them, shouting and pointing.

"Leave the horses," Taniel said, sliding from his saddle. He untied his saddlebags and threw them over his shoulder, taking his pistols and rifle, while Vlora did the same.

They slipped down a nearby alleyway, abandoning their horses and moving over to the next street. Taniel could see the soldiers flanking them, moving to keep up and spreading out up ahead. He put one hand on his pistol, ready to draw.

"We shouldn't have a running fight here," Vlora warned. "Too many people."

"To the pit with the people. I'll take first blood if they come any closer." Taniel knew they had to get out of there. Vlora was right. A fight in the middle of the city would just attract more attention and draw in more soldiers. There'd be no backup. Adopest was now hostile territory. If the soldiers goaded them into a fight, they would no doubt bring in a Privileged sooner rather than later.

Taniel had fought a Privileged in Adopest before. It was less than pleasant.

"You recognize this part of town?" Vlora said.

"We're near Hrusch Avenue, aren't we?"

"It's our old haunt."

"I didn't spend a lot of time in the streets," Taniel said.

"I did," Vlora answered. "And under them. There's an old bathhouse up ahead. We might be able to slip into the storm drains."

They crossed two more streets, watching warily as the soldiers continued to flank them while keeping their distance.

"What are they waiting for?" Vlora asked.

Taniel had just been wondering the same thing. They had the numbers. Even if Vlora detonated all of their powder—and she wouldn't, not with all the people around—she might miss a few and they would close in with bayonets and swords, or worse— some of them might have air rifles.

The old bathhouse was a ruin of a three-story building at the end of the street. The doors and windows were boarded up, with signs telling the local children it was a dangerous place to play. Taniel spotted a Brudanian uniform up ahead of them.

"They've gotten in front of us," he growled.

"Not only that." Vlora's face had gone pale. She didn't have to finish her sentence. Taniel could sense the Privileged moving in on their position, one behind and one ahead of them. *That* was what the soldiers were waiting for. How the pit had they gotten two

Privileged here so quickly? Either he and Vlora had been insanely unlucky, or the Brudanian commander had counted on needing reinforcements when Ka-poel's kidnappers returned.

"Quickly!" he said.

They headed around to an alley running behind the bathhouse. Taniel thrust his bayonet beneath the board barring the back door and wrenched it away.

There was a crack of a musket and Taniel flinched away from where a bullet struck the wall beside him. He ripped off another board as Vlora squeezed off a shot, dropping the soldier at the head of the alley. Taniel slammed his shoulder against the locked door, bursting it in two heavy hits, and they rushed inside.

"The Privileged are getting close," Vlora said.

"I know! Where's the damned storm drain?"

"In the basement. Down the hall. Go, go!"

Taniel sprinted down the dark, damp hall of the bathhouse and past the shadowed, sludge-filled baths. A voice called out behind them in accented Adran.

"Adran soldiers, surrender now!"

Taniel slowed, pushing Vlora on ahead of him, and brought up his rifle. He waited in the darkness of a doorway for a soldier to put his head into the back door of the bathhouse.

His bullet took the man between the eyes. There was shouting, and Taniel felt the pressure of sorcery being pulled into this world. He sprinted after Vlora, following her down the steps and into the blackness of the basement. An extra snort of powder gave him clarity in the depths. He found Vlora in the farthest room from the stairs. She had pried the grate away from the storm drain and tossed her own saddlebags down the hole.

Taniel could hear footsteps pounding along the floor above them. "Why haven't the Privileged attacked yet?" he demanded.

"Quiet!" she said. "Go, now!" He sensed her reach out toward the soldiers' powder, detonating a few choice charges to sow confusion. The sound of the explosions echoed through the building.

Taniel climbed into the storm drain, his hands slipping on the rusted ladder bolted to the walls of the drain. He lowered himself down until his feet touched water and then let himself drop the last foot to the drain floor.

"Come on!" he called back up to Vlora.

Vlora stood above the storm drain, her head tilted as if listening for something. "Wait," she said quietly. "There's something..."

Her words were cut off by a sudden trembling. Taniel threw his hand above his head, his heart leaping into his throat as he heard the foundation of the building give a deafening crack. There was a strangled scream above him. He choked on dust, wiping water from his face.

"Quick!" he yelled.

His voice no longer echoed. Peering up through the gloom, he saw nothing but stone above him.

The building had collapsed on Vlora.

CHAPTER

44

Adamat accompanied Police Commissioner Hewi and six officers to arrest Lady Cheris.

Hers was a beautiful manor on the outskirts of the Routs in Adopest, not far from Ondraus the Reeve's home. It stood three stories tall and overlooked one of the largest private gardens in the city. Adamat waited in the foyer, allowing the cool autumn air to blow over him from the open door while a pair of constables spoke with the butler.

"This is most unusual," the butler said, raising his voice. "Lady Cheris is an upstanding member of society and will not be treated like a common criminal."

Commissioner Hewi cleared her throat, interrupting a response from one of her constables. "My good man, I am the commissioner of the Adran police force. My presence here clearly indicates that

Lady Cheris is a most uncommon criminal. Now, tell me where she is, or you'll spend the next six months in Sablethorn."

The butler looked as if he would protest further, but a glance at the stone-faced constables seemed to convince him otherwise. He appeared to deflate. "She's in the sitting room. But Commissioner, she has guests. Surely this could wait for another time."

Hewi moved the man to one side with her cane and strode past him. Adamat followed.

A constable opened the door to the sitting room and Hewi walked in as if she owned the home. Two men sat in armchairs by the windows, while the two sofas were occupied by four women, one of whom was Lady Cheris. Their conversation stopped mid-stride and they all looked in surprise at Commissioner Hewi, while Adamat stood in the corner with his hat in one hand.

This particular arrest was one that he had no interest in doing himself. Everything, including Ricard's own word, indicated that Lady Cheris would be as hard to pin down as an eel.

"Commissioner Hewi!" Lady Cheris said, standing. "I wasn't expecting you today. May I introduce Lord Elmore of the Novi National Bank? I believe you know everyone else in the room."

"Charmed, Lord Elmore. Lady Cheris. Would you like to do this here, or see your guests out first?"

Cheris's face clouded and she blinked rapidly. "Whatever could you mean?"

Adamat cleared his throat and glanced significantly at the con-stables guarding the door, though he knew Cheris was only playing the fool.

"Ah." Cheris swallowed hard. "Lord Elmore. My friends. Would you be willing to resume this conversation tomorrow?"

The gentlemen and ladies all stood and Lord Elmore shook Cheris's hand while casting dark glances at the commissioner. "Of course. Please let us know if there's anything we can do for you."

They filed out the door and Adamat listened to be sure they had left the house. Once they were gone, Lady Cheris dropped onto one of the sofas.

"What is this all about, Hewi?" she asked.

"That's 'Commissioner,' my lady. And please remain standing. You are under arrest for the attempted murder of Ricard Tumblar. We can dispense with the wrist irons, I think, as long as you'll come along willingly."

Cheris's nostrils flared. "Attempted murder? I nearly died in that bombing! What are you talking about?"

"We have strong reason to believe you masterminded the bombing of the headquarters of the Holy Warriors of Labor."

Stronger reason than even Hewi would let on, Adamat reflected. Denni of Rhodigas had confessed in front of Commissioner Hewi's Knacked—the one who could determine a liar upon hearing. Lady Cheris had personally hired him for the job.

"Me? My arm was broken by a falling beam!" Cheris waggled the elbow of the arm she still held in a sling. "You have a damned lot of gall to accuse me of such things."

Hewi sighed. "We have ample evidence, my lady."

"Evidence? What evidence? There's nothing at all to tie me to such a crime! I was about to have dinner with Ricard tonight. Do you think I'd dine with a man I tried to kill? You, sir. Inspector Adamat, wasn't it? You're friends with Ricard. Does he think I've done such a thing?"

Adamat glanced at Hewi, who gave him the most imperceptible of nods. "He does, madam. As do I."

Cheris stood up straight. "I demand that you tell me the evidence you claim you hold against me."

Adamat scoffed. Surely she didn't think they would?

"I can't do that, my lady," Hewi said.

"Can't? Or won't? Because you don't have a damned thing. If you did, you would tell me. I know what condition the courts are in. Even with my connections, it'll be two weeks before I can get in front of a magistrate. Until that time I'll be rotting in Sablethorn with the gutter rats, my reputation in shambles and my—"

"We have the word of Denni of Rhodigas that you paid him to acquire blasting oil from the Flerring Chemical Company," Hewi said, her lip curled in disgust, "And to arrange for the bombing of the headquarters of the Holy Warriors of Labor."

"That lying cretin? Hah! As if I'd have anything to do with him. I hope you have something better than that."

"Transfer of funds amounting to one hundred and twenty-thousand krana from your personal account to an account belonging to Denni of Rhodigas," Adamat cut in. "We've already arrested and questioned your personal banker."

Cheris's mouth hung open for a moment, then she said quietly, "Those accounts are not open to government purview, nor are they admissible in court."

"They are now," Adamat said. "The law was passed a month ago. For the head of the bankers' union, I'm surprised you weren't aware of that. Commissioner?"

Hewi oversaw the arrest as Cheris was led out the side door by one of his constables and put into an unmarked police carriage. Adamat waited beside the carriage for the commissioner to join him. "Thank you for coming, ma'am," he said to Hewi.

"No, thank you, Inspector. If I had a thousand more officers prowling the city right now, I'd still be short. My people couldn't possibly have tracked all of this down. You really are one of the best."

"That's good of you to say, ma'am. And that law I mentioned…"

"It should be on the books by now. Backdated, of course. Not something I'd normally do, but after running Denni past our lie-Knack we have to cover our evidence."

"Thank you, ma'am."

"You sure you want to ride with her?" Hewi asked.

"Yes. It's best I question her in private."

"Nothing official can come out of it."

"Of course. For my own personal peace of mind."

Adamat said farewell to the commissioner and climbed into the carriage, where Cheris sat looking out the opposite window. Her façade of a baffled, outraged businesswoman had dropped to leave behind someone who looked tired and vaguely annoyed. The carriage began to move and Adamat took several minutes to examine her before he spoke.

"Why?" Adamat asked.

Cheris glanced over as if noticing his presence in the carriage for the first time. "Because Ricard's an idiot," she said. "And you can tell him I said so. He's a visionary, for certain, and that does give him something extra. But he's a fool and he'll be a terrible First Minister."

"So you admit it?"

"Sounds like you already know the truth, so I might as well." She sighed. "My resources have been stretched thin, Inspector. Having to rely on people like Denni makes my stomach turn. And you better believe that my banker will never work anywhere in the Nine again in his life."

"You think you'll still have that kind of power after this comes out?"

"My involvement will be forgotten in a year. Denni will go to the guillotine and I'll pay a heavy fine and lose my position in the union, but I'll climb back on top."

"And make your enemies suffer, I suppose?"

"I'm not normally a murderer, Inspector. I don't kill or maim unless I'm running out of options. But yes, I'll make them suffer. I'll destroy reputations if it suits me. You should know that if you've been investigating me."

Adamat's investigation had been a whirlwind that lasted only half a dozen hours between the time he took Denni in and the time he arrived at Cheris's door. He grunted a reply.

"In fact," Cheris added, "I'm amazed you'd allow me the knowledge of your involvement."

"I've dealt with worse." Adamat felt a bit of doubt in the back of his mind and wondered if this had been a good idea. Perhaps the commissioner's warning had held some meaning Adamat had missed. Nothing indicated that Cheris was the kind of monster that Vetas had been, but perhaps he should have taken precautions.

A knowing smile appeared at the corner of Cheris's mouth. Adamat narrowed his eyes, wondering if Cheris knew about Lord Vetas. Perhaps she did. With her relationship with Ricard, it was not out of the realm of possibility.

They rode into Elections Square and watched the black spike of Sablethorn Prison grow larger over their heads. The prison was full of dissidents and particularly loud royalists, but the guards had made room in one of the nicer cells for Cheris. Ricard had insisted upon that, though Adamat didn't know the reason. Sentiment, perhaps?

Cheris was escorted from the carriage. Adamat stepped out, wondering if he would now need to extend the length of SouSmith's contract, and watched her be led toward Sablethorn's doors. Cheris turned suddenly and looked back, throwing him a menacing smile.

"Have a good few weeks, Inspector. I'll see you soon."

The residence of Adro's former Arch-Diocel of the Kresimir Church, Charlemund, seemed bleak and bare.

Adamat remembered his first visit to the grounds. The vineyards had been full of workers, while horses practiced on the racetrack. It had been a sickening display of wealth, but Adamat almost preferred that pomposity to the overgrown hedges, deep grass, empty orchards, and cold, lifeless façade of the immense manor.

The only occupants of the manor were the dozen watchmen the city had assigned to keep looters and squatters at bay until the government got the chance to divide up Charlemund's wealth. His library would go to the university and Public Archives. His art collections would be sold off to private collectors or donated to the city museum. The building itself might be bought up by a wealthy merchant—Adamat had even heard Ricard express interest—or perhaps torn down and the stone recycled to help in the rebuilding of the city center.

"What you looking for?" SouSmith asked.

Adamat smoothed the front of his jacket. "I'm trying to find out what kind of man doesn't leave a shadow," he said.

Adamat showed his papers at a temporary guardhouse a few hundred yards from the manor and was waved on. At the front door, he remembered his second visit to the manor: during the battle in which Tamas fought and captured Charlemund. The burned-out remnants of a carriage still lay beside the gravel drive, and there were still muddy furrows where Privileged sorcery had dug up the ground.

At the front door another pair of watchmen lounged on the stoop, a game of dice between them. They stood as Adamat left his carriage and approached, with SouSmith behind him.

"They said that you would have a key," Adamat said.

"Right. We do," one of the watchmen said. She was a young woman, no more than twenty-five, and she held a musket and wore the light blues of the city police. "Papers?"

Adamat presented his papers once more. "Did I see smoke coming from one of the chimneys?"

"Probably," the second watchman said, rubbing a thumb under the rim of his hat. He was an older fellow with gray in his mustache.

"I didn't know the manor was occupied."

"The state employs a few of the former staff in order to keep the building tidy until they can get around to selling it," the first watchman replied, handing Adamat back his papers. "Don't worry about them, they stay out of sight. The library is in the south wing, all the way at the end. Head inside, past the first staircase, and take a left. That hall dead-ends in the library."

"Thank you very much," Adamat said. He waited for them to unlock the door and then slipped inside, followed by SouSmith.

The foyer still held evidence of the fight that had taken place there many months previous. Someone had tidied up the mess Adamat remembered, but there was no hiding the chips in the marble from bullets, nor the empty pillar where a bust of Charlemund had once stood.

SouSmith paused and gave a low whistle. "One man lived here?"

Adamat had forgotten that SouSmith had never been allowed inside on their previous visit together. "Kind of off-putting, isn't it?"

SouSmith ran his thick thumb over a chip in the marble banister. "Nah. Should have gone into the clergy."

They left the foyer and followed the watchman's directions toward the library.

"You said Charlemund escaped," SouSmith asked.

"That's what Ricard told me."

"Think he could be here?"

"What? In hiding?"

"Yeah."

"They've got watchmen and servants. He couldn't go unnoticed."

SouSmith stopped suddenly and looked up and down the hallway. It was over two hundred yards long, the ceilings twenty feet high, and had no less than thirty doors. He cocked an eyebrow at Adamat.

"Okay, it's big," Adamat conceded. "But Charlemund is... well...you've met him. He's used to command. To luxury. I don't think he could 'hide' anywhere if his life depended on it. My best guess is he's already fled to Kez or Novi or someplace farther. We'll hear about him sooner rather than later."

Their voices carried as they spoke, giving the place a strange echo and sending a chill up Adamat's spine, which he attributed to the autumn cold.

The hallway ended in a pair of closed double doors. Adamat jiggled one handle, finding it unlocked, and pulled. The room inside took his breath away.

Charlemund's library was a rectangular room several times larger than Adamat's house. Books lined every wall, sorted neatly on cherry bookshelves. There were wooden ladders on runners to reach the high shelves, and each corner had an iron spiral staircase to reach the second floor. There was a grand, marble-trimmed fireplace at either end of the room.

There weren't as many books here as there were in the Public Archives or the university library, but this collection was nearly as big as, if not bigger than, the late king's library. It baffled Adamat how one man could have acquired so many books. Charlemund had been far from a "man of learning."

"I don't have any bloody idea where to start."

SouSmith grunted and threw himself down into one of the leather wingback chairs by the cold fireplace closest to the door. "Wake me when you're done," he said.

"You're no help at all."

By the time Adamat had a grasp of Charlemund's indexing methods, SouSmith was already snoring loudly.

Uskan had sent him a list of a dozen books that might be of some interest. Adamat started with those, finding them and pulling them down, stacking them on a table in the middle of the library. When he had collected them all, he began to skim each book quickly, casting each page to memory in order to examine it more closely later, all while looking for words like "shadow" and "shade."

He finished with the first dozen books by one o'clock and returned, somewhat on edge, to the rest of the library.

Adamat's Knack allowed him to move through the library at what most would find a startling speed. To him, it was frustratingly slow. The library was sorted according to the name of the author, which was very little help. He was forced to look for titles that stood out as religious books, or for authors he recognized as scholars. He took down another stack of a dozen books and began to run through those.

He was on his third stack of books by four o'clock. SouSmith had awoken and fallen asleep again, and the lengthening shadows told Adamat he wouldn't have much more time to read by daylight.

"SouSmith," he said, shaking the boxer's shoulder.

SouSmith opened one eye. "Eh?"

"Do you have a match? I need to light the lanterns. Or a fire, or something."

"Nope." His eye closed.

Adamat sighed. SouSmith wasn't going to be a lot of help here. Adamat still had him working as a bodyguard for another week, but the real danger had passed, and SouSmith knew it. He also knew that Ricard was footing the bill. Adamat couldn't bring himself to blame SouSmith for slacking off.

"I'm going to find one of the servants," he announced.

SouSmith grunted.

Adamat remembered that the smoke had been coming from a chimney in the north wing. He envisioned the house in his mind's eye, remembering his brief inspection after the battle with Charlemund. The north wing had a ballroom, an observatory, the dining room, the kitchens, and the servants' quarters.

That was his best chance for a match. Maybe they'd even light the library fireplace for him.

He gathered his hat and cane and headed down the main hallway. He climbed the foyer stairs and continued down the main hall on the second floor, where he came to the servants' quarters. This part of the house was warmer, and he found himself looking forward to the heat of a fireplace. The autumn chill was more pronounced in this place than he'd expected.

He knocked on several of the servants' doors, but received no answer. Three of the doors were unlocked, and inside he found evidence of habitation, but there were no servants present.

Frustrated, he took the servants' stairs down toward the kitchens. Back on the first floor, he could hear the sound of voices. Finally!

He entered the kitchen from the back. It was an immense room, some thirty paces across, and he was startled to find it rather well stocked, despite the skeleton crew of servants. Herbs hung from the ceiling, there was canned meat on the shelves—dusted, no less—and sacks of grain unmolested by rodents. A figure at the opposite end of the room, wearing a white apron and a tall white hat, was singing to himself in front of the only lit oven.

"Excuse me," Adamat called.

The figure turned, giving Adamat a good look at his profile, and Adamat's feet suddenly felt like lead. He grabbed his cane in both hands and twisted it to draw his sword. His mouth was dry, and he pointed the tip of his sword at the fugitive Arch-Diocel, Charlemund.

"You," Adamat hissed.

Charlemund's eyebrows rose. His apron was covered in flour, and his hands full of bread dough. "Uh, yes?"

Adamat's mouth moved, but he wasn't exactly sure what he wanted to say. The Arch-Diocel was a national traitor and a villain, and he had wounded Adamat twice in their last encounter. But he didn't appear to be armed. If anything, he was more surprised to find Adamat here than Adamat was to find him.

"Put down the bread dough."

"All right."

"Wait! Never mind. Keep a hold of it. Keep your hands where I can see them."

"Fine." Slowly, Charlemund began to knead the dough between his fingers.

"Stop that."

"I'd rather not ruin this loaf," Charlemund said.

"I don't give a damn!" The words came out a shout. Sweat poured down the small of Adamat's back.

Charlemund squinted at him, but he didn't stop kneading the dough. "Have we met?"

"What kind of a question is that? We have met on several occasions." Adamat's heart hammered in his chest, but his annoyance was beginning to overcome his nervousness. This was Charlemund, was it not? He had put on perhaps two stone since their last meeting—an awfully large amount in just a few months—but otherwise it was the same man. Unless Charlemund had employed a relative in his kitchens?

And had he been singing to himself earlier?

Charlemund seemed to grow thoughtful, and his eyes focused on something over Adamat's shoulder. "Oh, that's right. We *have* met." He grimaced. "Not on the best of terms with this body, though. I really do apologize. Let me help you."

"Help me?"

"With your search. You're looking for a book. I think *The Compendium of Gods and Saints* should be the right thing. Mostly superstition and rubbish, but it answers your question. It's back in the library, northwest corner. About three feet from SouSmith's elbow, actually."

Adamat felt his sword arm waver. "How could you possibly know any of that?"

Charlemund grinned. "Just trying to be a good host. Can I offer you something?"

"Offer me what?"

"Something to eat. I made some squash soup last night. I may have leftovers."

Tamas stood atop the blasted ruins of the walls of Budwiel with the noonday sun in his face. His body ached and his leg throbbed, skin feeling tight against the stitches. A slash along his cheek itched and he had to remind himself not to rub at it, or the damned thing would never heal.

The Deliv army approached, a snake of Kelly-green uniforms winding down the highway and into the immense camp of Adran soldiers outside the walls. Tamas's men lined the highway in their parade uniforms as a sign of respect for their Deliv allies. Sulem and his cabal rode at the head of his army—Tamas could see their banners from this distance even without a powder trance—and he could hear the distant beat of their drums tapping out the march.

"Sir."

Tamas spared a glance for the young corporal who had come up to join him at the wall. "Yes?"

"Colonel Olem is here to see you."

"Send him up right away." He waited until the corporal was gone to sag against the fortifications and breathe a sigh of relief. Olem had survived. That was good. Too many quality men and women had died these last several weeks.

A few moments later he heard a halting step on the stone stairs behind him, and then Olem joined him at the ramparts. His face was black and blue, and he bore several visible wounds on his neck and hands. Olem stood slightly hunched, his shoulders curled inward, and Tamas could tell he was in a great deal of pain. He'd seen that stance many times in his long career. It was the look of a man who had been flogged severely. Tamas didn't even want to know what Olem's back looked like under the uniform.

There were several minutes of silence, and then Tamas heard a small sound like clattering coins. He looked down to see Olem's colonel pins lying on the stones.

"Did you fail your mission?" Tamas asked.

"It didn't go well, sir."

"Did you fail?"

"The magebreaker is dead. His men are killed or captured."

Tamas took the colonel's pins and set them in front of Olem. "If you try to give these back again, I'll shove them up your ass."

"But…"

"That was your only warning."

Silently, Olem returned the pins to his lapels. Tamas glanced out of the corner of his eye to see Olem struggling with the pins, one of his arms in a sling. His face was one large bruise, and his brows and lips between them had dozens of stitches. The bottom of one earlobe was gone.

"You look like the pit," Tamas said without reproach.

Olem finished putting his pins back on one-handed and managed a wan smile. "You don't look so well yourself, sir."

"I've had better days." Tamas's memories of the battle were a blur of blood and steel and he could not recall where he'd gotten half of his wounds, but he *could* remember the faces of hundreds of his men whom he watched die. He wouldn't sleep well for some time.

"My report's going to be a bit late, sir. I can't write left-handed."

"Don't worry too much."

"I can give it to you now if you'd like."

"Later. Wait. How did the Privileged girl do?"

"Very well." Olem hesitated. "I don't know much about sorcery, sir, but Privileged Borbador said she's going to be the strongest Adran Privileged in six hundred years."

"Bo has been known to exaggerate."

"She set fire to a magebreaker, sir. With sorcery. At least, that's what Bo said."

"That's… remarkable." Tamas remembered Taniel's report of the magebreaker Gothen being slain by what turned out to be one of the Predeii. Tamas had barely believed him at the time and might not have believed this either but he felt too tired to doubt Olem. After all, he had seen things in the last ten months to shake the foundations of the Nine.

He realized with a start that Olem was still talking, and waved him off. "That's enough. I'll get the rest later."

"Of course. Congratulations on the victory, sir."

"We're not done yet."

"Sir?"

Tamas lowered his voice. "Ipille's betrayal of the parley? It wasn't him. It was Claremonte's men in disguise."

"We'll feed him his own shoes, sir." Olem's eyes hardened, and his one good hand tightened into a fist.

Tamas turned to gaze back over the Adran camp and the incoming Deliv procession. There was a trumpeter at the front of the Deliv column now. The sound grated on his nerves. "I intend to."

They watched the procession draw near, and Tamas guessed that Sulem had just five thousand men with him, the rest of his forces camping up north with the captured Kez brigades. He wondered how many soldiers the Deliv had lost during their battle.

"They look like conquering heroes," Olem said, a note of bitterness in his voice.

"They should. They met the bulk of the Kez army to the north of us. Surely you passed the battlefield on your way here?"

"I saw it at a distance."

"They provided the distraction so we could take the city."

"To hazard a guess, they had a much easier fight. The Grand Army wasn't hiding behind the walls with Ipille's personal guard."

Tamas wasn't going to debate that. "I need them, Olem. His soldiers and his Privileged."

"Sir?"

"We captured nearly seven thousand Kez soldiers the other day. There's just over six thousand left alive. I can't keep the peace, not even with my best men. Word has gotten around about the atrocities committed by the Kez in Budwiel, and vengeance is taken out upon them every night. I'm going to hand these prisoners over to Sulem as quickly as possible, or there won't be any left."

"I'll do what I can to bring order among the men, sir."

"Save your strength. We leave for Adopest in the morning."

"You won't stay for the treaty negotiations?"

"I have to discover what's happening in Adopest. Claremonte is playing at some larger game and I need to find the end of it. I will make him answer for the attack that disrupted our parley, but I have to do it carefully. He's holding my capital—he has the knife to our throat. I don't know if it'll take a fight to unseat him or if he wants something else." Tamas shook his head. "I'm leaving General Arbor in charge here. The negotiations will take months at best. If Ricard Tumblar has managed to scrape together some manner of civil government, I'll have him send a delegation to join them."

"Very good, sir. Will the Deliv help us with Adopest?"

"Sulem has no fight with Brudania. We're on our own."

"Unfortunate."

"I thought so as well."

"Do you have orders, sir?"

"Find one of the Deliv Privileged and get yourself healed. I need you by my side. We may yet have killing to do before this is all over."

CHAPTER
45

Adamat wound his way through the thick crowd gathered in Laughlin Square on the north side of the city.

It was a gorgeous autumn day with barely a cloud in the sky and although the wind had picked up, Lord Claremonte's Privileged had used their sorcery to create an umbrella of calm around the entire square for his biggest public appearance since his arrival in the city. It looked to Adamat's eye that over five thousand people had turned out for Claremonte's speech—and the promised announcement of his newest and reportedly most groundbreaking endorsement.

He'd already been going on for almost an hour when Adamat arrived. From the rapt attention of the crowd and the frequent cheering, Adamat guessed it was going quite well for the head of the Brudania-Gurla Trading Company.

Claremonte himself stood upon a wooden podium erected at the south end of the square. Adamat had to admit that he made a dashing figure dressed in the finest suit and tails, gesturing for emphasis as he promised inheritance tax reform, more public services, and the establishment of a national museum in Skyline Palace.

Adamat gave up trying to get closer to the podium after twenty minutes of working his way forward and receiving dozens of elbows in his ribs. He retreated to the next best place—a raised walk along the east side of the square that was mostly filled with schoolchildren and shoppers, who had forgotten about the row of stores behind them and now watched Claremonte speak.

It gave Adamat a clear view of the podium and, more interestingly, of the tent behind the podium. No doubt it doubled as a shaded location for Claremonte's most prominent supporters, who would also give speeches after the main address, and as a hiding place for Claremonte's new endorsement.

Adamat wondered if he could slip around the back and glance inside, but dismissed the notion immediately. Claremonte's security was tight—Brudanian soldiers were stationed at every possible approach.

He watched as one such soldier sternly rebuked a young boy who had gotten near the tent, likely with the same aim in mind as Adamat.

This promise of a public-figure endorsement had been the buzz of the city for weeks.

The speech itself held little interest for Adamat. He half listened for the big announcement as he let his eyes wander over the crowd, trying to get a sense for Claremonte's supporters. There were the fervent believers near the front, applauding at every small thing. These could have been either paid performers or the real thing.

There were the wealthy donors, who had rented balcony rooms in the town houses along the north side of the square behind Claremonte. Most of the crowd seemed to be working-class men and women of all walks.

Adamat judged Claremonte to have a rather good spread of

supporters, with a definite leaning toward the common man, which was more the pity. It meant that Ricard's command of the union was giving him less traction than one might think.

Adamat's eyes caught more than a few familiar faces. Government employees. A couple of soldiers. A large number of the lesser nobility who had avoided Tamas's cull. His eyes continued to roam until they stopped on one particularly interesting figure.

It was a woman with dark hair and a narrow face, dressed in black pants and a matching jacket. She stood stoically in the crowd, ignoring her fellow listeners when they cheered, her hands clasped behind her back. Her name was Riplas, and since the eunuch's death several months ago she had taken over as the Proprietor's second-in-command. The rumors were that it was not a permanent position. Yet.

Adamat didn't have time to wonder at her presence. Claremonte shushed the crowd after a particularly long round of applause and said, "Ladies and gentleman, I am pleased—no, I am honored—to receive the endorsement of one of Adro's leading citizens and one of the architects of this new government: Ondraus, the Reeve of Adopest!"

Some members of the audience gasped audibly. Adamat felt his mouth fall open, and sure enough, Ondraus the Reeve emerged from the tent behind Claremonte. He wore the very best finery and sported a gold chain at his breast pocket. He approached the podium while Claremonte stepped to the side, and held his hands up for quiet.

Ondraus removed the glasses from his pocket and what looked like a ledger from beneath his arm, setting it on the podium. He examined the crowd for a few moments.

Adamat's mind churned. What was Ondraus up to? Ondraus was one, no *two* of the remaining members of Tamas's council. Didn't he know that Tamas would wring his neck once he found out? Adamat looked through the crowd until he found Riplas once again. He was one of the only men in the Nine to know that

Ondraus and the Proprietor were one and the same, but he couldn't come up with a connection in this situation.

Surely there had to be one.

Ondraus cleared his throat and Privileged sorcery made his voice boom. "My friends and neighbors. I am here today to tell you that I endorse Lord Claremonte for First Minister of Adro. I am not a public man, as surely you may all know, but I thought this campaign important enough to not just show my face but to lend my voice to Lord Claremonte."

Adamat was flabbergasted. For Ondraus to say he was not a public man was an understatement. His likeness had never once appeared in any newspaper, even though he was one of the richest and most influential men in Adro. Adamat knew it was because of his double life as a crime lord, but most people assumed he was just reclusive. If anything in Claremonte's campaign was going to get attention, it would be this.

Ricard would be furious.

"I have done the numbers," Ondraus said. "I have projected the financial future of Adro, and Lord Claremonte's proposed reforms and laws are the best course for this country, and believe me, I am not unfamiliar with the ebb and flow of coin." Behind Ondraus, Lord Claremonte stood beaming, hands held high as he led the applause.

What's his game? Adamat asked himself. Had Ondraus really changed sides in the campaign?

There was a commotion in the crowd and Adamat looked for the source of it but could find nothing as a round of applause erupted at Ondraus's words.

"If Lord Claremonte is elected, I give you my word that—"

Ondraus was suddenly cut off as a man threw himself up on the podium. A couple of soldiers rushed forward as the man got to his feet, and a gasp flew through the audience as he suddenly brandished a pistol.

Three things happened at once: The gun went off, the bullet flying over Ondraus's and Claremonte's heads and striking the building behind the podium. Second, one of Claremonte's Privileged leapt forward, his fingers dancing, sorcery slicing the assailant to bloody ribbons. And third, a gunshot went off somewhere over Adamat's head.

Lord Claremonte went down in a spray of blood just as the screaming began. Sorcery lashed out, destroying the roof off the building behind Adamat and forcing him to leap from the raised walkway to get away from the rain of wood and stone.

Crouching, eyes on the sky, Adamat began to run, forcing himself against the suddenly panicked crowd. The frightened stampede began almost immediately. He felt himself jostled and thrown, and he stopped to help an old woman to her feet. Then forced himself against the crowd once more.

Everyone was yelling. It was a chaotic mess. There were more gunshots, and Adamat heard the concussion of sorcery blasts and had no way of knowing if they were attacks upon the podium or reprisal from Claremonte's men.

He managed to reach the spot where he last saw Riplas. He forced himself through the throng, cursing and shouting and elbowing. Where was she? Had she fled? If so, where to? Adamat had the immediate feeling that something had been engineered by the Proprietor. If Riplas had been going with the flow of the crowd, she would be up ahead.

He plowed onward until he reached the main street, and threw himself into the nearest alleyway to get out of the chaos. Catching his breath, he worked his way down the sidewalk until he spotted a familiar black coat. Crossing the street was a chore, but he made it only a moment later to find Riplas strolling along, letting the fleeing crowd pass her by.

Adamat snatched her by the elbow and was startled to find himself suddenly pressed up against a shop window, her forearm across his throat and something sharp jabbing him in the ribs.

Her eyes searched his for a moment.

"Riplas," he said. "It's me, Inspector Adamat."

"I know who you are, Inspector." She slowly released him.

He dusted off the front of his jacket. She had begun to walk again, and he jogged to catch up. "I need to see him," he said.

"Him?" she asked innocently.

"*Him*," he repeated.

"Well then." She scratched at her chin. "That's harder than you'd think. My lord is pretty busy these days and—"

"Now, Riplas! This is a matter of national security! Or would he rather I make a house call?"

Riplas stopped suddenly and turned. "You be careful, Inspector."

"I am being careful. He'll want to know what I have to tell him, and you know enough about me to realize I wouldn't lie about something like this."

"I hope you don't regret it. Come with me."

Adamat was carted around the city for almost two hours by a pair of the Proprietor's goons, and he was not allowed to take off his blindfold until he was standing in the foyer of the Proprietor's headquarters.

He brushed off his arm as he was unhanded, removing his blindfold and tossing it to one of the men. "That's no way to run a business," he said.

"Sorry, Inspector. Riplas's orders."

"Does everyone have to be blindfolded?" he asked. "How the pit do you get anything done around here?"

"Not everyone," the man answered. "But you're an inspector, Inspector. Be glad we didn't give you ether."

"I am, thank you. That happened last time. Now I must see your master."

One of the goons nodded to the other, who went off down one of the halls of the immense building. As with Adamat's last visit, he was left with the impression not of a den of iniquity, as one might expect of a crime boss, but of a place of business. The marble floors gleamed, the plaster walls were freshly painted, and the candlesticks had been shined. Bookkeepers ran to and fro, while big, no-nonsense thugs lurked in the corners.

He was about to check his watch for the third time, when the second goon reappeared and gave him a "come hither" gesture. Adamat followed him down a hall to the nondescript door on their right. The man opened the door with his back to it, eyes averted, and pulled it shut after Adamat had stepped in.

The fine wood paneling was the same as it was on Adamat's last visit, as were the few decorations. Only the rug had been changed—a fact that he noted with interest. The desk was still covered by a screen, while the chair that the Proprietor's "translator" had occupied was empty.

Ondraus the Reeve stepped around the screen and sat in the translator's chair, gesturing Adamat to take a seat across from him. "I think we can dispense with the usual procedure, can't we, Inspector?"

"I believe so."

"Good. Secrecy is a necessity in this game, of course, but I will admit that it's a relief to talk to someone who knows my identity. There are only three of you left, with the poor eunuch dead."

"Riplas knows, I assume?"

"Yes. She and my translator are the only ones." The words were spoken without menace, but Adamat wasn't slow to note that it left very few people in the world who needed eliminating if Ondraus wanted to destroy his second life as Adro's criminal overlord. "Now," Ondraus continued, "what is it you needed so urgently?"

"I was at Claremonte's speech today."

"Were you, then?" Ondraus leaned forward, steepling his fingers beneath his chin. "What did you think?"

"I thought it was an interesting career choice, what with word that Tamas has returned."

Ondraus rolled his eyes. "You think I'm that stupid? Is that what you're here for? You were curious about my endorsement of the late Lord Claremonte? You only have so much of my goodwill left to feed upon, Adamat. Especially after you got my eunuch killed." There was something smug about the way Ondraus said "late," and it gave Adamat a thought.

" 'Late,' you say? He's dead?"

"You saw the assassination, didn't you?"

"Considering your endorsement of him, you don't seem very broken up about it."

"Because I ordered his death, of course."

Adamat barked out a laugh. "You did? Why bother endorsing him, then?"

"Oh, my dear Inspector. That's very naïve. I wasn't just endorsing him. Claremonte named me as his Second Minister. We didn't get to that point of the speech, I'm afraid. My men may have gotten ahead of themselves. All the paperwork is done, anyhow. It's quite official."

"And now that he's out of the way, you'll be in position to take his place."

"It'll be in the papers tomorrow morning, I suspect."

"And what will Field Marshal Tamas say about this? I read that he should be here in the morning."

"Indeed he will. And I think he'll be far happier to hear that it is Ricard and me running against each other rather than Ricard and Claremonte."

Adamat snorted. "I imagine he will. But you're a private man. Why First Minister? Why now?"

"Tastes change. You know how it is. My spot as First Minister would afford many benefits to the Proprietor. Or I may enjoy it enough that the Proprietor fades into obscurity." The Reeve shrugged. "Who knows?"

Adamat drew a book from his jacket pocket. "I think that you may have a problem there."

"And what is that?"

He held up the book. "This is *The Compendium of Gods and Saints*. A very old book. Written during the Bleakening, the time after Kresimir first left our world. Supposedly. I'm told that it's mostly superstitious nonsense, but there is one thing that caught my eye." He cleared his throat and read, "'Lord Brude, saint and god of Brudania, is unique among his siblings in one particular way in that he has no shadow. His shadow, it is said, is his other face: a unique condition of sorcery in which he occupies two separate bodies, making him not a single but rather two different gods.'" Adamat closed the book.

Ondraus looked impatient. "What does that have to do with me?"

"Lord Claremonte has no shadow."

"Hah! Are you claiming that he's the god Brude?"

"I am."

"I'm aware that this has been a strange time in our history and that the impossible may very well be possible, but this seems to be a long leap for you, Inspector."

"Not too much of a leap. A god told me."

"Oh?" Ondraus rolled his eyes.

"The god Adom."

Ondraus didn't seem convinced. "He's supposed to be dead, isn't he? The report is that Kresimir killed him."

"He's still very much alive." Adamat leaned forward. "I think it's far more difficult to kill a god than that."

Ondraus scoffed. "If that were the case, Claremonte would still be alive. I've sent a man to the hospital to find out. I suppose we'll discover the case soon." There was a knock on the door, then another distinct high knock and one low. "Come," Ondraus said.

Adamat recognized the Proprietor's translator. She was a severe-looking woman, her knitting tucked under one arm, her face expressionless. She closed the door behind her.

"What is the news?" Ondraus asked.

"You have to go."

"Excuse me?"

Still expressionless, the woman said, "Privileged on the street. Brudanian soldiers. You have less than thirty seconds."

Ondraus leapt to his feet like a man half his age. "Get out of here, go!" The woman fled, leaving Adamat alone with Ondraus. "You, Inspector. Come with me." Ondraus strode to the fireplace behind his desk and turned one of the candelabras halfway in its socket, then lifted up on the corner of what looked to be a solid mantelpiece. There was a click, and a panel beside the fireplace sprang open. "Inside."

Adamat followed his instructions, ducking inside a low but well-used passageway. They were suddenly plunged into darkness as Ondraus closed the hidden panel behind them. "Faster!" Ondraus ordered. "The Privileged will be able to see us moving. We tarry too long here and they'll suspect who we are. Watch your step."

Adamat stumbled, nearly falling down a flight of stairs despite Ondraus's warning. He followed those down almost thirty steps, the air becoming cold, close, and damp. They rushed along, splashing through puddles, and Adamat heard the unmistakable sound of a scream somewhere above them. There was a great wrenching noise and a crash, followed by more screams and the sound of gunshots.

"Quickly!" Ondraus poked Adamat hard in the back, forcing him on ahead, half-crouched, for well over a hundred yards. The passage was stoned in with an inch of water on the bottom, and Adamat could not tell in the darkness where it would end.

"Up," Ondraus ordered suddenly.

Adamat's foot hit a step a moment later, and his legs carried him up another flight until he could discern a source of light.

"Head," Ondraus said.

"What—ow!" Adamat's head hit a plank, and he reached up to push a trapdoor out of his way. They emerged into some kind of a basement that smelled of hay and the rich, grassy smell of horse manure. They went up another flight of wooden steps and emerged into a stable.

"Into my carriage," Ondraus said quickly. "Driver!" he shouted.

A moment later and Ondraus's carriage shot into the light, carried down the streets of Adopest and into the normal daily traffic.

Adamat leaned against the wall of the carriage, breathing a sigh of relief, his heart thundering in his ears.

"Turn here!" Ondraus shouted.

The carriage turned and they drove past a street that ended in a small but well-appointed courtyard and a three-story brick building. The courtyard was full of soldiers and the façade of the building had been ripped apart by sorcery, fire flaring into the air from the roof. Bodies were being dragged out of the building—some Brudanian soldiers, but mostly the Proprietor's goons.

"You keep a carriage on hand at all times?" Adamat asked as they drove on past the Proprietor's headquarters and into the anonymity of the midday streets.

"Three, actually," Ondraus said. His eyes were glued to the window and he was grinding his teeth. "Decades of work down the shit hole. Must have caught one of my lieutenants."

"We're in the banking district," Adamat said with surprise, recognizing the main thoroughfare they'd just pulled onto.

"Of course we are. I—and I mean Ondraus the Reeve—works here. I couldn't have it on the other bloody side of town." Ondraus pounded twice on the roof and the carriage pulled off to the side of the road. The driver got down and opened the door. "The council is meeting with Field Marshal Tamas tomorrow at four. Be there. Be ready to explain to Tamas your theory about Claremonte. And try to be more convincing than you were to me."

Adamat stepped out and the door slammed shut behind him. He turned, mouth open, but the carriage was already rolling away.

He waited for a few moments before hailing a hackney cab. He had the distinct feeling that Tamas would more readily believe the news than Ondraus.

CHAPTER
46

Tamas's soldiers deployed their camp two miles outside the walls of Adopest.

He watched the city through weary eyes, noting the absence of the once-prominent spires of Kresim Cathedral. The black tooth of Sablethorn Prison rose above the city and seemed to lean even more since the earthquake last spring. He made a mental note to mention it to the council. The building might have to be taken down before it could fall.

"Sometimes when we're out on campaign," Tamas said, "far away from the lands we love, it's easy to forget why we go on fighting." He gestured to the city sitting serenely at the tip of the teardrop of the Adsea. "Coming home always reminds me why I fight."

"It's a beautiful sight, sir," Olem said. Olem seemed to have recovered well enough, thanks to the Deliv Privileged, but Tamas knew it would be some time before he had the spring back in his step. "You have any more orders for the boys?"

"Spread the camp wide. I don't want a surprise attack by their Privileged to be able to wipe out more than a single brigade."

Olem lifted his spyglass to one eye. "They don't seem like they're looking for a fight. Crowd's gathering on the walls, though. Only see a few Brudanian soldiers."

"That doesn't mean anything. Spread the camp and post my remaining powder mages on guard duty. Any Privileged comes within a mile of the camp and they are not under a white flag, they're to put a bullet through their eyes. And get me a guard. We're going in."

"Yes sir."

Thirty minutes later Tamas was riding out of his camp and toward the southwestern gate of Adopest. His guard consisted of sixty men: Olem's best Riflejacks as well as Nila, Bo, and Gavril. He loathed going anywhere without his powder mages at his back, but they were better suited to keeping watch over the army.

"You sent messengers?" he asked Olem as they approached the open gates. People watched him from the crowded walls and children waved flags. He could hear their cheering from a mile away.

"Yes sir. They'll be ready for us."

"Good."

They rode beneath the arches and Tamas found the people lining the streets, calling his name. His messengers had been for his council alone, so this crowd would have had to gather since this morning. *Not a bad welcome*, he decided.

They rode through the Factory District and across the Ad, from whose bridge he could clearly see the ruins of Kresim Cathedral— cleared away but for the immense cornerstones and the footprint of the outer wall. City folk turned out to wave him past as word spread of his arrival, but Tamas paid them little mind. His eyes were on the rooftops and the alleyways, watching for Brudanian Privileged or soldiers.

None showed themselves but the few stationed upon the old walls, who simply watched him pass.

"Olem, I—"

"Sir," Olem interrupted, tapping him on the shoulder. He pointed into one of the alleyways along the street and then tugged on his reins, dropping back behind Tamas with a hand on his pistol.

A horse emerged from the alley and fell into step beside Tamas. Tamas eyed the rider in his dark Adran blues. "Good to see you, son."

Taniel nodded in response. He looked haggard and tired. His uniform was dirty and rumpled, but he'd managed to brush out most of the dirt and his boots were polished. Tamas noted a distinct absence of Taniel's usual Hrusch rifle, but he did have two pistols in his belt.

"Where have you been?" Tamas asked.

"Hiding. Gavril make it to you?"

"Yes. He's at the back of the column."

Taniel gave a relieved sigh. "Vlora's dead."

"What?" Tamas had to grab his saddle horn as a wave of dizziness swept over him. "No. Surely not."

"She is. At least, I think she is. We tracked the Privileged and Ka-poel to the city and got into a fight in High Talien. Whether the Privileged had reinforcements waiting for her or we were just unlucky, I don't know. We were trying to escape into the city drains when the building came down on her."

"Oh, pit." The words came out a whisper. Tamas swayed in his saddle. Another powder mage. Another friend. Pit, Vlora was family. He wanted to let out a sob, but he forced himself to fight it down, maintaining his stony demeanor. Claremonte's men were watching. He could feel hostile eyes upon him and he couldn't—he wouldn't—show weakness.

"Promoting me was a bad idea."

Tamas glanced out of the corner of his eye. Taniel's jaw trembled and his eyes were bloodshot. He was barely holding it together.

"That's not true. That's... Look. You tracked them this far. I'm proud of you."

Taniel didn't look like he believed him, and Tamas had to admit that the words were halfhearted. Taniel had gotten Vlora, two powder mages, and a dozen Riflejacks killed. He should have known better! Walking into a trap and...

No. No, no, no. Tamas could feel the grief turn to anger, could feel the corners of his mouth turn down in a scowl. He couldn't do that. Not now. Not to Taniel.

"Have you found Ka-poel?" Tamas asked.

"Claremonte's headquarters are in Skyline Palace. He's renting it from the city. It's crawling with soldiers and Privileged. I think I glimpsed her aura in the Else, but it was hard to tell at a distance. She must still be alive."

"Or else Kresimir would have killed us all by now, I suppose."

Taniel gave him a queer look. "Is the war over?"

"Yes. It's in negotiations right now."

"Do you have Kresimir's body?"

"I do."

Taniel nodded to himself. "Good. What about Claremonte?"

"I'm going to proceed cautiously. Are you coming to my council meeting?"

"Will Ricard be there?"

"I imagine so."

"I probably shouldn't, then."

"You can't run from being Second Minister," Tamas said. "You gave your word."

"I was bullied into it."

Tamas set his teeth, trying to rein in his anger. "You took advantage of what avenue of escape was available at the time. You'll follow through on your word."

"Or what?" There was defiance in Taniel's eyes.

"Or no one will ever respect you."

Taniel looked away.

"It's part of the game," Tamas said, trying to soften his tone. "Part of life. You think I wanted to be the Iron King's lapdog when I was not much older than you? No. But I did what I had to do to survive. We're here. Come upstairs."

They had arrived at the western entrance to the People's Court, Sablethorn looming over them from across Elections Square. Tamas dismounted, and his soldiers took their places by the doors, Gavril in command, while a core group of them followed him inside.

It had been only a few months since he last set foot in the cavernous building, but it felt like half a lifetime. He didn't recognize most of the staff they passed in the halls, and the corridors felt vaguely alien, as if he were walking them for the first time.

They climbed to the sixth floor and approached Manhouch's former office, and Tamas could hear shouting from a hundred paces down the hall. He doubled his pace.

He pushed open the door to find Ondraus sitting in one of the wingback chairs in the corner, looking crossly over his reading glasses at Ricard Tumblar. Ricard was red in the face, his beard unkempt as he shook his fist beneath Ondraus's nose. Lady Winceslav stood behind Ricard with a fan in one hand, trying to look dignified.

"You damned dirty traitor!" Ricard was shouting. "You prig! You villain! I'll kill you with my own hands!" Lady Winceslav leapt forward to grab Ricard's arm, pulling him away from Ondraus.

"What's going on here?" Tamas demanded.

Lady Winceslav opened her mouth, but Ricard cut her off, thrusting a finger at Ondraus. "He's gone over to the other side! He's put his support behind Claremonte. He's running as Claremonte's Second Minister!"

"I'm sure there's a perfectly reasonable explanation for this," Lady Winceslav said.

Ricard rounded on her. "Don't get me started on you, Lady.

Your people abandoned the army before the war was over. Do you know how that looks to public perception? We're supposed to be a unified face!"

"I had every right." Winceslav drew herself up. "My advisers felt that Field Marshal Tamas had lost his perspective, and his series of blunders had given us—I'm sorry, Tamas, I don't mean this to be personal."

Tamas crossed the room to Manhouch's immense desk and sat himself down behind it. He gave all three of them a cold smile. "No, no. Go on, please."

"We felt that our losses—"

"You got scared and you pulled out of the fight!" Ricard said accusingly. "I thought we were all in this together and now I learn that this crazy old coot is one of Claremonte's stooges!"

Ondraus sat up straighter. "Now, listen here—"

"No, you listen!" Lady Winceslav's voice rose to a shout. "We all have our own reasons for what we've done! I don't think—"

The room devolved into a jumble of heated shouting and finger pointing. Tamas rested his chin on his palm, listening for a few moments before he pointed at Olem and snapped his fingers. Olem removed his pistol and carefully loaded it without a bullet. He crossed from the door and handed the pistol to Tamas.

The blast of the shot brought everything to silence. Three sets of eyes stared at him, the members of his council frozen in their places.

Tamas breathed deeply of the powder smoke from the end of his pistol and set it on the desk. "Can you win the election?"

Ricard tugged furiously at his beard and began to pace, eyeing the Reeve suspiciously.

"Just answer the question," Tamas said.

"I have the best people in all the Nine running my campaign. They tell me it's a close thing. I've been matching Claremonte penny for penny as he bribes, threatens, and cajoles his way toward Election Day, and I'm almost out of money. He's not."

"That's not the reassurance I was looking for," Tamas muttered. More loudly he said, "What do you need to win?"

Ricard glanced at Taniel, who stood near the balcony windows, looking out over Elections Square. "The election is on the last day of autumn, which is just a few days away. Appearances from my running mate would help things. An endorsement from you would be enormously beneficial."

"You'll have it in the newspaper tomorrow morning," Tamas said. For all the things he didn't like about Ricard, the man was a gifted businessman. If he could run a country halfway as well as he ran the union, Adro would be the jewel of the Nine for decades to come. "I suppose just killing Claremonte would be out of the question?" he asked mildly.

Ricard stiffened. "Absolutely. We have worked far too hard for this election. We made the rules and we must play by them, else we've accomplished nothing."

"I agree," Lady Winceslav said.

"Well, at least there's that." Tamas gazed at his still-smoking pistol. The world was changing, and in a few days' time he wouldn't have the power he once had to silence his enemies. He had to relinquish that power willingly.

"Besides, the Proprietor already tried that," Ondraus added. "It didn't work."

Ricard slammed his fist down on the back of a sofa. "I *knew* he was behind it! Blast him!"

"Where *is* the eunuch, anyway?" Tamas asked. "And Prime Lektor?"

"The eunuch is dead," Ondraus said shortly. "The Proprietor has not yet appointed a replacement to this council."

"Nor will he. It's too late in the game for a replacement. After the election this council will be dissolved anyway. As," Tamas said loudly, raising his hand to forestall protest, "we all agreed when this began. How about Prime?"

"Prime has fled," a voice said.

Tamas turned to find Adamat in the doorway, his face flushed and breath short from a run up the stairs.

"I'm sorry I'm late," he said, closing the door behind him.

"Were you invited?" Tamas asked.

"I invited him," Ricard said.

Tamas wiped his brow with a handkerchief. "Thank Adom you did. This council needs a voice of reason."

"I'm afraid I have very little of that to offer," Adamat said.

"Olem, see to the door. Go on, Inspector."

"Wait!" Ricard said, pointing at Ondraus. "He's not one of us anymore. He shouldn't be here to hear any of it."

Adamat leaned heavily on his cane and swept his gaze across the room. "He already knows."

"Oh."

Tamas nodded. "Inspector."

"Prime Lektor has fled the country. Perhaps even the Nine. His assistant claims that Prime muttered about something worse coming before he went, then stole away in the middle of the night."

Tamas cocked his head to one side. "What the pit could he have meant? The man stood at our side when Kresimir was knocking at our door. What could frighten him more than that?"

"I thought he was supposed to be some kind of ancient Privileged," Lady Winceslav said. "Was that a hoax? Was he just an addled professor after all?"

"No hoax, I believe, my lady," Adamat said. "I suspect that Prime fled because he discovered what is really going on."

"And what is really going on, pray tell?" Ricard asked.

"Lord Claremonte is the two-faced god of Brudania. Brude himself."

The room was silent for several moments, and Tamas put his chin in his hand, considering the implications.

"Surely you can't be serious," Lady Winceslav said.

Tamas said, "We've already met two gods. Why not more in this mad fray? Claremonte has been behind the scenes for some time, manipulating events. It would make sense." Even as he said the words, he didn't want to believe it. Another god, here in Adopest, playing with mortals like they were pieces on a game board? The very thought made his blood boil. "What evidence do you have?"

"I'd rather discuss that with you alone, Field Marshal," Adamat said.

Ricard stood up. "Oh, come now. We are all on the same side! What could—" There was a knock on the door and Ricard stopped midsentence. "What is it?" he yelled.

Olem stuck his head in the room and addressed Tamas. "Sir," he said. "Someone to see you."

"Who is it?" Tamas snapped.

"It's Lord Claremonte, sir."

Adamat had the very sudden and very powerful urge to hide beneath the sofa. He looked toward Tamas, who, to his credit, remained stone-faced.

"What does he want?" Tamas asked.

"A moment to speak to the council."

Tamas lifted a finger to his bodyguard, who crossed the room and leaned down. Tamas whispered something in his ear and the man gave one nod, touching the butt of his pistol, before he returned to the hallway.

"This is a bad idea," Adamat said, almost without thinking. He glanced at Ondraus, who had nearly lost his life to Claremonte's men just yesterday. The old man was stiff, his fingers clutching the armrests of his chair, eyes on the door as a rabbit might watch a circling falcon. Adamat remembered Ondraus's suspicion that one of his lieutenants had been captured and wondered if perhaps Ondraus's other identity had been compromised. Claremonte would, rightfully, want his head.

Tamas didn't answer Adamat, but rather said, "We shall receive our guest with patience and courtesy. Is that understood, Taniel?"

Adamat glanced at the field marshal's son, having almost forgotten his presence. He was shocked by what he saw. Captain Twoshot's hands were balled into fists and he leaned forward on his toes like a dog straining at a leash. There was a hunger in his eyes, and fury. Adamat looked to the field marshal for reassurance that he would keep his son restrained, only to find a glint of that same hunger and fury in Tamas's eyes. It was well hidden, and the rest of the council seemed oblivious to it, but to Adamat it was plain as day.

He glanced at the sofa, wondering if he could fit beneath it, then eyed the walls for a closet door. Somewhere—anywhere—he could hide.

It was too late. The door opened and Tamas's bodyguard stepped inside. "Lord Claremonte," he announced. A moment later Claremonte came in, handing his hat and cane to Olem.

"Gentlemen. Gentlewoman," Claremonte said, an ingratiating smile on his face. "Thank you for seeing me on such short notice. It is a pleasure to—"

Olem unceremoniously tossed Claremonte's hat and cane on the sofa.

"—a pleasure to see you all. Ondraus, my friend! Are we still on for lunch today?"

"We are," Ondraus croaked.

Stop looking so guilty, Adamat thought, looking furiously at Ondraus. To his relief, the old Reeve shifted to get comfortable in his seat and repeated the words somewhat more confidently.

"Excellent! Lady Winceslav, it's an honor! Now that this dreadful war is over, we must discuss deploying your troops to Gurla. The Trading Company could use your soldiers badly. And Ricard, my esteemed opponent!" Claremonte dipped at the waist, managing a bow that was both graceful and seemingly unironic.

Claremonte's eyes swept over Taniel Two-shot. Adamat thought he sensed the slightest hesitation there. Then Claremonte stepped over to the desk and offered his hand to Tamas. "Field Marshal. I am your greatest admirer. I am so pleased to see you return from the disastrous expedition to Kez and end this war once and for all. It's a relief to us all."

"My Lord Brude," Tamas said, taking Claremonte's hand for a moment.

Claremonte's smile widened slightly, and Adamat would be damned if his eyes hadn't twinkled. "Don't tell me," he said. "Adamat discovered it. I told Lord Vetas that the good inspector was twice as clever as he gave him credit." He turned to Adamat and swept an imaginary hat from his head. "You did well, Inspector. What gave it away? No! Wait. Don't tell me. It's far more mysterious to let it go unsaid."

Adamat felt his teeth clench. He didn't trust himself to speak. All the fear and trepidation was gone, replaced by anger. All Claremonte had to do was mention Vetas's name to remind Adamat of all the horror that man had inflicted on Adamat's family.

Relax, he told himself. This was Claremonte's goal. To put them all on edge. And it was working. Lady Winceslav was uneasy, Taniel Two-shot looked ready to murder, Ondraus was queasy, and Ricard didn't seem to know whether to run or fight.

Only Tamas seemed unperturbed, and only just. If Claremonte's eyes twinkled from amusement, Tamas's twinkled as if he was imagining a very slow, painful way for Claremonte to die.

"Now." Claremonte clapped his hands loudly, making Ricard jump halfway out of his shoes. "On to business." He strode across the room and deposited himself in a wingback chair opposite Tamas's desk and eyed Taniel for a moment. "I'm the last god left in the Nine. Kresimir is restrained and Adom is dead. None of the rest of my brothers and sisters will join this fray, I can promise you that.

"I imagine you all think I'm about to make some inane threats, but you do me injustice with the thought. Unlike my elder sibling, I am a modern god. I understand that these things can't be forced. I *could* kill you all and enslave the Nine, but that would hardly be sporting. Within years there would be rebellion and powerful Privileged rising up to challenge me, and frankly I don't have the constitution for that kind of thing. I don't like confrontation. If Adom were here, he would tell you that's true."

"Convenient that he is not," Tamas said.

"Sadly, you should say," Claremonte reprimanded sternly. "I was always rather fond of Adom. He was the only one who ever took me seriously. And his food was to *die* for." He drew the word "die" out for several moments and dramatically threw his head to one side.

"Your point?" Tamas asked. "Some of us don't have aeons to live, you know."

Claremonte grinned fiercely. "Pit, you have spirit. That's what I love about you. Back in Kresimir's time, there was this general named—damn, I don't remember now. Anyway, he was a mortal, not even a Knacked, and he was the only one who would stand up to Kresimir when he thought he was doing something stupid. Novi used to say he had balls as big as South Pike. You remind me of him." Claremonte's face grew pensive. "Kresimir had him flayed alive, in the end. Stupid waste. Anyway, where was I?"

"Your point," Tamas said.

"Ah, my point! I am a modern god, as I was saying, and I play fairly. You have my word that this war is over. What's more, I'm only here for the election. Tomorrow morning I will withdraw my troops from Adopest as a gesture of goodwill. In three days the election will go forward as planned. I'm not even going to rig it. If I'm elected as First Minister of Adro, I will help usher this country into an era of prosperity the likes of which the Nine has never seen."

"And if you lose?" Adamat found his voice, and decided to try it out. The words only trembled a little.

"If I lose, my good Inspector, I will go back to Brudania and my Trading Company and continue trying to better mankind from my position of power there. I will molest you no further."

"Why should we trust you?" Adamat demanded.

Claremonte turned to look at him, eyebrows raised innocently. "Because you have no other choice. And because I just gave you my word. The word of a god is a solemn oath."

"You arranged all of this." Adamat felt his anger coming forward, straining as a powerful pressure in his chest. "Kresimir's return. The Kez-Adran War. You've had your fingers in it from the beginning. I've seen Vetas's notes. Don't try to deny it."

"Why would I deny it? Of course I've been involved with it. But you're being unfair. It was Julene, that misguided child, and the Kez cabal who conspired to bring Kresimir back. You think I wanted my elder brother here, poking his nose into everything? He'd send us all back to the Bronze Age! No, I simply put my fingers into the pot to try to mitigate his damage. The people I've used along the way, including your family, I'm afraid, are unfortunate casualties of a war you didn't even know you were fighting."

"Don't you reduce my family to 'unfortunate casualties,'" Adamat growled through his teeth. He gripped his cane so hard in his hand he thought he might snap the handle. If Claremonte cared for his fury he gave no indication.

"You attacked my forces," Tamas said, his fingers still steepled beneath his chin. "You tricked me into betraying a white flag of truce, and you took something that doesn't belong to you."

"Ah. That was...unfortunate," Claremonte said. "I did what I thought necessary. My spies told me about the savage girl and her restraining of Kresimir—remarkable, by the way—and I didn't know what to think. If she faltered even once, all of this would be for naught. I thought it necessary to take action and capture her. I assure you, the order was given without the knowledge that you had called a truce with Ipille."

"You keep using the word 'unfortunate,'" Taniel suddenly said, turning all the heads in the room. "It stinks of apologetic ingratiation."

"I'm a businessman, my boy. Apologetic ingratiation is what I do. Ask Ricard."

"Why are you here?" Adamat said. "The next week could have gone by without you revealing any of this and it would have proceeded just the same."

"I wanted to make sure that this council knew what and who I am. We don't need any more of that same hullabaloo that occurred with the Proprietor's men. That would be ill advised. As would you attacking me with your bare hands, Mr. Two-shot." Claremonte's eyes flicked to Taniel, who looked ready to leap.

"It worked on Kresimir," Taniel said breathlessly. "How do you think I got his blood for Ka-poel?"

Claremonte blanched at that. "I'd rather not find out. Now, I suggest a trade. The girl in exchange for Kresimir's body."

"Done," Taniel said.

Tamas stood, shooting Taniel a glance. "What makes you think we have it?"

Claremonte gave him a level look. "Come now."

"Ka-poel will be returned unhurt," Taniel said.

"Taniel, enough," Tamas barked.

"Not *that* girl," Claremonte said. "I need *that* girl. I'll give you another girl."

"Who?" Tamas's brow furrowed.

"Vlora."

"She's still alive?" Taniel asked.

"Quiet!" Tamas roared. "Taniel, wait outside. That's an order!"

For a few moments Adamat thought that Taniel would resist

his father, but with a glare for Claremonte he stalked out into the hallway.

"That's not a fair trade," Tamas said when his son was gone.

"Your powder mages killed many of my Privileged. The fact that Vlora is still alive is more than testament to my generosity."

"And the fact that I didn't let Taniel pummel you into next week is testament to mine."

Claremonte rolled his eyes. "We needn't resort to threats, Field Marshal. We aren't children."

Tamas drummed his fingers on his desk, eyeing Claremonte. "The trade would be conditional on the return of both Vlora and Ka-poel, and the withdrawal of every last one of your men from Adopest."

"You can't be considering this," Winceslav protested. "We don't know what use he'll make of Kresimir's body."

"If I wished to release him, I would only have had to kill the girl," Claremonte said. "Bring Mr. Two-shot back inside. He'll tell you." He shook his head. "I've already promised to remove my men, but I can't give you the savage. She's the only thing holding Kresimir in check and I want my eye on her. Once Kresimir is buried in the deepest ocean trench, where the weight of the sea above him would keep even him from rising, I will give back the savage. You have my word."

The room was quiet for several minutes while Tamas considered this, and Adamat wondered why Ondraus and Ricard hadn't protested. This was madness! If Tamas had Kresimir's body, it was not something he should let out of his keeping.

"Lady Winceslav is right," Adamat said quietly.

Tamas glanced at him and sighed. "I agree. I can't make that trade, Claremonte."

"Hmm." Claremonte got to his feet and collected his hat and cane from the sofa. "That is most unfortunate. Still, I will stand by my word. My men leave the city tomorrow, and then we wait for the results of the election. Until then, good luck." He bowed to them each in turn and then left.

The rest of the meeting was a somber affair. Adamat heard shouting a few minutes after Claremonte left, presumably when Taniel found out his father wouldn't make the trade. An hour went by before Ondraus followed Claremonte, presumably for their meeting at lunch, and an hour after that Adamat was alone with the field marshal.

"The books say that Brude has two faces," Adamat said. "Not just some kind of allegory, but two actual presences."

"So Claremonte isn't the only enemy we have to focus on?"

"No. He's not. I'm looking for the other one."

"It could be anyone?"

"Yes."

Tamas let his head drop into his hands. "That just made my day infinitely worse, Inspector."

"Sorry, sir. Do you trust Claremonte?"

"Not at all. I'll believe he's going to leave of his own volition ten years after he actually does it." Tamas held his head in his hands, staring at his desk. "Please tell me you have any information to make this better."

"As a matter of fact, I do."

Tamas glanced up, a look of disbelief on his face. "Oh?"

"Yes. See, when Claremonte said he was the last god left in the Nine, he wasn't precisely correct. Adom is still alive."

CHAPTER
47

Tamas gazed up at the doors to the manor, then down at the two uniformed guards who had stopped snoozing on the front step and now stood at attention before him. They were city policemen, who seemed to know who he was.

"As you were," he said. "I'm not officially here."

The two guards exchanged glances and seemed to relax.

"Just having a look around." Tamas dismounted and handed his reins to one of the guards, while Olem handed his to the other. "Probably best not to mention my presence to anyone."

"Yes sir," one of the guards said.

Tamas slipped in through the front door and stood in the foyer, soaking in the eerie silence. Olem came in behind him, holding up a lantern, which threw shadows across the marble floors.

"You seem pensive, sir," Olem said.

"The last time I was here, I almost died. That kind of thing makes a man pensive. In fact, shouldn't you be just as pensive?"

"I just think this place is in bad taste."

"It belonged to Charlemund," Tamas said. "He was more concerned with opulence than with good taste. At least his damned bust isn't here staring me in the face anymore."

"You broke it, sir."

"Ah. That's right. Come on."

They left the foyer and took a right, heading down one of the great hallways toward the kitchen per Adamat's instructions. As they drew closer, Tamas could hear a distinct humming and felt his step quicken involuntarily. They reached the end of the hall and he gestured for Olem to wait for him, then stepped inside.

Unlike the rest of the empty manor, the kitchen was full of warmth and light. Two of the ovens burned brightly, and Tamas was hit by the smell of warm bread, roasting mutton, and squash soup. His mouth watered and his fingers twitched in anticipation.

The main baking table was clean at one end and set with silver tableware for two.

"Good morning, Field Marshal."

It was a shock to see Charlemund in a chef's apron, white hat on his head, and for a moment Tamas reached for his sword. Charlemund had put on at least two stone since Tamas had shot the Arch-Diocel in the gut and then thrown him under guard until he could figure out what to do with him. His face was broader, and he wore a grin that Tamas had never seen on Charlemund before.

He let his hand fall away from his sword. "It's really you? Mihali?"

"Mihali is dead." The grin faltered for a moment. "Unfortunate to say. I am Adom, in my purest form." He looked down at himself. "Well, I never looked quite like this. I'll admit that Charlemund was a little handsomer than me, in my original body."

"How?" Tamas asked.

Adom tugged at the strings of his apron and swept it to one side.

"Come! Break bread with me. I can hear your stomach from here and I haven't eaten in at least a couple of hours."

There were no chairs, and the table was too high for them anyway, so Tamas stood opposite Adom while the god ladled him a bowl of squash soup. A few minutes later, Tamas was asking for another, which Adom happily supplied, before serving the main meal of mutton, sliced thin on toasted bread.

"Your son," Adom finally said, breaking the silence.

Tamas stopped chewing for a moment, having forgotten he'd even asked a question. "What about him?"

"After he shot Kresimir, the counterstroke almost killed him. It would have killed anyone else instantly, but Ka-poel's wards were tight enough to block even Kresimir's fury. It put him right on the brink, and even I couldn't bring him back. But that darling girl." Adom shook his head. "I've never seen anyone learn so quickly. Not even Kresimir himself."

"What does that have to do with you?"

"I'm getting there. She figured out that Taniel's coma would require a life. So she took Charlemund's. She stripped his essence from him, leaving his body nothing more than a husk."

"That's terrifying."

"Yes. Yes it is, and I have lived hundreds of lives over thousands of years. I *know* terrifying."

"But how do you know all this?"

"She told me. While you were in Kez."

"She can't speak."

"She's a very good communicator. Anyway, I stole the body, and when Kresimir killed Mihali, I transferred myself into it." He slapped his belly happily. "It was a crude transfer. I usually put myself into a brand-new vessel, an infant still growing inside a mother's womb, one that might otherwise be stillborn. But this method worked just as well!"

Tamas looked down at his meal to find it almost gone. He

reached for the platter between them, but Adom was faster, slicing off several pieces of mutton and depositing them on Tamas's plate.

"Why didn't you come back?" Tamas asked.

Adom chuckled. "Well, I'm in the body of the most hated public figure in Adro, so that would have been inconvenient."

"Brude," Tamas said.

Adom sobered. "Brude," he confirmed.

"Did you know he was involved?"

"I didn't. Not until after Kresimir killed me. There is an instant, flashing between consciousnesses, that I am more aware than when inside a body. That's when I felt his influence. It explains a lot, really. Him trying to keep Mihali under wraps at the asylum, for one thing. He wanted to keep an eye on me. Keep me out of the way." Adom scowled.

Tamas leaned forward. "What does he want? He claims—"

"I know what he claims," Adom said, waving his hand. "I've seen that much. But whether he's telling the truth, I can't tell you."

"You're not a lot of help."

Adom let out a booming laugh at that, and Tamas found himself grinning. That laugh was all Mihali.

"Brude. Brude, Brude, Brude." Adom shook his head, wiping tears of mirth from his eyes. "He's the youngest of us, you know. A prankster. He had the ambition to match Kresimir, but he lived in Kresimir's shadow. He bickered with everyone. Even the two of us had our quarrels, though none as serious as he had with the others." Adom popped a bit of bread into his mouth. "I can't pierce the veil he's raised around himself, but I can tell you that he's now far more powerful than he ever was in Kresimir's time. That scares me."

"Confront him with us," Tamas said. "We can force his hand. Find out what he wants."

"Oooooh no. Forcing his hand would be a grave mistake. I'm no match for Brude."

Tamas leaned back, his food turning sour in his mouth. "Then what do we do?"

"You find out if he's going to keep his word or not. Brude was always the most forward-thinking of all of us. He might actually be telling the truth. But I'll warn you: There are always two sides to everything he says and does, just as there are two sides to Brude himself."

"And if he doesn't keep his word?"

Adom lifted a chestnut from his plate and popped it in his mouth. He looked up to meet Tamas's eyes. "If he doesn't keep his word, there's not a lot we can do about it."

"You're just going to hide here, aren't you?"

"That was my plan. I'd rather he not know that I'm still alive, to be honest."

Tamas threw his fork away in disgust. "What happened to standing beside us? What happened to being the patron saint of Adro?"

Adom picked up Tamas's fork and cleaned it with the corner of his apron. He set it carefully back on Tamas's plate. "Something scares me about Brude, Tamas. Something that was never there when we were young. I can't put my finger on it. An instinct deeper than my age or my sorcery is telling me to stay away."

"I've fought too long and too hard for this country to step aside and let someone have at it. Even a god." Tamas wiped his face with a napkin and stepped away from the table. "I don't know why I came here."

"For advice."

"It was a wasted trip."

Adom gave him a sad smile. "I'm glad you came. I worried for you."

"Not enough to help, it seems."

"You have so little faith that things will work out, Tamas. Here." He held out a round metal canister.

"What's this?"

Adom blinked back at him. "Olem's dinner. I may be a fat coward, but do you take me for rude?"

"Am I doing the right thing, Olem?"

The moon was full and bright above them, even though daylight was only an hour or two away, and Tamas barely noticed the smell of Olem's cigarette. They stood in a grove between two farms a few miles outside of Adopest, their presence sheltered from the casual eye by the screen of old-growth trees. It was chilly, and Tamas tightened his jacket at the collar.

"Not for me to judge, sir."

"You're as useless as Adom."

"Now, that's unfair, sir. He did give us something to eat. Pit, I miss his cooking."

Tamas shook his head. "I was so mad he wouldn't help that I forgot to ask his advice on this."

"You think it would have changed your mind?"

Tamas hesitated. "No."

"I thought not."

"Shut up and smoke your damn cigarette. And stop looking so smug. Where's Bo?"

"Over there."

Tamas made his way to the edge of the grove, where Borbador and his apprentice stood just inside the trees, watching the road that led to Adopest.

"They're late," Tamas said.

Bo looked up from fiddling with the straps on his fake leg. "They're out there about a mile off. Watching us as we watch them."

"Is it a trap?" Tamas asked.

"Not enough men for it to be a trap," Bo said. "Not unless they brought Brude with them."

Tamas looked at Nila, who was watching the darkness silently, then back at Bo. He took a step closer to Bo. "I'm sorry," he said.

"Hmm?"

"I'm sorry I sent Taniel to kill you."

Bo looked surprised, then like he might laugh. "Don't be. It's in your nature. If our positions had been reversed, I would have done the same. Ow!"

Nila had kicked Bo in his one remaining shin.

"Well," Bo said. "I *would* have."

"It's rude to say so," Nila chided.

"Which one of you is the apprentice?" Tamas asked.

Bo sniffed. "Not another word, old man."

Tamas watched Bo. "You haven't called me that since you were fifteen."

"And it's all the more applicable now."

"You're still a bratty upstart."

"Yes." Bo grinned. "I do my best."

"Thank you as well for convincing Taniel not to go after Ka-poel himself."

"He was champing at the bit." Bo looked off to the north, where Taniel now crouched in another such grove, his rifle aimed at Clare-monte's representatives still waiting down the road. "I'm hoping he doesn't shoot one of them tonight."

"Me too."

"They have Privileged with them, by the way."

"How many?"

"Six. Claremonte doesn't particularly trust you, it seems."

"Nor I, him. That's why we have you and Nila here. As well as Taniel, Norrine, and Andriya in the bushes."

Bo was tapping his wooden leg. It gave Tamas an uneasy feeling. "Don't tell me you're thinking about revenge."

"I really miss my leg. And she's down there. The one who did this to me. I can tell. And I recognize her now. Her name's Lourie. We've got a little bit of history."

"Is there a woman in any of the cabals of the Nine that you don't have a history with?" Nila asked.

"A few," Bo replied.

Tamas swore. "You better not jeopardize this entire operation."

Bo made a calming gesture. "Of course not. I'll keep myself reined in, thank you. Here they come."

Tamas put powder on his tongue to increase his trance a little, and watched as the group on the road split in two, the smaller half coming across the farmer's field toward their hiding spot. Tamas called quietly for Olem and they walked out of the grove.

The Privileged at their head was a woman he had not met before. She had pale skin, large eyes, and hair so blond it might have been white. She was wearing her gloves, and she eyed Tamas suspiciously.

"Mage," she said.

"Privileged."

"You have something for us?"

"I do."

"And we, for you." The woman raised her hand, and a figure was brought forward. Tamas stifled a sigh of relief at the sight of Vlora. Her uniform was ripped and dirty, one cheek scraped raw and one eye bruised, but she was still alive.

"What are you trading for me?" she demanded.

"Nothing I want to keep," Tamas said. Olem went to Vlora's side, taking her arm and leading her away from the Privileged and back toward the grove.

The Brudanian Privileged raised one hand. "Your half of the bargain?"

"Olem! Bring it out."

Olem disappeared into the grove with Vlora and came back a moment later, alone.

"Well?" Tamas asked.

"She's objecting strenuously to the deal."

"Would she rather go back with them?"

"That's what she says."

"I never wanted daughters, Olem. You can quote me on that."

"I'm growing impatient, mage," the Brudanian Privileged growled.

"I'm still here, aren't I? Olem, go get it."

Olem returned to the grove. A few minutes later Tamas heard the sound of wooden wheels trundling over dirt, and soon a wagon came into view from around the opposite side of the grove. It was pulled by two oxen and had a stone sarcophagus in the bed. Olem pulled it up and jumped down from the wagon.

"All yours," Tamas said.

One of the Brudanian soldiers leapt into the wagon and opened the sarcophagus. He closed it a moment later, and nodded solemnly to his leader.

"Your Knacked can see in the dark," Tamas said. "That's handy."

The Brudanian Privileged gave him a tight-lipped smile. "I should kill you right now."

"What would your boss say to that?"

"I'm sure he'd find it in his heart to forgive me."

Tamas took a long step forward, then leaned into the Privileged until their chests were almost touching. "Try it," he whispered.

The Brudanian Privileged gave a low chuckle. "You think I'm scared of your powder mages hidden on the horizon? Or your pet Privileged hiding in the grove? I've already fought him once. He'd be dead if I hadn't been in a hurry and feeling generous. Tell Borbador that he owes me his life."

"I think you *are* afraid. Otherwise you'd have tried it already. Get out of here, Privileged dog. Take Kresimir back to your master. Remind him to keep his word."

One of the soldiers took the reins to the wagon and the Privileged turned away. "He'll keep whatever he desires. Even this miserable country."

Tamas watched until the Privileged were long gone before he returned to the grove.

"You shouldn't have done that," Vlora said.

"I've done a lot of things I shouldn't. This isn't one of them." Tamas leaned over and kissed her on the forehead. "It was worth it. Bo, that Privileged sends her regards."

"I bet she does."

"Bo," Tamas continued.

"What?"

"A fight is coming. I can feel it. If you see her again, wipe the floor with her."

Bo's fingers flexed, his jaw clenching, and he exchanged a glance with Nila. "That would be my pleasure."

Adamat sat on the northern section of Adopest's old wall, his feet dangling off the thirty-foot precipice.

He crunched into an apple, feeling the juice run down his chin as he watched the Brudanian troop transports load by the evening light. The largest oceangoing ships had already set off up the Ad River, hauled against the current by teams of twenty oxen each on their long journey to the lock system over the mountains, while the troop barges were still only half full.

"I confess," he mused aloud, "that I'm shocked to see him leaving."

SouSmith didn't reply. The big boxer leaned against the battlements. He wore a butcher's canvas pants and white shirt, the bloodstained sleeves rolled up to his elbows. He removed a pipe from his shirt pocket and lit it with a match, puffing to get it lit. A few moments later the air was full of the sweet smell of cherry tobacco.

"*He* hasn't," SouSmith finally pointed out.

"True, true. The man himself is still here. But the fact that he is keeping his word about his soldiers boggles my mind."

"Think he's up to somethin'?"

"Of course I do. He's a salesman and a politician. If he's not up to something I'll eat my boots." Adamat felt in his pockets for a moment before remembering that he'd left his own pipe at home. He eyed the troop transports as the Brudanians filed onboard, then looked down the Ad to the south. From this position it was impossible to see where Kresim Cathedral once stood, but he remembered its destruction as starkly as he remembered everything else.

"He left his mark," SouSmith said.

"Yes. Yes he did." And so many unanswered questions as well. Claremonte claimed that everything he had done was only to mitigate the damage Kresimir could do. It didn't feel like an outright lie, but even an idiot could see that Claremonte had only his own gain in mind. The First Ministry of Adro seemed like such a pitiful goal for a god. Was there something else he wanted? Something greater?

And where was Brude's other half? *Who* was Brude's other half? He had played off of Tamas's ambitions from the very beginning, which suggested someone inside the council. The thought sent chills up Adamat's spine. Lady Winceslav? The Reeve? Perhaps it was Tamas himself! The thought was enough to give him a stroke, but he knew he had to dig deeper.

Lord Vetas had worked at cross-purposes to Tamas and the council. What had he once said? One hand not knowing what the other is doing? As far as Adamat knew, Vetas had done nothing to prevent Kresimir's return. In fact, he had been working with Charlemund, who by all accounts had known about Kresimir's return. An accident? Or on purpose?

"I have a hunch," Adamat said.

"Huh?"

"Come with me to Sablethorn tonight. Do you have time?"

SouSmith glanced down at his clothes.

"Go get changed," Adamat said. "Meet me at Sablethorn in two hours."

SouSmith descended from the wall, leaving Adamat alone.

Adamat kicked his heels against the stone wall, watching as the first of the transports left, considering his options. He had to rule out the central members of the council. If Brude's other half was one of the council, he would have done far more damage than he already had.

He waited until the last of the transports had left before he got to his feet and headed down to the main street to find a hackney cab. Thirty minutes later he arrived at Sablethorn, and the sun set over his shoulder as he went through the main doors and approached the guard station on the first floor. SouSmith sat in the stone hall-way, back to the wall, hat tipped over his face.

"I'm here to see Lady Cheris," Adamat said to the guard on duty.

SouSmith climbed to his feet, and the prison guard checked Adamat's papers before letting them through.

"I think Claremonte has another agent in the city."

"You think?"

"Of course he does, I'm not an idiot. But I mean another agent of the same rank or higher than Lord Vetas. Someone working autonomously. Completely apart from Vetas or Claremonte." *The other half of the god*, Adamat thought silently.

"Why?"

"We interviewed Claremonte with a Knacked who could see through lies, and Claremonte didn't know anything about the attack on Ricard's headquarters. But no one benefits more than he with Ricard dead. If Claremonte has another agent in the city, working independently, it explains why he could truthfully say he didn't plan the attack."

"Lady Cheris?"

"I think that Cheris might know who it is."

They reached a room near the top of the spire and Adamat paused to catch his breath while the jailer unlocked the ironbound door. They were admitted to a small but comfortable room with a fireplace, two lanterns, a bed, chair, and side table.

Lady Cheris stood beside the window, looking out onto Elections Square. She glanced curiously at Adamat but remained silent while the jailer lit the lanterns and then left.

"Lady Cheris," Adamat said.

She waved her hand without looking away from the window. "I've told you everything you're going to get from me," she said.

"I don't think you have. Who are you working for?" Adamat asked.

"Me? Working for someone? Hah! You must not know me very well, Inspector. I'm no one's stooge."

"So you claim you plotted Ricard's fall all on your own?"

She remained silent.

"If you help me, I might be able to keep you away from the guillotine," Adamat said.

"I don't believe that they will send me to the guillotine, Inspector. And even if they did, you don't have that kind of power."

Adamat felt a cold sweat break out on his brow. He blinked several times, then rubbed his hand over his eyes. "Can you risk that?"

"I've risked everything, and I've lost. This conversation is over."

Adamat's throat was dry. He stared at Cheris for several moments until she turned to face him.

"What is it, Inspector? Can't think of something to say? Am I a dead end? Forgive me for not showing any sympathy. You can tell Ricard I'll be the downfall of him yet."

Adamat found his voice and stood up, managing a half bow. "I'm sorry for wasting what little time you have left, my lady."

Out in the hallway, Adamat gestured for the jailer to lock the door. He leaned against the wall, shivering.

"Adamat?" SouSmith said.

Adamat drew the jailer to the side and gave him a hundred-krana note. "Let me be clear. You are not to let Lady Cheris out of that room. But if she does get out, you are not to stand in her way. Your life may depend on it. Tell the field marshal I gave you those instructions."

Adamat found himself running down the stairs, with SouSmith hurrying to keep up. Outside, Adamat practically leapt into his waiting hackney cab. "Go home, SouSmith," he said. "I think we're done here. You've been the greatest of help." He banged on the roof. "Across the square," he ordered, and they took off, leaving Sou-Smith with a confused expression outside of Sablethorn.

Adamat ran up all five flights of stairs to the top of the People's Court, his lungs near to bursting when he reached the top. He showed his papers to Tamas's soldiers and ignored the secretary who told him to wait, shoving his way into Tamas's office. His chest was tight, and he was spurred on by sudden fear.

Tamas looked up from his desk, where he was reading by the light of a lantern. "Inspector?"

"Lady Cheris," Adamat gasped. "She doesn't have a shadow. She's Brude's other half. And that's not all."

Tamas shot to his feet. "Tell me."

"Claremonte's troop transports are riding high in the water. He's left behind at least five hundred men."

CHAPTER

48

The election was held early on the morning of the last day of autumn.

Adamat stood near the window of Ricard's office in the Kinnen Hotel. To his great consternation, he was unable to keep from wringing his hands as he watched the constant flow of people passing in the street below. Today was the second of two days of a national holiday. The polls had been opened at six in the morning the day before and had closed well after midnight. A delegation of Novi vote counters had spent all night with the ballots. By noon, word should come back on the results of the election.

And then they'd find out if a god could keep his word.

There was so much left unanswered. Adamat didn't like the loose ends. No explanation of Claremonte's involvement in the Kez-Adran War, or Cheris allowing herself to be imprisoned, or even why Claremonte cared about the election in Adro to begin with.

It was giving him heart palpitations.

He heard the door behind him open, and the sounds of Ricard's election party floated in. Adamat turned to see Privileged Borbador slip inside the room. It was the first time Adamat had seen him since he returned to Adopest. He walked confidently with a cane despite the prosthetic on his left leg, and he was dressed well enough to make a banker blush. He wore his Privileged's gloves despite, or perhaps because of, the heavy crowds at the election party.

Their eyes met and the half-patronizing, half-predatory smile that Bo had plastered on his face for the party slid off to be replaced by a somber visage. "Our deal is complete."

Adamat swallowed a lump in his throat. "You're sure?"

"Nila killed a Black Warden in Brude's Hideaway. It was missing its ring finger. Looked like it had been nothing more than a boy, around fifteen or so, when it was turned. I can't be more certain than that."

"You saw it yourself?"

"I was there when it happened."

"Did—?"

"It was quick."

"Thank you."

Bo gave him a short nod and slipped out of the room. Adamat took a deep breath, steadying himself. Josep was at peace. Adamat could now be at peace as well. Or at least he could try.

He didn't have time to think through his grief. He heard Bo exchange words with a familiar voice outside the door, then it opened again and Fell appeared in the doorway. She looked him up and down, then stepped back outside. "He's in here!" he heard her shout.

Ricard entered the room a moment later, mopping his brow with his handkerchief. "Pit, that's a lot of hands to shake. Adamat, what are you doing up here? Your wife is looking everywhere for you, and Astrit got away from her nanny and has been terrorizing the kitchen staff."

Adamat shook himself out of his thoughts. "I'm terribly sorry, Ricard, I'm coming."

"I joke, I joke! Your children are angels. All except that orphan kid, what was his name?"

"Jakob."

"Jakob keeps going into the basement to play with what's left of my wine collection."

"He's a good lad."

"He might be. But keep him out of my wine."

"I thought you hired more than one nanny?"

"I did. Not enough, apparently. You already have too many children. Why did you have to take on a stray?"

"Faye wants to adopt him," Adamat mused aloud. He wondered whether this was Faye's way of dealing with Josep's death, or whether she genuinely cared for the Eldaminse child. It was something they'd agreed to talk about later. Only a handful of people even knew of his importance, but Adamat worried about the possible ramifications of adopting the closest living heir to the Adran throne.

"How is Faye holding up?" Adamat asked.

"She's been yakking with the new head of the tailors' union. What's her name again? Maggie?"

"Margy. I'm glad you picked her."

"I can't really account for your taste. She hates my guts."

"It's good to have some opposition," Adamat said. "I'm sure she'll come around."

"You're too confident. Anyway, I'm glad you're alone. I want to talk to you."

"Oh?"

"How would you like a job?"

Adamat swayed on his feet. "Ricard, you know I'd do anything for you. But I'm exhausted. I'm getting too old to run all over the city. The money from you and Privileged Borbador will keep us alive for a while. If I told Faye I had another investigation job, she'd skin me alive."

"Investigating? Pit, Adamat. I want you to be on my staff."

Adamat sensed some kind of a trap. "Isn't that conditional upon your winning the election?"

"Well. Yes."

"I see." Adamat hesitated. "I'd have to ask Faye."

"Well, she'd be hypocritical to say no."

"What do you mean?"

"I offered her a job on my staff already and she said yes. The position comes with full-time nannies for the children and a lot of foreign travel. If I hire you both, you can take those trips together."

Adamat tried to blink away his exhaustion. "She did? I . . . well. I suppose I could do that."

"You suppose?" Ricard thumped him on the back. "Have a little enthusiasm. I wouldn't let you say no."

"You seem awfully confident in a win."

"Pit, no. I think I'm going to lose, Adamat. Pretty confident, actually. But I'm a little drunk right now, and I've done everything I can. No sense in worrying over it anymore. See you downstairs?"

Adamat gave his friend a crooked smile and watched him stumble out the door. Fell remained there a moment longer.

"Fell," Adamat said as she followed Ricard out.

"Yes sir?"

"Thanks for taking care of him."

"It's my job, sir."

"And sober him up a bit."

"Next on the list. I have more confidence in his winning than he does."

Adamat was alone for only a couple of minutes before he heard someone else enter the room. He turned, a smile on his lips, expecting that Faye had come looking for him finally. Instead he found Taniel Two-shot standing with his back pressed up against the door, a look of terror in his eyes.

Adamat frowned and listened for some kind of commotion downstairs. The sound of the party continued on, and then he realized, "You're not used to this kind of thing, are you?"

"I'm going to break the next person who asks me to shake their hand."

"You look tired."

"I am." Taniel wore a new dress uniform, his colonel's pins at his collar, his hat under one arm. "Haven't slept in about six days."

"That's enough to kill a man," Adamat said, stepping forward. Perhaps he should call for Fell. Taniel was potentially less than an hour away from being Adopest's new Second Minister and he had a wide-eyed unsteadiness to him that said he'd either run off after his lover or pass out at any moment.

Taniel waved him off. "I can't do it. I can't keep shaking hands and smiling at sycophants while the pressure builds. We may have another war on our hands the moment the election ends, and no one seems to care. This time we won't have a god on our side. And Claremonte still has Ka-poel."

"No one knows about Brude," Adamat said. "Except for us."

"Ricard knows. How does he keep going on with the farce?"

"Habit?"

Taniel looked at him sharply. "Do you think this is over? This whole thing with Claremonte? Will he really just walk away?"

"I don't know."

There was a rap on the door. Taniel leapt away, then put a finger to his lips, shaking his head.

Adamat rolled his eyes. He opened the door a crack. It was Fell.

"It's almost time," Fell said. "Ricard needs Taniel Two-shot."

Adamat gave her a nod and closed the door. He stepped over, taking Taniel under the arm. "Let's go."

Taniel allowed himself to be dragged down to the hotel lobby by Inspector Adamat.

He thought about fighting the man off and finding a closet to hide in, but he knew that wouldn't be what most people called "mature." Instead, he tried to take Bo's advice and put a smile on his face as they reached the main floor.

Behind the smile, his mind raced. Ka-poel was still with Claremonte. If he lost the election, would he kill her? Would he release her? Would he do either of those if he *won*? There was no way to know, and he was going mad. *Something* needed to happen.

Adamat slipped off to the dining room, where Ricard was holding court, leaving Taniel to greet the constantly flowing river of well-wishers. He didn't know any of their names, but they all seemed satisfied with a handshake and a kind word muttered from behind gritted teeth.

"I've seen that look before. You look like a hare cornered by a pack of hounds," a voice said from behind him.

"I'm glad to see you're doing better," he said.

Vlora stepped up beside him and returned a passing merchant's smile. "Me too. For the record, I don't think Tamas should have made the trade." She hooked her arm into his and he stiffened, but he let her lead him into one of the hotel's sitting rooms, where local officials spoke quietly over their drinks, out of the main hubbub of the crowd.

"I do."

"You're both idiots, then."

"Were you treated well?"

Vlora gave him a flat look. "Don't try to change the subject."

Taniel shrugged. "Kresimir's fate is out of my hands. Handing over the body was Tamas's call. I had no input."

"I know." Vlora let out a sigh and met his eyes, watching him silently for a long time. "I miss you."

Taniel hesitated. "I miss you too."

"Is there any chance things could ever go back to the way they were?"

Taniel had to confess that from time to time the same question had occurred to him. He remembered their childhood and their courtship, going through training together, stealing off to be alone, and all the time they spent together. But the fragile thread that had held them together had been snapped, and there was nothing that could mend it. "I don't think so. Ka-poel. She and I..."

"Yeah."

What if Ka-poel dies? Vlora didn't ask the question out loud, but he knew it had crossed her mind. He didn't even want to consider it.

"I saw your savage," Vlora said.

Taniel turned. "Is she all right?" The panic he felt for her kept rising to the surface and he had to fight it back down. Tamas had told him how important it was to play Claremonte's game, and only a direct order and assurances that contingencies had been made kept Taniel from running off to try to rescue her.

"As far as I could tell." Vlora gave him a sad smile. "If the opportunity comes up, I'll help you get her back."

"Thanks." Taniel reached out and squeezed her shoulder. There was a part of him that wanted to hold her, that knew that she would welcome it. He shook his head to banish the thought. "Vlora, I..."

She held up a hand and he fell silent, frowning. She tilted her head, and it took a couple of moments before Taniel caught on. The chatter from the foyer and dining room had died down. "The results?" she asked.

They left the sitting room to find the crowd from the foyer huddled around the entrance to the dining room, and Taniel had to elbow his way through. He reached the center of the dining room to discover a messenger in a powdered wig, white frock coat, trousers, and black riding boots standing between Ricard and Fell. Taniel tried to melt back into the audience, but Ricard had spotted him. Ricard beckoned eagerly and Taniel felt himself pushed forward.

Tumblar's brow shone with a sheen of sweat and his eyes looked tired. He took Taniel by the arm and directed him to his right hand.

One of the hotel's kitchen lads brought in a wooden crate and the messenger climbed up, while Fell clinked a spoon on her glass.

"Ladies and gentlemen!" the messenger said. "It is my honor as representative of the vote counters to reveal the identity of the First Minister of Adro." He paused, removing an envelope from his jacket and breaking the seal.

Taniel licked his lips, wishing he had something to drink, and wiped his palms on his trousers.

"I am pleased to announce that the First Minister of Adro...is the honorable Ricard Tumblar!"

A cheer went up through the crowd more deafening than cannon fire. Taniel stumbled as Ricard suddenly grabbed him in an embrace. His hand was snatched by a dozen different people and shaken until he thought his arm would come off at the elbow. He heard a cork pop, and a champagne glass was thrust into his hand and then immediately taken away so he could shake hands with someone else. Congratulations were shouted in his ear and he was shoved around the room by well-wishers until he thought he might snap at any moment.

The silence that suddenly swept through the room hit Taniel like a punch to the gut. Someone's laugh cut through it, then dissipated awkwardly. Taniel blinked away the haze of the excitement as the crowd scattered and Lord Claremonte stepped into the dining room.

Claremonte was dressed in the sharpest of black suits with tails, a top hat held in one hand. His eye wandered lazily over the assembled guests and he lifted his hands to gently clap. "I see that the messengers reached me faster than they did you."

Ricard gazed back at Claremonte warily. Taniel put his hand on the hilt of his smallsword and set his jaw. Tamas's stern command to hold it together kept running through his brain.

"You know the results?" Ricard asked.

"If I didn't already, I do now. I heard the cheering from the streets."

Taniel could hear nothing but the pounding of his own heart. The room was deathly silent, and though the guests didn't know Claremonte's true nature, there was a palpable air about him that threatened danger. Taniel caught Vlora's eye, and saw the pistol in her belt half drawn.

"And," Claremonte continued, "well earned, I say." He swept one leg back in a graceful bow. "Congratulations, Mr. First Minister, and to you, Second Minister. I wish you all the greatest success!" He stepped forward suddenly and shook Ricard's hand, ignoring the shocked look on Tumblar's face.

"You'll be leaving the city, then?" Taniel asked, his voice low.

Claremonte met his eye, the corner of his mouth lifted slightly. "As I gave my word. I just have a few things to wrap up before I go. Well done, Mr. Two-shot. Enjoy your victory."

Claremonte was gone before Taniel could respond. He withdrew graciously, offering congratulations to Ricard's staff and waving all the way out the door. Slowly, the conversation resumed, and Taniel pulled himself out of the middle of the room and made his way over to Vlora. Just as he reached her, he heard another champagne cork pop and turned to find Ricard holding the foaming bottle.

"Fell," Ricard shouted. "Tell Tamas to start the parade!"

Taniel gripped the hilt of his sword and turned to Vlora. "Get to your position."

Tamas lay his hand on the neck of his charger to calm the horse as it stepped nervously in place at the head of a long column of sharply dressed Adran soldiers. The column snaked along the main road leading out of Adopest in the midst of a great crowd.

He could sense the excitement of his men. Though every one of them stood at parade rest with feet apart and eyes forward, bayoneted rifles down, he could feel the buzz of energy that emanated from and surrounded them as Adran citizens gathered along the streets ahead laughed and children ran up and down the sides of the column, throwing garlands of fresh flowers, trying to loop them around the bayonets.

"Field Marshal Tamas!" a voice shouted above the din.

Tamas looked up, and it was Olem, who pointed out one of Ricard's men riding toward them down the main avenue out of the city. The man shouted, but his voice was drowned out by the mob of revelers.

"Speak up!" Olem shouted back.

The messenger pulled up a dozen paces away. "We've won! Ricard Tumblar is the First Minister of Adro! Lord Claremonte has admitted defeat." Tamas could hear the news being relayed by the citizens lining the street and watched the exclamations and the curses. There was a clamor as the information was spread, opinions barked back and forth. A fistfight broke out, but was quickly put down by the people themselves.

Tamas exchanged a look with Olem, and could see his own optimistic trepidation reflected in the bodyguard. "Well. That's that, then."

"We hope," Olem said.

"We hope," Tamas echoed. "Colonel, if you'll do the honors."

Olem pointed to a nearby drummer boy, and a long, steady beat suddenly broke through the noise. People all along the road paused in their celebrations.

"General Arbor, the parade is at your command."

General Arbor swung his horse around to face the column behind them. "Parade!" he bellowed. "Attention!" The sound of five thousand pairs of boots shuffling together rang out as every man came to attention. "Parade advance!" The drummer boy clicked his sticks four times on the rim of his snare, then snapped out the beat, and the column moved forward.

Tamas sat straight on his charger, sword over his right shoulder, as they marched into the crowded city streets, the path clearing ahead of them. He could hear happy shouts, and saw flower garlands thrown from the tops of buildings to float down onto the marching soldiers.

The parade led through the Factory District and the New City, winding up and down a dozen streets as the people cheered and waved. Women reached out to touch the soldiers as they passed, and men shouted congratulations. Tamas saw more than one tavern owner running up and down the column to tell the soldiers they could drink for free all night at his pub.

Tamas kept his back straight and his bearing regal, but he watched the crowds and the shop windows and the rooftops with trepidation. Every time he thought he could give in to his pride and let himself relax, he felt as if hostile eyes were on his back. He tried to tell himself that old instincts never died. He tried to tell himself that it was finally over.

The parade proceeded toward the bridge over the Ad River, and Tamas raised his fist at the sight before him.

"Parade halt!" General Arbor yelled.

The brigade came to a stop and Tamas eyed the lone wagon abandoned in the middle of the road not far from the bridge. He felt his hand creeping toward the butt of his pistol and could see Olem's sword half drawn.

"Orders, sir?" Olem said.

"Wait." Tamas glanced at the surrounding buildings. There was no sign of ambush, no Brudanian uniforms flashing in windows.

Suddenly, a dozen revelers ran out into the street and surrounded the wagon. With some effort, they managed to push it out of the way, and a young girl climbed to the top of the wagon waving an Adran flag, planting herself like a conquering hero.

"Parade advance!" Arbor called.

They passed over the river and continued on to Elections Square, where the greatest part of the crowd had gathered. The balcony of Tamas's office—now the office of the First Minister of Adro—was festooned with Adran blue and red, banners stamped with the teardrop symbol of the Adsea draped halfway down the building.

The crowd was cleared away from the middle of the square as the parade marched in and fell into rank before the People's Court. Tamas looked up to see Ricard Tumblar on the balcony, decked out in his finest suit, Taniel standing beside him looking somber in his uniform.

Tamas let a smile crack his stony visage.

"Sir?" Olem asked.

"My son. Second Minister of Adro. Strange twist of fate."

"He doesn't look happy about it."

"He's not. Not at all. He'll keep his promise, though." *He had better*, Tamas added mentally.

The soldiers had fallen in, and a hush descended on the square, quieter than the day Tamas had stood on that same balcony and announced to the crowd that the reign of Manhouch was over. Tamas let out a slow breath, blinking away the wonder, and realized that he'd now come full circle. The plans of so many years had finally come to fruition.

"Is it over, Olem?" he asked, hearing the emotion in his own voice. "Is it finally over?"

Olem didn't answer. Ricard had raised his hands. "People of Adro! Friends! Brothers! Sisters! I'm humbled to stand before you today as your new First Minister." The cheers lasted for several minutes before Ricard could finally speak again. "My friends, the tyranny of kings is over. The doubt and anticipation of the last eight months of tragic war is over. Today, on the last day of autumn, we have become a republic. I am proud to be here, the first among equals.

"My friends, none of this would have been possible without the extraordinary efforts of the Protector of Adro, Field Marshal Tamas, and his powder mages and soldiers. You owe them your freedom. Your lives. Your love."

The cheers were deafening. Tamas felt a tear roll down his cheek, but he did not move to wipe it away. He kept his eyes fixed on Ricard.

"My friends! I . . ."

A sound reverberated across the square, cutting Ricard off and causing a stir among the gathered crowd.

"My friends," Ricard started again.

The groaning and creaking continued, and Tamas turned to see the crowd chattering restlessly. A cloud cast a shadow over the assembled masses, and Tamas removed his hat to look about him. Where was the sound coming from?

The groaning grew in intensity, and the slightest movement caught Tamas's eye as a creak gave way to the grinding of stone on stone.

"Scatter!" he bellowed.

Sablethorn, the mighty prison of the Iron King, tilted and wobbled like a wooden top before ponderously tipping and falling across the square. He sat upon his horse transfixed, watching it descend upon him as if reality itself had slowed. His mouth opened, and he stared for a moment before he was suddenly jerked to the side as his horse bolted, and he looked to see Olem galloping ahead, Tamas's reins in his hands.

He twisted in his saddle to see the spire topple, the structure crumbling as it fell. Black basalt blocks the size of oxen tumbled across Elections Square. The tip of the spire smashed through the balcony and ripped through the front of the People's Court.

Tamas jerked his reins from Olem's hands and pulled up, whirling toward the destruction. "Taniel!"

He threw his arms up to protect his face as the dust cloud enveloped him.

CHAPTER

49

Inside, inside!" Taniel yelled, grabbing Ricard's delegates and advisers and shoving them through the balcony door into the office. "Run!"

A female voice screamed, "Ricard!" and Taniel turned to see Adro's First Minister gaping at the black spire as it plummeted toward him. Taniel dashed across the balcony, snatched Ricard by the shoulders, and lifted him bodily, plowing both of them through the glass of the balcony window and into the office behind it. They landed in a heap among a shower of glass. Taniel rolled them both across the floor to get farther away from the window, looking up in time to see the black stone slam through the balcony where they'd just been standing. The air erupted into a blast of plaster dust.

Taniel felt a surge of sorcery so close it tickled the back of his neck, and he threw Ricard off of him. He leapt to his feet, sword in hand, only to find Bo standing near the office fireplace with his fake leg braced, hands outstretched.

"Taniel," Nila said. "You should move."

Taniel looked around, then up, to find the roof above him split by the spire's capstone, a black chunk of basalt the size of a small house suspended just above his head. Ricard was on his feet now and Taniel shoved him back, out of the way.

Bo grunted, and rolled his gloved fingers. The stone lifted and was flung out into Elections Square.

Ricard brushed himself off. "There are people down there!"

"People up here, too, and I wasn't gonna hold that very long," Bo said.

Ricard seemed to think better about arguing with Bo and instead called for Fell. "Is everyone safe?"

"I think so." Adamat's voice came out of the gloom of the dust.

"Downstairs, quickly," Ricard said. "There will be people trapped beneath the rubble. Dear Adom, what the pit happened? Was that an accident?"

Taniel followed Ricard out into the hallway where the dust had begun to clear, and Adamat was pale as a ghost. "No," Adamat said. "That was no accident. Brude's other half was in Sablethorn."

Taniel froze in his steps. "Fell. Get my rifle. Now!" He began to run toward the stairs, everything else forgotten. If Brude was down there, whatever half it was, there would be no one to stop him. Taniel didn't think even he could do much, but he remembered Kresimir's blood on his knuckles. If he really was a god-killer, then he might be the only one who could do anything.

Taniel felt something hit him from behind, knocking the breath from him and slamming both him and his attacker against the wall. He threw the other person away from him and struggled to his feet, only to find Nila crouched beside him, both her bare hands wreathed in blue flame.

The sorcery that cut through the air where he had just been

standing had sliced a cannonball-sized hole in the floor and the ceiling. The blast had come from beneath him, and he could sense multiple Privileged somewhere below. Taniel scrambled along on his hands and knees. "Back to the office!" he yelled.

Bo, crouching awkwardly with his prosthetic, snatched him by the sleeve. "Get your rifle and take the back stairs. They'll need you out there. I'll take care of this."

"You're sure?"

"Trust me." Bo slapped him on the shoulder, and Taniel ran back down the hallway, taking his rifle from Fell and fixing the bayonet as he ran, passing through two doors until he reached the servants' stairwell behind Ricard's new office.

He took the stairs a flight at a time, leaping like a madman from landing to landing. At the bottom he ran down a short hallway and kicked a side door open, then sprinted out into the dust-filtered sunlight. He stood blinking for several moments, trying to get his bearings, when the concussion of an immense blast threw him straight back into the building.

"She's down there, Nila. The bitch who took my leg."

Nila was about to ask how Bo knew, but the awareness at the edge of her newfound sorcerous senses told her enough. There were Privileged two floors beneath them. Their presence was muted in the Else, as if they'd been taking great care to conceal themselves, but they were most certainly there. And based on what Bo had told her about cabal Privileged, they probably had a company of soldiers with them as well.

"What do we have protecting the People's Court?" she asked.

Bo responded, "Two companies of Adran soldiers."

"They'll get torn to ribbons by three Privileged."

"Five Privileged. And I agree."

Nila tried to think of who they could depend on to help them, and found a knot in her stomach. She and Bo *were* the Adran Cabal. And Tamas's powder mages had their hands full with whatever power had just toppled Sablethorn. Her heart thundered in her ears. She had her back to the marble banister and there were five floors of the People's Court between her and the ground. After watching the top of Sablethorn destroy the balcony and nearly flatten Taniel, she felt as exposed as if she were stripped naked. "What do we do?" she asked. "Follow Taniel out the back?"

"Good idea. Get everyone out that way as quickly as possible, and hope that their soldiers haven't already cut us off. This is my fight."

"This is *our* fight," Nila corrected. "Fell! Get everyone out the back. Empty the top floor if you can, because there's no going this way."

Ricard's secretary gave a sharp nod and began to urge the people back down the hallway.

"You sure you're here with me?" Bo asked.

"Of course, you fool. I'm your responsibility now. Who the pit else is going to teach me how to be the best Privileged of the century?"

"This isn't a few thousand Adran infantry. These are cabal Privileged."

Nila swallowed hard. "I know."

"All right. Here we go." Bo climbed to his feet, his prosthetic jerking and wobbling beneath him. "Lourie! Hey, Lourie!"

"Borbador!" A voice came back from downstairs. "Why aren't you running yet? That last shot could have been for you, but I figured I'd give you a sporting chance. Is your powder mage friend dead?"

"You missed, actually."

There was a pause. "That's a pity."

"Lourie, do you have a favorite eye?"

"What?"

"Just answer the question," Bo shouted.

"Why?"

"Because I'm going to keep that one in a jar after I strangle you with your own entrails."

"What are you doing?" Nila hissed.

"Just having a conversation," Bo said. "What does it sound like?"

Lourie's voice returned, "Oh, come now, Borbador. You weren't using that leg too much."

"You won't be using your eye too much either."

"Bo," Nila said. "What the pit is going on? Why aren't they trying to kill us?"

"Because they're taking up positions. The moment we open up on each other, people are going to die. They want to be very certain it's not them." Bo leaned back, closing his eyes, hands held out in front of him with one elbow on the marble banister for support. His fingers twitched and moved, tracing tiny patterns in the air.

"What are you doing?"

"A few quick wards," Bo said. "And finding out where they're all positioned."

Nila could feel him tugging at the Else. Whereas her own experiences with sorcery had been torrents of power pulled from the other side, Bo seemed to be threading the Else carefully, using just a trickle of sorcery for his purposes. She couldn't tell exactly what he was doing with the wards, or even how he was making them, but she marveled at the quick, almost casual precision.

"Borbador," Lourie shouted, "why don't you join the Brudanian cabal and I'll come up there and we can kill the bloody minister together? You're wasting your talents, Borbador. You can't fight a god. Why I—"

Bo's fingers twitched and there was a terrifying scream from below them. Silence followed for a moment, and Bo said, "I was also trying to figure out which one was Lourie."

"I'll take that as a no," Lourie shouted up to them.

"Damn it," Bo grunted. "I missed. Run."

*   *   *

Tamas struggled to his feet, coughing and choking, thrashing blindly in the dust that filled the air. He briefly spotted his charger running from the wreckage of Sablethorn, following the fleeing crowds of revelers, and checked himself to be sure nothing was broken as a result of being thrown off his horse. He seemed whole, but his head was pounding and his left elbow didn't want to bend.

How many had been crushed by the collapse? How many were dead, or trapped beneath the rubble?

The tower had been leaning ever since the earthquake many months before. Had this been a freak accident? He hoped—he prayed—that it was. But instinct told him it had been arranged by Claremonte and that something else would follow. For now all he could do was regroup and prepare for the worst.

Tamas pulled a handkerchief from his pocket and tied it around his mouth against the dust. "Olem! Olem! Pit."

"Sir, are you all right?" It was General Arbor, emerging from the rubble, a soldier a quarter his age limping along with his help.

"Fine, fine. Do we know how many are buried?"

"I think most of us got away in time, though we can't be sure. Lost my damn teeth!"

"Glad that's all you lost. Have you seen Olem?"

"No."

Tamas was suddenly launched from his feet. One moment he was speaking to Arbor and the next moment he was on the ground, his own voice sounding distant as he shouted for a report. He shook his head, ears ringing, trying to figure out what had happened. It felt, and sounded, like a munitions depot had exploded beneath his feet.

His vision swam and his head pounded, the whole world sounding like a muffled bell. He put his hands on his ears and hid his head, trying to regain his senses. With some effort he got to his feet.

General Arbor was up already, the body of the infantryman he had been helping crushed beneath a piece of basalt. Arbor's face was red, and spittle flew as he barked commands that Tamas couldn't hear. Arbor took him by the elbow and Tamas pointed to his ears. The general nodded.

"Sir." The voice seemed small and distant, but Tamas turned to find Olem at his side. The bodyguard was coated in dust and splattered with blood, but it didn't look like it was his own. "Sir, we've got to go! We're under attack!"

"Who?"

Before Olem could answer, Arbor raised his hand and pointed toward the rubble of Sablethorn. Tamas flinched away from a sudden blinding light, and he held up one hand as he tried to see. Slowly, the light faded and resolved itself into a glowing figure a dozen feet above the wreckage. Sorcery swirled around her in white ribbons, and the clothes she wore dissolved beneath her own unveiled power.

Tamas gaped. Never had he seen anything like this. Not from Adom or from Julene or even from an entire royal cabal working in concert. He didn't recognize the woman, but he could guess all the same; this was Cheris, Claremonte's other half, the second face of the god Brude.

"Get the people back!" Tamas shouted. "Arbor, bring my soldiers into line. I want everything you can give me. Rifles, artillery. Everything!"

"Sir, we should retreat," Olem said.

"Blast your retreating. I fight here and I die here. Get to the brigades waiting outside the city. Tell them to sack Claremonte's headquarters at the palace. Kill everyone wearing a Brudanian uniform. For pit's sake, avoid Claremonte himself!"

"Sir, you can't—"

"That's an order, man. Go!" As Olem sprinted away, Tamas drew his pistol and leveled it at the god, squeezing the trigger. The bullet disappeared into the swirling sorcery and had no visible effect. Tamas threw a powder charge into his mouth and chewed, feeling the power course through his veins.

The god rotated toward him, her face serene. Tamas drew his other pistol, aiming it at her eye, and pulled the trigger.

She was gone in the blink of an eye. Tamas stared hard at where she had just been, his pistol still held warily before him. "Where'd she go?"

"Here," a voice whispered in his ear.

He whirled, but he was too slow. A hand like a steel vise closed around his neck and he felt himself lifted in the air, the breath choked from him. He was turned so that he looked into the eyes of the god.

"I gave you a chance." Her voice was silky and feminine, but with an echo to it as if spoken inside the immense halls of a cathedral. He could hear the resonance of Claremonte within it. "I did not want this." Tamas was lifted higher. He grasped at the fingers holding him, but he might as well have tried to pry away the unyielding hands of a marble statue. He struggled with all his strength, the power of ten men flowing through his veins, but it was as nothing to this god.

Cheris shook him like a doll. "I did not want this," she repeated. "I wanted to do this the easy way. I would have led Adro to greatness. I would have united the Nine once again, toppled the rest of the monarchies, ushering in a modern era of prosperity and unity. I would have erased all memory of the old gods and created a utopia that Kresimir could never have accomplished.

"I could have done this all with bloodless revolution. I told myself that the people would choose wisely. That they would unite behind a man like Claremonte. But they didn't, and now you've forced my hand. I *will* unite the Nine. I *will* unite the world. Even if I have to kill half the people on this planet to do it."

Tamas felt his eyes bulging, his mind screaming from the lack of oxygen. He could feel his own struggles growing weaker. A bullet hit Cheris in the cheek and shattered without leaving a mark, pieces of lead ricocheting into Tamas's shoulder.

"You obstinate shit," Cheris said. "I would have had you lead my armies. What a waste." He felt her fingers squeeze and he knew any moment his head would pop off his shoulders like the head of a dandelion torn off its stem. He thrashed and tore, and out of the corner of his vision he saw the swinging rifle stock.

Cheris did not.

The stock hit her in the side of the face hard enough to shatter the whole length of the weapon. Her head jerked to the side, if only slightly, and she turned to face Vlora with a look of disgust. Tamas was thrown, suddenly able to suck in a breath for only a moment before he hit Vlora and the two of them rolled across the cobbles of the square.

Tamas gasped, air cutting like knives through his injured windpipe. Vlora scrambled to her feet.

"Don't you see that this is just a game to me?" Cheris demanded. "Do you not see how insignificant you are?"

Andriya, covered in blood and gravel and dust and screaming like a pit-born devil, ran at Cheris with his bayonet fixed. He thrust with enough force to skewer a bull. The blade struck Cheris in the belly, bending like it was made of rubber. Cheris twitched a finger and Andriya's head exploded, showering Tamas and Vlora in blood. The body stumbled and fell, neck still spurting crimson.

"Fire!" Arbor's voice bellowed.

The crack of two hundred muskets shattered the air, and Cheris turned toward the sudden hail of bullets and faced the ranks of Adran soldiers, as unperturbed as a man walking into a gentle rain. She lifted her hands, and Tamas opened his mouth to scream a warning to Arbor.

*   *   *

Taniel ran at the goddess with all the speed he could coax out of his body. She turned toward Arbor and the soldiers, and he knew that it would take her but a wink to do the same to them as she'd done to Andriya.

His fist connected with her chin and he heard an audible crack. The goddess spun fully around from his blow, toppling to her knees. She shrugged off the punch—a punch that might have put down an elephant—and was back on her feet in a moment, her face an expression of shock and outrage.

So he punched her again.

Cheris's head jerked back. She raised a hand, and he felt a sudden pressure build in his ears, but he slapped her hand away and slammed his fist into her gut. She doubled over and he brought his elbow down on her shoulder, dropping her to her knees. He drew his fist back, ready to come down on the base of her spine.

Her punch to his stomach felt like he'd been hit by the prow of a Brudanian ship of the line. He stumbled, blood trickling from the corner of his mouth as he tried to regain his footing, but her second punch snapped his head back, sending him soaring through the air. It was with great surprise that he found himself still alive, forty feet away from the god. He stumbled to his feet, preparing to run at her again, but he could see that he now had the goddess's undivided attention.

She flexed one hand, and Taniel felt as if a steel cage had snapped in place around him. His arms could barely move. His legs wouldn't respond. The sorcery closed in on him. His bones and muscles protested against the pressure and it took all the strength he could summon to take one step forward.

Sweat poured off his brow and into his eyes. How was this possible? Not even Kresimir's magic was this strong against the sorcery

Ka-poel had woven into Taniel's bones. Was Brude really stronger than Kresimir? What if Ka-poel's wards weren't powerful enough to hold off this god's power?

He took another step forward and felt a scream of agony wrench itself from his lips. His vision blurred. He could feel the sorcery pushing down on him with the force of a mountain, but he knew that he had to end this. It was the only way to get back Ka-poel.

Suddenly the goddess was in front of him. He swung one fist and she stepped out of the way, catching his arm and slamming the tip of her finger into his shoulder. He groaned and she reached out one hand, grasping his face, and threw him away from her with an angry grunt.

She raised her hands and leapt into the air. He waited for her to come down upon him with the force of a mortar shell, but she stayed in the air, hovering well above his head. "Your lives are nothing to me. Surrender this battle now or I will lift this entire city into the air and drop it from a hundred miles up. Everything you've ever known and loved will die at once and there will be nothing you can do to stop it. Surrender!"

Taniel bared his teeth and looked toward his father, who was now on his feet, leaning against Vlora.

"Why don't you do it, then?" Tamas demanded. "If we're so insignificant, why do you hesitate to kill us? Go to the pit."

The goddess laughed. She spread her arms, and the air began to shimmer. Taniel felt a sudden nausea in the pit of his stomach as his entire body grew weightless. Rubble and paving stones suddenly lifted off the ground. His heart leapt into his throat. There was a groaning, wrenching sound and the earth began to quake. Soldiers were lifted off their feet. Horses panicked and screamed as their hooves left the ground, and an immense cannon rose six feet into the air.

The goddess suddenly fell to the ground. She landed in a crouch

and blinked at the world around her as the rubble and dust all settled back down to where it had once been. There were shouts of
relief, and some of pain, as men fell back to the ground.

"What is this?" Cheris demanded.

A figure appeared in the haze and the goddess turned to face it.
Taniel squinted, trying to make out its identity.

"You're dead," the goddess said.

The figure was tall and fat, with black hair. One moment he
looked like Charlemund and the next like Mihali. His features
warped and slid into something vaguely in between. He wore a
white apron and a tall hat and stood with his hands on his hips.

"You're mistaken," he said.

Tamas stumbled over to Adom, his senses still reeling from Cheris's
attack. "I'm glad to see you show up," he said hoarsely.

Adom didn't respond. He raised his chin at Cheris and she
sneered back.

"Get out while I let you leave," she hissed. "I've never been as
fond of you as my other half has."

"You've killed them all," Adom said sadly. "I went looking for
them. All of our brothers and our sisters. Novi and Ishtari and
Deliv and all the rest. You've managed to lure them all back here
and murder them. All right under my nose. Only Kresimir and I
are left. And you."

The goddess snorted. "Kresimir won't last the day. I'll spare you
his fate if you stand down now."

Adom seemed to consider her threat. He turned to Tamas. "You
should go."

"What do you mean?"

"To the palace. Claremonte—Brude—he's going to kill Kresimir. You can't let that happen."

"But this..."

"You won't be any help here. Taniel's the only one who can hurt her, and Ka-poel will need his help at the palace. If Brude kills Kresimir, he'll do the same thing he has done with all the rest of my brothers and sisters and absorb a portion of his power. Don't let that happen."

Tamas tore himself away and began to run. He flinched as a wall of the People's Court suddenly exploded in a shower of plaster and stone and sorcerous fire flared through the hole. "Vlora, get inside. Get the new minister to safety. Taniel, come with me. General Arbor, evacuate the city center! You're in command here!"

Tamas turned as he reached the edge of Elections Square and looked back toward the two gods who were now facing off.

Adom drew a ladle from his apron string and leveled it at the goddess.

"Get out of my city!"

CHAPTER
50

Nila ran back down the hallway toward the minister's office, only to stop and dash back to help Bo along. Sorcery enveloped them both and a blast rang in her ears, nearly knocking her off her feet.

"Caught it in time," Bo said, sweat beading on his forehead. "Keep moving."

The blasts continued. Each time magic came close to incinerating them, she could feel Bo's threads into the Else suddenly pull his own sorcery into the world as a counter. Marble flooring erupted behind them, spraying shards and dust into the air, knocking holes in the walls and ceiling. Flame and wind buffeted the air around them, but it all bounced harmlessly off of Bo's shields of air.

"Wait, wait!" Nila said. "If we go this way, we'll lead them straight to the minister."

"Can't be helped." Bo hobbled on ahead, out the back of the office and into the servants' stairwell. Nila looked down the stairs and could still see the fleeing minister's staff. Back out in the hall-way Brudanian soldiers had gained the landing and were taking up positions in doorways and behind columns.

Nila stepped away from Bo and leaned into the hallway, stretch-ing out one hand, plucking at the air with the other. Flames shot from her fingers, rolling and snaking through the doorway. A bul-let splintered the door frame beside her head, but she didn't allow it to distract her. She focused on the heat of the flames, dragging sorcery through the Else and into this world.

She stiffened suddenly as an icy feeling crept up her spine, as if she had suddenly found herself plunged into shadow on a sunny day. "Bo, what just happened to me?" Her fire trickled off, expunged by her sudden doubt, and she dared not move.

Bo hobbled up beside her, his prosthetic clicking. "Well done," he said. "You've set the building on fire, but I'll give you points for the effort. That thing you felt was me, by the way. Come on." He grabbed her by the arm and they made for the back stairwell.

"What did you do?" she asked as she helped him on the stairs.

"Quiet," he whispered. "Trick an old lover taught me. I took a tiny bit of your aura and left it where we were just standing. Leaves a splash of color in the Else that burns like a person and covers our tracks. They'll see through it quickly, but it might give us time to get behind them."

They passed the fourth floor and Nila rushed through the door and into the office beyond, approaching the door to the main hallway. Soldiers stood down the hall, gathered around the main staircase, muskets pointed cautiously upward. Among them was a female Privileged—Lourie, she had no doubt.

"Now?" she asked.

"No, down one more floor."

"We'll give up the advantage of height."

"I'd rather give up the high ground if it means we're not trapped. Besides, you set fire to the top floor."

They returned to the stairwell and descended to the third floor. Bo approached the servants' door, sweat now pouring down his face, grimacing with every step on his prosthetic. He'd lost his cane somewhere in the chaos. Nila ran ahead of him and grabbed the door, but was suddenly thrown backward by a burst of sorcery. She slammed into the wall, plaster falling on her shoulders, the breath knocked out of her.

A man strode through the remains of the door. He wore Privileged gloves and he was big, as big as Colonel Etan. Bo made a warding gesture, which the man seemed to brush away. He grabbed Bo by his wrists and swung him around and into the banister. It cracked beneath Bo's weight and both men toppled backward and plunged from sight.

Nila gathered herself off the floor and ran down the steps after them. They lay on the next landing, Bo underneath the behemoth of a Privileged, wrists pinned at his sides. The big Privileged laughed and cracked his forehead against Bo's nose. Bo screamed with pain.

Nila grabbed the man by the back of his neck. He whirled, spittle flying from his mouth as he threw her off of him. His eyes twitched toward her hands, checking for gloves, before he turned his attention back to Bo.

"Shouldn't be looking at me," Bo said, blood bubbling from his nostrils.

Nila's burning fingers seared through the man's spine as easily as a shovel through snow. He gave a strangled scream before she was in his lungs, and he died with her hand around his heart. She shoved the body off of Bo.

"Are you all right?"

"I've felt better." He wiped at the blood streaming from his nose. "Up, quick."

She helped him to his feet, and then there was a great whining sound. The building trembled, and blades of hot iron suddenly leapt through the wall above their heads, raining wood and plaster upon them.

"Run, run!"

*   *   *

Tamas didn't bother to find his horse, but rather threw another powder charge into his mouth and ran all the way to Skyline Palace.

Taniel ran beside him, rifle clutched in his hands, blood caked around his nostrils and at the corner of his mouth. They reached the winding road that snaked its way up the hill to Skyline. Tamas stopped them both there, gasping for breath. The powder trance spiked his adrenaline, giving him strength and energy, but he was far too old to do this for long. He could hear cannons and muskets firing, and smoke rose from the hill above them.

Olem must have started the attack.

"Find the girl," Tamas said. "I'll look for Kresimir's body."

"Do we have a plan?"

"If we can get Ka-poel out and maybe Kresimir himself, we might have leverage over Claremonte," Tamas said. "I'll distract him."

"That's suicide."

"That's why I'm doing it."

Taniel clutched at Tamas's jacket. "I can survive his sorcery." Tamas could hear the earnestness in his son's voice, the insistent, almost pleading tone. He wanted to be the one to go in after Claremonte. Tamas would not allow that.

"Cheris almost squashed you like a bug, Taniel. You won't do any better against her other half. Get Ka-poel. Get her out of the building. If we have her, we have leverage. Those are your orders."

Taniel let his hands fall from Tamas's sleeve. There were several moments when Tamas thought his son might argue. Taniel gritted his teeth, anger slowly turning to resolution. Finally, he nodded.

They continued up the road until they reached the extensive gardens in front of Skyline Palace. It looked like a war zone. The cannons had stopped firing, but the crack of rifles and the screams of men filled the air. Tamas heard a very un-powder-like detonation and could sense the sorcery emanating from the building.

"Too small for a god," he said. "Claremonte must still have some of his Privileged here. Keep an eye out."

"I see her," Taniel said, his eyes focused on something far away, half-lidded from looking into the Else. "She's in the throne room."

"If Claremonte is still hiding his true power, he might be impossible to find. I…" Tamas opened his own third eye and swept his gaze from one end of the palace to the other. Opposite the throne room, all the way at the other end of the palace, the Privileged wing where Tamas had slaughtered the royal cabal shone like the sun in the Else. The power felt like it might burn his face, and he knew that it could only be Brude. "Never mind. He's not hiding."

A fact that couldn't mean anything good.

Tamas searched until he spotted some of his soldiers crouching behind one of the immense marble fountains in the garden. "Taniel, do you remember the trapdoor in the gardens behind the throne room? I showed it to you when you were a boy."

"Vaguely."

"It's behind a statue of Manhouch the First—old man, big ears. Go in that way. You'll come out in a passage right behind the royal throne."

"All right."

"Get at it, soldier."

Taniel nodded and stepped away, only to stop and look back. Tamas met his eye.

"Dad?" Taniel said.

"Yes, son?"

"Be careful."

"You too."

Taniel was off at a crouching run as he ran from bush to bush, covering his approach. Tamas went the opposite direction, toward the group of his soldiers he'd spotted earlier. He came up behind them and threw himself down behind the fountain where they hid. "Report!"

One of the soldiers, a woman of about forty with a major's stripes on her uniform, snapped to attention. "Sir! We've encountered heavy resistance, sir. They've got marksmen in all the windows and at least three Privileged inside. They had around a thousand men in the gardens, but we were able to sweep through with our superior numbers."

Tamas had expected Claremonte to have some kind of contingency for if he lost the election. After Adamat's information that the ships hadn't been fully loaded, Tamas had had his men follow them up the river to where they disgorged the rest of their troops. Those troops had then circled back around to garrison Skyline Palace.

But Tamas wasn't making the same mistake he'd made attacking Charlemund's manor. He now had over twenty thousand men closing in on the palace.

Whether that would mean anything in the face of a god... "Casualties?" he asked.

"No idea, sir, but it has to be at least fifteen hundred men. Those Privileged were unleashed the moment we took the gardens."

"Where are they?"

"North side of the palace grounds, where the fighting is heaviest."

Tamas craned his neck to look out from behind his cover and toward the north. At the north wing of the palace was the throne room. Taniel was walking into a full-on battle. "Where's Colonel Olem?"

"We cracked the main palace door in two volleys from our cannon. Five minutes ago he led two companies into the palace to try to clear it out. Haven't heard from him since, but the marksmen's fire on this side of the building has died down."

"Have your men tighten the perimeter. I'm going in after the colonel."

"We'll send a company with you."

"Excellent."

Just a few minutes later Tamas approached the front doors of Skyline with two hundred soldiers at his back. The mighty silver-plated doors had been rent asunder by light artillery. The entryway was littered with the bodies of the dead and dying, both Adran and

Brudanian alike, and he left ten of his men to move the wounded back out into the relative safety of the royal gardens.

He paused in the mighty foyer and, by the pattern of the dead and wounded, could see the progress of the battle heading off to his left and up the stairs around one corner. Olem had led his men toward the throne room to try to come out behind the Brudanian soldiers who were holding the northern palace doors. The sheer size of the palace could easily swallow up Olem and his two companies. The thought made Tamas wish he'd brought an entire brigade with him.

He felt tired, his strength waning. Every old, sorcery-healed scar ached, and the memories of how he got them all seemed to flow together. He remembered the campaigns in Gurla and the countless charges and battles. He recalled his flight from Kez after his attempted assassination of Ipille, and the years of planning his own monarch's fall that ended in Manhouch's head in a basket. The battle against the royalists and his flight across northern Kez toward Alvation all seemed to blend together.

He was so tired, and this needed to end.

"You, Captain," Tamas said, splitting his force in two, "bring your platoon and come with me. Major, take the rest of the men up to the second story and work your way north. There are a half-dozen galleries between here and the throne room that will give you the high ground. Give Colonel Olem what reinforcement he might need from above."

"Sir?" the major asked. "Where are you going?"

"I have a score to settle."

Taniel worked his way through the gardens and hedgerows, past the fountains and statues, over the decorative walls and around the north face of Skyline Palace.

The fighting grew thicker, bullets whizzing over his head, black powder smoke hanging like a fog over the ruined gardens.

The smoke gave him strength and clarity of mind as he avoided the clusters of Brudanian troops and sprinted behind the lines of Adran soldiers slowly advancing on the palace.

He moved like a man possessed as he rounded the northeast corner of the palace, sprinting with all his strength. He cut across a polo lawn and heard the crack of muskets and the whiz of bullets cutting through the air behind him. Out of the corner of his eye he saw a squad of Brudanian soldiers leave their cover in pursuit, but he left them behind as he cut through a hedge maze, throwing himself through the prickly walls of greenery with an arm over his face.

He came out on the other side of the maze and descended a hill into a grove of birch trees in a hollow behind the palace. The sound of fighting was muffled and distant, and this part of the garden was overgrown but untouched by the conflict. A dry streambed, once fed by the same pumps that kept the fountains going, meandered through the grove.

Taniel approached the back wall of the palace, passing the statue of the old King Manhouch the First. He ran his hands over the thick stone blocks of the foundation, ransacking his memory for an image of the entrance his father had showed him sixteen years ago.

He continued along the wall for twenty paces, feeling every crack and nook to no avail, his heart beating harder with every second that passed without finding the entrance. Back at the statue he gazed for several moments at the wall—all that lay between him and Ka-poel—before taking a step back.

The fall might have broken his neck if he hadn't dropped his rifle to catch himself. His leg plunged into a hole in the grass below his feet, and he wiggled his foot in the empty space, unsure if his eyes were playing tricks on him. Reaching down, he cleared away the grass to find an opening easily big enough for a man worked into the landscaping in a way that made it impossible to see.

He crawled in on all fours, sliding his rifle along ahead of him. Within ten paces the passage turned and opened up into a narrow corridor. He was able to stand and keep moving forward. The ground was damp beneath his feet, cobwebs tugging at his face and arms.

The corridor ended abruptly, leaving Taniel at a dead end. The only sounds he could hear were his own nervous breaths and the distant, almost inaudible cracks of musket and rifle fire.

Putting his ear to the wall, he waited for several moments of silence before he pushed gently with both hands. There was a click and the wall gave way to reveal another dark hallway. He could see a source of light at one end, which proved to be the hairline crack of what Taniel could only assume was another hidden doorway.

This door slid to one side in complete silence, leaving Taniel with a view of a well-lit, curtained-off corner of a room. He recognized that corner. The tall windows, the blue-and-crimson trim, the tapestries gilded with the dueling lions of the Manhouch family crest.

He was in the throne room, directly behind the throne itself.

He crept forward until he reached the curtain, moving it to one side cautiously with his finger. A sudden blast made him jump, withdrawing behind the curtain and pointing his rifle ahead of him. A few shouts followed the blast, and musket shots echoed somewhere nearby. When he was certain those blasts weren't meant for him, Taniel leaned forward to peek past the curtain again.

The throne room appeared deserted. Dust covered the floor, though it was crisscrossed with footprints, and a couple of the torches were lit. The big double doors at the far end of the room were open about a foot. While Taniel watched, two Brudanian soldiers rushed inside and threw their backs to the door. They wore the uniform but neither held a weapon. Taniel could sense sorcery, and his suspicion that they were Privileged was confirmed when one held up his rune-covered glove.

He said something to his companion, then leaned into the crack of the door, and a blast of ice slipped from his fingers and disappeared. The other Privileged's fingers danced in the air, and Taniel heard another concussion beyond the doors.

Taniel wasted no time. He wrapped a bullet in cotton and rammed it down the barrel to join the one already loaded, then stuck a spare powder cartridge between his teeth. He got down on one knee and with an elbow propped on the opposite knee he slid the barrel of his rifle through the curtain. He opened his third eye to see the Privileged clearly, then pulled the trigger.

In one instant he burned the powder charge between his teeth, sending the energy behind the foremost bullet. The lead balls flew out of the chamber, one after the other. He let the first fly true and put his focus behind the second, nudging it with his sorcery, adjusting his aim by just a few feet.

The two Privileged dropped together, their brains scattered across the inside of the throne room door. Taniel swept the curtain aside and ran forward. He had to find Ka-poel and get her out of here. He could sense her nearby, he—

"Ahem."

The sound made Taniel spin.

Ka-poel sat on the throne, her legs dangling above the dais, hands on the armrests, leaning back like she owned the chair. She was wearing new pants and a shirt beneath a brand-new duster, and appeared unharmed, though she was flanked by a pair of Brudanian soldiers. One of them held an air rifle, leveled at Taniel, while the second held a pistol pointed at Ka-poel.

"Lower your rifle, powder mage," the soldier with the pistol said.

"Ka-poel, are you all right?"

"Lower it!"

Ka-poel seemed unbothered by the pistol barrel pressed against her neck. She gave Taniel a thumbs-up.

Slowly, his eyes on the two soldiers, he lowered his rifle to the ground. Reaching out with his senses, he found no trace of powder on the two men. The pistol looked off, and though he'd never before seen its like, he guessed it operated on air cartridges as well.

"Pistols," the soldier said, while his partner took two steps down the dais, his aim unfaltering. "Take them slowly from your belt and throw them over there."

"Just wait a minute," Taniel said. Both soldiers were big men, as big as grenadiers, with weathered faces and the lean, muscular build of professional killers.

"Do it now!" the soldier shouted. He grabbed Ka-poel by the arm roughly and jerked her from her seat on the throne. "You even twitch and I will—" His sentence cut out in a cry of pain.

Everything happened at once. Ka-poel slipped the soldier's knife from his belt while he talked and rammed it into his groin. Taniel drew his pistol while the soldier with an air rifle whirled toward his partner.

Taniel's shot was rushed and went wide, blasting a chunk of wood out of the throne. He tossed the pistol aside and drew his spare, and in the time it took him to do that, Ka-poel stepped forward and smacked the barrel of the air rifle to one side and slid the knife across the second soldier's throat.

Taniel leapt onto the dais, kicking the air pistol away from the bleeding Brudanian. He snatched Ka-poel up in his arms and kissed her, breathing hard. "You're unhurt?"

She rolled her eyes and wiggled out of his arms.

"Pole, we've got to go. Tamas wants you out of here. We're going to try to negotiate with Claremonte."

She shook her head vehemently.

"What do you mean?"

She drew her finger across her throat.

"Kill him?"

A nod.

"We can't, Pole. He's a god. He's Brude."

Another nod.

"You know?"

She rolled her eyes again.

"Look, Pole, I've got to get you out of here so I can go help Tamas. He's going to get himself killed."

Ka-poel rounded the throne and reached beneath it, dragging an iron strongbox out and onto the dais with a thud. Taniel helped her pull it around in front of the throne. "What's this?"

As an answer, she went to the soldier holding his blood-soaked groin and rummaged through his jacket, batting away his feeble attempts to stop her. She took a large iron key and used it to open the lockbox. Inside, Taniel recognized the container she'd made of branches to hold Kresimir's doll. Gingerly, she removed the casket and set it to one side.

"Good," Taniel said. "Bring that too and we'll get out of here." Taniel staggered to one side as sorcery shimmered around him, shaking the entire building. "Was that you?"

No, she mouthed, pointed at his rifle still lying in the middle of the throne room.

Taniel fetched it for her. "We have to hurry," he said. "Something is happening. That sorcery feels so..." He tried to work moisture into his dry throat. "I've never felt anything like it. It's emanating from the other end of the palace. Where Tamas is."

Ka-poel pulled the ring bayonet off the end of the rifle, then used the Brudanian's knife to slice the tip of her finger. She let her blood drip all over the slender blade. The color drained from her face and Taniel had to leap forward to keep her from collapsing. "What are you doing?"

She pushed him away and took a deep breath, steeling herself. Stepping over to the Brudanian soldier, she looked down upon him like a priest might look upon a sacrificial victim, then plunged the bayonet into his heart. The man twitched once and fell still, and Taniel watched as his skin seemed to wrinkle and sag, aging fifty years in a heartbeat.

Taniel couldn't help but feel ill. There was a part of him that knew he'd just witnessed sorcery as dark as anything the royal cabals did in secret. "Pole?" he said, reaching toward her.

She drew the bayonet from the soldier's chest and handed it to

Taniel. It had not a drop of blood on it, but a thin red line ran from the very tip to the ring. He recognized that red line.

"This is what you did for the redstripes, isn't it? And to contain Kresimir?"

A nod.

"Did you kill people for those, too?"

Ka-poel shook her head, then mimed a pair of tall ears.

"Rabbits?"

She shrugged her shoulders and made a wheel-like motion with one hand. Taniel got the message: *and other small animals.*

"This will kill a god?" he asked.

She raised her eyebrows as if to say, *I hope so.*

"That's very reassuring, Pole. I don't suppose you'll get the pit out of here on your own so I can go help Tamas?"

She shook her head.

"All right. Stay close."

Nila put a shoulder beneath Bo's arm and they ran down the next two flights of stairs, spikes of hot iron as big around as Nila's wrist raining around them.

"How the pit can she do that?" Nila demanded.

"Her primary element is earth. Every Privileged likes to get good at something that's both effective and physically terrifying. Mine is ice. Those bloody bolts are hers."

They reached the bottom of the stairs. She headed for the door leading outside, but Bo stopped her with one hand.

"There are worse things going on out there," he said.

"What could possibly be worse than raining iron?"

"It's not strictly iron. It's compressed matter. Iron is just easier to say. And outside you'll find a pair of gods fighting."

"You're joking."

Something suddenly shook the building, followed by a deep

groaning sound. "That would be them." Bo grimaced. "Pit, be glad you're not attuned to the Else like I am. I feel like I'm walking naked through a battlefield. I wish Adom would just kill her already."

"Well, I think I would have preferred to remain ignorant of what's going on."

Bo limped on ahead, leading her through a series of servants' rooms and out into the main hall of the first floor. "Keep close," he said. "I'm losing strength. I can only do so much." His fingers twitched and Nila ducked involuntarily as the ceiling above her exploded. The iron spike that plunged down through the ceiling would have impaled her from head to foot if Bo's sorcery hadn't slapped it aside, sending it clattering down the hall.

"What can I do?" she demanded. "I can't form shields, I'm not that quick!"

"You'll learn."

"If I survive this!"

"Good point. Air, can you do air?"

"Only a little."

"Air behind your fire. The hottest fire you can make. The fire will melt the iron, air will spread the molten metal around you."

"And shower anyone nearby? That's mad!"

"This is sorcery!" He stopped her with an arm across her chest. "Shit." The building shook and they both nearly fell. "One of those bloody Privileged is trying to help Brude. I don't know if it'll do anything, but to pit with me if I let him." He reached out one hand. Nila noted his fingers moving slower, his eyelids drooping. "Damn it, I'm getting tired. This damned leg!"

"Tell me what to do."

"Privileged. There." He pointed up and to his right. "Two stories up. Do you feel him?"

Nila reached out with her senses. She could feel that Privileged and she could sense something greater outside the building. It was thick and ominous, far stronger than the Gurlish magebreaker's sorcery nullification. This turned her bowels to jelly.

"Okay," she said, her voice shaking.

"Kill him."

"How?"

"Be creative."

Nila scowled. Reaching up, she flung her sorcery at the ceiling, her own fire splashing back to singe her clothes before melting through marble, wood, and plaster and boring a black hole right through the guts of the building.

She felt the Privileged wink out of existence, his light in the Else snuffed out. "I did it. I did it!"

"I'm very proud of you. Just don't let it go to your head. He would have countered you if he had been paying any attention. Keep going, there are still two more of them. Lourie's still on the fifth floor, but she won't stay up there long."

The iron spike came from nowhere, slamming through Bo's shoulder and flinging him across the hall. His response was almost immediate, his fingers twitching even as he was thrown, spikes of ice flying through the air and impaling the Privileged who had appeared in the stairwell ahead of them.

Bo tried to wrench the spike from his shoulder, screaming as it seared his flesh. His wrists were suddenly pinned to the wall by air, and then a smaller spike went straight through the palm of his right hand.

Nila stared in horror as Lourie strode into the hallway, ignoring her comrade pinioned to the wall with ice like some kind of insect. Nila sneered, raising her hands, but was instantly batted down by an invisible fist.

Her head pounded as she struggled to regain her feet, and watched helplessly as Lourie approached Bo. The Brudanian Privileged stopped in front of him, then turned to regard Nila for a moment. "What are you, his apprentice? You should have carried extra gloves, little girl. A fight like this will burn them off." She turned to Bo and put a finger under his chin. "I'll make the offer one last time. But if you want to survive this moment, you'll beg me to kill this imp you call an apprentice and you'll laugh as she screams."

Bo choked a couple of times.

"Well?" Lourie demanded.

"Nila," Bo croaked. "Remember the magebreaker?"

"You're not answering me," Lourie said. "You have five seconds."

"You have my answer, you bitch."

Nila struggled to her feet and reached for the Else.

"And what is that answer?" Lourie said, tilting her head forward in a mocking manner.

"Burn," Bo replied.

Nila tapped into all of her fury, spurred on by memories of her fear and helplessness at the hands of all who had abused her. She used that strength to wrench sorcery from the Else. It poured through her, more power than she could possibly hold. Lourie turned toward the danger, molten matter compressing into a spike above her shoulder and soaring toward Nila. But Nila threw air behind her fire just as Bo had said, and the spike melted to her flames and was splashed away by the air. She heard herself scream as the flames washed over Lourie and plowed on ahead, blasting through columns and walls.

It went on for several seconds before, with a thought, Nila extinguished it, her eyes on the ash that remained of the Brudanian Privileged.

Bo clung to the wall, his mouth slightly open. "Air, huh?" he said. "I'm really glad you figured that out. Now, would you come help me get this out of my shoulder?"

CHAPTER
51

Tamas and his squad of soldiers went through the Diamond Hall, passing the shattered windows still unrepaired from the night of Tamas's coup earlier in the year.

They moved through half a dozen large galleries, passing staircases and countless side rooms, but they met no resistance along the way. There was evidence of animals taking up residence in this wing of the palace—chewed curtains, birds' nests, and scratched plaster walls. Tamas had heard that Claremonte's headquarters had been in the royal apartments on the north side of the palace, near the throne room. Apparently this wing had gone untouched by his staff.

The battle seemed far away now, the palace almost peaceful. Tamas thought that perhaps he'd made a mistake.

Opening his third eye confirmed that he had not. Claremonte

was still up ahead of him, beyond the two scepter-wielding statues that flanked the entrance to the Answering Room.

Tamas motioned for his soldiers to split into two groups and flank the doorway. They rushed forward, rifles at the ready, and took up their positions. Tamas moved forward to open the doors.

He sensed a flare of sorcery behind him and only his preternatural speed allowed him to dodge the ice spike that flew down the hallway and slammed into the door where he had been standing a moment before. Tamas whirled, pistol ready, and grunted as a second spike slammed into his shoulder, throwing him against the wall with enough force to make him see stars.

There were a few moans and a cut-off scream as his men died, nailed to the walls where they stood with sorcery-formed spikes jutting from heads and hearts.

Tamas fought against the pain, feeling the cold deep in his muscles as he snapped the spike off the wall and pulled the broken piece slowly from his shoulder. He jammed his fist into the wound and searched for the source of the sorcery, waiting for a second attack. There, coming down one of the staircases they'd passed a hundred paces back down the hall. It was a slender woman in her fifties with graying brown hair trimmed above her ears.

"Field Marshal Tamas," she said with a heavy Brudanian accent. "My lord Brude said you would—"

Tamas's pistol jerked in his hand, and the bullet took her between the eyes. He breathed shallowly for several moments, inhaling the powder smoke, waiting to see if her fallen body would stir. It did not.

He removed the handkerchief from his pocket and shoved it into his wound. It was bleeding too much, the wound too wide. He could barely move that arm, and he was sure that the ice had chipped a bone. Slowly he straightened, feeling his strength wane, and let his eyes wander over the bodies of his men. Not a single one still drew breath.

The door to the Answering Hall swung ponderously at his touch, and Tamas stepped inside the cavernous room, still lit by Privileged sorcery long after the deaths of the men who weaved the spells.

A raised altar draped in velvet dominated the center of the room, upon which Kresimir's body had been laid out. Lord Claremonte knelt before the altar, his back to Tamas. He was dressed in a fine suit with tails, his hat and cane on the ground beside him.

"Good afternoon, Field Marshal," Claremonte said. "I'm sorry about all this."

"No you're not."

"A little. Come in. Would you like to know how to kill a god?"

Taniel and Ka-poel rushed through winding corridors, back rooms, secret passages, and servants' halls.

He could sense the power up ahead of them and he charged forward, with Ka-poel leading their way through the maze of rooms. They passed through small apartments and dark hallways, cutting across marble floors littered with Brudanian and Adran bodies and rooms that had been destroyed by sorcery. He could hear the triumphant yells of the Adran soldiers as they gained ground, but he soon left all sounds of battle behind him.

They entered the cabal's wing of the palace, marked by ancient runes on the doorposts. This part of the building seemed deserted. They passed a dozen rooms, ascending to the third floor and then going back down to the second before Ka-poel finally slowed in a long hallway that ended in a large, well-lit room.

Taniel could hear voices coming from the room ahead of them. They crept to the end of the hallway and then across to a banister to find themselves looking down into the Answering Room.

Kresimir lay on an altar in the middle of the room and Tamas, holding one blood-soaked shoulder, stood in the doorway. Between him and the altar was Lord Claremonte, and he was speaking in the low, pleasant tone of a man discussing the weather over tea.

Taniel tightened his grip on his bayonet.

Claremonte stood and faced Tamas. He held something in his hand, and Tamas squinted through his pain to make out a piece of sharp flint.

"First of all," Claremonte said, "we're not really gods. No more than you are. We're just very, very old. We were the very first Privileged to walk this planet, back when men had only just begun to live in mud huts. Kresimir used to say we were the first humans, brought into existence by some kind of mysterious maker, but I know that's bullshit. I remember my parents."

Claremonte tossed the stone up in the air and caught it. "I remember when Kresimir killed them. He made them scream for hours. Afterward, he said that their deaths were necessary because they wouldn't let me go with him. That they wouldn't let him teach me how to wield this great power inside of me. Once again, bullshit. He did it because he liked to see lesser creatures suffer."

"I thought you were brothers." Tamas's strength had fled him. He was weak with loss of blood, and he fumbled with a powder charge, lifting it to his mouth, only to drop it.

"Brothers in sorcery alone," Claremonte said. "My other half, the one you call Cheris. She was my twin, conjoined at the hip. By all rights we should have been exposed to the elements, left to die after birth. But our parents loved us and kept us. Kresimir killed our parents and then he separated us with sorcery. We mourned for months. We clung to each other until he pulled us apart by force. Without him, we would have always been one, as we were meant to be."

Claremonte looked behind him, frowning up at the second-floor balcony.

"What was I saying? Oh yes. Killing a god takes either raw sorcery, like when Kresimir killed Adom's mortal form a couple of months ago, or it takes something like this." He held up the sharp stone again. "This bit of flint is tens of thousands of years old. It was struck in a land far from here, long since swallowed by the sea. Kresimir cut himself on it when he was a child and that blood will be his undoing."

"That's no sorcery I've ever heard of." Tamas's vision grew hazy. He tried to press his hand harder to the wound in his shoulder. It must be far worse than he thought.

"The blood loss is getting to you, Tamas. Of course you've heard of this kind of sorcery. It's magic long lost to this part of the world, older than me or Kresimir, and never really understood by any of us. But it exists, and is still used today in a land halfway across the world."

"Dynize."

"Yes. All the way on the other side of Fatrasta. Your son's little savage girl is the strongest practitioner of this sorcery that I've ever stumbled across, and that includes even myself. I've used artifacts like this to kill all but two of my siblings."

"Adom..."

"And Kresimir. Yes. I like Adom. He was always kind to me, back before I came into power. I've left him unmolested so far. I'm afraid my twin won't feel so magnanimous, though, with Kresimir out of the way. Speaking of which."

Claremonte paused, and there was a distinct popping sound. Coughing, smoke rising from her skin and hair, Cheris appeared from beyond a translucent veil of sorcery and stumbled into Claremonte, who caught her with one hand. "Hello, my love," he said. "What is the matter?"

Cheris hacked, then went behind Kresimir's altar and heaved noisily. "Our damned brother has gotten his filthy sorcery inside me. I had to flee, but I don't think he'll follow."

"I told you not to eat anything in this city," Claremonte said, his pleasant voice sounding slightly cross. "It won't kill you. Adom is too gentle for that."

Tamas took a step forward. The world seemed to tilt in his vision, the floor spinning. "This doesn't have to go any further," he said.

Cheris pointed at Tamas. "Why haven't you killed him yet?"

Claremonte rolled his eyes. "I had other plans," he said, addressing Tamas. "In case I lost the election. Plans within plans within plans. Weakening Ricard's position, toppling the Adran currency. I planned on having power within twelve years, but my other half is less patient than I, it seems."

"You're the one who left me in that bloody tower," Cheris said to her brother accusingly.

Tamas took another step. "Kill Kresimir. Go ahead. I won't stop you. It sounds like he deserves to die. But leave us out of your machinations. Leave Adro in peace."

"You won't try to stop us?" Cheris scoffed.

"Now, now," Claremonte said. "Don't dismiss the field marshal entirely, Cheris. Tamas, I plan on uniting this world for a new era. I'd like you to lead it. Say yes and you will be healed. I'll lengthen your life. I'll spare your friends and your family. You will hold a place of honor. You will bring peace to every nation on this planet."

It was growing harder for Tamas to breathe now. He could feel the blood in his lungs, and wondered if he'd been cut in more places than just his shoulder. It took every last bit of strength to grasp the spare pistol in his belt and draw it. His hand wavering, he lifted it and aimed it at Claremonte. "No."

The pistol evaporated in a splash of light, and along with it Tamas's hand. There was no pain from the destroyed limb, just a sudden numbness. Tamas stumbled backward, felt the sorcery grip and tear his body. The pain filled his head until he thought it might burst, and then he fell.

*   *   *

The appearance of Brude's other half gave Taniel pause. He waited for several moments, watching them speak.

"Pole?" he hissed. "There's two of them. Even if I can get close enough, I only have one bayonet."

Ka-poel seemed to consider this a moment. She gave him a nod and tapped her chest with one finger.

"You?"

Another nod.

"What can you do?"

She smiled at him, but didn't have time to give an answer. Out of the corner of Taniel's eye he saw a quick movement as Tamas drew his pistol. The pistol exploded in Tamas's hand, and Taniel could feel the sorcery spear through his father's body.

Taniel leapt the balcony and landed in the hall on the opposite side of the altar from Brude. He saw Tamas's body topple. "Dad!" The word wrenched from him as a sob, a searing, painful cry of fear and anguish. He stepped forward and felt Brude's sorcery turn on him, snaking around the altar like a python and snatching at his bones. The pressure was incredible. He instantly felt as if he were wading waist-deep through mud, the same crushing feeling that had held him at bay in Elections Square.

He held the ring bayonet in one hand, the blade between his fingers. He plowed forward, using the bayonet to cut through the sorcery as if it were the prow of a ship slicing through the sea. Cheris rounded the altar to meet him while Claremonte, his face calm, stepped up to Kresimir and raised the flint dagger in his hand.

"Pole, a little help!"

Kresimir's casket—the small one that Ka-poel had been carrying—soared through the air in an arc above Taniel's head. The sticks and string burst apart, the bonds around Kresimir's doll unraveling in the blink of an eye. Sorcery suddenly erupted from Kresimir, blasting both Cheris and Claremonte across the room.

Kresimir rolled off the altar and Taniel froze in place, afraid of the madness in Kresimir's eye as the god's gaze came to rest upon him. But there was no madness there. In fact, there was nothing. Kresimir's face was blank, expressionless. Ka-poel's doll floated above his head, and Kresimir jerked as the doll moved, mimicking its motions.

Taniel rushed toward Claremonte, only to find himself driven to his knees. He tried to stand, but he felt as if the weight of the world were pressing down on his shoulders. His eyes bulged and his heart thundered as he shoved against the unrelenting, invisible force. Through the slits of his eyelids he could see Claremonte and Cheris, both on their feet, jaws clenched, fighting back against Kresimir's sorcery.

Taniel realized that the pressure he now struggled against wasn't directed at him, but was rather the strength of the two gods suddenly pushing against each other. He was only caught in the middle. His whole body shook as Ka-poel's magic fought to protect him. He could feel every sinew straining, bones ready to snap at any moment. Ka-poel worked her way down the stairs at one end of the room. Sweat poured off her face and her fingers danced like a puppeteer with her hands on the strings.

Claremonte and Cheris moved toward each other with Kresimir between them. Kresimir himself seemed unaffected, but Taniel could see the doll above him dripping wax, the pressure turning it into a formless blob.

Claremonte raised his flint knife and brought it down on Kresimir's neck. The god toppled before him, and Taniel suddenly lunged forward, freed of the oppressive conflict of sorcery. He gained his balance and grabbed Claremonte by the front of his jacket, thrusting Ka-poel's bayonet through the soft part beneath his chin and through his brain.

Cheris's scream made Taniel release Claremonte's body and clutch at his ears. She ran toward him, hands raised, and he braced himself for the power of her fury.

Cheris stumbled. Taniel looked to find Tamas at her feet, Claremonte's flint dagger in his remaining hand. Blood poured from Tamas's ears, nose, and mouth, and black powder stained his chin. He thrust the dagger through her leg.

She yelled again, but more in anger than in pain. "You think that will kill me?" she demanded. She snatched Tamas by the collar of his jacket and lifted his broken body only to recoil as he spit blood in her eyes.

"Let him go," Taniel roared.

"You have no power to command me," Cheris said. "I will drink the blood from your father's corpse. I will slaughter you and your savage and then I will bring my love back. I have that power!"

"Let him go, and you win."

Cheris hesitated. "What do you mean?"

Taniel drew the bayonet from Claremonte's lifeless body and flipped it around in his hand. "Here," he said. "You win." He tossed the bayonet.

Cheris dropped Tamas and reached up, but the bayonet arced over her fingertips. She whirled, hand extended.

Ka-poel snatched the bayonet from the air and rammed it through Cheris's heart. The god gasped once and toppled to the ground. Ka-poel straddled her body and drew the bayonet out, ramming it in again and again until Cheris had stopped moving.

Taniel grabbed her arm. "She's dead, Pole."

Ka-poel sneered at Cheris, but let Taniel pull her away. He left her to check Claremonte's and Kresimir's bodies while he went to Tamas.

His father lay on his side, soaked in blood. Both legs were broken, his left arm shattered and left hand gone entirely. He still clutched the flint dagger in his hand. "Dad," Taniel pleaded, feeling desperation grab hold. "Dad, come on!"

Tamas's eyes fluttered. "Lost one of your pistols," he croaked.

"It's fine, Dad," Taniel said, cradling his father's head in his hand. "Come on. Stay with me."

"Is it over?"

"Yes. They're dead."

"Bloody gods."

"Stay with me, please," Taniel sobbed.

"No, Tan," Tamas said, blood on his teeth. "I don't think I will."

Taniel's vision blurred. "Please, Dad."

Tamas groped blindly for the front of Taniel's jacket, his fingers gripping the bloodstained lapel. "I'm proud of you, Taniel."

"Nothing to be proud of, Dad. I'm a terrible commander. An awful soldier."

"You're a good man. A good fighter. That's all that matters."

"Just stay alive, Dad. You hear me? Stay alive."

"I've earned this, my boy. I'm ready to rest."

"No you're not. You've got so much more to do." There was a rumble and the building shook around them, but it didn't matter, not anymore.

"I'm going now, son. Get out of here. Brude's going to have a death rattle, and it won't be pleasant."

"You're coming with me."

Tamas's breathing slowed. His fingers loosened and his arm went slack. Taniel ignored another insistent rumble, ignored Ka-poel tugging at his sleeve. "Dad..."

"Hey," Tamas whispered. His lips curled into a faint smile, and he softly said, "Your mother says hi, my boy. We love you."

CHAPTER
52

Adamat reined in his horse in the palace gardens, not far from the twisted remains of Skyline Palace's front doors. He dismounted beside a squad of Adran soldiers tending to their wounded.

"Where's the field marshal?" he asked.

A captain got to his feet. "He led a company of men inside the palace not fifteen minutes ago. What do you—?" He was cut off by a low rumbling sound. The soldiers exchanged nervous glances.

Adamat replied, "I'm here with news from Adopest. The enemy has been driven off and the new First Minister is safe."

"Pit, I didn't even know we were under attack in the city," the captain said. "We've been hunkered down out here all night and morning. Tumblar won the election?"

"He did."

"Glad to hear it. I'll send a squad in after Field Marshal Tamas to let him know the news."

There was another rumble and Adamat looked down at his feet. "Did you feel that?"

"Earthquake?" another soldier asked.

"Someone find Colonel Olem," the captain said. "And find out what the pit that was. If there's more sorcery about to spew out across the battlefield, he'll want to know about it."

Adamat eyed the palace gates and wondered if he should take the news in himself, but quickly dismissed the notion. Best to leave this to the professionals. Last time Adamat charged into a battle he'd gotten stabbed. Twice.

"Get back!" a voice bellowed.

Adamat turned to find a figure running up the road, approaching as fast as a powder mage in a full trance. He was tall and fat and soaked with sweat, his long black hair flying in loose, wet ribbons around his head.

"What is it?" Adamat asked.

"Get everyone back," Adom shouted. "Now!"

"Who the pit are you?" the captain demanded.

Adom seemed to shimmer and grow, towering over the captain. "I am your god, man, and if you don't order a full retreat right now, every single one of you will die."

The order was passed on by a nearby sergeant before the captain could even choke out a reply. He sputtered once, then said, "Tell everyone to get away from the palace. Run!"

Adamat went to Adom's side. "What's happening?"

"You remember what happened to South Pike when Kresimir was shot?"

"Yes."

"That."

"You're bloody well joking."

"Do I look like I'm joking, Inspector?" Adom seemed to notice for the first time that his apron had come loose and reached back to retie it. "Faster!" he bellowed. "Get everyone away!"

Though the palace gardens were thick with smoke and confusion, the order seemed to work its way through the Adran lines. Adamat saw a man ride his horse into the palace, straight through the big doors. The ground shook again. A minute later the same man returned, followed by two companies of Adran soldiers hauling their own number of dead and wounded.

Men leapt from palace windows as the tremors came in increasingly more powerful waves, and Adamat had to brace his legs to keep from being thrown to the ground.

"You may want to run, Inspector," Adom said.

"Will it help?"

Adom seemed to consider this. "No."

"I'll stay here, then." Standing next to a god didn't seem to be such a bad idea if the world was about to collapse.

The southern wing of Skyline Palace dropped out of sight so suddenly that Adamat leapt back in fright. The section of the building dropped in on itself, and it took a moment for Adamat to realize that the ground itself was falling away, swallowing the palace whole.

The walls caved inward and disappeared, and a plume of plaster dust shot upward from the growing destruction like the steam from an erupting geyser. Adom braced himself, face shining with sweat and grime, legs spread for balance, arms at his sides with palms held open toward the palace, fingers gripping the air. Veins stood out up his arms and his muscles bulged, but whatever sorcery he brought to bear failed to slow the destruction.

Crimson leaked from the corners of Adom's mouth and nose. A bloody sheen replaced his sweat, and his eyes looked like they might pop from his skull. The wreckage of the silver palace door toppled, swallowed into the widening sinkhole.

Adamat stepped back nervously. That sinkhole showed no sign of stopping, and though he could not see inside, he had the vague perception of depth that made him want to run. He glanced at

Adom, whose whole body now trembled like a twig about to snap, and though he was only a Knacked and hardly adept, he could feel the sorcery rolling off of the god.

The sinkhole swallowed more rooms of the palace and continued to widen, reaching toward the throne room and the northern wing. Adamat closed his eyes and stared at the blue sky above him, wishing that he was at home with Faye and his children.

The rumbling stopped. The ground grew still. Scarcely daring to breath, Adamat looked toward the earthen maw and found that it had stopped growing. The air was full of dust and soil, reducing his vision to only fifty yards or so, but he could see the shadow of the northern wing of the palace still standing.

A marble fountain cracked and slid into the sinkhole and then the air went still. Adamat felt as if the entire Adran army had breathed a sigh of relief. Cautiously, the retreating soldiers came to a stop and began to trickle back toward the palace, looking on with horrified curiosity.

"The field marshal!" someone shouted.

Adamat found himself running forward with a dozen soldiers. The dust began to settle and clear as he threw himself to his knees beside the bloody body lying on the gravel drive not far from where the palace door had recently stood.

Field Marshal Tamas was missing a hand, and his clothes were black with blood. The blood on his brow was smeared as if someone had held him. His body lay alone, broken. Adamat pressed his hand to the field marshal's neck, feeling for a pulse. He felt his stomach fall as he relayed the news. "He's dead."

Someone let out a choked sob. The quickly growing crowd split, and Adom plodded to the body, kneeling opposite Adamat. He scooped his arms beneath Tamas, lifting the body the way a child might lift a doll.

"Where's Taniel Two-shot?" a soldier asked.

Another shouted, "Get Colonel Olem!"

Adom cleared his throat and looked toward the gaping ruin. "Taniel Two-shot is dead. There lies his grave. You may look, but you won't find the body." He ignored the questions thrust at him by the gathered soldiers and pulled Tamas's body tight to his chest.

And there, among the ruined splendor of Skyline Palace, Adamat saw a god weep for the hero of Adro.

CHAPTER 53

Nila paced the marble floors of the People's Court, her footsteps echoing in the early morning silence. It was less than a week since she and Bo had bested what remained of Claremonte's cabal, and memories of the fight still gave her nightmares. She never wanted to set foot in this building again. Yet here she was.

"Why are they making us wait?" she asked.

Bo sat on one of the hard benches nearby bouncing a rubber ball off the opposite wall of the hallway, pausing every other bounce to squeeze the ball experimentally. He did not wear his gloves, and his right hand had a pink scar from the healing job done by the Deliv Privileged. "Because," he sighed, "they're trying to show us who holds authority now."

"That's arrogant."

"Welcome to the world of politics, my dear," Bo said.

Nila stopped pacing and crossed her arms. She'd had very little sleep and she had a full day ahead, and she could feel her mood already beginning to turn for the worse. "I'm not going to play their games."

"This is your life, now."

The thought made her want to retch. For five days they had been interrogated by politicians and pulled into late-night meetings with Vlora, Ricard Tumblar, and a hundred men and women whose names she couldn't possibly remember as they tried to force some kind of order onto the government in the wake of Tamas's death.

"I should just leave," she said.

Bo frowned. "You're welcome to whenever you like. I would be very sad."

She resumed her pacing. "You'd get over it."

"I would never!"

You got over Taniel's death awfully quick, she wanted to say. But she dared not utter it out loud. No sense in driving a wedge between them when they so desperately needed to present a unified front to the world.

"You must admit," Bo said, "while less exciting than being shot at and chased, and battling sorcery, at least spending all day in meetings won't make you shit your pants. In there"—he pointed to the closed door down the hall—"they won't try to take your life. Just destroy your career."

"The joke is on them," Nila said. "I don't want this career."

"Then you're the best woman for it. Come on, they've kept us waiting long enough." Bo got up, adjusting his prosthetic and pulling on his gloves.

Nila drew a pair of gloves out of her pocket and tugged them on. She didn't need them, but she'd found in the meetings over the last few days that people took her far more seriously when she wore them.

Bo held the door for her, and she brushed past the secretary who tried to stop her as she went into the inner chamber.

Nine sets of eyes looked up as she and Bo entered the room.

Nila only recognized two of the men and three of the women, but she knew these were the newly elected regional governors of Adro. They, the new Hall of Magistrates, and First Minister Ricard Tumblar made up the three legs of the new Adran government.

The governors sat around a half-moon table, a light breakfast being cleared from before them. Governor Ratchel, a woman of about fifty with short gray hair and hands curled and bent from rheumatism, scowled.

"We're not ready for you yet," Ratchel said.

"Yes," Bo said with a charming smile, "but we're burying Field Marshal Tamas in less than six hours in a ceremony in front of millions. We don't have time for your shit. If you want something from us, get on with it."

A round of indignant scoffs went up from the governors. Ratchel, to her credit, merely fixed Bo with an annoyed squint. "The time has come to determine the place of the Adran Cabal within our new government," she said. "Or to determine if the cabal even has a place among us."

"Are you trying to tell me the Adran government would dare continue in this strife-laden modern era without a cabal?" Nila asked, feigning shock.

"It sounds," Bo said, looking equally surprised, "like they're trying to put us out of a job!"

"If you'll just . . . ," Ratchel said.

"Well." Nila threw her hands up. "I got my wish. Thank you for calling us in here to let us know. I think I'll go spend the rest of the day in bed."

"I'll join you!" Bo said with a wink, linking his arm with hers and turning them both toward the door.

"Where the pit do you think you're going?" Ratchel demanded.

Nila and Bo both turned back toward the governors. "If you don't want us," Bo said, "we're more than happy to leave."

Ratchel shuffled the papers in front of her angrily. "It's not that we don't want you," she said. "It's that we have yet to determine how the cabal will serve our government."

"Ah," Bo said. Prosthetic clicking, he went and grabbed one of the chairs from beside the wall and dragged it noisily into the center of the room, plopping himself down in it and leaning forward on his cane. Nila took up a position behind him. "The cabal," he said, "intends on serving as it always has. But instead of the king, we will serve the best interests of the people."

"That's very vague."

"I'm glad you noticed."

"It's too vague. The cabal must report to someone."

"We do. We report to the army, who reports to the First Minister, whose actions are answerable to both the Hall of Magistrates and the esteemed governors before me."

"There *must* be more direct oversight."

"And you," Nila said, "propose that we report directly to the governors' council?"

"Yes," Ratchel said curtly, fixing Nila with that same annoyed squint she'd used on Bo earlier.

"We've already gotten similar offers from both the First Minister and representatives of the Hall of Magistrates." Bo laughed. "And we've decided that it is in the best interest of Adro for the cabal to remain independent. We will fight the nation's wars. We will fight for the people's interests. We will not be lapdogs to any single group of politicians."

"And who decided this?" Ratchel demanded. "The two of you?"

Nila said, "The two of us, as well as the recently promoted General Vlora and the remaining half-dozen members of Tamas's powder cabal."

"We've combined, you see," Bo said. "So if you want to have this conversation again, you can do it with a handful of war heroes in the room in addition to the last two Privileged you have left." He slapped his hands on his thighs. "Well, out of time. Good day to you all."

Nila helped Bo to his feet, taking satisfaction in the stunned silence that followed as the two of them left the room.

Outside the office, Nila watched men scrub at the blackened marble farther down the hallway while Bo adjusted the straps on his prosthetic, wondering if it was her fire that had caused the stains or fire from one of the Brudanian Privileged. Frankly, she was shocked that the entire building hadn't been condemned after that fight.

"I thought that went rather well," Bo said cheerfully.

Nila nodded. Part of her agreed. Bo was right. The spirit of this new government would be crippled from the beginning if any one branch of the legislature had the cabal at their fingertips. Going it alone, however, meant there was no one else to blame for their failures and shortcomings. Sometimes taking orders was the easiest way.

"Borbador!" a voice echoed down the long hall.

Nila turned around to find Inspector Adamat heading in their direction. The inspector wore a new suit, and his eyes had dark rings beneath them from lack of sleep. He gave Nila a half bow, then turned to Bo.

"Inspector," Bo said. "How are you?"

"Well, thank you. Tired. Busy. But well."

"Your family, how are they?"

Adamat covered his grimace well. "Wonderful. Thank you for asking."

"And Jakob?" Nila asked.

"Faye considers him one of her own."

"That item that we discussed...?" Bo said.

Adamat handed him a folded piece of paper. "You'll find her here."

"Very good."

Nila glanced curiously at Bo, but his face gave away nothing. "You're making this poor man run errands still?" she asked.

"Thank you for the consideration," Adamat said, coughing into his hand, "but half a day's work for fifty thousand krana seemed like an opportunity I couldn't pass up."

"How do you feel about a more permanent position?" Bo asked.

"I have one, thank you," Adamat said. "I'm an ambassador now."

"Congratulations," Nila said. "To where?"

"We haven't quite gotten that far, actually."

"You'll get it sorted out, I'm sure," Bo said. "I promise, though, that I pay better than the government."

"Ricard is very generous with his friends." Adamat paused, clearly cautious. "Just out of curiosity, what did you have in mind?"

"Spymaster for the new Adran Cabal."

Nila raised her eyebrows. Bo hadn't mentioned this to her.

Adamat shook his finger at Bo. "Not a chance. Far too dangerous. Far too political."

"I'll leave the offer on the table for a week," Bo said.

Adamat bowed and took a step back. "I should be flattered by the consideration, but I won't do it. Thank you, Privileged."

"Shucks." Bo removed an envelope from his pocket, no doubt stuffed with krana notes, and handed it to Adamat. The inspector bowed again and made his retreat, Nila and Bo watching him go.

"That man is eminently employable," Bo said. "I'll get him eventually." He seemed to forget about the inspector, though, turning to Nila and giving her a look up and down. "Time to get ready for the funeral. Then we have a trip to make tomorrow."

"Oh?" Nila asked.

Bo unfolded the paper Adamat had given him and looked it over. "South. Not too far."

The Deliv army had made their camp in a small town halfway between Adopest and Budwiel. Only about fifteen thousand Deliv soldiers remained, the rest having already begun their march to be home before the winter took a turn for the worse.

The camp was semipermanent, meant to last through the winter, as most of the occupants were the wounded and dying, and the surgeons, nurses, and support staff from both the Adran and Deliv armies, as well as several thousand Kez prisoners. The place reeked of blood, disease, and death, and the burial grounds on the plains outside the town seemed to grow by the acre every day.

Taniel loathed it, and from the moment he and Ka-poel had ridden into the camp he had wanted to be gone.

But he had a promise to keep.

He strolled through the camp, rifle over his shoulder, tricorne hat pulled low over his face and the collar of his greatcoat flipped up. Just another Adran soldier on leave, looking among the wounded for friends or relations. No one stopped or questioned him.

Ka-poel clung to his arm, hidden in her own greatcoat. While he felt exhausted, his body spent from so long at war, she looked more vibrant than ever. Days of sleep had done her well, with her skin flushed and her eyes bright. The death around them didn't seem to bother her, but Taniel knew that, like him, she longed to be gone.

Taniel spotted a familiar figure waiting beside a carriage near one of the hospital tents at the center of camp and stopped to watch his oldest friend for a few moments.

"Did I ever thank Bo for saving my life up in the mountains?" Taniel asked.

Ka-poel nodded, then pointed at herself and shook her head.

"I did too thank you for saving my life! Did you ever thank me for saving yours?"

She cocked one eyebrow, and Taniel's face flushed. "All right, so thanks all around," he said.

She gave a perfunctory nod.

Taniel took a step toward Bo, then hesitated when he saw that Nila was with him. Taniel scowled.

Ka-poel tugged on his arm.

"I asked Bo to come alone."

Ka-poel seemed to reassess the situation, watching Nila for a few moments, then tugging on his arm again. She mouthed the words, *She's fine.*

They approached Bo and his apprentice, and Taniel tipped up his hat. Bo just smiled and stepped forward to embrace first Ka-poel, then Taniel.

"Tan. Little Sister. You look well rested."

"Being dead will do that," Taniel answered.

Nila scowled viciously at Bo. "Why the pit didn't you tell me he was still alive?"

"Does it matter?" Bo asked.

"I've spent the last week thinking you were a heartless ass because you didn't seem to think twice over the fact your best friend had been killed by a god."

"That was kind of suspicious, wasn't it?" Bo said. "I'll have to go into mourning when things quiet down."

Nila rolled her eyes. "Pit, you're insufferable. Taniel, why haven't you come forward? Everyone thinks you're dead."

"That's kind of the idea," Taniel said.

"But why?"

"Because," Bo answered for him, "Taniel would have lived beneath Tamas's shadow the rest of his life. I don't think either of us has any real concept of what that entails. They would not have let him be Taniel. They would have expected him to be Tamas all over again. Leading Adro. Being her beating heart every moment."

Taniel kept his silence. There were so many reasons to remain dead. He wondered if he was a coward, taking the easy way out and leaving everyone else to clean up the mess.

"That doesn't explain why you kept it from me," Nila said. "You think I can't keep secrets? Pit, there's no one for me to tell! You're my only confidant."

Taniel waved a hand between the two of them. "I asked him not to tell anyone," he said. "Bo is a man of his word, but I'll let the two of you work that out later. Every moment I linger is a greater chance I'm recognized. Did you find her?"

"I did," Bo said. "Just inside."

"Good." Taniel pulled the pistol from his belt and double-checked to see if it was loaded while Bo tugged on his gloves.

"You sure you need me?" Bo asked.

"I'd feel better about this with you. Don't have to come inside, just . . . be here in case."

"She might have already sensed I'm here," Bo said. "She and I don't have the best of relationships. Remember, I threw her off the mountain last time we saw each other."

"*I'm* the one who threw her off the mountain," Taniel said. He could already feel his heart begin to pound and wondered if this was a mistake.

"She won't remember it that way."

"Who are you talking about?" Nila asked. "What are we doing here?"

"Confronting a demigod," Bo said.

Nila blanched. "Excuse me?"

Taniel lifted the tent flap to the hospital. "Ladies first," he said to Ka-poel. To Nila: "Don't worry. She doesn't have any hands. The two of you can wait out here."

The tent held three times as many beds as it did occupants, and Taniel wondered whether that was a good or a bad sign. Regardless, the lack of nurses fit their purposes, while none of the wounded seemed coherent. Well, almost none of the wounded.

Julene sat on a cot on the far side, the corner flap of the tent cracked so that she could see outside. She didn't turn as he and Ka-poel approached.

"I see they cut you down," Taniel said.

"No thanks to you." Julene's voice seemed to have recovered from months staked out in the sun without water. Taniel circled her cot, craning his head to look at her arms. They ended in bandaged stumps. A part of him had wondered if they would grow back after long enough. After all, her sorcery made her stronger than just about anything short of a god.

"You asked me to kill you. Not to cut you down," Taniel said. Nor would he have promised to do the latter. She'd killed friends. She'd tried to kill him. She'd summoned Kresimir into this world, causing so much death and destruction.

Julene shifted on her cot, lifting her right stub and jabbing it toward him. "And you've come to fulfill your promise?"

Taniel drew his pistol in answer.

"I see." Julene stared down at where her hands had once been, then glanced at Ka-poel. "You're just something else, aren't you? I can't believe I didn't see it. Have you loaded that thing with one of her bullets? The ones you used to kill Privileged up on South Pike?"

"I have," Taniel said. He licked his lips. He wanted to lift the pistol and pull the trigger, but something was holding him back. Perhaps it was regret. Caution. Unwillingness to further the bloodshed. He was not certain. "Did they know what you are when they cut you down?" he asked.

Julene shrugged. "The Deliv cabal has been glancing in on me, but I just told them I was a mercenary who'd offended Kresimir, and he kept me alive with his sorcery."

"And they believed you?"

"Why wouldn't they? It's mostly truth. Besides, even if they knew I was a Predeii, they'd know I'm not a threat without hands."

"You have a lot of knowledge, though."

"That's why I'm not telling them," Julene said, the scar on her face tugged by her shallow smile. "Best get on with it, shouldn't we?"

Taniel glanced at Ka-poel. Her face was placid. He lifted his pistol.

"I don't suppose you'd consider going back on your promise, would you?" Julene asked mildly.

Surprised, Taniel lowered his pistol. "You think I would? After all the grief you've caused?"

"It was worth asking." Julene shrugged, as if she didn't much care one way or another.

"You want to live like this?"

Julene turned her arms over. "I might be able to get it back. The Else, that is. I can still see it, I just don't have fingers to touch it. And even if I didn't, maybe I deserve this. Maybe I deserve spending the next thousand years on the Deliv cabal's torture racks, giving them every ounce of my knowledge."

Taniel examined the side of her face for several silent moments. He wondered if Julene was truly sorry for what she'd done, or if this was all an act. She regretted summoning Kresimir, that's for certain. But the murder? The chaos? Did she regret all that?

Taniel stuffed his pistol back in his belt.

Julene's eyes flicked from him to Ka-poel, then back, widening slightly. "Don't toy with me, Two-shot. Finish it or don't, but for those months I spent hanging from Kresimir's beam, for these hands of mine, you owe it to me not to toy."

"I don't owe you anything," Taniel said. "But I'm no executioner. I'm only here because I promised to kill you when you wanted an end. Now that you don't want an end...I'm tired of the blood. Tired of the fighting. Another gunshot won't solve anything. But you have to promise me one thing."

"What?"

"Let it all go. Any grudges you hold for Borbador or anyone else in Adro, they're finished. Over. You've no business here."

"Agreed," Julene said, almost too quickly. They watched each other for some time before she raised her chin to Taniel. "I'll remember it, Two-shot."

He and Ka-poel left Julene in the tent and joined Bo and Nila outside.

"I didn't hear a gunshot," Bo said.

"I didn't kill her."

"Is leaving her alive a good idea?" Bo asked, looking slightly nervous. He had begun to peel off his gloves but now had stopped.

"I don't know. Maybe. Maybe not. I don't think she'll bother you any more, though."

"You better believe I'm going to have her watched, regardless."

"Don't blame you," Taniel said.

"Is that it, then?" Bo asked. "Are you leaving?"

Taniel exchanged a glance with Ka-poel. It was almost time for that, yes. But not quite. "I've got one last thing to do," he said.

EPILOGUE

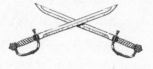

Vlora stood outside of her carriage, looking up at the three-story town house situated on a quiet street on Adopest's east side.

It was late in the afternoon, almost four o'clock, and Vlora cocked her head to listen for the church bell that had been rung every hour for the many years that she'd lived in this home. It was several moments before she remembered that every church in Adopest had been destroyed, and the thought of never hearing that bell again brought her sadness.

"Would you like me to come in?" Olem asked from the carriage.

"Give me a few minutes," she said, closing the carriage door. She walked past the overgrown garden and up the front steps, slipping a brass key from her pocket.

Long practice made her stop in the foyer and listen for voices to call her name, but nothing answered her presence in the old home but the familiar creak of the floorboards beneath her feet. Dust filled her nostrils, and she wondered if anyone had been here since before the night of the coup so many months ago. Her inquiries had told her the servants were dismissed last winter.

She was a general now, but felt no sense of accomplishment from it. The newly minted House of Ministers had showered her with praise and given her the promotion with Tamas only a week in his grave. Now, six weeks later, it didn't seem any less strange. The youngest general in Adran history, even younger than Tamas himself when he first achieved the rank. She wondered if everyone else saw it as the political stunt that it was.

Use them before they use you, she heard Tamas's voice say in the back of her head. *Show them you earned it.*

She went up the stairs and sought the first room on the right—her room for six years of her life, after Tamas had saved her from the street. She remembered a time from before the coup. Before Taniel was sent to Fatrasta and before that blasted nobleman.

Laughter echoed in her memory and she tilted her head, wondering if she had heard it for real. No. Of course not.

The bed seemed so much smaller than she remembered. How had she and Taniel fit in there on those nights when Tamas was gone? Had Borbador still been in the house? Or had that been after he was taken away by the cabal magus-seekers?

The memories seemed distant now, and she left the room and continued down the hall, pausing beside the door to Tamas's office.

His desk was coated in dust, a map of Adopest still held down at the corners by Tamas's favorite teacup and a handful of musket balls. Vlora crossed to the desk and rolled up the map carefully before returning it to its place on Tamas's bookshelf. She unbuttoned the gold epaulets on the shoulders of her uniform and set them on the desk where the map had been.

She felt tired. Dizzy. Weeks straight of shaking hands. Of parades and memorials. Tamas's funeral as well, which had been attended by two kings, a queen, and what the newspapers had said were eight million mourners. It had even been presided over by the newly pardoned Arch-Diocel Charlemund.

She opened the window of Tamas's study and watched the dust swirl in the sunlight. Slowly, she went through the various knick-knacks Tamas had collected in Gurla. She ran a finger down the spines of his leather-bound books on warfare, religion, and economics. She remembered the contents of this study like she remembered the palm of her own hand, and tried to recall the first time she had ever been in this room.

The memory seemed distant. Perhaps even manufactured in the back of her mind, pieced together from the scraps of a hundred other memories. It was a faded thing, like cloth left in the sunlight for too many years.

There was a creak on the floorboards and Vlora opened her eyes, not remembering that she'd closed them. Her cheeks were streaked with tears, but she did not wipe them away.

"You don't have to go," she said to the figure in the doorway.

Taniel wore faded buckskins and held an old, secondhand rifle in his hands. He had grown out his beard and his hair. His eyes were brighter than she'd seen in years and he looked as if a weight had been lifted off his shoulders.

"I do," he said with a smile. "I'm free, Vlora."

She stepped around Tamas's desk and walked up to him, examining his face and eyes. She glanced back at the epaulets she'd left on the desk and she thought she understood.

"They made you a general," Taniel said.

She glanced at the epaulets again, a bitter taste in her mouth.

"The country will need you. Tamas's death has left a gap."

"One I can't hope to fill."

"Just concentrate on the tasks at hand," Taniel said.

Vlora responded, "Beon je Ipille has gone into hiding and there are rumblings of a Kez civil war. General Hilanska still needs to be brought to justice. Bo wants to combine Privileged and powder mages in the new republic cabal, and Gavril wants to make sweeping reforms to the Mountainwatch. There is...a lot to do."

Vlora had expected a more emotional response from Taniel at the mention of Hilanska, but he just nodded and reached over to touch the gold epaulets she'd left on the desk.

"Tamas would be proud."

Vlora looked down at her uniform, at the variety of accolades that she wanted every day to rip off the front. "You sure?"

"I am. Will you sell the house?"

Vlora blinked at him. "What do you mean?"

"I read about the will in the newspaper. With me dead, Tamas left everything to you and Bo," Taniel said, touching the door frame with two fingers. "I'd sell it, personally. Too many memories."

"Pit, no. I'm moving into it."

Taniel seemed surprised, but after a few moments he smiled again. "That makes me glad, for some reason. We had a good time here, didn't we?"

"We did." They stood quietly for several moments before Vlora said, "Forgive me?"

"Only if you forgive me."

"I already have."

They hugged, and Vlora felt Taniel's lips pressed to her forehead. She felt dampness in her hair, and when they separated, Taniel wiped tears from his eyes.

Vlora took his hand. "Good luck. Take care of yourself."

"You too."

He left her in the quiet of her new home.

She remembered a night not long after Tamas had taken her in, when she'd had nightmares. Tamas had come to her room and put her back in bed. He had kissed her on the forehead, which no one had ever done for her before, and told her that nothing would ever harm her or Taniel while he lived.

Even with the blood and slaughter and death, she hadn't had a nightmare since.

"Were you talking to someone?" Olem asked, entering the office.

Who would keep the nightmares away now, she wondered, but even as she did so, she could hear Tamas's voice in her head. *You will*, he seemed to say.

"No one," she answered Olem. "Just shadows of the past."

ACKNOWLEDGMENTS

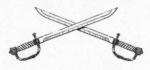

Thank you so much to my editor, Devi Pillai, for the patience and foresight to help me get through my first series of books. She doesn't get nearly as much credit as she should for being the best at what she does. Also thanks to my agent, Caitlin Blasdell, for talking me down from the ledge on multiple occasions during the writing of this series.

My wife, Michele, was there for me along every step of the way, from tossing around ideas for the magic and characters, to going over my copyedits before I sent them back. She's the greatest, and shouldn't let anyone tell her otherwise.

Thanks to Howard Taylor, Justin Landon, and David Wohlreich for looking over and discussing early drafts of the book with me. Friends like that are invaluable.

Thanks to my parents, who listen to me prattle on at great length about the tiny details of my job so that my wife doesn't have to listen to it too much. Also thanks for their unending support and love for my writing. Similar thanks goes to all my friends and family, who come to my signings and listen to me yap.

Finally, the utmost appreciation goes to Gene Mollica, Michael

Frost, and Lauren Panepinto for their work on the amazing covers for all three books in the trilogy, and to James Long, Alex Lencicki, Ellen Wright, Laura Fitzgerald, Lindsey Hall, and all the rest of the staff at Orbit and Orbit UK who do all the thankless work to make these books into something awesome.